Romantic Suspense

Danger. Passion. Drama.

Protecting The Littlest Witness
Jaycee Bullard

Undercover Colorado Conspiracy
Jodie Bailey

MILLS & BOON

PROTECTING THE LITTLEST WITNESS
© 2024 by Jean Bullard
Philippine Copyright 2024
Australian Copyright 2024
New Zealand Copyright 2024

First Published 2023
First Australian Paperback Edition 2023
ISBN 978 1 038 90269 6

UNDERCOVER COLORADO CONSPIRACY
© 2024 by Jodie Bailey
Philippine Copyright 2024
Australian Copyright 2024
New Zealand Copyright 2024

First Published 2024
First Australian Paperback Edition 2024
ISBN 978 1 038 90269 6

MIX
Paper | Supporting
responsible forestry
FSC® C001695
FSC
www.fsc.org

Published by
Harlequin Mills & Boon
An imprint of Harlequin Enterprises (Australia) Pty Limited
(ABN 47 001 180 918), a subsidiary of HarperCollins
Publishers Australia Pty Limited
(ABN 36 009 913 517)
Level 19, 201 Elizabeth Street
SYDNEY NSW 2000 AUSTRALIA

Cover art used by arrangement with Harlequin Books S.A.. All rights reserved.

Printed and bound in Australia by McPherson's Printing Group

Protecting The Littlest Witness
Jaycee Bullard

MILLS & BOON

Jaycee Bullard was born and raised in the great state of Minnesota, the fourth child in a family of five. Growing up, she loved to read, especially books by Astrid Lindgren and Georgette Heyer. In the ten years since graduating with a degree in classical languages, she has worked as a paralegal and an office manager, before finally finding her true calling as a preschool Montessori teacher and as a writer of romantic suspense.

Visit the Author Profile page
at millsandboon.com.au.

When I consider thy heavens, the work of thy fingers,
the moon and the stars, which thou hast ordained;
What is man, that thou art mindful of him?
and the son of man, that thou visitest him?
—*Psalms* 8:3-4

DEDICATION

To my mum
And with great thanks to my editor, Katie Gowrie,
for her support and kindness.

Chapter One

Etta Mitchell had learned about the block party from one of the neighbors. The details had followed two days later in an invitation shoved under her door.

Come early. Leave late. And bring a smile and a hot dish to share.

Not to be rude, but it didn't sound like her kind of scene. She'd tossed the flyer in the trash and hadn't given it another thought until, days later, a steady buzz of music and laughter leaking through the windows reminded her of the event.

"We'll make our own party," Etta said to the little girl perched next to her on a stool. "What do you think, Polly? Pancakes for dinner sound okay?"

She wasn't surprised when her niece didn't

answer. Polly wasn't talking much these days. Actually, she wasn't talking at all.

Etta tried again with a singsong rhyme set to an old tune she remembered from preschool.

"Patty cake, patty cake, baker's man. Bake me a cake as fast as you can. Count the eggs out, one, two, three. Just enough to make pancakes for my sweetheart and me."

A ghost of a grin lit up Polly's face, causing Etta's heart to leap in her chest. Maybe this was the day she'd break through the wall of silence hampering her attempts to communicate with her niece. But as Etta gripped the cast-iron skillet hanging over the stove, the pan slipped from her hand and clattered against the countertop, causing Polly to dash from the room.

A wave of exasperation pulled at Etta. She closed her eyes and tried to picture her sister's face. *Oh, Lilly. I'm making a mess of this. I'm trying my best, but Polly misses you so much. And every time I start making headway, she runs away.*

The creaking of hinges sent Etta's senses on high alert. It didn't take much to set her heart racing these days, not after what had happened to her sister. But it seemed unlikely that Polly had gone outside just now. Her niece knew the rules, having been told more times than Etta could count that she should never leave the house without permission. But maybe she had forgotten. After all, she was only five.

"Polly…?"

There was a movement to the left, followed by the thudding of heavy footsteps by the patio door. Not Polly, then. Panic threaded through Etta's veins as her eyes darted toward her phone lying on the desk. But as she moved to grab it, stubby fingers cuffed her wrists and a calloused hand clamped across her lips.

"Relax, and no one gets hurt," the man said gruffly.

Etta didn't believe that. Her survivor instinct took over, and she opened her mouth and bit down hard.

"Oww!" the burly intruder howled as he released his hold.

"Help!" she screamed as her attacker's left hand pressed against her throat. "Help," she cried out again, her voice gurgling like water circling a drain.

Terror threatened to overwhelm her. And fear—not just for herself, but for Polly—gnawed at her senses. She could only hope and pray that the little girl was curled up in one of her favorite hiding places, safe from the assailant. She raised her foot and bent it backward, kicking the man in the groin, and then took off toward the front door.

She rounded the corner into the hall. But her pursuer was close and getting closer, muttering threats as he closed the gap between them, gaining ground with each thunderous step.

"You can run, but I'm gonna catch you."

Her brain registered the details of his heavy footfalls and booming voice even as she realized she'd never make it out the door.

She ducked into the powder room, quickly turning the lock as her pursuer's fists began to hammer against the door. She tamped down her panic and focused on her next move. The only path of escape was through the window above the toilet, seemingly too high to reach and too narrow to shimmy through. But she had to try.

Climbing onto the tank and stretching on tiptoes, she strained her fingers toward the ledge. She could almost touch it. Almost. But not quite. It remained mere inches away.

Bending her legs, she sprang upward, stretching her arms out, and this time she was able to grab hold of the windowsill. She dangled for a moment to catch her breath and then pulled herself up on her elbows. With the cuff of her sweatshirt tugged across her left hand, she slammed her fist against the sealed window. A cobweb of cracks formed on the glass.

She punched back again. A red stain of blood soaked through the cloth as she brushed aside the jagged glass in the frame. A gust of wind blew through the opening, stinging her face with an exhilarating slap of fresh air.

She swung her right leg upward so that she was straddling the ledge. The crack of the bathroom door crashing off its hinges fueled her desperation. She took a deep breath and readied for the dismount.

But before she could make her move, a cold hand grabbed hold of her ankle, and fingers clenched around her calf. She screamed for help even as her captor held her tight, and she slowly slid down and away from the window. The hand reached up now and encircled her waist, heaving her backward and tossing her to the floor. Pain exploded through her body as she looked up into the sullen eyes of her attacker.

Steven Hunt walked slowly down the flagstone path that led to the house at 411 Dogwood Drive. The Google map on his phone claimed that this was the right address, but now that he was here, he was second-guessing his decision for the impromptu visit. As for the bouquet of yellow roses he'd purchased on impulse at the bus station, he didn't feel so great about those, either. The flowers had seemed like such a good idea when he'd hopped the bus from Dallas to Silver Creek. Now, not so much.

He wasn't ready for this. Maybe he should just turn around and take his roses along with him. A deep breath brought a sharp jab of pain that ricocheted across his chest and reminded him of what it felt like to be trampled by a two-thousand-pound bull. The doctor had said that it would take a few months for his ribs to heal, but patience had never been his strong suit. He glanced at the front door again, resolution firming in his gut. Wouldn't he regret it even more if, after traveling all this way, he didn't even make the effort to see Etta? Besides, what else was he going to do? Return to South Dakota and his family's smothering sympathy? No, he was here now, and he wasn't ready to go home. He took a step forward, and then froze at the high-pitched and desperate sound of a woman screaming.

Was that Etta?

It was hard to tell amid the cacophony around

him—he seemed to have stumbled upon a block party. There was music playing, and people milling about. Another scream came from within the house. He dropped the flowers, sprinted up the steps and pulled at the handle of the front door.

Locked. Following the voices down the hall, he dashed toward the back of the house and raced across the patio and through the half-open glass door, stopping short at the sight of Etta's body sprawled on the kitchen floor.

A huge man hovered beside her, and he didn't look pleased to see someone new preparing to enter the fray.

Steven propelled himself forward, managing to knock the behemoth off balance by the sheer force of the attack.

But Steven's success was short-lived as, a second later, he found himself summarily tossed onto the floor. Fresh pain exploded through Steven's chest as he skidded into a shelf. Books rained down on his back, adding insult to injury. He pushed himself up off the ground and staggered toward the larger man, his arms raised and his fists ready. It had been a while since he'd been in a real brawl, but growing up with a twin brother, he'd been in his share of fights.

He swung his right arm in a hook, his fist connecting with his opponent's chin. He followed with an upward thrust from his left side into the gut. Once again, the element of surprise gave him an initial advantage as the big man staggered backward. But he managed to steady himself and pop a punch at Steven. With a quick step to the right, Steven dodged the blow, but a second one landed squarely against his jaw. The impact made his eyes water and brought a new throbbing ache. He couldn't afford another direct hit. Not in the condition he was in. If his opponent landed a punch to his chest, it would be game over. But how long could he dodge the blows from the man lunging after him?

All of a sudden, Etta appeared behind his attacker, a cast-iron skillet in her hand. She raised her arm and brought down the heavy pan on the man's head. His assailant froze for a moment before his body crumpled to the floor, a thin pool of blood forming around his jaw.

A gasp formed in Steven's throat. Grim-faced with tension, Etta lifted the frying pan a second time and held it above her head. "Don't move," she said, pointing at him. "Who are you and why are you here?"

Not quite the reception he'd been hoping for.

"I know it's been fifteen years," Steven began, "but I was expecting at least a glimmer of recognition."

Etta glared back at him for a moment before a look of bewilderment played across her features. "Steven?"

"Got it in one."

The hardness was gone from her voice, but a wary edge remained. "What are you doing here?" she asked, lowering the pan.

"Fair question. But maybe we'd better deal with the matter at hand. What did I just walk into? What's going on?"

"In a minute, okay?" Etta blinked a few times as her gaze took in the body of the man lying face up on the floor. She had hit him hard, and he wasn't moving. Her face seemed to crumple as shock set in.

She kneeled beside her assailant and checked his vitals. From the frown creasing her lips, Steven assumed that there was no pulse and no sign of breathing. Etta waited a few seconds and then placed the palm of her hand in the middle of the fallen man's chest. Placing her other hand on top of the first, she pushed down hard to perform several dozen compressions.

"Etta…" Steven said.

She looked up at him and shook her head.

He watched as she tilted the man's head and checked his airway, pinched his nose shut and, with her mouth against his, executed two quick rescue breaths. When his chest failed to rise, she repeated the procedure a second time and then a third. She seemed to be preparing for a fourth round of compressions when he realized that he needed to intervene.

He took a step toward her and touched her shoulder.

"Etta, he's gone."

"Pease, God. No," she whispered, dropping her face to her hands.

Steven took a step closer and pulled her toward him. He could feel the drum of her heartbeat as she gulped in a fresh lungful of air.

"I'll call nine-one-one. And when the police get here, I'll explain…"

"No!" Etta pulled away from his embrace and shook her head.

"Etta…you killed the guy. In self-defense, but it needs to be reported."

She glanced down at her fallen attacker and then raised her gaze to meet Steven's. "I can't do that."

Frustration bit at the corners of his mind.

How had he forgotten about Etta's stubbornness? He tugged at his beard. "Why not? What's going on? What is it that you aren't telling me?"

"What am I not telling you?" Etta's voice was tinged with hysteria. "What are *you* not telling me? What are you even doing here? You show up at my sister's house fifteen years too late and ask what I'm not telling you."

Fifteen years too late? What did that mean? But now was not the time for that sort of question. He needed to convince Etta to be sensible, to think of the consequences before she committed to a reckless course of action.

"I saw on the news that Lilly died, and I wanted to reach out and tell you that I—"

"No," she said shaking her head. "Lilly didn't just die. She was murdered." She looked as if she was trying to keep her face from crumpling on those words.

"I know that. And I'm sorry for your loss." But the way Etta was acting didn't make any sense. A man was lying dead in the middle of the kitchen floor. They had to call 911 and report the accident to the police. "Are you worried that the break-in today is connected to what happened to your sister?"

"I don't know. I don't know anything for sure.

Except that I won't involve the police. If I do, I'll end up arrested, just like Greg."

"Wait. Who's Greg?"

"Lilly's husband. The police think they have him dead to rights for the murder. But they're wrong." She pinned him with her gaze. "Greg would never hurt Lilly. He loved her more than life itself."

Okay, this was getting complicated. Steven raked his chin with his hand and tried to figure out what to do next. "Let's see what we can find out about this guy who attacked you. Then, we really need to talk about reporting the incident. Okay?"

He didn't wait for an answer as he leaned over and patted the man's pockets, pulling out a billfold and reading aloud the information on the license. "Reginald Taylor, age thirty-two, with a home address in Dallas. Ring any bells?"

She shook her head.

He continued his search. A fifty-dollar bill was tucked under one of the side flaps of the wallet, and as he pushed it back into position, a photograph fluttered to the ground.

"Any idea of who this is?" he asked, holding up a picture of a little girl.

All the color seemed to drain out of Etta's face. "That's Polly," she said.

"Polly?"

"My niece. Lilly and Greg's daughter."

A thread of foreboding snaked its way down his spine. "And where is Polly now?"

"Probably hiding in her room. Just like she did when Lilly was murdered. I should see if I can—"

Ding dong.

Steven's eyes met Etta's as the chime of the doorbell echoed through the house.

"What now?"

Chapter Two

Etta peered through the peephole on the front door. "It's my neighbor, Lynn Weber," she whispered. "She's kind of a busybody."

Bad timing for them. "Will she go away if you don't answer?"

"Maybe. But she'll probably come back to make sure everything is okay."

"Better see what she wants then."

Etta clicked the lock and cracked the door, pressing her body tightly against the opening.

"Hi, Lynn. How are you? Sounds like the block party is going strong."

"Everyone seems to be having a blast. I'm just sorry that you can't join us," the woman replied. "But I totally understand. After all, you're still dealing with the pain of losing your sister. The last thing you need is all that noise and commotion. But I wanted to bring over some cookies for Polly before they all disappeared. Oatmeal-raisin. She's not allergic or anything, is she?"

"Not at all," Etta said, taking the foil-wrapped plate from her neighbor's hand and setting it on the table next to the door, giving Steven a quick view of an older woman with neatly coiffed hair waiting on the threshold. "I'll find Polly and tell her you brought her a treat. Thanks for thinking of us, Lynn. Maybe I'll see you sometime later in the week."

Etta didn't wait for a reply as she pushed the door closed and then turned to face Steven. "We need to find Polly and get out of here now."

Get out of here now? Why was Etta so insistent about cutting the police out of the equation? Wouldn't fleeing the scene make her appear guilty? It wasn't like she had intentionally murdered the guy.

"But, Etta…"

"You need to trust me on this, Steven." Etta's tone was tinged with impatience. "Greg's in jail, and Lilly's gone. That leaves me. I'm the only one left to take care of Polly. It's a mess, and I understand if you don't want to get involved. With this or with us. I can handle it alone."

Steven pulled in a long sigh. "Well, at the very

least, let me help you find Polly. If you called out and said you needed her, would she come?"

"No. And she's really good at hunkering down and keeping quiet. It's sort of her specialty. She hasn't spoken a word since Lilly died."

Steven suddenly felt overwhelmed by a situation that was becoming more confusing by the minute. "Is there a chance that she wandered out into the yard?"

"Maybe."

Steven glanced out the kitchen window. A chain-link fence enclosed a wide lawn with a large wooden play structure. No trees. Just a few scraggly bushes next to a raised flower bed. Unless the kid had dug a tunnel, there weren't that many options for her to hide out there.

"How about you check outside while I search upstairs? It might rouse suspicions if someone sees me wandering around the property."

"Okay. But Polly can be really high-strung. Especially around strangers."

"Don't worry. If I find her, I'll tell her that I'm a friend of her aunt's. I can even show her a picture to prove it." He pulled out his wallet and unfolded a photograph of him and Etta at the lake. Though he had been carrying that particular photo around for years, he couldn't recall the last time he'd looked at it. Wow, did they look young. And happy.

The staircase leading to the upper landing was lined with photographs. Lilly's blue eyes and curly hair—so different from Etta's—made her instantly recognizable as the surly teen he'd met long ago. The man standing next to her, with an arm swung across her shoulders, had to be her husband, Greg. And, of course, there were plenty of pictures of Polly.

At the top of the stairs, Steven paused and listened. It was a tactic he had learned playing hide-and-seek with his twin brother. If you stood completely still and waited, the person you were looking for would invariably make a sound.

But his tactic didn't seem to be working with Polly.

Four doors opened out to the upstairs hall—two bedrooms, a bathroom and what looked to be an office. He checked the bathroom first, flipping the lid on a hamper and scanning behind the towels on the narrow bathroom shelves, but had no success.

He moved toward the office, with its large window that overlooked the backyard. Glancing out, he could see Etta make her way to the top of the play structure to check under the green canopy roof. Even from a distance, he could see her shoulders tense as she bent to scrutinize the top of the slide. He scanned the rest of the office for likely hiding places. There was no closet, but he checked under the desk and even inside a filing cabinet.

There was no sign of Polly.

Two down and two to go. He headed down the hall and into what was clearly the little girl's bedroom. Piles of stuffed animals, most of them horses of every shape and size, covered a large swath of the braided rug that encircled the floor. After pushing aside a handmade quilt, he bent and looked under the bed and then moved on to the closet, determined not to let even the smallest space go unchecked.

Next door was the larger bedroom belonging to Lilly and Greg. Muted gray curtains and crisp white sheets showcased a well-coordinated decorating effort. On the top of a pale wood dresser, Etta's suitcase was open, her clothing still neatly folded with a leather-bound Bible on top of her things. Well, that was new. The Etta he used to know never had a whole lot of time for the Lord. Not that she had ever been hostile to his own faith, just coolly ambivalent.

He once again checked under the bed and in the closet with no success. Where could the little girl be?

The pit in Etta's stomach felt emptier with each passing second as the reality of what had happened seeped into her brain.

She had killed a man. She, Etta Mitchell. A nurse. Someone whose job was to save lives. Instead, she had ended a life in a moment of need and panic and fear.

A case could be made that her that actions had been justified, that if she hadn't grabbed that frying pan, the intruder probably would've killed both her and Steven. And Polly, too, once he found her. After all, her niece seemed to be his target. Fear crept along her spine—she'd felt sick seeing that photo of Polly pulled from the man's pocket. Why would anyone be after her niece? Unless…she and Greg were right that the little girl might have seen something the day Lilly was murdered. What Steven said about her actions being in self-defense was true, though it didn't make dealing with the reality of what she'd done any easier. But there was no way around it. The only thing that mattered was protecting Polly. But with all her hiding and not talking and the nightmares and the fear, that was proving to be difficult.

She clenched her fingers in frustration. She had checked every nook and cranny in the yard that was big enough to fit a five-year-old child. And given the fact that she hadn't heard from Steven, she could assume that he hadn't found Polly, either.

She was getting ready to head back into the house when her gaze settled on a gray plastic storage unit nestled flush against the sidewall. How had she missed it? The container wasn't huge, but it was certainly big enough to accommodate a little girl. Beads of perspiration formed on her forehead as she hurried across the lawn, her knees buckling beneath her as she tore open the lid. But the only thing inside was a coiled-up hose, cracked and forgotten—yet another sign of her failure as keeper of the home. Since Greg had been arrested, not once had she even thought about watering the bushes along the fence. No wonder their leaves were brittle and anemic. A young neighbor kid stopped by weekly to mow the grass, though at this point it was brown and dry as well.

Why hadn't Greg given her better instructions about her duties before he was hauled off to jail?

He probably assumed she understood the basics—buy groceries, water the plants, check the mail. And he did have more important things to think about, like mounting an effective defense against the charges being brought by the DA.

From the beginning, Etta had believed there was no way that Greg could have been involved in her sister's murder. He'd always been the rock in their relationship, steady and patient as a foil to her sister's more tempestuous temperament. But lately, she had started to wonder. The police seemed convinced that he alone had both motive and opportunity. What if it turned out they were right? Then, Polly would be left without a mother and a father, forced to live with a hapless aunt who couldn't even remember to water the lawn. And that was best-case scenario. What if Etta herself was arrested for killing an unarmed man? What would happen then?

Etta knew the answer without even pausing to think. Polly would be taken to Child Protective Services, where she would be assigned to a caseworker and become a part of the system. She had seen it all before, firsthand, with Lilly. Sure. There were great foster homes with kind people who loved kids. But her own experience was hardly a recommendation for that type of care.

Tears formed in the corners of her eyes, but she quickly brushed them away. It wouldn't do to have Steven see her crying. No doubt, he was already confused by the current situation. Why had he come to Silver Creek, anyway, especially today, of all days? She supposed she should be grateful to him for saving her life. But seeing him brought back too many painful memories, and she couldn't cope with any of that today.

And how odd that he still had that old photograph of the two of them, taken at the lake. Her own copy had been tossed in the trash immediately after he'd left town in an angry huff, furious that she'd broken their engagement just one day after he had proposed. Why would she keep it? What was the point of holding on to such a tangible sign of love so quickly lost?

There was no point. And the last thing she needed to do today was to get tangled up in regrets about the past. Right now, she needed to find Polly.

An idea she had dismissed just a short time ago as unlikely suddenly seemed reasonable and...likely. Polly knew about the block party and the pony rides for kids eight and under at the end of the block. And the chance for even a few minutes in the saddle would be like catnip to a horse-crazy little girl.

Etta slipped out the gate and headed toward a group that had congregated in her neighbor's front yard. A tall bespectacled man, whom she recognized as the owner of the duplex two doors down, welcomed her with a wide smile.

"Hi. Etta, right? I'm Griffin Galvin. We met at the funeral, though I don't suppose you remember. I'm so sorry for your loss." His smile faded briefly. "Lilly and Greg were good people, and I know I speak for all the neighbors in offering to help in any way possible. Why don't you grab something to eat and come on over and join us at our table?"

Etta barely had time to make her excuses when a young woman approached her, her forehead pleated with concern.

"I was hoping to see you today, Etta. Not sure you remember, but I'm Jenny Sandquist. I was a friend of Lilly's." There was a slight pause before she added, "And your brother-in-law, too. How is he doing? When's the trial? Sorry. I just launched right in without even asking about you. How are you getting along?"

The neighbors' compassion touched her, though she was in a rush. "I'm doing okay."

"I'm glad to hear it," Jenny said. "My kids have been begging for a playdate with Polly. We're totally open to any day next week. Whatever works with your schedule."

"Can I get back to you on that? I'm actually looking for Polly right now. Have you seen her anywhere on the block?"

The woman's blond ponytail swung back and forth as she shook her head. "No-o-o. But I've been a bit distracted snapping pictures of the party to post on the neighborhood-share app. Come to think of it, your niece might be in one of the photos. Let's see if we can spot her." She opened the camera on her phone. "Oh, look at this one. John Pearnin with his chef's hat and apron cooking burgers for the crew. Cute. Oh, and here's one from this morning, before the party got started. That's my older daughter, Ellie, holding baby Mae…"

A series of loud bangs and crackles split the air, sending Etta's heart lurching in her chest. Fireworks exploded at the end of the block.

"Those dads are all just kids at heart! Oh, and take a look at this one," Jenny said, once again holding up her phone. "It's from last summer. Kids from the neighborhood in Lynn's pool."

Etta pulled in a deep breath. She didn't have the time or patience to watch as Jenny scrolled through every single picture on her phone, especially since Polly might still be out here, somewhere, in the middle of the crowd.

"Thanks. Maybe I could look at your pictures later," she said. Suddenly, the idea of milling through the crowds of neighbors at the block party didn't seem like a good idea. But before she could return to the safety of the house, a tall man with a full gray beard stepped in front of her, barring the way.

"You seem upset," he said, positioning himself directly in front of Etta. "Sorry to be so blunt, but I pride myself on reading people's moods. I can always sense if something is wrong."

Etta stared at the man, confused. He was acting as if they were acquainted, but she didn't remember meeting him at the funeral. Maybe she had forgotten. She had forgotten quite a bit about that day.

"Thank you for your concern, but I'm fine. I was just, um, looking for my niece. I thought she might have wandered off to see the ponies."

The man stepped closer. "I'm headed there

right now. Why don't you come with me, and I can help you look for the kid."

Etta took a short step backward and eyed the stranger. Maybe he was exactly who he claimed to be, a neighbor that wanted to help. But she couldn't take that chance. She glanced around, desperate for an excuse to escape.

"Excuse me, I just remembered that I need to talk to Jenny," she said. "But thanks for your offer to help. Maybe I'll talk to you later."

She turned and began to jog toward the adults gathered by the dessert table, but swerved at the last minute and headed toward the gate. Was the bearded man following her? She didn't stop to check.

It was only after she reached the safety of her yard that she was finally able to breathe. But fear still threatened to overwhelm her senses. Her stomach roiled, and her throat tightened. Suddenly, she was running as fast as her feet could carry her. She stumbled into the house, careening into Steven as she turned the corner into the hall.

"There's a man out there, Steven." Her breath came out in sudden bursts. "He has a long gray beard, and there's something about him that just doesn't seem right. We need to find Polly and escape." She bent over, her hands splayed out across her knees as she struggled for breath.

"I found her, Etta. Don't worry. She's okay," Steven said.

"What? Where?" Even as relief flooded her veins, she couldn't yet trust him, couldn't let herself believe that what he was saying was true.

"She's curled up in the back seat of the black Mustang in the garage, fast asleep."

"That's Greg's car. I should have known she'd hide in a place where she felt safe."

Steven blew out a long breath. "Okay, so I was thinking... Given everything that's been happening, maybe we should get away from all the neighbors and the noise, and discuss what to do next. I'd still like to persuade you to talk to the police. But, for the moment, I suppose that can wait."

Chapter Three

Etta hadn't been behind the wheel of her brother-in-law's Mustang Mach 1 since her sister's funeral. That was three weeks ago, but the memory of that day still burned.

Friends had been invited to stop by the house after the church service, and Greg, knee-deep in grief and denial, had asked her to go out to buy food for the mourners. Of course, she had agreed to make a quick stop at the local grocery store, where it had taken all the fortitude she could muster to make it through the checkout and then load her purchases into the car.

If only she'd known then that her hurried shopping trip would turn out to be the best part of a nightmare day. But she could never have anticipated the scene that waited for her as she pulled up the driveway, just in time to see Greg being led away in handcuffs. All in front of Polly and the dozens of guests arriving for the luncheon.

What if something like that happened today? What if the police showed up in the next few minutes to arrest her for murder?

Impossible, she decided as she buckled her sleeping niece into her booster seat. At this point, no one knew about the intruder. While she had been outside, Steven had moved the man's body into the pantry, where it would be out of sight.

Steeling her nerves, she inched the Mustang down the driveway and past the block party, which was still in full swing. No one gave them a second look as they cruised toward the stop sign, not even the kids playing cornhole in the street. She made a wide arc around the game and then stepped out of the car to push aside the wooden barricade cordoning off the block.

She glanced over at Steven, whose eyes were fixed on his phone. "I wish I could help with directions, but I'm not sure which way to go," she said. "Except for the trip from the airport and a couple of stops at the grocery store, I haven't seen much of the town. Lilly kept inviting me to visit, but I've been working out of Tucson, fifteen-hour shifts with hardly a break. I should have made an effort to get here. But something always seemed to get in the way." The weight of that truth felt heavy on her shoulders. She hadn't spent any time with Lilly in the months before she died.

"Etta?" Steven set the phone on the console and fixed her with a steady glance. "You don't need to explain why you didn't visit your sister as often as you would have liked. I know about the sacrifices you made when Lilly was a teen, so no judgment here."

Of course. Steven had been around for a part of Lilly's awful adolescence. It was embarrassing now to recall how much of their time together had been spent discussing her sister's misbehavior.

"She cleaned up her act, you know," Etta said as she shot a quick glance at Steven. She didn't know why it mattered, but she wanted him to understand that Lilly had grown out of her teenage angst. "When she met Greg, she started reading the Bible and going to church. She walked away from the people that were influencing her bad behavior. And she really became her best self once Polly was born. She had a great part-time job working as a reporter for the local paper. And the last time we talked, she mentioned that she had started to do some free-lance work for the *Dallas Observer*. She was hoping it could turn into a regular gig."

"Glad to hear it." He looked at his phone. "I think we should drive downtown. Seems like the best place to find a quiet spot to discuss what to do next."

Etta nodded. She didn't blame Steven for not wanting to talk about Lilly. Her sister had been awful when they'd started dating, doing everything she could to undermine their relationship.

She made a turn, piloting the vehicle through an upscale neighborhood, where signs of the season were everywhere—baskets of geraniums hanging from porch rails, tufts of new grass popping up along the sidewalks and legions of walkers, clad in shorts and T-shirts, enjoying the early summer weather.

"Nice ride!" a group of teenage boys called out, pointing to the Mustang.

"We probably should have taken your car," Etta said, shifting her eyes once again to look at Steven. "Greg's Mustang is attracting way too much attention."

"I took an Uber to your place." He shrugged. "I'm still not driving because of the accident."

She eyed him briefly. "What accident?"

"That's a story that can keep for later. You just need to relax right now. No one is after us."

Etta shifted her focus to the rearview mirror. Steven was right. There were no police cars following behind her, just a tan Suburban, crawling along at barely the speed limit, two car lengths back from the Mustang. Once again, feelings of guilt and remorse threatened to overwhelm her thoughts. She had killed a man. And the fact that she hadn't intended to strike a fatal blow didn't count for much in the reckoning.

"When do you think the kid will wake up?" Steven craned his neck for a view of the back seat.

"I'm not sure. She didn't sleep that well last night, so she's probably exhausted."

Her gaze returned to the mirror. The Suburban had moved up and was now only a dozen or so feet behind them.

"Steven," she said, struggling to hear her own voice over the pounding of her heart. "That tan SUV has been tailing us for a while. The driver is wearing sunglasses and a ball cap, and so is the passenger, so I can't really see their faces. But neither one looks like the gray-bearded guy who talked to me in the yard."

Steven swiveled around to look through the

back window. "I see them." He leaned back, holding up his phone. "Smile, guys," he said, snapping their picture. He lined up another quick shot.

Etta took a couple of quick turns without signaling, circling one block and then another, but her serpentine route through the empty streets was not enough to shake the Suburban from their tail.

She tried to tamp down the panic threading through her senses. Maybe the driver really was just a harmless tailgater. But, as the SUV nudged even closer to her bumper, that theory made less and less sense.

She needed to do something...and fast. "Hang on. I have an idea."

Cranking the wheel hard, she took the curve as they veered off Northumberland Drive, blowing through a stop sign as she headed south toward the center of town. She had traveled through the area only once before, in the car with Greg on the way from the airport, and she didn't remember much. But she did have a specific memory of passing a two-level parking garage, adjacent to a municipal building that housed the library and city hall.

She floored the gas pedal, skidding onto the

ramp, but was heading the wrong way toward the top level. Just as she had hoped, the angle was too sharp for the SUV. Its tires screeched as the driver overshot the turn.

"Etta." Steven's voice sounded far away.

"I got this," she said.

A quick circle around the upper level, and they headed down the ramp toward the street. It was getting darker now, the once navy sky transformed into a gray backdrop for the tiniest sliver of a moon. She needed to use the shadowy dusk to her advantage. Beside her in the passenger seat, Steven reached back and looped a hand around Polly's car seat. She was still asleep.

"I think you lost them."

"Maybe. But just in case, keep an eye out for a crowded store or fast-food restaurant."

"There's a McDonald's up ahead," Steven said.

Etta veered into the lot, racing at top speed toward the back of the building. She pulled to a stop and cut the lights.

Then, she closed her eyes and said a quick prayer.

Steven released his grip on the car seat and turned back to face the front of the car. "You still okay?"

"Yeah," she said. As okay as she could be after

speeding through a parking ramp in the middle of the city.

"Something is clearly going on here, Etta. Something that is too big for us to handle. First, an intruder broke into the house, and now we have two men tailing us through town. We're less than two miles from the police station. What do you say we head there and go in and explain the situation to the authorities?"

"How can I do that when I don't even understand it myself?" Etta slumped against the seat, pushing back the tears that had begun to leak from the corners of her eyes. For so long after her sister's death, she'd done her best to hold it all together, not once breaking down, even on the day of the funeral when Greg was arrested. But this—the prospect of getting arrested and having Polly taken away from her for good— was too much to bear.

"I can't go to jail," she said. "I told Lilly that I'd be here for Polly. That I'd take care of her and love her if anything happened to her or Greg. And something did happen. And now I need to step up and fulfill my promise."

"Okay, Etta." Steven steepled his hand over the screen of his phone. "But let's not take anything off the table until we hash all this out.

What do you say we drive along the highway and find a motel? Get a room where Polly can sleep, and we can sit outside and sort through the options."

There was a rustling of movement in the back seat—Polly, awake at last, frowning and confused.

"Hi, sweet pea." Tenderness flooded Etta's tone. "Sorry about all the commotion. But a lot has happened since you fell asleep. This guy in the passenger seat is my friend Steven. He's going to be hanging out with us for a little while. Are you hungry?"

Polly shook her head, which was good since Etta didn't relish the thought of getting stuck in the drive-through and the chance of being spotted by the men in the SUV.

"Okay. Well, let me know if you want something to eat." She had a few fruit bars in her purse, but they were hardly enough to sustain a hungry child. At some point, she'd need to stop at a store, but priority one was convincing Steven that it would be a bad idea to involve the police. And if he didn't agree, she'd drop him off at the bus station and handle the situation on her own.

Steven looked up from the map on his phone.

"I found a place that isn't far. I should probably just go ahead and make a reservation."

She exited the lot slowly, looking carefully to the left and the right. But there was no sign of anyone following them. The GPS route led them through the north side of the city, past row after row of homes similar to the one belonging to Greg and Lilly. Etta released a sigh as the Mustang picked up speed, and she put more and more space between them and the last place they'd seen the tan Suburban. Relief flooded her senses. It felt like they had done something bigger than just completing a short drive to reach the outskirts of town. Etta imagined younger versions of herself and Steven bumping fists to celebrate the accomplishment.

Those kinds of moments were all part of the past now, although Etta did allow herself the luxury of a smile. It was a smile that lasted until a neon sign beckoned them toward the weather-beaten canopy shielding the entrance of the Tick Tock Motel.

"It looks pretty crowded," she said, glancing at the number of vehicles parked in the lot.

"Yeah. But crowded could be a good thing. I booked a room under the name of Cassidy Carruthers. That seemed like the best way to go.

And old Cassidy has always served me well on the circuit."

Right. Etta cast a sideways glance at Steven. He didn't need to explain why he often used a fake name when he checked into hotels. Because back in the day, as Etta had eventually realized after only a few weeks of spending time with him, when it came to bull riding, Steven Hunt was kind of a big deal. A handsome cowboy with a mop of dark hair tucked under his hat and a lopsided grin that made it clear that he didn't take much in life too seriously. Even now, he was just as handsome as she remembered, maybe even more so now, with the flecks of gray in his beard and the fine laugh lines around those eyes she knew so well from all the time she'd spent staring into them. How had she not recognized him when he first came running through the patio door?

"I have cash, so I'll check us in," she said. "Cassidy is a fairly androgynous name."

Her hands were shaking as she stepped out of the car and walked into the small office at the front of the motel.

Inside, a dark-haired teen behind a plexiglass barrier slid a form through the bottom slot when Etta announced she had a reservation. Etta curled her *C*'s as she signed in as Cassidy Carruthers. Then, she counted out four twenty-dollar bills and set them on the counter. In return, she received change and a key card marked with the number 6, which, she was told, was to a door at the far end of the L-shaped cluster of rooms on the property.

She shot a quick smile at the girl behind the check-in desk. "Can I grab a couple of toothbrushes and some toothpaste?"

"Sure," the teen said, reaching into a drawer and pulling out a few bags full of often-forgotten essentials. "This okay?"

"Absolutely. Thanks," Etta said, maintaining eye contact as she backed across the room.

Well, that was easy. She had almost made it to the door when a loud voice called out to stop her.

"Wait!" the girl practically shouted. "Something's wrong."

Etta froze in her tracks.

"You didn't fill out the make and license plate of your car. Any vehicle not registered with the office will be towed at the owner's expense."

"Right," Etta said, then muttered under her breath, "Wouldn't want that to happen after everything else today."

★ ★ ★

Steven's eyes blinked open, and he stared in confusion around the small room. An illuminated clock displayed the time—6:02 a.m. But where was he? And why were both his back and jaw throbbing? His limbs felt leaden, as if he'd been run over by a bulldozer. And more than anything, he wished he could go back to sleep. But after growing up on a ranch, the routine of waking up at six to complete chores was ingrained in his very core. He stretched his arms and realized he wasn't in a bed, but rather, was slumped in a chair. His eyes adjusted to the dim light, and he spotted the other two people sharing the space, both still asleep in a double bed. Ah. Right. The events from the previous day flashed across his brain. The long bus ride down from Dallas. The Uber to Dogwood Drive. The sight of Etta lying on the floor and the fight with the intruder. The harried search for Polly and the drive out of town.

He reached up to gingerly touch his jaw. It was definitely swollen, and probably black and blue, too. Good thing he was keeping his beard longer these days. Maybe no one would notice that he looked a bit worse for wear. The small motel room felt safe enough, but he had pushed the one chair against the door, just in case. And, truth be told, it wasn't the most uncomfortable place he'd ever spent the night. A soft chair beat a horse stall and a bale of hay any day. But, between all of his injuries, old and new, his body was sure feeling tender.

He glanced again at the bed. Dark brown hair spilled across a white pillow as Etta slept on her side, holding Polly against her chest. Etta was still as beautiful as she'd ever been, yet at the same time so different from the girl he'd known all those years ago.

Don't go there. The rational part of his brain blinked out a warning, but he was already gone. Back to that dusty road where he had pulled his truck over and tried to change Etta's mind about breaking their engagement. But she had been adamant, her *no* as sure as the *yes* she'd uttered just one day earlier, when she'd accepted his ring.

A twelve-hour engagement after a two-month courtship. Crazy to even think of that today. He and Etta had been on a roller-coaster ride filled with dips and turns from the moment they'd met to their last, angry argument, when she'd told him that rather than getting married, she wanted to work as a traveling nurse. Oh, she had her ambitions. Thinking back, he had to admire her drive. That girl had been fiery and fiercely independent, with big plans for her life—plans to get out of Texas and see the world. That girl had been biding her time, waiting for her kid sister to finish high school before she set off on her grand adventure.

But the Etta he'd met yesterday seemed like a different person. Part of it was superficial. She was wearing her hair longer now, and the bangs that used to hang down into her dark brown eyes and frame her open face had grown out. It made her seem more grown-up, more mature. Which, of course, she was. They both were. Fifteen years was a long time. But it was the worry in her eyes and the anxiety that tightened her face that had caught him by surprise. Twenty-one-year-old Etta hadn't had an easy childhood, but she'd always seemed fearless and impervious to the harsher realities of life. The Etta of today still radiated that same courage, but now there was a new layer of vulnerability.

He pushed his hands through his hair. If he had noticed changes in Etta, what must she have thought of him? She hadn't even recognized him when he'd shown up at the house. He knew all too well that his boyish good looks were long gone. Every day he grimaced at the stranger in the mirror—a stranger with deep lines around his eyes and threads of gray in his hair and beard, both of which needed to be trimmed.

He stifled a groan and pulled himself to his feet. It was time to stop stalling and face the morning. Don't Delay! Seize the Day! had been one of his dad's favorite mottos growing up. While it had certainly annoyed him when he had been an exhausted teen, trying to catch up on sleep, he had grown to appreciate the sentiment.

Last night had not gone the way he had hoped. He had imagined them putting Polly down in one of the beds, and then pulling up chairs outside the room so they could finally talk. He had it all planned out—what he would say to make her see that running away was the absolutely worst thing to do, how he would convince her that turning herself in to the police was the only logical course of action left open, given the circumstances.

But that conversation was put on the back burner as Polly fussed, thrusting her little body to and fro on the bed until Etta had agreed to lie down next to her. Moments later, they were both asleep.

But, hey, this was a new day. When Etta woke up, they could still have that talk while Polly holed up inside, watching cartoons. Maybe he could persuade her to turn herself in to the police. But first, coffee.

Stiffness shortened his steps as he pushed the chair away from the door and then quietly unlatched the lock. Sunshine was already streaming down against the parking lot as he stepped outside, his eyes squinting as he stared at the still-full lot. Last night, there were no parking spots in the front, so Etta had pulled around to the back lot.

A red Dodge Charger he hadn't noticed last night was parked in front of the main office. It was kind of early for check-in, and his gut instincts snapped to full alert. He pulled his worn ball cap out of his back pocket and tugged it down low on his head. His clothes were wrinkled from being slept in all night, but this motel didn't seem like it would stand on ceremony.

He pulled open the door to the office and walked toward the large urns of coffee, set out on a long table. The small room felt cramped, even though it was mostly empty. A family of four was sitting at one of the tables, two children eating cereal while their parents watched the news on TV. Two thirtysomething men were standing beside the check-in counter, drumming their fingers impatiently. There was no sign of the teenager who had checked them in the night before.

He pushed down on the lever and filled one cup with piping hot liquid, then fitted on a lid. He picked up a second cup and looked around. He took his coffee black, but, if he remembered correctly, Etta liked a splash of milk. Ah. The milk was over by the cereal. He quickly filled the cup and then carried the steaming drink over to the counter with the food.

"Hey," one of the men suddenly said.

Steven glanced over at them. An older man with curly red hair had appeared behind the counter and was offering a quizzical smile. "Are you here to check in? It's early, but we might be able to make accommodations."

"Nah, we don't want to stay at your motel. We're looking for someone. Or rather, a couple of someones who are in trouble with the law."

The hairs on the back of Steven's neck stood up. He finished pouring milk into the coffee, struggling to maintain an air of nonchalance as he took a few steps closer to the counter so he could hear the rest of the conversation and get a better look at the two men. He couldn't be sure if they were the driver and passenger of the tan SUV that had followed them yesterday through town. If so, they had probably changed cars. They were dressed almost identically, in pastel polo shirts and tan khakis. Both had short dark hair worn in a buzz cut. The one in the light blue shirt stepped closer to the counter and continued taking charge of the situation.

"Yeah," he said. "Can you tell me if you had a youngish woman check in last night with a small child? There may have a been someone else with them, too."

"Oh, I am sorry, but I can't give out information about our guests. Besides, I wasn't working the evening shift yesterday."

The skinnier of the two men reached into his pocket and pulled out a thick wad of bills. "Listen. We're in kind of a hurry here. That's our car parked out front, and we're anxious to get back on the road. I understand your reluctance, but this is very important. Is there any way that I could maybe make it worth your while?"

The proprietor stared at the cash for a beat and then nodded. "Let me get my daughter. She handles all of the late check-ins. Maybe she can help."

Chapter Four

Steven's first instinct was to rush back to the room, wake up Etta and Polly, jump in the car and get back on the road. But the inquisitive side of him wanted more information. Neither man had a gray beard like the guy Etta had encountered in the yard, but there was something about the thinner one that was oddly familiar. Steven took out his phone and pulled up the photo he'd taken the day before. It was hard to be certain, since both men had been wearing sunglasses and ball caps, but they could easily be the ones standing at the counter less than five feet away from him.

They had claimed to be looking for someone in trouble with the law, but neither had flashed a badge. Instead, they had offered a bribe. Not cops, then.

How much time did he have before the proprietor of the motel returned with his daughter? Two minutes? Five minutes? Still, if he could cause a distraction, maybe he could buy them some time to make their escape. His eyes scanned the small space again.

A buffet crammed with prepackaged breakfast foods—cereal, muffins, yogurt—and a stack of paper plates. Nothing useful. Then there were the coffee dispensers on the other side of the room. No help there, either.

Frustration pumped through his veins. If he was going to do something, he needed to act fast. He had already wasted precious seconds when he could be back at the motel room, warning Etta and packing the car. He turned on his heel, preparing to walk out the door, when his gaze fell upon something he had missed. An idea began to form in his mind. It was a long shot, but then again, wasn't he the king of long shots? Sure, his return to rodeo hadn't gone quite as planned, but that just meant he was due some success this time around. And if this move didn't work, then he would just head out of the office and hurry Etta and Polly on their way.

He trained his eyes toward the ceiling of the small room. No cameras. Good. If what he was about to do was to succeed long-term, he didn't want to leave any video evidence. These guys were smart. They'd found the motel before twelve hours had passed. The main advantage he and Etta had was the fact that the men were unaware of Steven's identity. He moved just a few feet to the side, then edged closer to the family having their breakfast, as the youngest son—a little boy of about four—approached the table with a full glass of orange juice.

Steven stepped forward and deliberately nudged his arm, causing the little boy to drop the plastic cup and sending a spray of liquid onto Steven's pants. "Whoa. Watch it there," Steven said as he tripped backward, stumbling against one of the two men, who were still waiting by the counter. Too late, the dad of the family cried out a warning, and that resulted in the little boy to bursting into tears.

The motel owner came hurrying back down the stairs without his daughter. There was a flurry of excitement and apologies. But, within in a matter of seconds, the tumult died away. Steven bent down to console the crying child, hoping to keep the men from seeing through his ploy. But the evasion wasn't necessary. Their only reaction was to pester the proprietor about his daughter's whereabouts.

"She'll be here in five minutes. I told her that

you were looking for information, and she said she'd come down here as soon as she can." Now the motel owner seemed far more concerned with wiping up all the spilled orange juice than appeasing the grumbling men.

That was Steven's cue to make his exit. With a final apology to the family, he headed out the door, his hands jammed into his pockets. His theatrics seemed to have worked, and no one seemed to suspect his stumble hadn't been orchestrated to pick the pocket of the man waiting by the counter. A smile curled on his lips. Some people looked down on rodeo folks, and sure, there were plenty of sketchy characters. Heck, he'd been one of them at seventeen. One good scolding from his mama when she'd found his collection of stolen keychains had put an end to his life of crime, and he'd never lifted anything again. Until now.

He pulled his own key fob out of his pocket and slipped open the blade of the small Swiss Army knife attached by a link. Then, just like he was out for a stroll through the parking lot, he sidled up next to the Charger and plunged the knife into the front tire.

He waited until he heard the satisfying hiss of air and then he continued on his way. Once he reached the motel room, he flashed his keycard to unlock the door.

The space was still dim as he stepped inside, but both Etta and Polly were sitting up in bed. His heart thumped as Etta, her hair matted down on one side and her face still soft and re-laxed from sleep, offered him a smile. No one should look that good after such a stressful day. But, then again, Etta always looked good. It was part of her charm.

"We have to hit the road immediately," he said as he set down the coffee, then scrambled around to collect their stuff. Etta didn't bother asking him any questions, but sprang out of the rumpled bed, pulling Polly with her.

"We're going back into the car now, sweetie." Her voice was calm as she spoke to the little girl. But already, the fine lines of worry were back as her jaw seemed to tighten.

Her gaze met his. "Problems?"

"Nothing we can't handle. There are two men at the front office asking questions. But since we parked in the back lot, they don't know which room we're in. Yet. We have to hurry."

Etta swept up the few items she had brought along for Polly as Steven opened the door a few inches and looked toward the office. No signs of the men yet. But their car was still parked in front.

He waited a moment and then checked outside again. Still clear.

"You and Polly start walking to the car while I keep a lookout."

Etta gave him a worried glance, but he shook his head. This wasn't the time to dwell on the negative. For now, their focus had to be on escape. The next time he glanced through the crack, Etta and Polly had turned the corner toward the back of the motel and were out of sight. Time for him to start moving. He stepped across the threshold, his eyes tracking the entrance to the motel. When he reached the edge of the building, he sprinted toward the back lot.

His chest hurt from the short jog to the car, but he tried to cover up how winded he was as he pulled open the passenger door.

He slid in. "Ready to go?"

Etta nodded as she pulled forward and drove to the far end of the lot. "Highway or back roads?"

He turned his head for a final view of the motel entrance. The men were standing on the front pavement, looking down at the Charger's flat tire. "Let's take the interstate down two exits, and then hop off the main road. I'll map out a route on my phone."

He pulled out his cell as Etta merged onto the highway. A quick glance behind him confirmed that no one was following them.

"Hey! We did it!" He gave Etta a smile. "Good thing you're not high-maintenance, or we might not have beat them."

But Etta didn't smile at the joke. Her fingers were curled around the steering wheel and her lips were pressed tight.

"Who are these people?" she asked. "And how did they find us?"

The same thought had been tumbling around in his own head. Not for the first time, he wished his twin brother, Seb, was here. As sheriff of their county up in South Dakota, his brother would have the resources to help them. "I have a few ideas about how they managed to track us down. But as to who they are? I'm not sure, but I might know a way we can find out."

Etta cast a glance in his direction. "How is that?"

"Well, when I first started working the rodeo, I went through a slight delinquent phase. I wasn't going to church, and, well, I acted like the rules didn't apply to me anymore since I was living as an adult. I had a friend who worked the side-shows at the rodeo. And he taught me some of his tricks. Long story short—" he reached into his pocket and pulled out the wallet he'd lifted from the burlier of the two men "—we might be able to get some answers from this."

Etta pulled in a deep breath. She had hardly recovered from yesterday, and now, once again, they were on the run, fleeing for their lives from men who seemed to have superhuman tracking abilities.

A shiver started at her shoulders and ran down her spine as the reality of their situation dawned on her. What would have happened if Steven hadn't been in the motel office when their pursuers arrived? She and Polly might be dead.

Just like Lilly.

"Hey! Look at that!" Etta shook off the feelings of fear and anxiety and pointed toward a rainbow arcing over the horizon. It was the perfect reminder that she needed to keep her focus on hope and trust in her Creator, even during the darkest times.

A rustling movement drew her attention to the back seat as Polly leaned forward, a deep frown etched across her lips.

"Did you see the rainbow, Pol?" Etta asked. Polly nodded.

"Is there something you want me to do?"

Another nod as Polly pointed to a disc wedged next to the console on which Lilly had written Favorite Hymns.

"Shall we give it a listen?" Etta asked.

Another nod. Etta pushed the CD into the slot on the player and music filled the car.

Steven was quick to identify the song. "'How Great Thou Art,'" he said.

"Lilly's favorite." Etta smiled. "They played it at her wedding." For a moment, she was transported to the small back room of the restaurant where they had gone to celebrate after the ceremony. Her sister had been so radiant that day, joyful and excited at the prospect of a new life ahead. Etta sucked in a long breath as guilt seeped into her memories. With Lilly happily married, Etta had taken a step back in their relationship, visiting once or twice a year, calling every couple of months to catch up on all the moments she was missing. New house, new job, new baby. She had listened as her sister talked about her jam-packed days and the challenges of raising Polly. Lilly's newfound confidence had offered Etta a reason to pull back, to be less involved in her sister's life. At the time, Etta had been grateful for the break. Now, she was filled with regret.

When the song ended, she ejected the disc and turned back toward her niece. "Your mama sure did love that one. I remember her singing it to you after you were born."

Polly smiled as she settled back in her seat.

Etta shifted her eyes toward Steven and said lowly, "Maybe it's a leap, but I think she knew I was fretting and wanted to cheer me up."

He nodded. "Well, she picked a good song."

"She did. So...what next?"

"Well. Let's see if the contents of this wallet will provide a few answers about the men from the motel." Steven flipped open the billfold and looked inside. "Apparently, the owner's name is Matt Bickler, age..." He slid the ID out of the plastic and squinted. "Thirty-four. Dallas address. Ring any bells?"

"I'm not sure. The name does sound slightly familiar."

He pulled out his phone and began to type. A moment later, he looked up and said, "I found a Matt Bickler. Attorney with the firm Thompson, Colfax and Bickler."

Of course...that was where she knew the

name. "Greg's lawyer is Sam Colfax. Odd co-incidence, don't you think?"

He took a moment to compare pictures. "It's the same guy. And *odd* is hardly the word for it." Steven shuffled through the remaining items in the wallet. "Credit card. Gym membership. Sticker for that guy who's running for reelection as Texas attorney general. Oh, and hey, look at this. Apparently, he's a customer at Pizza Roundup. Two more punches and he'll earn a free pie."

Etta turned again to face Steven. "How do you think they found us?"

"Most likely they pinged your phone. I turned it off when we got into the car, but it's possible that they're tracking the Mustang. I know you don't want to hear it, but I need to say it again. This is a job for the police."

Etta shook her head. "I've already explained why going to the police is not an option. Is there a plan B?"

Steven shot her a look. "Not really. Not if you want to keep Polly safe. Continuing to run is a huge mistake."

"But what if there was a way we could stay off the radar? I don't trust the police to handle this right. And the fact that Greg's lawyer is a partner of one of the men following us is troublesome, to say the least." Could she even trust Greg? Why was someone from the law firm representing him after them? Deep down, she knew Greg wouldn't do anything to harm his family—certainly not Polly. "Maybe the next step is to talk to Greg and see if he can fill in some blanks about the situation."

Steven frowned. "Etta, no. That's not a good idea. And I have to ask—what's the endgame in all of this? I thought the goal here was protecting Polly."

"This *is* all part of that goal. We don't know who we can trust yet. I'd like to ask Greg a few questions."

"Consider this as an alternative." Steven seemed to be having a hard time hiding his exasperation. "You asked about a plan B. How about we head north to my family's ranch in South Dakota? My brother, Seb, is the sheriff there, and he can help us look into your sister's case."

Huh. During their long-ago courtship, she had heard a lot of stories about Steven's twin brother, but she didn't know he was a sheriff. But as interesting as that was, she still didn't think it was good idea to involve Steven's family in her personal problems. She had killed someone and fled a crime scene. It all just seemed too risky.

She looked at Steven and shook her head. "The last thing I want to do is put your family in danger by asking them to shelter me and Polly."

"I'm one-hundred-percent certain that they'd want to help. But, if it makes you feel better, I can call and run the idea by them before we show up on their doorstep."

"It's a kind offer. But before we do anything, I'd still like to discuss all of this with Greg. This situation with his lawyer is so sketchy. Sam Colfax and Matt Bickler could be leading Greg down a rabbit hole that would make it impossible for him to prove his innocence or for there to be justice for Lilly." She couldn't run away if there was a chance of that happening. She wanted justice for her sister as much as she wanted to protect her niece.

Steven sighed. "Well, whatever we decide, we're going to need to ditch this car as soon as possible. I'm just thinking out loud here, but I'd say that the best place to do that would be at the airport. We can leave the Mustang in the long-term lot and rent a new vehicle to drive to South Dakota."

"With a quick stop afterward at the prison," Etta persisted.

The landscape got bleaker and bleaker as they headed north, toward the airport. Tall scrub grass leaned down by the side of the road. The drought had been hard on this part of the county, and the farmers had to be looking for some much-needed rain.

But just that quickly, the freshly plowed fields gave way to a more suburban landscape as they reached the outskirts of the big city.

"I just thought of something," Etta said. She'd been too distracted to think of it before. "You can't rent a car without a license, and it's probably risky for me to do it in my name."

Steven glanced at her. "What makes you think I don't have a license?" Steven shuffled through the cards in his wallet. "Actually, I have three. One in my name, one for Cassidy Carruthers and the last one courtesy of Matt Bickler."

"I thought you said you couldn't drive."

He raised an eyebrow. "How have you not heard about this? It was on the news, and it was featured in a four-page spread in *People*."

"I've been busy," she said defensively. "And since when was there national interest in something that happened at a rodeo?"

There was a long pause.

"Okay, fine," she said, fighting the urge to roll her eyes. "I'm guessing you got wrecked again in the ring. Was it worse than what happened the first time we met?"

He shrugged. "Nah. Not nearly that bad. Just enough to sideline me for the season."

"Hmm." Etta pressed her lips together, unsure of whether or not to believe him. Steven had always been a little reckless. "How long ago did this take place?"

He ran a hand across his beard. "End of February."

"And you still can't drive?"

"Okay, counselor," he said, raising his hands in a gesture of surrender. "You are correct that my injuries were a bit worse than I've been letting on. But can we ease off on the interrogation just a bit? Because none of that matters in light of the rest of this stuff that's going on."

She let the subject drop, at least for the moment. Following the signs, Etta parked the Mustang in the airport's long-term lot and helped load their gear on a luggage cart. Now that she was paying attention, she noticed that Steven was walking with a decided limp, and she resolved to find out what had happened in February.

After a fifteen-minute shuttle ride, they reached the rental-car center. So far, so good. But once inside, they were faced with a choice of more than ten companies offering a variety of packages and a selection of different vehicles. Security cameras were everywhere, and Etta's eyes locked on one particular revolving lens with a wide-angle view. Steven must have noticed it, too, because he stepped sideways to avoid getting tagged in the picture.

An intercom crackled with announcements as they made their way toward the line in front of the Hertz rental counter. "We don't have a reservation, so this might take a while," Steven said. "You two grab a seat. I'll try to be as quick as I can."

Etta pointed to a row of chairs by a window. "We'll wait for you over there." She tugged at Polly's hand, but the little girl refused to move. Her lower lip trembled, and her eyes filled with tears.

"Would you like to ride in the baggage cart while I go get our car?" Steven asked.

Polly nodded.

He turned to Etta. "Will you help me get her up here?"

"Of course." Her gaze tracked Steven's efforts

as he bent to lift Polly. The cowboy she had known so long ago had been wiry and fit. But the rough life of the circuit had taken its toll on his body. And that last injury must have been a lot worse than he was letting on.

Etta found a quiet corner where she could wait. Polly's face remained impassive as Etta tried to explain what was going on. She had gotten quite adept at making up stories centered around the small details of home life, but it wouldn't do to mention that they would soon be headed to the prison to see Polly's dad. Every so often, she glanced at her watch. As the minutes ticked by, it became harder and harder to understand the delay. Finally, Steven ambled over to join them, smiling as he led them through a dark parking lot toward a blue minivan.

Polly's forehead wrinkled as she pointed to the van and shook her head.

Steven bent to reassure her. "Don't worry, kid. It's only a loaner. Your dad's car will be here, waiting for him here when he comes home. Until then, this will be more comfortable for all of us, but especially for our new friend." He pulled open the sliding door to reveal a small stuffed rabbit perched on the back seat. "He looked kind of lonely, and I was hoping he could hang out with you for a little while."

Polly's smile was pure sunshine. Grinning, she climbed up and settled back against her car seat. Then, after snapping the safety strap into the clip, she put on her headphones and pulled her bunny close to her chest.

Etta slid into the driver's seat, and Steven handed her the keys. "When did you find the time to shop for that?"

He grinned. "You're not going to believe it. The guy behind me in line saw me talking to Polly. He had bought the rabbit at the airport gift shop for his niece, but he must have realized that Polly needed it more than she did. Nice guy."

The gesture, from both Steven and the stranger, touched her heart. "Absolutely. So, next stop, the prison?"

He pulled in a deep breath.

"I don't think we have a choice here, Steven. It's actually a practical solution if you think about it. Greg could have some information that will help us keep Polly safe."

"Fine...but I'm going to be the one who goes inside." She was about to protest when he held up a hand. "I know that you're convinced of your brother-in-law's innocence, but with his law firm being involved in all this, I'd like to get a read on him myself. Besides, the police are probably looking for you, and, so far, anyway, I've been staying off the radar. The only hitch will be if Greg refuses to see me because he doesn't recognize my name."

Etta bit down hard on her lip, recalling what her sister thought of Steven Hunt. "He's heard of you, of course," she said diplomatically. "But maybe not in a good way."

Steven met and held her glance. "Glad to know. Do you have a set time when you talk to him each week?"

Etta snuck a peek at her niece in the middle seat. Since the headrests were thick and high enough to muffle most sound, even if Polly slipped off her headphones, it was unlikely she could hear what was being discussed in the front. Still, Etta lowered her voice as she turned toward Steven.

"He calls when he can, but it's usually about Polly. Before he was arrested, he and I talked about getting Polly in to see a counselor in the hope that she might open up about what happened when Lilly was killed. It's possible—likely, in fact—that she saw something the day of the murder. It happened in the morning, and Polly was home at the time, so she might have been there when the killer came to the door." Etta still shuddered to think about her little niece, terrified and worried about her mother. "But what exactly she witnessed, we don't know. Greg tried to talk to her about it, of course, and so did the police. I tried as well. But you've seen how it is. She just won't speak."

Steven frowned, his countenance grim. "I suppose it would explain why Polly has become a target. Poor kid. I can't imagine how difficult that would be for her if she was, in fact, a witness to her mother's murder."

Etta turned her head to the side and pushed back tears. Everything had happened so fast that there had been barely time to formulate a plan to help Polly deal with the sadness and confusion of her mother's death. Her cheeks were wet when she turned back to face Steven.

"I can't even think about it without breaking down. Polly has been through so much. I know she misses Lilly, but she misses Greg, too. That's one of the reasons to talk to him. Maybe there's something he can tell us that will help put an end to all of this."

Steven sighed. "Fine. But let's just not get our

hopes up, okay?" He paused for a moment. "I just had an idea that might be a game changer. While I was waiting in line at the rental counter, I took another look at Matt Bickler's license. He and I are close to the same age and build, give or take a few inches. The main difference is that Bickler looks like a hipster rock star, and I look like..." He shrugged. "Me. But with a little help from a razor and some bleach, I think I could do a fairly good impersonation. Greg might agree to see me if he thought I was affiliated with his law firm. And masquerading as Matt Bickler will allow me to keep my real identity hidden for the time being."

As ideas went, it wasn't the worst. This way, neither of them would be spotted at the prison while trying to lie low. But a lot would be riding on Steven's ability to assume a false identity. "But what if the guards at the prison see through your disguise?"

"We'll cross that bridge when we come to it. But we should talk about something before I meet with your brother-in-law. Are you positive that he had nothing to do with your sister's murder?"

Etta nodded. A twinge of doubt poked at her, but she pushed it away. "I know the facts don't line up in Greg's favor, but I can't see him deliberately trying to hurt Lilly in any way."

"Okay, then. We should move forward on that assumption. But we need to keep an open mind and not view anything as a given. And once we finish up at the prison, we'll set the GPS for the ranch in South Dakota."

Chapter Five

Visiting Greg would have to wait. First up was perfecting Steven's transformation into Matt Bickler.

"Second exit and turn left," Steven said, reading the directions to Walmart on his phone.

"Got it," Etta said. She wasn't completely sold on the idea of Steven disguising himself to gain entrance to the prison. But he had insisted that it would be too risky for her to take the lead on this. And though he didn't say so directly, she suspected that he wanted to make his own decision about her brother-in-law's involvement in Lilly's death.

"I've used an alias countless times when I was out on the circuit, and no one questioned me at all."

"But Cassidy Carruthers is you, just with a different name. This time, you're pretend-ing to be someone completely different, both in appearance and in mannerisms. That's a big enough challenge. But what if Greg has met Matt Bickler and knows what he looks like? He won't be fooled by bleached hair and a pair of hipster glasses."

Steven waved off that possibility. "I'm not concerned. One guy with short, spiky hair looks like a dozen others. Even if their paths did cross at some point, Greg wouldn't have been focused on details. Panic does crazy things to the psyche. Consider the fact that you didn't recognize me when you saw me at your sister's house. That took me down a few pegs."

"But…"

"Stop worrying, Etta. You need to trust that I can do this, okay?"

Etta bit back a sigh and trained her focus on the road ahead.

Even after all the changes of the past fifteen years, Steven still had an extremely healthy ego. Could he really be offended that she'd failed to recognize him at first glance? Given the fact that she was being beaten by her assailant, she might be excused for not rolling out the welcome mat to greet an old friend. And then, of course, once again, the efficient file system of her brain eas-ily turned up another example of Steven's self-centeredness—there was his shocked reaction when he discovered she hadn't been following his accomplishments on the rodeo circuit. What was that all about? Had *he* been following *her* career?

Not likely.

Though to be fair, her work as a traveling nurse didn't garner headlines in the national media. So she supposed he had a point there. But she really had been busy, stuck in an endless cycle of work, sleep, repeat. She could almost hear Steven's retort, that her single-mindedness had always been the root of her problems.

Was that true? She worked hard at her job, which was often gut-wrenchingly sad and always challenging. Etta had to constantly deal with illness and tragedy—being a nurse certainly didn't involve spending evenings out with pals from the circuit.

"Here's our exit, straight ahead." Steven's voice pulled her out of the imaginary argument she was having with herself. An argument that, sad to say, she seemed to be losing. If nothing else, she prided herself on being self-aware.

She flicked on her signal and made the turn toward the Walmart, looming in a half-acre lot straight ahead. A quick glance toward the passenger seat took in Steven's strained countenance and brought a sudden realization that maybe the past few years hadn't been all fun and games for him, either. There had to be more to the story about the most recent injury to his leg.

"What did happen the last time you rode in the ring? Did you pull an ornery bull that no one could handle?"

He shook his head. "Nothing like that. I actually stayed on for the whole eight seconds, and my dismount was sweet, if I do say so myself."

"And then..." she pressed.

He raised a brow. "A buddy got thrown, and I jumped in to help him. His bull didn't like that, and he showed his displeasure by trampling on my leg."

"Oh, Steven." Her voice quavered as she thought about how much that must have hurt. But he shook off her sympathy with a shake of his head.

"It hurt at the time, but it's much better now."

Once they parked and went inside the store, Steven turned to face her, his eyes bright with anticipation.

"I'm going to check out the hair dyes and then look for some clothes to complete my disguise.

You should pick up some things for you and Polly. And also shop for groceries." He waved her toward the grocery aisles. "Once I get the stuff I need, I'll head into one of the private family bathrooms and bleach my hair. We'll keep this stop as quick as possible and then meet at the front so that I can pay."

"But first, shouldn't we…" she began, but then, with a wave and a wink, Steven disappeared into a crowd of shoppers waiting to check out in the front of the store.

Classic. That move captured Steven in a nutshell. One minute, humble about his past heroics; cocky, the next.

Etta's brain flashed back to those early days when she was working the night shift at the hospital, a new nurse with no seniority but plenty of dedication when it came to her patients. She had a special interest in the cowboy she had helped, however briefly, when he'd been hurt in the ring at the country fair. Steven had been pretty out of it after a complicated surgery to repair a punctured lung, a lacerated liver and to set more than a dozen broken bones. But when she had stopped by his hospital room to see how he was doing, he had opened his eyes and immediately shot her a crooked smile.

"Here you are again. Tell me, what did I do right to get the best-looking nurse in the hospital?"

She had smiled back at him. Flirting with patients was frowned upon by the administration, but what was she expected to do when the patient was flirting with her?

He was good-looking and charming. And back then, he was different in every way from most of the guys she knew. Serious and lighthearted at the same time. And supremely self-assured. He was a twin, he told her, the child of a happy family who all still lived on a ranch in South Dakota. Her polar opposite in so many ways.

She had liked him immediately.

Although, that was fifteen years ago. A lot had changed since then. For both of them. Even though she hadn't been following Steven's bull-riding career lately, she knew enough to understand that the sport had been good to him, at least when it came to paying the bills. But maybe not so much in terms of the toll it had taken on his body. That limp looked pretty serious, even as he had moved through the crowd, away from her and Polly. She made another mental note to herself to look into the circumstances of his latest injuries.

"C'mon, Polly," she said, shaking herself out of her reverie. "Let's go find some carrots for your new rabbit. After we get the groceries we need, we'll have plenty of time to look at the clothes and the books."

With a firm grasp on Polly's hand, Etta pushed her cart toward the fruits and vegetables. There, she sifted through bags of apples and oranges, marveling at the freshness of the display. It had been weeks since she had been in a proper grocery store. While staying at the house, she had arranged to have most of their groceries delivered, often dealing with surprising substitutions. The knowledge that today Steven was paying the bill made her more extravagant than usual as she added a bunch of bananas and a large chunk of cheddar cheese to the growing pile of items in her cart.

Soon, they had everything they needed for the days ahead, including two new outfits for Polly and a pair of jeans and a couple of T-shirts for herself. Etta checked her phone and glanced around for Steven. They should have time to quickly check the books.

She was pleased to see that an ample number of picture books filled the shelves, all suitable to the taste and ability level of a precocious five-year-old girl. She hovered near Polly as her niece checked out the selection, taking a moment to eye a display of current bestsellers for herself. She had always enjoyed a good mystery, and she scanned the covers for one that was not too cozy but not too grisly. A difficult balance to find, for sure. But who was she kidding? It wasn't like she was going on a vacation to the islands. There would be little time for reading in the days ahead.

With Polly still looking at books as she sat cross-legged on the floor, Etta's eyes flitted to the bank of TVs along the back wall, and a gasp stuck in her throat as a picture of Greg and Lilly's house flashed across a half-dozen screens. What followed were photos of Etta and Lilly, taken years ago, before Lilly's marriage, with text underneath providing close captions. *Police continue to investigate an apparent homicide in Silver Creek in the four hundred block of Dogwood Drive. Still missing is five-year-old Polly Sanderson, who had been left in the care of her aunt, Etta Mitchell...*

Etta had seen enough. She grabbed Polly's hand and headed for the front of the store.

★ ★ ★

Steven ran his fingers through his now-buzzed hair as he caught his reflection in the bathroom mirror. Well, he might not look exactly like Matt Bickler, but he sure didn't resemble himself anymore. Gone were his trademark dark hair and ever-present stubble, which had grown out into a fuller beard of late. He probably hadn't been truly clean-shaven like this since his twin brother's wedding a few years back. It would be good to get to the ranch and see Seb and and his wife, Tacy, again, even though it would mean asking his twin for a pretty big favor. But it wouldn't hurt to have the full force of the law on their side sooner rather than later, given the ruthlessness of the men who were after Etta and Polly.

He studied the picture of Matt Bickler again and fitted the clear glasses he'd purchased on his nose. The green tortoiseshell frames didn't exactly match the ones Matt Bickler was wearing in his picture, but they had the same hipster vibe. And, best of all, they hid the bruises from his earlier fight.

Satisfied, he exited the bathroom in search of Etta. The brown dress shoes pinched a bit and the new pants felt even tighter as he headed for the front of the store.

He spotted Etta. "Excuse me, miss," he said, tapping her on the shoulder.

He had expected a good reaction. Maybe a burst of laughter. Certainly, a smirk and an eye roll. What he had not anticipated was for Etta to flinch away from his touch and shrink into herself.

Or the look of fear as she turned to face him. It felt like a sucker punch to the gut.

"Etta, it's me. Steven."

She blinked up at him, and then she seemed to pull herself up as understanding flickered.

First, her eyes narrowed and she took a step back, her gaze roaming from the brown tips of his tasseled dress loafers up to the tucked-in metallic shirt and ending at his bleached hair. Her lips quirked, and her eyebrows rose. Steven shifted back and forth, feeling just a bit uncomfortable under her scrutiny. But then, as if a bubble of mirth had risen up from her diaphragm, Etta's mouth curved into a perfect smile. A second later, she doubled over, her entire body shaking with laughter.

"Hey now, it's not that funny." Steven tried to make his voice sound gruff, but he was beaming in her direction. He was happy to lighten her mood, if only for the moment.

He turned to Polly, who was looking at him with her usual gaze of dubious skepticism. "Do you think I look ridiculous? See, Etta, the kid thinks I look as handsome as ever."

Etta pulled in a gulp of air. "Sorry. Sorry. Honestly, I'm impressed. It's just that you usually seem so…" She paused as if trying to think of the right word.

"Good-looking? Manly?" he ventured.

"Rugged," Etta offered. "And this—" she gestured toward his clothing "—well, this is different."

He smirked. Rugged. That seemed like a compliment. He'd take it. For sure. "You ready, then? I already paid for all my stuff, and I even remembered to pick up a couple of burner phones in case we need them. But let's check out your gear and get going. What's with the ball cap, by the way?"

At the mention of her hat, Etta blanched. And, just like that, all the joy on her face evaporated, replaced by pinched anxiety.

"Lilly's house is on the news," she said lowly. "Which means they found the body. No big surprise there, I suppose. But they have a picture of me. It's an old one, but it won't be long before they find one that's more up-to-date. The police are going to be looking for me now. And they'll probably arrest me and take me to jail."

"We'll figure this out before that happens, Etta."

"How can you know that for sure?"

He couldn't, and that was the problem. Twenty years ago, he would have given vent to his feelings with some choice words. But he wasn't a delinquent teen anymore. And he knew that there was only one thing to do when the road became difficult. One person to seek. *God, please give us guidance. Help me to know how to help Etta and Polly and make this right.*

"I'll take Polly and finish up here while you head to the car," he said, as he guided Etta toward the exit door.

Etta nodded and pointed to her hat. "I haven't paid for this yet," she said.

He reached over and ripped off the tag. "Keep it on for now. I'll ring it up at the register," he said, then he watched her walk out the door.

Steven raked his fingers through his hair. Two minutes ago, he had been reveling in the absurdity of his altered appearance. Now, the feel of the spiky strands just served as a reminder of the impossible situation they were in. No, *impossible* wasn't the right word. Challenging. Unexpected. Scary.

For some reason, he hadn't expected the police to be looking for Etta this quickly. What had he been thinking suggesting that she and Polly accompany him into Walmart? Stupid mistake on his part. He pushed any lingering questions out of his brain as he went to the checkout counter. He passed the health and beauty aisle on the way, and on a whim, he grabbed a second box of hair color, this one for Etta. It seemed like a good idea to buy it just in case. He snuck a glance at Polly. Her gaze seemed fixed on a display of Doritos on an end cap. He grabbed a bag and tossed it into the cart. It wasn't the healthiest snack, but the kid deserved a treat.

Steven self-scanned and then bagged the items Etta had selected. He wasn't surprised at her choices. Frugality had always been Etta's way. He could still remember her look of horror the first, and only, time he'd tried to take her to a fancy restaurant, where the entrées ran fifty or sixty dollars a person. He'd been trying to impress her, and instead she had insisted on ordering a salad.

He pulled out his credit card, paid, and then

he and Polly headed out the door. Etta was waiting in the van. As he loaded the groceries into the trunk, she buckled Polly into her booster seat. Two minutes later, they were back on the road. He flexed his hurt leg, wishing he could take his turn behind the wheel. It wasn't right that the burden should fall entirely on Etta.

"It won't be long before we reach the prison." Her voice broke the silence that had descended in the vehicle.

"Great," he said, craning his head to check out his appearance in the side mirror. Gone was his earlier confidence in his disguise. In its place was the realization that he looked strange and artificial, like someone pretending to be something he was not.

He was starting to wonder if this was going to work.

Chapter Six

The prison was as intimidating as he had imagined, with its massive concrete buildings and high fences with swirling loops of barbed wire on top. Etta pulled into a parking space in the visitor lot and cast a look in Steven's direction. She appeared to be exhausted, with worry lines etched across her brow. No doubt, she was thinking the same things he was. Could they really pull this off? Would the guards actually believe that he was Matt Bickler?

And what if, after all of this—the delay in leaving town and the risk to Etta, who had now become a person of interest—Greg didn't have any additional information? Or, worse, what if he was actually guilty?

Twice during the drive to the prison, he'd considered telling Etta to turn the car around. That the risk wasn't worth it. That they should forget the visit to the prison and instead just hightail it to South Dakota. But he doubted she would agree to that. She remained convinced that her brother-in-law was innocent and that he might have answers about who was after them.

Steven pulled in a deep breath and placed his fingers on the handle of the van's front door. "Okay. Here I go."

"Steven." Etta's voice was little more than a whisper.

"Yeah?"

"Just be careful. Okay?"

He tried for his most reassuring look. "It'll be fine. You know me. I'm a master at getting out of sticky situations."

"I do know you. And I know that look. It's the same swaggering smile you'd plaster on your face seconds before you got tossed by a bull."

A ripple of pleasure pinged him. Somehow, even after all these years, Etta was still able to penetrate his usual bravado. He allowed his phony grin to slip as he placed a hand on top of Etta's fingers, which were still clutching the steering wheel.

"I got this," he said. "Really. I'll be back before you know it."

Etta gave a weak smile as he stepped out and pushed the door closed behind him.

He covered the walk toward the prison quickly as dread, anxiety and adrenaline coursed through his veins. Not for the first time, he realized that, but for the grace of God, he could have ended up spending quite a few years in a place like this. He had certainly been headed down a path of crime and delinquency when he was eighteen. But, thanks to his mama's stern warnings and constant prayers, he found his way out.

He pushed open the doors and walked toward the guard behind the counter. He fished Matt Bickler's wallet out of his pocket and handed over the license. This was the first test.

"I'm here to see Greg Sanderson."

The guard glanced down at the ID, and then up at his face. A cold, clammy feeling slithered through Steven's insides, but he forced his face to remain impassive. As the uniformed deputy rechecked the license, his confidence wavered. Why hadn't he thought of a way to contact Etta if he got caught? He clenched his fingers into a fist. Should he turn around and make up an excuse to justify a sudden departure? No. That would surely alert the guards to the fact that something wasn't right. He shifted his weight. His leg was really starting to hurt.

The guard glanced up. "New glasses?" he asked with a raised eyebrow.

"Yeah. It was time for a change."

The deputy jotted something down and then directed him toward the metal detector. Once on the other side, another set of guards reviewed his ID again before allowing him through the double security doors and escorting him into a large room with tables and chairs. Wary of the scrutiny involved in an official request for an attorney-client visit, he opted to meet with Greg as part of regular visiting hours. Most of the tables were already occupied, but there was an empty spot on the far edge of the room.

Trying to act as casual as possible, Steven surveyed the plain gray walls, the linoleum floor and the half-dozen cameras mounted to the ceiling. He drummed his fingers against the table and thought about the man he was about to see. Etta was convinced that Greg was innocent. But he'd reserve judgment about that, at least for the moment.

"Who are you?" a loud voice asked, interrupting his thoughts.

Steven looked up. Greg Sanderson was not what he'd been expecting from the curated photographs he had noticed at the house along the stairs. The man standing before him, in an orange coverall and flat slippers, looked older and stressed, as if he was carrying the weight of the world on his shoulders.

"Let's keep our voices down." Steven stood up and extended his hand. "I'm Matt Bickler, a partner of Sam Colfax. Sam's out of the office today, but he asked me to come by to discuss some new information that has come up in your case."

Did any of that make sense? Steven didn't think so. But he blew out a quick sigh of relief that Greg didn't question his claim to be Matt Bickler.

"What happened?" Greg Sanderson sat down across from him at the table.

"Well, the facts are a little hazy right now, but it appears that your sister-in-law, Henrietta Mitchell, has disappeared and taken your daughter with her to—"

"Nope. No way." Greg was shaking his head before Steven had finished his sentence. "If Etta left town with Polly, she had a good reason. Maybe she needed to return to her apartment to pick up something."

"It's a bit more complicated than that. Your home was broken into, Mr. Sanderson, and your sister-in-law was attacked."

"Wait. What?" Greg's head whipped up. "Is Polly okay?"

"We have every reason to assume so."

"What's that supposed to mean?"

"Your daughter's fine," Steven said reassuringly. "We're just trying to figure out why this happened and how it affects your case."

"Probably, it's the same reason why Lilly got killed, right? And since I'm in here, what just happened can't have anything to do with me."

"True. But who is to say that you don't have an accomplice?"

Greg's brow furrowed. "An accomplice? What are you talking about? Aren't you supposed to be on my side?" The ferocity of his anger seemed to reverberate off the walls.

Steven cast a glance around the room. A few of the other visitors were looking their way, so he lowered his voice to almost a whisper. "It doesn't matter what I think. Sam just wanted me to find out if you knew anything about the break-in."

"This is the first time I'm hearing about any of this! I'm innocent. I don't think I want to talk to you anymore." Greg pushed himself up from the table. "I'll wait until Sam is available.

He's my attorney. And I know he's definitely on my side."

Steven paused for a moment and took a deep breath. He needed to remain calm and not panic. He had made it this far and gained entry to the prison. But it would still be a challenge to secure Greg's trust.

He met and held Greg's gaze. "I think you should talk to me."

"Why should I?"

"Please. Give me two minutes. There are additional details I need to share."

Greg hesitated a moment, and then sank back down onto the chair. "You have sixty seconds to convince me that it will be in my best interest to discuss my case with you, Mr. Bickler." He pointed to the clock. "And your time starts now."

Steven leaned forward in his chair. The truth was all he had left, but he wasn't certain how Greg would react to it. Still, he needed to try.

"I came in here under a false identity." He leaned in. "My real name is Steven Hunt. I'm a friend of Etta's. What I told you about the home invasion is true. She and Polly are with me now, and we're trying to find out what is going on. But we need more information."

Confusion flickered in Greg's eyes. "Why not say that up front? Why come in here, claiming to be a partner of my attorney?"

"It's complicated. Matt Bickler is one of the men involved in the incident. We don't know why, but we thought you might be able to help us in some way."

Confusion marred Greg's face. "I don't know why Bickler would be involved...and I still don't understand why *you* are involved in our family situation. Last I heard from Lilly, you were still riding in the rodeo and had nothing to do with Etta."

Steven nodded. "That's true. But when I heard Lilly had died, I came to see Etta...and stumbled into the middle of the break-in. I knew your wife, too, back in the day. I heard all the stories about how their dad left when she was born, how their mom skipped town eight years later." He twisted his mouth into a wry grin. "Lilly never liked me. I think she viewed me as a threat to her relationship with Etta."

"You're right about that. She actually prided herself on helping undermine your relationship. She used to claim you were the reason that Etta was still single. That you broke her heart."

Steven couldn't help snorting. "More like the

other way around. But that's ancient history. At this point, I just need for you to trust me enough to answer a few questions. Will you take me through the events of the day of the murder?"

Greg rubbed his jaw and then leaned in closer. "Can't hurt, I guess. You've probably heard it already from Etta. I woke up as usual and got ready for work. Made a pot of coffee, talked to Lilly. I was supposed to take Polly to pre-school that day to give Lilly a break. But she was complaining of a stomachache, so we decided to scrap the plan. Polly was not happy about that, let me tell you. She stomped off and went to hide, but I didn't have time to go after her. When I think about how things might have been different if..." His voice trailed off as he wiped his hand across his eyes. "She used to be such a happy kid. And now she's so silent and closed off."

Steven could feel his own chest tighten in response to Greg's palpable grief and the pain he was feeling at being stuck in jail and separated from his daughter. "Okay. So you went to work. What happened next?"

"I came home at lunchtime and found Lilly on the couch. I checked her pulse, but she was already gone. I called for Polly, but she didn't come. I thought… I thought…" Greg closed his eyes and took a minute to compose himself. "I was afraid she had been hurt as well. Then, I called nine-one-one. The emergency responders arrived in minutes, but I could tell by their faces that they knew she was dead. Of course, there was an autopsy. The medical examiner found traces of poison in Lilly's coffee. And in the pot that I had admitted to making that morning. And just like that, I became suspect number one."

"It was a logical deduction."

Greg's eyes flashed as he pushed away. "Etta knows I didn't kill Lilly. But you seem to be taking the side of the police."

Steven shook his head. "Cool your jets, man. I may not be a lawyer, but I'm pretty sure the questions are going to get a lot more heated at trial. And at this point, it doesn't matter what Etta thinks about your guilt or innocence. I'm just laying out the facts."

Greg slumped back in his seat.

"You say that you didn't notice anything unusual in the weeks leading up to the murder?" Steven asked.

"Nothing that set off warning bells. But Lilly was acting different."

"Different, how?"

"It's hard to explain. She just seemed more self-pleased, like she had a secret that she didn't want to share." Greg shot him a look. "She sometimes got like that when she had some sort of big scoop involving her job at the paper. Given the normal goings-on in Silver Creek, that usually meant one of the council members was planning to resign or, most recently, some sort of scandal involving special treatment of the mayor's son. But this seemed bigger and more consuming. When I pressed her to explain, all she would say was that she was working on something big. I knew that she had consulted with an old friend of hers from juvie, a PI named Jordan Shapiro who lived in Sulphur Springs. But that's about it."

"Jordan Shapiro." Steven repeated the name to himself, committing it to memory. "Had you heard the name before?"

"No. Lilly didn't talk much about people she knew from that time in her life."

"You told the police all this?"

Greg blew out a sharp breath through his nose. "Of course. But they didn't seem interested. They had made up their minds I was guilty right off the bat, especially after they interviewed one of the neighbors who said that Lilly and I argued a lot about our finances. But it was never anything serious. We were both pretty strong-willed, so it tended to get heated when we disagreed. But once the cops heard about that, it was case closed. In their minds, Lilly's murder was just another deadly domestic dispute."

"You had money issues in your marriage?" Steven pressed.

Greg shrugged. "Who doesn't, right? But we were doing okay. Even though Lilly had always been fascinated with all sorts of get-rich-quick schemes, she was a stickler about justice. I think it had something to do with the time she spent in juvie. She really believed that no one was truly above the law. After she was killed, I searched through her things, hoping to find some clue about what she was up to. I hit a dead end on that, so I thought about asking around the neighborhood and got a recommendation for a good lawyer."

"Right. Sam Colfax. What did you hear about him?"

Greg smirked. "You mean your pseudo partner? What do you want to know?"

Before Steven could answer, the guard tapped

him on the shoulder and pointed at the clock. His time was up.

"Maybe we can talk later. But one last thing before I go." Steven lowered his voice to a whisper. "It would probably be best if you didn't say anything about my visit. It might come out eventually, but as far as you know, the only person you spoke to today was an attorney from your law firm."

Greg made a motion of sealing his lips as Steven stood up and walked toward the door. Was it his imagination, or was one of the guards following his movements with his eyes? Maybe it was all part of the job. Still, the faster he got back into the car, the better. There had been a couple of dicey moments, but his meeting with Greg had proven to be worth the risk.

Etta adjusted her position in the driver's seat and, for the fifth time in as many minutes, peered out the window at the near-empty parking lot next to the prison. What was taking Steven so long? At this point, she was fairly certain that he'd made it inside. But then what? She could easily imagine Greg making a fuss and refusing to answer any questions.

And what if a vigilant guard had allowed Steven to enter but then called the law office to double-check his identity? The police could at this very moment be on their way to arrest Steven for impersonating a member of the bar.

Was that even a crime? She wasn't sure, but she could not allow herself to think that way. *Focus on the positive.* She closed her eyes and tried to imagine the best-case scenario. But her moment of peace and quiet was interrupted by a man in a tan uniform knocking on the driver's side door.

Uh-oh. Had he somehow recognized her from the picture that had been on TV? She pulled down her ball cap and rolled down the window.

The man's thin gray hair fluffed up in wisps along his sunburned scalp as he held up a laminated state ID. "I noticed some movement inside the van, so I thought I'd come over and make sure everything's under control."

Etta took a deep breath, relief roiling though her senses. So far, anyway, he didn't seem to have connected her with what had happened in Silver Creek. She just needed to stay calm and not act suspicious. And to stick to the truth as much as possible.

"Everything is fine, sir. My niece and I are

waiting for a friend who's inside visiting an inmate. Is that okay?"

"No worries. We keep tabs on all vehicles parked in the lot, but when I ran your plates, I saw that you were driving a rental. Not that there's any problem with that. I just wanted to check things out and make sure you were okay."

Etta waited until the man had moved on to the other side of the lot before turning to check on Polly. Poor kid. Etta could only hope that Polly hadn't fully comprehended most of the events of the past few days. "Do you want anything to eat or drink?" she asked.

Polly stared back. A slight shake of the head was the only sign that that her words had registered.

Etta fought the desire to sigh. Showing exasperation wouldn't help Polly feel more comfortable. "Do you want to play 'I spy'?" she said, trying again.

Another minuscule shake of the head from Polly.

Well, that was probably just as well since there wasn't much to see in the prison parking lot. Etta scanned the area. What would it be like to be confined within these walls for years at a time?

A shiver ran up her spine. Maybe now, she'd find out sooner rather than later.

She had been so adamant about not involving the authorities when she had first been attacked. Was it really only yesterday that she had killed that man in self-defense? She shook her head. It seemed like weeks. Maybe Steven was right. Maybe it would have been better to call 911. She hadn't done anything wrong. But she knew only too well that law enforcement didn't just mean the police. It also included social services. And there was no way she was going to let anyone take Polly away from her.

A rustle from the back seat reclaimed her attention. She swiveled her head to see Polly, clutching her stuffed rabbit.

"I like your bunny. Does she have a name?"

Polly blinked back.

A knot of sorrow tightened in Etta's chest. Not for the first time, she regretted letting time slip by without visiting Lilly and Greg. If only Polly trusted her a bit more. Maybe talking about Lilly would lessen Polly's wariness.

"Did you know that your mom and I had a pet growing up?"

A flicker of interest seemed to glint in Polly's eyes.

"Yes," Etta continued. "Except it wasn't a rabbit. It was a dog. And it wasn't really our pet. She was a stray who lived in the neighborhood. Your mom named her Jane. I tried to tell her that wasn't a proper name for a dog, but she didn't care."

Polly blinked. She seemed to be waiting for more.

"Actually, Jane saved my life. Jane and your mom." Etta paused. For years, she hadn't allowed herself to dwell on memories from her childhood. Everyone, including Lilly, had advised her that denial wasn't healthy, but so far it had been working just fine for her. Well, one story wouldn't hurt. Not if it gained her some trust with Polly.

"Jane was quite a silly dog. She used to wander through the streets sniffing for food. But if someone tried to feed her something, she would back away. Oh, and she never barked. When she saw your mom, her tail would wag, and she'd trot over to be petted.

"Well, one Thanksgiving, when I was about thirteen, I'd been sent to the grocery store to buy dinner." She could well remember how much she'd dreaded waiting in line and having to pay with food stamps. Of course, they tried to make it less embarrassing with the pre-paid cards, but she knew that the checker knew what it meant. That she was poor. That her mama couldn't hold down a job. Not that the grubby jeans that were two sizes two small and hit above the ankle weren't a giveaway. Or the sneaker with a hole at the toe. But buying groceries was somehow the worst. A new level of humiliation.

"Anyway, on this particular afternoon, I'd saved up some of my own money from weeding our neighbor's garden and bought a turkey. A real, frozen turkey." Again, the memory wrapped itself around her. Her pride in making the purchase with her own money. They hadn't had a real Thanksgiving dinner for a few years, and she'd had all sorts of lofty dreams of cooking it for hours and then serving it to her family for dinner. Why she'd thought that she would be able to cook a turkey without any experience was still beyond her, but, at thirteen years old, she hadn't been quite as worried about the details.

Too bad those good feelings hadn't lasted.

The touch of a hand on her arm called her back to the present. Polly had reached out to her. Etta stared down at the tiny fingers and fought back the desire to cry. She and her sister had spent most of their childhood confused and lonely. And now the cycle seemed to be continuing for Polly. It wasn't fair.

But, obviously, Polly was expecting some sort of happy ending to the story. Etta tamped down her feelings. She needed to keep it light and not scare Polly more than she already was.

"Well, a turkey is cold and heavy, and I had to walk home. It wasn't far. About a mile and half. But by the time I had gone just a few blocks, my arms were getting tired. A part of me wanted to just give up and leave the turkey in the street and go home. But I had been so excited, so I kept trudging on. Well, I must not have been paying attention, because all of a sudden, I stubbed my toe on the sidewalk. The turkey slipped from my fingers and landed on my foot, and then I fell down. It was like a chain reaction of unfortunate events. Bing, bang. Boom."

Etta willed her voice to make the event sound funny and was rewarded when a ghost of smile wavered on Polly's face.

"But when I tried to get up, my foot hurt too much to walk. So I just had to sit down by the side of the road. A couple of people drove past and offered to help, but I said no. I just sat there and waited. And waited. And waited. And then, guess who came by? Jane. She walked right up to me and let me scratch her ears. It was starting to get dark, so I was a little scared. Jane sat right next to me, and I put my arm around her neck and really wanted to cry. But after a little while, she stood up and walked away, too. And then I was really lonely." She smiled down at Polly.

"Meanwhile, your mom was at home waiting. She knew that I usually brought her a couple of lollipops when I went to the store, so she was on the lookout for my return. Well, I didn't know this at the time, but Jane didn't actually abandon me on the side of the road. She went to find your mom. Lilly told me later that Jane trotted up, but instead of greeting her with a handshake, she pawed the ground. When Lilly saw that, she knew something was wrong, and she went to get help from one of our neighbors."

A movement from outside the van caused her eyes to dart toward the window, and a wild fluttering of relief and joy erupted in her chest. There was Steven, strolling back toward the car, as relaxed as someone out for a walk in the park. She turned back toward Polly. Time to wrap up her story. Steven didn't need to hear any more details about her dysfunctional childhood. Not when his own had been so picture-perfect.

Probably best not to describe what had really happened next, how she and Lilly had eaten cereal for Thanksgiving dinner, and a cold towel had been wrapped around Etta's swollen foot. Polly needed a happy ending. So did she, for that matter. She forced her lips to curve upward. Except that it actually didn't seem fake. Her mouth wanted to smile.

"Well, the neighbor found me and gave me a ride home. And there was your mom and Jane waiting for me. Together they had saved me. Can you imagine? My baby sister and a dog that wouldn't bark were able to get help."

Polly pulled her rabbit closer to her chest and gave a little sigh. For once, it didn't sound like a sigh of worry or anxiety, but one of contentment.

A second later, Steven pulled open the van door and climbed into the passenger seat. He gave a discreet thumbs-up to Etta and then turned to smile at Polly.

"How did it go?" Etta asked.

"Better than expected," Steven said. "How did you do with Polly?"

Etta shrugged. "Okay, I guess. I was worried

that they would see through your disguise, so I got really nervous when a guard came by and knocked on the window. But he was just interested in the van because he had run the plates and saw that it was a rental. When I explained that I was waiting for someone, he left."

Steven let out a long sigh. "This is not good, Etta."

"But he didn't recognize me. And he didn't ask who I was waiting for."

Steven shook his head. "Maybe we're okay for the moment. But we can't take the chance that he won't eventually make the connection."

Chapter Seven

Etta was sitting ramrod-straight as she clutched the wheel, her eyes fixed forward. To say she looked tense would be an understatement.

What happened at the prison was his fault, not hers. He shouldn't have asked her to wait for him in the lot. But what was done was done. Their options were becoming more and more limited. He needed to think outside the box.

Inspiration struck as he remembered a text from his buddy who was riding this week at a county fair in Leesburg, which was only about an hour or so away. Donny was a good guy, and it didn't take much convincing to talk him into a temporary swap of his Airstream camper for the rented van. In theory. It seemed like a perfect solution. Once they made the switch, they would once again be off the radar. They could head north without any worries about stopping and being recognized at restaurants or motels.

"Don't worry, Etta." He reached over and touched her hand. "This is a good plan."

"I don't know, Steven. It seems like everything we do is one step forward, two steps back. I just hope there was something positive that came out of your visit with Greg."

"There was. Definitely. Your brother-in-law did share some interesting information about Lilly. Are you familiar with the name Jordan Shapiro?"

Her forehead creased. "No."

"Well, apparently, she's a PI friend of your sister, living in Sulphur Springs. Lilly reached out to her for advice about something she was working on. Said it could blow up into something big."

"What was it about?"

He shrugged. "Greg didn't know."

"Sounds like we need to talk to this Jordan Shapiro and get more information."

Steven shook his head. "Uh-uh. Remember? You agreed that we would drive straight to South Dakota once we found out what Greg had to say."

"I know I did." She glanced his way. "But now that we know about this, we can't leave Texas without checking it out."

"Sure we can." They couldn't stay here—
the men following them would catch up soon
enough. And the sooner he got home, the sooner
he could get Seb's help with this mess. "When
we get to the ranch, you can call Lilly's friend
and find out what she has to say."

"She might not talk to me on the phone, Steven. Our best hope would be for me to make a
personal appeal as Lilly's sister. Besides, Sulphur
Springs isn't far off the route to South Dakota.
In any case, it can be a quick stop. Not much
more than an hour delay."

An hour delay? Not likely. And right now,
his main concern was making it to Leesburg
without being pulled over by the police. He
could tell Etta understood the risks as she kept
the speed at a steady two miles over the limit.

Truth to tell, this was not the way he had
planned to spend his six-month recuperation.
He remembered the wary smile on the doctor's
face as she signed his release forms from the hospital. "You'll be fine," she had said. "As long as
you take it easy. No vigorous exercise or undue
stress. Grab a stack of good books, and settle
back and relax. Better yet, do your reading on a
deck chair under an umbrella on a warm beach."
Toes in the water… Now that sounded good.

Well, Texas was warm. Or, warmish. But getting knocked around in a fight with a thug with at least thirty pounds on him wasn't exactly what the doctor had ordered. He'd realized that the moment the first punch was thrown at Lilly and Greg's house in Silver Creek. So why had he stuck around?

Once again, he shifted his eyes toward the driver's side of the car, hoping to check out Etta's current mood. Hmm. Hard to say. She was frowning as she peered at a cluster of signs ahead.

"Our turn isn't for a dozen or so miles," he said.

"Thanks," she answered without turning her head. He had never been an expert when it came to women, but was it possible she was annoyed at him? Why? Unless, of course, she could read his mind and sense his regret.

His mood was less regretful and more circumspect. Wary of risks.

Bottom line, he had decided to come to Texas on a whim. Hop a bus south and see the country from the inside of a Greyhound. Spend some time thinking about life and love and his next thirty years. Yeah, he had wanted to see Etta, but with no illusions that their eyes would meet and the years would fall away. He was smart enough to know that what had happened be-tween them was part of a past that could not be reclaimed.

"Steven?" Etta turned suddenly to face him. "Can we take another minute to review the plan?"

Not mad, then. Just anxious. He could deal with that.

"Sure." He checked the time on his phone. "We'll be in Leesburg within the hour. The fairgrounds are on the north side of town, and Donny's Airstream will be parked in the area adjacent to the main lot. He flies a POW/MIA flag, so the trailer should be easy to spot. The key's under the mat, and he said we should go in and make ourselves comfortable. I'll head off to visit with Donny, and you can color your hair. As soon as I get back, we can hit the road."

She gripped the wheel. "But what about our visit to Jordan Shapiro?"

Frustration bit at his senses. He had given in to Etta every step along the way. His suggestion that she turn herself in to the police had been met first with stonewalling and then an out-right refusal to even consider the option. And while the decision to seek shelter at the ranch had been made, the drive north kept getting re-routed and delayed.

"I don't think so. Etta. It's getting too danger-ous for us to stay any longer in Texas."

She shook her head. "Fine. We can talk about it later. Look!" She pointed to a sign up ahead that showed the exit to Leesburg. "We're al-most there."

Once they were off the main road, it was just a short drive to the fairgrounds and a cluster of caravans and tents that formed a small city to the left of the main lot. Etta honed right in on the distinctive black-and-white flag flying next to the front door.

"Does your friend Donny know someone who was a prisoner of war?"

Steven nodded. "His dad was in Vietnam. Some of his friends went missing and never came home."

"Flying the flag is a good way to keep their memory alive."

The Airstream looked smaller than Steven remembered, but the keys were right where his buddy had left them. He had a moment of trepi-dation as he pushed open the door. But inside, the tiny home was compact and tidy. Two adults and a child in such a small space would be tight, to be sure, but it would do just fine. Besides, beggars couldn't be choosers. Steven smiled as he recalled his mom's favorite words of wisdom for him and his brother.

Etta paused on the threshold as she spotted a black-and-yellow gun on a shelf next to the door. "Is that what I think it is?"

Steven stepped forward to check it out. "A Taser? Yeah. Donny must have bought it to deal with vandals who sometimes roam around these kinds of fairs. I'll put it in the glove compartment and lock it up. That way we won't need to worry about Polly getting hurt."

"Good idea… If we take the Airstream, where will your buddy sleep? Isn't this where he's been living?"

Steven shrugged. "He'll bunk in with one of the other riders. Most of the guys travel in campers, so there's always room for a friend in need. Speaking of which, I better change my clothes and head over to the fairgrounds to meet Donny." He reached out and grabbed one of three cowboy hats that were hanging next to the door. "I was wondering what happened to this. Must have left it here last time I stayed with Donny." He pulled the brim low on his head.

"I'll probably be gone for about an hour or so. Will you guys be okay?"

Etta nodded. "I think so. I'll bring in the groceries and make Polly something to eat. Then, maybe I'll take a shot at coloring my hair. It just feels odd to be poking around in someone else's home."

"If you knew Donny, you'd realize he's happy to help. Here. Take these just in case." He handed her a set of keys and watched as she slipped them into the pocket of her pants. "It would probably be best not to wander outside. It's just a guess, but I assume that a more up-to-date picture of you is now being shown on the news. Best to keep a low profile and stay inside the Airstream."

Etta stared at the description on the box of hair dye that Steven had purchased at the mini-mart along the road. Intense dark red. "Ugh," she said out loud, shaking her head. Polly sidled up next to her, anxious for a peek. "What do you think, Polls? Maybe a bit too flashy for your stodgy aunt?"

A wisp of a smile creased Polly's lips.

"I agree. I'm not sure why Steven thinks I can pull off being a redhead."

She spread out the instructions and began to read. It looked complicated, especially the part about sectioning the hair and clipping it out of the way on the top of her head. "Maybe I should do the cutting part first. That way, I won't run out of dye."

Polly picked a picture book from the pile Etta had hauled in from the car and settled down on the floor to read.

The Airstream, though compact, was as fully functional as any of the places she found herself living on the job as a traveling nurse. There was a tiny kitchen with a two-burner stove, a sink, a refrigerator and even a small microwave tucked under the counter. Two small couches could quickly be converted into pullout beds, and under the windows was a folding kitchen table. The place was fully air-conditioned; though today, with the temperature outside hovering in the sixties, a bank of open windows next to the door provided a refreshing breeze. "I could be very happy living in a place like this," Etta said as she headed into the tiny bathroom, scissors in hand.

This was going to be difficult, but it needed to be done. Her long, flowing hair had been a part of her for so long. On the job, she often wore it pulled back in a French braid, or, if she was pressed for time, a simple ponytail. But this was not the moment to be sentimental about an old hairstyle. A new color and cut were the quickest way to change her appearance.

Fifteen minutes later, the bathroom trash can was filled with strands of long dark hair. Etta frowned at her reflection in the mirror. A short new style. Not bad, but not all that good, either. Back in the day, she remembered someone calling that particular cut a "pixie," and she had to admit that there was something elflike about her new look.

She took one last glance in the mirror and reached for the instruction sheet for the dye. It seemed simple enough. Mix the tube of applicator cream with the developer and then use the brush to paint it on the hair. A pungent, ammonia-like scent assailed her nostrils as she worked methodically to cover each section with clumpy, grayish dye. When she finished, she slipped on the clear plastic shower cap that came with the kit and looked at the clock. Well, she had gone and done it. In thirty-five minutes, she'd be a redhead.

With nothing else to do, she wandered out to the main living area and sat down next to Polly, watching the little girl as she carefully turned the pages of her picture books. It was a strangely relaxing activity, and she found herself drifting off to sleep. She awoke with a start to see that she had only a few minutes to go before the final step in the coloring process. She was on her way to the bathroom to rinse off the solution when high-pitched cries from outside in the campground stopped her in her tracks. What was going on? The view out of the front window was split by a stand of dusty evergreens, but the body of a young boy crumpled on the ground could be seen clearly a dozen yards down the dirt road. Two women stood beside the child, pacing and shouting.

"We need a doctor! Now!"

Etta sprang into action. She wrapped one of Donny's red, white and blue scarves around her head. Steven's reminder that she shouldn't leave the Airstream flitted through her mind, but how could she ignore a cry for assistance? It would only take a few minutes to assess the situation and call 911. Besides, no one would recognize her with a scarf tied over her hair.

"Wait here, Polly. I'll be right back," she called out as she slipped into the late afternoon shadows of the campground. A crowd had already gathered around the body of the small child. The boy was moaning, a good sign since it meant he was conscious. But her relief turned into concern as she saw the blood pooling next to the arm that he was clutching to his chest. A pair of hedge-trimming sheers, with telltale blood spatter, was lying inches away in the dirt. An accident, then. But had the sharp blades hit an artery, and if so, should she apply an emergency tourniquet to staunch the flow?

"I'm a nurse," she said as she kneeled down beside the child and applied direct pressure to the wound. "Did someone call for an ambulance?"

"We dialed nine-one-one, but no one answered," one of the women claimed.

"Keep calling, Joann," an authoritative voice urged. "They have to be there."

"It hurts!" the little boy wailed, and Etta's adrenaline kicked into overdrive.

"I need a piece of thin cloth to make a tourniquet," she said. Someone tossed her a white T-shirt, and she twisted it into a triangular band, which she wrapped around the little boy's arm. "Can one of you find a stick? Or a pencil or a spoon? Something that will allow me to increase the pressure and stop the bleeding."

Someone in the crowd handed her a metal spoon. It was small but sturdy, and it would do as a windlass for the tourniquet. Etta tied off the ends of the cloth and inserted the spoon as she prepared for tightening. She leaned in closer to reassure her patient. "This might hurt a little," she whispered softly. The kid stared back at her with worried eyes.

A loud commotion caused the crowd to part, and a short woman in a colorful dress appeared beside her. "I'm Ricky's mom," she said, her voice shaking. She glanced at her son. "Hang in there, hon. This lady is going to help you until the ambulance gets here. Just squeeze my hand if the pain gets too strong."

The little boy nodded, his wide eyes full of tears.

Etta knew from experience how the increased tension of the tourniquet often caused a patient to cry out from the discomfort, but Ricky seemed brave. The 911 call must have finally been answered because soon the sound of a siren split the air, the wail growing louder and louder as a small fire truck and an ambulance blew up clouds of dust on the road.

Moments later, a team of paramedics arrived on the scene. "We'll take it from here.

But that sure is a nice tourniquet, lady," one of the EMTs said.

"You got it on there real good," the taller of the two added as Etta scrambled to her feet, yielding her place to the professionals.

Gaze firmly fixed on the ground, she took one step back and then another, slowly fading into the background as the firefighters made a first attempt at crowd control.

Well, that was that, then. It was reassuring to see the flashing lights of the rescue vehicles and to hear the squeaking of the wheels of the gurney as it was pulled across the dry dirt road. She had done her best to help, and she hadn't been recognized. No one had stopped her to ask any questions about who she was and what she was doing here. All eyes were glued to the brave little boy still holding his mom's hand.

Etta retreated toward the Airstream, and, with one final glance to make sure no one was watching, ducked inside. Overwhelmed with exhaustion and relief, she leaned against the wall and pulled in a long breath. Polly's gaze met hers in a tacit sort of understanding. If her niece could speak, Etta imagined her saying, *Glad you're back. Now tell me what happened.*

She needed to remove the headscarf and rinse

the now-tacky color solution out of her hair. With wet hair, it was too soon to reveal the consequences of the fifteen-minute delay. There was nothing she could do about it, so she returned to Polly's side and began to describe the brave little boy who had accidentally cut his arm and the triumphant arrival of the first responders.

Suddenly Etta had a sensation that the pockets of her pants felt just a bit lighter than they had earlier, and she realized that she had dropped the keys to the Airstream. She remembered bending down to apply the tourniquet and feeling something slide out of her pocket and onto the dirt. She peeked again out the window. The crowd appeared to be breaking up as the paramedics loaded the boy into the ambulance.

So what to do about retrieving the keys? She had avoided detection the first time around. Could she do it again? She could wait until Steven returned and ask him to help search, but she was still hoping they could leave as soon as he got back from visiting with his friend.

Maybe she was overthinking this. The keys were probably still in the exact spot where she had kneeled down to assist the little boy. But just in case they weren't, she'd take Polly along to help with the search.

With the shrill scream of a siren, the ambulance and the fire truck departed and the crowd dispersed. Now that the excitement was over, there was nothing more to see.

"Hey, Polly. I seem to have dropped my keys outside. Will you come along and help me look for them?"

Polly stood up, and Etta reached for her ball cap and tightened it so it fit her little niece's head.

As they made their way toward the site of the accident, Etta swept her gaze across the flattened patch of new grass and fresh tire tracks, past the crimson stain of blood pooled on the ground, and the rusty hedge trimmers still lying half-open in the dirt.

But there was no sign of the keys.

"Someone probably picked them up," Etta mused. "Maybe a neighbor…" She lifted her eyes toward the front of a nearby trailer. The curtains twitched.

A youngish man with a scraggly goatee answered on the first knock.

"I just got home from work," he barked gruffly once she explained the reason for the interruption. "But I heard about the commotion from my wife. And now that I think about it, she may have mentioned something about finding some keys. Said she had an idea who might have dropped them, but she thought it would be best to turn them in at the lost and found at the grandstand."

Chapter Eight

There was something strangely comforting about the dusty paths lined with fairy lights, the pop-up vendors selling fried food and the throngs of people swarming around the grandstand. It had been more than a decade since Etta's last trip to a county fair. But the sounds and smells that permeated the air reminded her of the evening she'd first met Steven.

Then again, maybe *met* wasn't the right word to describe that first encounter. She had been twenty-one back then, out for a day of fun with a group of fellow nurses from the hospital. Her mood had been relaxed and nearly carefree, though as guardian of a sulky teenager, she hadn't had the luxury of ever being completely free of worries. But it was definitely one of the less stressful times in her life. It had been purely happenstance that they had stopped to watch a bull-riding competition. A fluke that she had gone down to buy peanuts at a stand near the ring when a cowboy climbed onto the back of a bull named Midnight Mansion, only to be bucked off the enormous animal's back and then trampled into the dirt.

She shivered to imagine how much worse it would have been if Steven hadn't been wearing a helmet, a face mask and a protective vest. Even so, the spectacle in the ring had caused the crowd to gasp in horror as a trio of cowboys worked to distract the bull so the medic on call could attend to Steven.

It was horrible, even worse from Etta's close-up perspective. She recalled the anxious hush, followed by high-pitched shouting as the gates were pushed wide for a small ambulance.

Etta had pushed forward into the ring, certain she could help in some small way. Even now, as she replayed the scene in her head, she wondered why she had been allowed to pass through the gates. But there she'd been, kneeling next to the staff doctor, offering a weak smile as Steven's eyes blinked open and then closed as he winced with pain. And then, as the rest of the medical team arrived, she had taken a step back, quickly consigned to the role of spectator. That moment in the ring would forever remain seared in her memory.

Now, as she approached the grandstand, it was the scent of those roasting peanuts that still made her mouth water after all these years.

Would it be foolish to stop at one of the vendors to purchase a few snacks for herself and Polly? With her short choppy red hair tickling the back of her ears, she felt like a new person, but she resisted the temptation to stop as she trudged forward, searching for a sign that would lead her to the lost and found.

"What do you think, Polly? Do you like the fair?"

The little girl replied by wrinkling her nose.

Etta laughed. "Yeah. It does have a different smell. But you get used to it. Steven used to say this is real life. And that the city is what smells wrong."

She could picture him wrinkling his nose just like Polly when she would sit with him in the hospital, his dark hair rumpled and his lips quirked in his trademark half smile. He'd claimed to hate being confined to a bed, explaining that the air was too clean, too artificial, too plain. That he belonged in the country, riding a horse, or better yet, hanging on for dear life on the back of a bucking bull.

Well, look where that had gotten him, she'd been tempted to say. But she'd offered no criticism. How could she—her heart was already melting at the sight of those teasing dark eyes.

Yeah, those had been the days. More good than bad in a lot of ways. For years, she hadn't allowed herself to dwell on the past, to recall stories from her childhood or to relive that whirlwind romance. Lilly used to say that Etta played things close to the vest. Even at her sister's funeral, when friends and neighbors had gathered to celebrate her life, Etta hadn't offered up any old memories of the bond they had shared, always as sisters and sometimes as friends. Yet somehow, spending time with Steven, it was as if the lid she had kept so carefully locked on her past had suddenly been blown off, and it all came flooding back in a torrent.

She shook her head and tightened her grip on Polly's fingers for a moment. This is exactly what she didn't need. It was time to face some cold, hard facts. Lilly was dead. And Steven hadn't sought her out intending to rekindle their past relationship. Instead, he'd been hijacked into helping them by the circumstances of his arrival. He was kind. She had always known that. And it was his kindness that had caused him to get involved in her problems, just as it had been his kindness that had instigated his proposal all those years ago. Oh, sure, he had claimed to be in love with her, but he had also fancied himself her knight in shining armor, rescuing the girl from the wrong side of the tracks and offering her a better life. She hadn't wanted that then, and she didn't want it now.

She and Polly needed him right now, she'd admit that. But she couldn't allow herself to dwell on a misty dream of what could have been. Steven was still the same overly confident, cocky bull rider, and she was the same independent-minded nurse who was determined to have her own career.

A tug on her arm brought her back to the present, and she realized she was squeezing Polly's hand.

"Sorry, Pol." She relaxed her fingers, looking down at the little girl. "Do you think you can be my helper? We're looking for a table or a stall with a sign that says 'Lost and Found.'"

Polly stared up at her, blank-faced. Right. Polly's reading skills were limited at best. But the kid was smart, she'd give her that. The way she put her fingers over the words in her books. Almost as if she was trying to pull them off the page and keep them for herself.

If only Polly would talk… Etta couldn't begin to imagine what she would say. The little girl's face—alternately happy, sad, lonely and content—had been Etta's only window to what was going on inside her head. And right now, her niece's expression revealed deep dismay. Etta stifled the sigh welling up in her chest. It was the same old story. One step forward, two steps back. That was what her interactions with Polly felt like. Every time there was the hint of a breakthrough, something would happen that would cause her niece to pull inward again.

And just like that, her excitement at exploring the fairgrounds dimmed. Who was she kidding? She was completely out of her element here. It was as if all the stress and exhaustion from the last two days had suddenly thrown a heavy mantle around her shoulders, physically pulling her down. She needed to find the keys and return to the Airstream. Steven was probably already back there, wondering where they had gone.

"Excuse me, sir," she said to an official-looking man in khaki shorts and a white shirt.

"Can you point me in the direction of the lost and found?"

"You just passed it," he said, pointing toward a building behind them. "It's in a little booth to the right of the entry door. You can't miss it."

Etta muttered a quick thanks, then turned to retrace her steps. "C'mon, Polly!" She injected some forced pep into her voice. "We're almost there."

As they stepped back inside the open barn, her nostrils were once again assailed by the scent of animals and hay as she led Polly past cows of all shapes and sizes awaiting a best-of-breed competition. The signs on the front of the stalls identified them as Holsteins, Angus, Shorthorn and Longhorn. And from the size of the crowds milling around, there seemed to be much interest in comparing the unique characteristics as well as the size and coloring of each breed. Following the official's directions, Etta headed to the right. There, just as the man had said, was a little booth claiming to be the lost and found. Etta quickened her steps, pulling Polly along with her.

"Can I help you with something?" a dark-haired woman behind the counter asked.

Etta nodded. "I lost my keys at the campground, and someone suggested they might be here."

"Oh, of course. Are you the lady who helped little Ricky?" The woman's eyes were fixed downward as she rummaged through a drawer. "We heard all about his accident and how you arrived out of nowhere and knew just what to do. Actually, dear, Ricky's uncle stopped by. His parents are at the hospital. But he asked me to thank you for saving his nephew's life."

Etta smiled. "I just did what anyone would do."

"Hmm," the woman murmured, still looking through the drawer. "I'm not finding any keys in here. Now, where did I put them? Oh, I know! I stuck them in the jar with the lost lighters." She turned toward a cabinet on the back wall but kept up her steady stream of chitchat. "Well, it was certainly providential that you were able to help. From what I heard, you really saved the day. I told Carl, that's the uncle, you can't be too careful. Kids can get hurt in the strangest ways. My neighbor's son almost died when he was run over by his riding lawn mower. And don't even get me started about all the crazy people in the city. Carjackings and assaults. I'm just grateful to live in the country. Oh, here they are!"

The woman swung back around as Etta stretched her hand over the counter, eager to claim the keys the woman held in her hand.

"Now, what was I going on about? Oh, right, can't be too careful these days. Why, did you see that story about the little girl who went missing in that town outside Dallas?"

An icy shiver ran up Etta's spine. "I must have missed that one." She made a show of looking down at her watch. "But, oh, I'm sorry. I've got to run. I'm meeting a friend at the grandstand."

The lost-and-found lady was staring now, her eyes fixed squarely on Polly. The silence stretched for only a few seconds, but for Etta, it felt like she had fallen into a void of growing dread as the woman set the keys out of reach on the back counter and pushed a form in front of her instead.

"Actually, you need to sign this before I hand over your property. We keep a record of all transactions. That way we don't have people trying to claim something that isn't theirs."

She could tell that the woman was stalling, and she realized with a start that Polly had removed the ball cap covering her hair, making her instantly recognizable as the missing child in that Amber Alert.

Etta shifted back on her heels. The quicker she and Polly got out of here, the better.

The lost-and-found woman excused herself, scooting around the counter as she hurried toward one of the khaki-clad officials standing by the door. The man took out his walkie-talkie, his glance shifting slyly toward Polly.

Etta had seen enough. Just then, a large group shuffled past the area, and she reached over the counter and snatched back her keys. After lifting Polly into her arms, she jogged toward the exit.

Khaki-clad officials appeared to be everywhere. She could spot four without even turning her head. And they all seemed to have their ears glued to their walkie-talkies.

"Some people are looking for us, Polly," she said as she edged closer to the exit of the building. "But we don't want them to find us because we've planned an adventure. We're going to hide for a while and then go back to the Airstream, okay?"

Polly's head slowly bobbed up and down.

Etta stepped quickly through the door. A worn path led to another barn with a sign that claimed it was closed to the public. Perfect. She quickly ducked inside. Rows of small stalls lined the back wall, and Etta headed for one in the farthest corner, where a half-dozen bales of hay were stacked in a pile. "Good cover for hiding," she whispered to Polly as she sank to the ground and settled the little girl on her lap. Tucking her knees up, Etta lowered her head, trying to make herself as small as possible. She squeezed her eyes closed for half of a second, and then forced them open, letting out a squeak of surprise as she stared into the beady eyes of a scraggly goat. "He—or she—seems friendly," she said. The goat held her gaze, trying to size up the unexpected intrusion.

With all the bleating and chomping and rustling of hay, it was hard to hear what was happening outside their little stall. As the minutes passed, she entertained herself by imagining that no one was looking for them, that she had overreacted, that the woman at the lost and found hadn't recognized her, after all. A bubble of relief began to grow in her chest as she allowed herself to dwell on that pleasant possibility. She stroked Polly's hair and waited. The little girl was getting impatient as seconds turned to minutes, and then minutes to almost an hour. She stretched out her foot and kicked the hay into a pile. Etta checked her watch. If another fifteen minutes passed without any signs of activity nearby, it ought to be safe to move on.

"Hey!" A voice broke through the noises around her. "Did you see a woman with a little girl?" The beam of a flashlight made a long pass through the barn's interior, stopping for a moment in the stall to the right.

Etta froze. The voice was strangely familiar. She had definitely heard it before, but she wasn't sure where.

"Nah, we didn't see anyone," someone responded even as the yellow circle of light passed inches from the spot where Etta and Polly were hiding. "We closed up early today. Not too many people are interested in goats, you know. The horses and the pigs are the popular spots." There was a long pause. "What's going on? Are you with the police?"

"What do you think?" was the gruff reply. "Why else would I be mucking around in a goat barn? This is serious business, bucko. This woman is known to be armed and dangerous. She killed a cop and kidnapped a kid. So you better watch your back and take some care."

Killed a cop? No. That wasn't true. The man who assaulted her had broken into her home, attacked her and Steven. Clearly, *he* was the criminal—bent on kidnapping Polly.

Etta waited a few minutes longer and then snuck a peek over the hay. The gruff-voiced man appeared to be gone, and in his place was a woman wearing a straw hat and carrying a baby goat. An older man with a shaggy moustache followed behind her, lugging a large crate.

"What did that guy want?" the woman asked her companion.

"Information about some lady and kid. Claimed to be a cop, but he sure didn't look like one with that wild gray beard and those crazy eyes. In any case, this sounds like trouble. Last time something like this happened, they shut down all the exits to the fair."

Where were Etta and Polly? Not inside the Airstream, that was for sure. Steven had figured that out in a matter of seconds. But it was hard to believe they would have gone far.

It was too soon to panic. At least not yet. He was tempted to ask a few of the neighbors if they had seen a woman and a little girl. But he'd rather not say too much—not unless he had to. And, at the moment, he was tired and anxious and slightly on edge. It had been great to see

Donny, but he had felt vaguely uncomfortable reliving the glory days when they were major competitors in the ring. It seemed that he no longer had the heart for it.

It had taken a long time to understand, but eventually it had dawned on him that, while he loved riding bulls and he enjoyed the camaraderie of his fellow riders, he no longer relished the notoriety that came with winning championships. His first love had been for the adrenaline rush he experienced whenever he'd strapped onto a bull. But the more time he spent on the circuit, the more he had come to realize that it was the bulls themselves that were his passion.

Since his vaunted comeback, he was more popular than ever. Apparently, the only thing more impressive than winning the championship was jumping into the arena to save a friend. Now he was being hailed, not as a great bull rider, but as a hero. And he felt like a fraud.

Where was Etta, anyway? Maybe if he strolled around the campsite, someone would offer him information rather than him having to seek it out. Actually, hadn't he noticed a uniformed police officer along with members of the security team strolling around the fair? A tickle of apprehension nudged him. In and of itself, it wasn't unusual for there to be guards in the area, since campers could become rowdy. But a uniformed police officer was definitely not the norm.

He began to pick his away along the road, hoping to encounter a friendly stranger who might have seen Etta and Polly.

He spotted a boy, about fourteen, walking with an older man who looked like his father. Both of them were decked out in camo-patterned overalls and sporting hats with the logo of the Professional Bull Riders circuit, PBR. "Hey, there," Steven said, trying on his best smile. "I just pulled in for the night. What's with the extra security?"

The teen smirked. "You know these rent-a-cop types. They're all a bunch of tools. Think they're going to catch a big-time criminal just because Mrs. Swallows claims she spotted a fugitive."

"Kenny…" The older man's voice had a rebuking tone. "Don't be telling tales that might not be true." He held out his hand. "Name's Carl. Carl Deering. And who are you? You don't sound like you're from Texas."

"You're right about that." Steven nodded. "I'm from South Dakota. But I used to ride the circuit."

"You don't say. Kenny here is hoping to make the cut the next couple of years. So you were asking about the police. I don't know the story, but they're wandering around asking all sorts of questions about this woman they say is a fugitive. Plainclothes and uniformed cops. Not that anyone is talking. Whoever the lady is, she saved my nephew from bleeding out. We all saw it. She's good, in our book."

Steven sighed. So that explained why Etta had disregarded her own safety—to help a hurt kid. But what happened after that?

It would be smart not to act too interested. Best to change the subject and then circle back to the stuff he wanted to know. "I get it. I saw some of the craziest stuff when I was trying to make it onto the circuit. One time, a friend of mine found a pig inside his Winnebago eating his sheets."

Carl threw back his head and laughed. "I've never heard that one before. But there sure are some good tales." His face sobered for a minute. "This was real serious, though. Ricky was bleeding all over, screaming his head off. None of us knew what to do, and this woman comes running from one of the nearby trailers and offers to help. She managed to get the bleeding to stop. But then she disappeared. One of the by-standers—Charlene—found some keys that she thought the lady might have dropped. I went with her to drop them off at the lost and found. Thought maybe the lady might turn up while we were there, and I'd get a chance to say thanks for what she'd done."

Steven nodded. The story was a bit con-voluted, but he was following so far. His eye caught Kenny, who was staring at him as if try-ing to suss him out.

"Anyway," Carl continued. "Word travels real quick around here. Turns out, we were right that the keys belonged to the lady. 'Cause she did come by to get them. And then that's when Dottie Swallows, who was working the lost and found, got it into her head that the little girl she had with her looked like a kid on that Amber Alert. It all happened pretty quick after that. Dottie notified fair security, who contacted the police, but in the meantime, the lady and the kid slipped away. Crazy story, right?"

Steven nodded. Crazy and worrisome. But Etta would be quick to recognize the danger. And if she thought the police were looking for her, she'd definitely take care. The question was, what could he do to help them?

"Well," he finally said to Carl and Kenny, who were clearly expecting some sort of reaction, "if the lady saved your nephew, it seems unlikely she'd be kidnapping some kid."

"That's what I said," Carl exclaimed.

"Hey, I know who you are!" Kenny interrupted. "You're Steven Hunt! You won the PBR Championship. Twice." His face suddenly fell. "But you got really badly hurt last time you rode, didn't you? Jumping into the ring to help your friend."

Steven inclined his head. "Yep. That's me. But as you can see, I'm pretty much recovered. Not that I'll be climbing on the back of a bull anytime soon. But I sure do miss it. That's why I'm here."

"Wow! Mr. Hunt. It's honor to meet you." Carl seemed equally excited. "I can't believe that you're staying at the campground. You let us know if there's anything we can do for you. My wife would be more than happy to have you over for dinner."

Steven could feel his lips quirk into a smile. This was one of the things he loved about rodeo people. The generosity and kindness of men like Carl Deering. "That won't be necessary. But I tell you what," he said, deciding to take a gamble, "that girl who helped your nephew, if you could keep quiet about her presence here, I think she might appreciate that."

Steven felt the stirrings of unease as a quizzical expression danced across Carl's face. Maybe he should have stayed mum instead of taking a chance. Was it his imagination or did the man have a canny, knowing look in his eye? Should he try to backpedal and retract his request? It was probably too late for that. He had already said too much.

"Don't look now, but I think we're about to have some company…" Kenny's whispered comment broke through his thoughts. Steven looked up to see two police officers headed their way.

Chapter Nine

Steven's eyes darted toward his companions, a pit of unease forming in his gut. A knowing smile was twitching on Carl's lips. And, as for Kenny, well, the boy didn't seem to have put two and two together, at least not yet.

The officers were getting closer. Steven's mind scrambled to weigh the options. Should he admit the truth to Carl? Or would that just make it worse? Maybe he should just back away from the group and pretend there was something that required his attention.

"Hey there, folks," a burly officer said. He stepped in front of Steven, blocking his exit.

"What do you want?" Kenny's voice was aggressive.

The thinner, shorter cop gave the boy an amused smile. "We're just asking around to see if anyone has seen a woman with a small child."

Carl chuckled. "We've seen lots and lots of

women and children. You're going to have to be a bit more specific than that."

The first officer frowned. "Average height. Short red hair. The kid is about four or five."

"Is she in trouble?" Carl's voice held just a hint of malice.

"At this point, we just want to ask her some questions. We think she may have helped an injured kid earlier today."

"Oh, *that* woman!" Carl seemed to be relishing the attention. "Yeah. I saw the whole thing. She saved my nephew's life. But I don't recall seeing a child with her."

"Hmm." The shorter officer took off his hat and scratched his head. "And you haven't seen her since then? Any of you?"

Steven shook his head. It wasn't even a lie. He hadn't seen Etta or Polly since he'd left to talk to Donny.

"Nah. Nah. I haven't seen her," Carl said, "but there was some young fellow around here who was asking about her."

The office stepped closer. "Really? And did you get the name of this man or have any idea where he was headed?"

"He wasn't from here. That's the reason I'm telling you this. I'm pretty sure that all three shoved off already, though. The man claimed he had come up from El Paso to get some parts for his tractor. You know, you can find great deals at these fairs. One time, my boy Kenny, here, and I were able to get diesel motor for a quarter of its cost just 'cause it was slightly used."

Steven slowly blew out a breath and un-clenched his hands. It seemed that Carl wasn't going to give him up. But Etta and Polly had to be stuck somewhere on the fairgrounds, prob-ably waiting for the commotion to die down. Given the police presence and the level of se-curity, that didn't seem likely anytime soon. Which meant that he needed to extricate him-self from this conversation and find them imme-diately. Carl was still rambling on about engines to the taller officer, who, from his follow-up questions, seemed engaged by the subject. Ste-ven cast a quick peek at the other officer. Arms crossed and foot tapping, he clearly wanted to move along.

"Hey, man…" Kenny's voice, previously belligerent and forceful, was soft and discreet when he whispered to Steven. "You may want to head back to your Airstream to check on your woman."

What did that mean? The adrenaline that had

been simmering in Steven's chest again surged through his limbs. Was the kid trying to send him a message? If so, he didn't understand. He scanned the area around them. No sign of Etta or Polly. His eyes flicked toward the boy, who gave the slightest tilt with his head toward a row of picnic tables and grills set about a hundred feet away. Steven squinted in that direction. There weren't too many people around, but maybe one of them could be Etta.

"Well, I guess I better be on my way, then." Steven turned toward the officers. "I hope you find the people you are looking for." Then he turned toward Carl and held out his hand. "Thanks for your help."

"Don't mention it." Carl returned the firm handshake. "You know how it is here in the country. One person needs an egg, you just ask the next campsite over. We look out for each other. Here, take Kenny with you. He's actually planning to make a cake, so maybe he can borrow a couple from you. I'm going to show these officers the new Hemi I just installed in my truck, and Kenny is sick to death of hearing about it. C'mon, fellas, my Chevy is parked over here behind my camper."

Carl headed off toward a large pickup, still

bending the ear of the burly officer. The shorter policeman trailed behind, looking less than pleased.

"She's over there." Kenny started to walk toward the picnic site. But before they reached the tables and grills, the teen veered toward the lavatories. Serious doubts started to form in Steven's mind. Should he trust this kid? Did he even understand that the person the police were looking for was his so-called woman?

"She went in there." Kenny pointed to the door to the ladies' bathroom.

"You're sure?" Steven didn't mean to sound skeptical, but he could hear a tinge of disbelief in his voice. "You saw her go in?"

"I've got good eyes. My mom thinks I should become a pilot because my vision is so sharp, but I want to see how I do on the rodeo circuit first."

"Right." Steven stared at the door with uncertainty. "I guess I better go in."

Kenny smirked.

Really, after everything that he and Etta had been through in the last twenty-four hours, it was ridiculous to be wary of entering the women's bathroom. Still, with Carl distracting the officers, this was his chance to get Etta and Polly back to the Airstream without being caught. With a final sigh, he pushed open the door and stepped inside.

Etta crouched against the ceramic tile of the toilet in the farthest stall. Her arms wrapped tightly around Polly, she squeezed her eyes shut and offered up a silent plea to God. Terror was knotted in her gut as, just moments earlier, she had heard the door to the bathroom swish open and then bang closed. Was it just another woman, coming in to use the facilities? Or was it one of the relentless pack of security officers she and Polly had been dodging for the last forty-five minutes as they made their way back to the Airstream?

The sound of booted footsteps echoed against the floor. Blood pounded in her chest, and she tightened her grip on Polly. *Please, please, God, let us be safe.*

"Etta? Are you in here?" a familiar voice whispered.

Relief flooded her senses. "Steven."

"Yeah. It's me. We need to get you out of here now."

Her fingers trembling, Etta reached up, pushed the lock back and opened the door. At the sight of Steven's familiar face, Etta felt an intense desire to burst into tears. But no. That wouldn't solve anything.

"Here, let me help you." Steven reached in and lifted Polly up into his arms. The little girl stared at him with solemn eyes and then laid her head down on his shoulder as Etta scrambled to her feet.

"He's here, Steven." Etta's voice trembled.

"Who's here?"

"Gray Beard. I heard him when we were in the goat barn. He said I killed a cop."

Steven shook his head. "I'm sure he'd say anything if he thought it would help track you down. But I wish I knew how he found out that you were at the fair. He must have some sort of pipeline to the police."

A gasp stuck in her throat. "Are the police here, too?"

"Yeah. But don't worry. We'll be on the road before they even know we're gone."

Still holding Polly, Steven walked to the door of the lavatory and pushed it open. After the harshness of the fluorescent bulbs, the dusky darkness caught her by surprise, and she blinked for a moment as she took in her surroundings. The coast was clear. No police. No security guards. No gray-bearded man determined to find her. The only people around were a couple of kids roasting hot dogs on a grill.

She sighed with relief.

But a second later, her heart resumed its frenetic pounding in her chest. She had nearly walked straight into a teenager lurking beside the door. He looked at her for a moment and then turned to Steven.

"Dad will keep the cops distracted for a while. That should give you enough time to get back to your camper and be on your way."

Steven nodded. "Thanks, Kenny. You're a good kid."

Etta exhaled in relief. Steven seemed to know this person.

"Where are you parked?" the kid asked.

"About two spots down from you. Donny Gage's trailer."

"I know the one." The boy paused, as if thinking. "You want me to drive it down here, so you can avoid the police?"

"That would be great. Etta, can you give Kenny the keys?"

"Huh? Oh, right. The keys." The cause of all this trouble. Etta reached inside her pocket and fished them out. "You don't look old enough to have a license."

The teenager rolled his eyes. "Ma'am, I've been driving since I was nine. I'm not exactly official, but, trust me, I'm a good driver."

Etta cast a glance at Steven. He nodded.

Reluctantly, she placed the keys in the boy's outstretched fingers.

"I'll be back as quick as I can," the boy said. "It might take a little while to get everything unplugged and packed up." A moment later, he was bounding away.

"Friend of yours?" Etta asked after a few seconds of silence.

"Seems to be."

"Seems to be?" Etta said, echoing back Steven's words. "What does that mean?"

"Well, I just met him and his dad, so I suppose you can call him a friendly acquaintance."

Steven's offhand manner was beginning to grate on her nerves. "You just met him, and we gave him the keys to the Airstream?"

Steven adjusted his hold on Polly. "Look, you're going to have to trust me on this. If Kenny or his dad were going to turn us in, they've already had the opportunity."

Another silence descended between them as

Etta considered what Steven was asking of her. *Trust.* That was something that had never come easy to her. Too many people in her life had let her down when she needed them most. Her father. Her mother. Even Lilly during her delinquent days. Steeling herself against inevitable disappointment had become a survival technique for most of her life. And when Steven had come to her rescue during the home invasion, she had initially felt that same sense of wariness and mistrust. But in the course of time, Steven had come through for her, risking his own freedom and doing everything in his power to keep her and Polly safe.

"I like your hair." Steven's voice interrupted her thoughts.

"Oh." She reached up to touch the short tresses. "Thanks."

"I heard you saved some little kid's life. Well done on that."

His praise warmed her. Suddenly embarrassed, she turned her gaze away. "Slight exaggeration. I just helped stop the bleeding."

"I figured you had a good reason for leaving the trailer. When I got back and couldn't find you, I was worried."

"I'm grateful that you found us. I think my

heart actually leapt when I heard you call my name in the bathroom."

"Glad to be of assistance." He smiled, and there it was again—that flush of joy along with the crazy feeling of her heart beating double-time in her chest.

"How did you manage to make it this far without being caught?" he asked.

Where to begin? After hiding with the goats, she and Polly had snuck out and attached them-selves to a large family group. That had gotten them as far as the birthing stables. There, they had dodged in and out of buildings and barns, slowly making their way back to the campsite. She gave him the condensed version.

"We just kept to the edge of the crowd and tried to stay hidden," she explained.

"Well, I'm impressed. I wasn't back at the campsite for more than ten minutes before I was pulled into a conversation with two police of-ficers. So, clearly, you have better evasion skills than me."

Etta cast a sharp glance in Steven's direction. Was he being patronizing? No, Steven never said anything he didn't mean. Suddenly, the hairs on the back of her neck started to stand up. Who was that man in khaki shorts over by the picnic benches?

"Steven," she said, lowering her voice to a whisper. "I think that security guard is getting closer."

Steven glanced at the man and nodded. "Right. Maybe you and Polly should go back into the bathroom to hide until Kenny gets here with the Airstream. I'll wander away, so it doesn't look like I am loitering in front of the women's lavatory."

"Shouldn't Kenny have gotten back already? The trailer is close by." Apprehension was again pricking at her brain. She didn't want to question Steven's decision to trust the teenager, but she couldn't help the jolt of uncertainty.

Steven grimaced. "Yeah. But he did have to unplug the connections and whatnot. Actually, I think I see him coming. Yeah, there's the POW flag. It's definitely our ride."

"Good." She hadn't wanted to go back into the bathroom to cower on the floor. She glanced toward the picnic tables. The two security officers were involved in a conversation with the teens at the grill. She turned her gaze back toward the road. She had to concede—the kid was a good driver. On an uneven surface barely wide enough to accommodate the Airstream, Kenny seemed to be having no difficulty navigating the dusty lane.

The RV came to a shuddering halt just a few feet from the lavatory, and Kenny popped out of the Airstream.

"I left it running. Sorry it took so long. Dad was still talking, but he got a little information from the police as well. Apparently, they're checking vehicles as they leave the fair, but only at the north entrance. They don't have enough officers to cover the other gates yet."

"Right," Steven said, pulling open the side door and setting Polly down to find a seat in the back of the trailer. He turned to face his new friend with a smile. "You and your dad have been a great help, Kenny. Here—" He tugged his cowboy hat, pulled a Sharpie out of his pocket and signed the brim. The kid pulled off his ball cap and replaced it with the Stetson, then offered a half salute and a grin as he walked away.

Etta wished she had something to give him, too.

Steven opened the front door and claimed the seat behind the wheel.

Etta shook her head. "Let's change seats. You're not supposed to be driving."

"I'll be fine. There still could be some sort of security checkpoint, so I should probably sit up front alone while you and Polly hole up where you won't be seen."

She wanted to argue with him, but his logic made sense. Besides, she didn't have any energy left for a fight. She hustled back to the side door and scampered inside. Even before she had pulled the door closed completely, they were on the move.

"C'mon, sweet pea." She held Polly's hand, and they walked toward the back. Would it be reckless to turn on the overhead light? Probably. But sitting in the cramped darkness was too depressing. Willing herself to find the positive, Etta fished around for a blanket and then draped it around Polly's shoulders.

"I think it's time for a story. You already know the one of the three little pigs, but have you ever heard the story of the three little wolves?"

Polly shook her head.

"Well, once upon a time, there were three little wolves..." Etta kept her voice to a soft murmur, hoping her lilting tone would help lull Polly to sleep. She could tell from the vibrations below her feet that they were still on a dirt road. Then, there came a sudden, jerking stop. Etta cut off the story and held her breath. It seemed like at least three minutes passed, but finally the Airstream began moving again. She looked down at Polly. The little girl had fallen asleep.

Etta adjusted Polly's position on the pullout bed, tucking the blanket around her, and then peeked out from behind the partition. All appeared clear.

Once they'd exited the fairgrounds, she slid into the passenger seat next to Steven and offered him her best smile. "What do you think of heading to Sulphur Springs where we can find a place to pull in for the night? Tomorrow morning, we can see if we can arrange to visit with Jordan Shapiro."

Chapter Ten

The brass plate in the center of the town house's front door was very discreet. Jordan Shapiro. Private Investigator. Discreet Inquiries Welcome.

When they left the fairgrounds in Leesburg, Etta had been adamant that they needed to head straight for Sulphur Springs. But Jordan's office hours didn't begin until ten o'clock the next day, so they had driven to a nearby Walmart lot where they had spent the night.

Now, after two trips around the block, counting back and forward, looking for the address, they had finally found the right place. But it remained to be seen whether or not this additional detour would yield information that would be worth the risk.

Steven locked eyes with Etta, who was standing beside him, holding hands with Polly. He shifted his gaze toward the high-tech camera, its black lens focused on the threshold.

"I saw it, too," Etta muttered under her breath, taking a step sideways and turning her head.

"Not a great start to our adventure. But ready or not, here we go." He lifted his hand and rang the bell above the mail slot.

A few minutes passed before a prim, older woman in a fitted blue suit opened the door. She seemed more annoyed than intrigued to see them waiting on the front steps. "I assume you're here to see Jordan. Do you have an appointment?"

Steven nodded. "Yes, of course. Matt Bickler of Thompson, Colfax, and Bickler." His white lie caused Etta to flinch as she waited beside him. While it was true that the voice-mail message he'd left a half hour earlier had been a bit fuzzy on details, he had correctly estimated their arrival time to be around ten o'clock. He pointed at his watch. Three minutes early. Perfect.

The woman disappeared, returning a few moments later, a deep frown creasing her forehead. "Jordan just saw your message, and she apologizes for the inconvenience. But she's extremely busy at the moment, and she won't be able to see you today. Would you like to reschedule for next week?"

Steven shook his head. "We're only in town for a few hours, so now is our only option."

"I'm sorry, Mr. Bickler. But 'now' is just not possible."

"I understand. But perhaps you would ask Ms. Shapiro if she could spare just a couple of minutes to talk to the sister of an old friend," he pleaded. "We're willing to wait for as long as it takes."

The stylish woman disappeared inside once again, this time pulling the door shut behind her.

"She's not going to see us," Etta whispered. "Maybe it was a waste of time coming all this way."

"Let's see what happens," Steven said. As they waited, he snuck another glance at Etta. With her short, very red haircut and oversize glasses, she reminded him of the confident girl he had fallen in love with years ago.

He pulled his gaze away. This wait felt like an eternity. Out of the corner of his eye, he checked out the CCTV recording device above them in the entryway. Was someone inside watching their every move? No doubt, the camera had already captured a full-on shot of all three waiting on the threshold.

At long last, the door swished open. Gone was the older woman in the blue suit. In her place was a younger, spandex-clad female with spiked pink hair.

"Yes? What do you want, then? I believe my assistant already explained that I have no openings, but, apparently, you won't take no for an answer."

"Ms. Shapiro?" Steven asked. "We were hoping to talk to you about Lilly Sanderson, or Lilly Mitchell, as you knew her in the past."

The woman's face darkened. "Lilly's dead. I have nothing to say on the subject."

"Maybe not," Steven said, "but surely you can take a moment or two to answer a couple of questions about the situation."

"Fine." The woman pulled the door open wider. "But I only have a very small window of time before my next appointment. I suppose you better come inside."

A few minutes later, Steven found himself sitting next to Etta and Polly on a white leather couch in a small office. Modern art graced the ivory walls, and hundreds of hardcover books were stacked in untidy piles throughout the space. Seated behind a glass desk, Jordan Shapiro tented her arms and leaned forward, training her gaze on Steven.

"My assistant tells me that your name is Matt Bickler. And I recognize your companions from pictures on Lilly's Facebook page—her daughter Polly and her sister Etta with drastically different hair."

Steven cleared his throat. So, much for the efficacy of Etta's new look. But, whatever. They had the Airstream now, so there would be no need for her to venture out in public. And, on the plus side, Jordan's claim to familiarity gave them a logical place to start.

"Cards on the table here since we don't have much time. We know that you and Lilly were friends. And we know for a fact that she had reached out to you about some sort of scheme that was going to make her rich."

"You know for a fact, huh? I don't like talking to lawyers, Mr. Bickler, especially when they choose to adopt a confrontational tone."

"Perhaps I should explain," Etta interjected. "Matt is part of a team representing Lilly's husband Greg who has been arrested for her murder."

"So, Lilly's daughter has become your ward?"

"I'm taking care of her, yes. But only until Greg is proven innocent."

"How old are you, kid?" Jordan turned her attention to Polly.

No answer.

"Shy. I get it. Your mama taught you not to talk to strangers. Smart lady." Jordan turned her gaze back to Etta. "I seem to remember that she's around five, am I right? Maybe old enough to have learned some facts from watching her mother."

"What Polly knows isn't the issue," Steven interjected. "We understand that Lilly reached out to you before her death. We have no idea what that was about, just that it was something big. We're not saying that it's anything illegal. But her connection to you is one of the few credible leads we have at the moment. So if you know anything at all that can help us understand what or who Lilly was investigating, we'd appreciate you sharing it with us today."

Jordan blew out a long sigh. "Okay, listen. Against my better judgment, I'm going to tell you what I know. But don't get your hopes up that it's going to break open the case against her husband Greg. According to the papers, the evidence appears to be stacked against him."

"But…"

Jordan held up a hand to forestall Etta's question. "I first heard from Lilly in January. She claimed she was on the verge of making a huge score. Same old Lilly. Always thinking she was smarter than everyone else. Sorry," Jordan said, looking at Etta and Polly. "She was my friend but she sometimes acted a little too self-pleased. Anyway, she told me that she had stumbled across something that has the potential to be a major game changer. What that is exactly, she wouldn't say. 'A blast from the past' was how she described it at the time. I remember how she was always so fascinated by true crime stories in juvie, and I knew she had a part-time gig reporting and wanted to make it big. If I had to guess, I'd say that her big scoop involved something like that. But that's all I know."

"But that was your first contact," Steven pressed. "We know that you heard from her more than once. Did she offer any explanation as to why what she was working on was top secret?"

Jordan shot him a look. Clearly, she preferred Etta's gentle inquiries to his pointed questions. "No names. No details. I told you. Lilly didn't like to share. And I've learned to be discreet as well. I did offer her advice about protecting the data she had gathered in the course of her investigation. Nothing specific. Can't you pull these details from her computer or cell?"

Etta shook her head. "There was nothing on her hard drive. The police checked into that."

"See what I mean?" Jordan held up her hands in resignation. "She was paranoid about anyone uncovering her secrets." She paused for a moment and then continued, "We spoke again in mid-February, and she claimed that she was close to reeling in a big fish. I told her to be careful and keep a record of everything she found out. That made her giggle in that crazy way I remember from the time we spent together in juvie." Jordan smiled momentarily. "She told me not to worry, that she'd downloaded her notes on a USB that was tucked away in a spot where it wouldn't be found. Said that she has a kid now and caution is her middle name. That's it. I was out of the country on an extended vacation for most of March and half of April. And when I got home, I heard she was dead."

"Thank you... You've been very helpful." Steven saw Etta trace a glance from him to Polly. "Um... Matt, would you mind stepping out for a moment? I have one last question for Jordan."

Steven pulled himself up and turned to face Polly. He had a good idea of what Etta wanted to ask, but he wasn't sure she'd get the answer she was expecting.

"C'mon, kid. How about we wait for your aunt Etta out in the hall?"

As the door of the office quietly slid closed, Jordan made a show of looking at her watch. "Tick tock, Etta. I agreed to meet with you because I genuinely cared about your sister. But there isn't anything more I can say. I just wish I hadn't said those things in front of the kid. I know from the things that Lilly posted that she loved her daughter very much."

Inexplicably, Etta felt her eyes fill with tears. What Jordan said was true. Lilly would have walked across fire for Polly, so whatever she was up to in her investigation, the end result would have benefited Polly in some way.

"I know you don't have much time to chat," Etta began, "but I did want to ask you one thing. You said you were out of the country when Lilly got killed. But when you heard what had happened, did you realize that you had evidence you ought to be sharing with the police?"

Jordan shot her a withering look. "Of course,

I did. But when I thought about it, I decided there wasn't much to tell. All I knew was that Lilly had some sort of scoop. I didn't have any specific information."

"Maybe you were also thinking—" Etta had to force herself to be brave "—that you might want to cash in on it for yourself."

"I won't even grace that remark with an answer. And, honestly, Etta. You ought to be more circumspect about tossing out accusations since you yourself are currently on the wrong side of the law."

Etta's chest tightened.

"Did you really think I would agree to meet with you without checking out your credentials? I am a PI, after all. And your story has been front-page news. The short red hair and fake glasses were a momentary distraction, but hey, I'm not about to bust you on this. At least not today. Tomorrow will be time enough to contact the authorities and tell them about your visit. Sorry, Etta, but I don't have a choice. I knew I was walking a thin line by not notifying the authorities about Lilly's attempts to reach out to me. But this is a lot more serious. I could lose my license for withholding information about a fugitive from the police."

Jordan walked across the room and opened the office door. "No hard feelings, eh? It is good to finally meet you, Etta. You remind me of Lilly in all the best ways. Even in the small things, like the way she tilted her head to the side before asking a question that she had no right to know." The woman sighed. "You were a great sister to Lilly while she was in juvie. All those amazing packages you sent full of chocolate bars and the newest books on the bestseller list. I owe you for that, too. And that's the reason I'm giving you a twenty-four-hour head start before I talk to the police. And tell your friend—Matt Bickler, is it?—that I don't plan to share the CCTV footage with the cops. Once you're gone, the tape will be erased, and the system set to reboot. Consider that another gift in honor of Lilly. Take care, Etta. And watch over that kid."

Etta paused on the threshold. She had one more question to ask Jordan, and it was a difficult one to voice. But knowing the state of her sister's finances, she was hoping the PI could offer a small bit of reassurance about Lilly's motives. "This may be impossible for you to answer, but do you think my sister intended to use her information as blackmail?"

Jordan shrugged. "The Lilly I knew was clearly capable of that. But she had a kid to consider. I honestly don't know. There's a chance she was planning to write some sort of tell-all article or book about whatever it was she'd been digging into. I can see how that might get her into trouble, especially if the person she was investigating didn't want that information out there."

Etta stepped out into the hall, and Jordan closed the office door behind her. Hovering in the shadows was Jordan's assistant, who then led her toward the entryway.

There was sympathy in the woman's eyes as she held open the front door. "Your friends said they'd wait for you outside."

"Thanks," Etta said. She rushed down the front steps of the town house and around the corner, where they had left the Airstream. She opened the driver's door and climbed inside, turning to take in the sight of Steven and Polly playing checkers at the table.

"Batten down the game pieces," she said, gunning the motor. "We need to get out of here—now."

A few minutes later, Steven took a seat next to Etta. "What's the rush? It will take a few minutes for me to pull up the map. What did Jordan say when you accused her of trying to profit off Lilly's investigation?"

In spite of herself, Etta grinned. "How did you know that was what I wanted to talk to her about?"

He shrugged. "It's what I would have asked if I thought I could have gotten away with it. Good call in sending me out with Polly, though. The conversation was getting pretty heavy for her to hear." He glanced back at Polly, who was settled with a book, and added, "But she seemed okay when we got back to the trailer, and she was happy to play a few games of checkers. Danged if she didn't beat me two out of three, though. When that kid finally starts talking, I want to be around to hear what she has to say."

Etta shook her head. "Jordan is planning to report us to the police. She claims to be giving us twenty-four hours head start to get out of town. But she did promise to erase the CCTV footage from the camera at the front door." Etta was glad they'd parked around the corner from the town house. That was one less way they could be tracked.

Steven pulled his phone from his pocket and

peered at the screen. "Clearly, we need to get out of Dodge—I mean, Sulphur Springs—as quickly as possible. I'm thinking it will take around fifteen hours for us to get to the ranch if I take a turn behind the wheel."

She opened her mouth to protest, but he shook his head. "No argument. But I promise we can switch it up if my leg starts to hurt."

Etta glanced at Steven, trying to gauge his reaction to what she was about to say. "I was actually going to suggest a quick stop in Silver Creek."

"Why?" His voice contained an edge of disbelief.

"You heard Jordan say that Lilly downloaded her information to a USB. So now we know what we're looking for." She knew it. This was evidence that would finally crack Lilly's murder case—the truth about what her sister was working on and why she was killed.

"You've got to be kidding, Etta." She could tell he was fighting for calm. "It's a big house. And Greg and the police have both already searched it thoroughly. Even if we make it inside without anyone noticing, it's a dangerous move. And keep in mind that we're talking about a thumb drive. A two-inch gizmo that could be hidden anywhere."

Etta shrugged. Obviously, it would be hard to find. But Steven was forgetting that she had an advantage over Greg and the police. She knew how her sister's mind worked, the way Lilly saw things and looked at the world.

Steven ran his hand through his short hair. "I'm kind of confused here, Etta. I thought the goal was protecting Polly. How can you not recognize the risk in what you're suggesting? If we get caught, you could land in prison. Tell me. How would that help Polly?"

"We can't give up now when we're this close." Etta's voice shook with emotion. She owed it to Lilly to see this through. She hadn't been a great sister these last couple of years, and this was her chance to make things right, to find the evidence and justice for her sister and for Greg. "The final piece of the puzzle is out there, just beyond reach. I can feel it in my heart."

He shook his head. "I still don't think it's a good move. We should be heading to the ranch stat. My brother can help us, and we can continue our investigation. But we'll be doing it from a safe place."

"I hear what you're saying, and I understand that you have qualms about what I'm suggesting. But…"

"Qualms, Etta? I'd say my objections are a bit more serious than qualms. Going back to that house is the last thing we should be doing if the goal is protecting Polly."

"I disagree. And, no matter what you decide, I'm determined to see this through, even if it means doing it on my own. Go big, or go home."

"That's exactly what I've been saying, Etta. In South Dakota we'll find a safe haven at my home."

A deep sadness overwhelmed her senses. Since entering the fray and saving her life during the home invasion in Silver Creek, Steven had been at her side every step in the way. But as a team, they had come full circle in their quest to find the truth about Lilly's murder, and her heart hurt at the thought of setting off on her own. Maybe she'd hire a lawyer to help her once she had the evidence. It wouldn't be easy but she'd figure it out. She looked over at Steven and forced a smile. "We knew all along that our partnership was temporary. I'm grateful for your help and for everything you've done for me and Polly along the way. Given the circumstances, I'm actually surprised you didn't bail sooner."

Chapter Eleven

"End of the road? What does that mean?" Steven's tone was sharp, almost cutting. "Are you going to abandon me at the bus stop while you and Polly drive the Airstream to Silver Creek? And what's all this about being surprised that I hadn't bailed already? Isn't that your specialty? I mean, you're the one who quit on us."

Etta winced. She had known that she'd gone too far almost as soon as the words left her mouth. She allowed a brief moment of silence to pass before offering a defense. "What I meant to say was that Polly and I have been nothing but trouble these past few days, and almost everyone I know would have left us a long time ago."

Steven cast a long look in her direction. "Sounds like you have the wrong kind of friends."

"Look," she began, trying again. "When Lilly's body was found, the house was also ransacked. Which means that the killer was searching for something, right?"

"Why are you so certain that he didn't find it?"

"Maybe he did. Maybe going back for a second look will just be a colossal waste of time. But if it's still there, I can find it. I know my sister. When she was four, a neighbor gave her five lollipops, and she hid them all in different places throughout our house. Eventually, I found them all, even the one Scotch-taped to her mattress when I was changing the sheets on her bed."

"So Lilly was really good at hiding things. It sounds like you're making my point."

"Yes… I mean no. You're deliberately misunderstanding me."

"Etta, I'm not. I care about you, and I'm just trying to make you see reason. Maybe claiming that you understand Lilly's mindset helps you feel connected to her. But, over the years, she changed, and so did you."

Steven was right about that. Lilly had changed…but in a good way. And even if he had correctly nailed her motives, that wasn't a reason to give up.

"But what's the endgame for me and Polly if we don't discover Lilly's secret? Greg goes to

jail and then what? I know you're all in on trying to protect us. But how long can we hide out
at your family's ranch? Five years? Ten? Maybe
until Polly's old enough to go to college? We
can't run forever. And every day we let pass,
clues that will help solve Lilly's murder might
disappear."

"Can you give me a little credit here?" Steven shifted in his seat. "All I'm saying is that we
need to get somewhere safe where we can put
our heads together and try to figure this whole
thing out."

"But how can we do that if we don't have a
clue about a motive for the murder? Everything
you say sounds so reasonable, but without any
idea of what Lilly was working on, where do
we even start? We need to find the USB and
see what is on it."

A tap on her shoulder interrupted their argument. Etta turned in her seat to see Polly standing behind them holding a piece of paper. "Hi,
sweetheart. Did you draw a picture?" Etta took
just a second to glance away from the road. "Oh,
it is a flower. Pretty." It was quite a nice drawing for a five-year-old, with purple petals and
dark green leaves. But what really pulled at Etta's
heartstrings were the painstakingly written-out

letters, *P O L L Y*, printed at the top of the page. "I didn't know you could write your name."

Polly pushed the paper toward her.

"Is it for me? Thank you, sweetie. I'm going to set it right here." She propped it up on the dashboard. That seemed to satisfy Polly, who headed to her seat in the back. An uneasy silence settled between her and Steven. Etta felt an itch to continue the discussion. But something told her that Steven needed a break.

Yet a few minutes later, he was the one who brought the subject back up. "If we do this, it will have to be when it's dark out, obviously."

Etta nodded.

"And we'll need to go in with flashlights and be really quick."

Etta nodded again.

"In and out, twenty minutes, tops. No stopping to grab clothes or books or toys for Polly."

Twenty minutes. That wasn't a lot of time. But it was better than nothing.

"Thank you, Steven." She placed a hand on his arm. "We really would be lost without you. Well, I'd be in jail, and Polly would be in foster care. Or worse."

"And," Steven said, pressing his point, "as soon

as we finish our search, we're driving to South Dakota. No more excuses. No more delays."

"Agreed," Etta concurred. She had no desire to stick around at the house any longer than necessary.

Steven took a turn behind the wheel so that she could make a list of Lilly's favorite hiding places. There were a lot of them.

They pulled into a deserted park for dinner— salad and chicken sandwiches from Chick-fil-A—and settled back on folding chairs next to the Airstream to watch the sunset. Both Polly and Steven dozed off, but Etta felt too keyed up to settle down. This could be a make-it-or-break-it moment in solving Lilly's murder. She didn't have a choice. She had to find that USB.

As the sun set, they packed up their stuff and made the short drive to Silver Creek. Steven pulled into a spot a half block away from the address on Dogwood Drive.

Etta headed to the back of the Airstream and kneeled down next to her niece. "Polly...we're going back to your house because we're look-ing for something. We're not going to turn the lights on, but we'll have flashlights. And we have to be really quiet. Okay?"

As Polly's eyes darkened with fear, Etta felt a

chill go through her own body. Maybe Steven was right. Returning to the scene of the crime was too big of a gamble. The memory of the body of the man she had killed, lying inert in the hall, flashed across her brain, but she blinked it away. She needed to stay strong. They could do this. No one would see them as they crept under the cover of darkness down past the other homes on Dogwood Drive. And once they were inside the house, the rest would be easy. Relying on her sisterly instincts, she would quickly find the USB.

That was the plan.

She glanced over at Steven. He had slipped on a hoodie from Walmart and was standing by the Airstream's door. "Ready to go?"

Etta pulled in a long breath. She looked at Polly, whose face was a mask of terror. And as the implications of what they were about to do hit her, all of her resolve evaporated, and she realized that there was no way that she could take this child back into that house. And she couldn't for one minute leave her alone.

"Steven," she said, her voice tentative and soft enough for only him to hear. "I've changed my mind. I can't do this, not with Polly."

Steven nodded. "Okay. Give me the key and your list, and I'll do the search?"

"No." She shook her head. Steven's kind gesture touched her heart, and it was tempting to take him up on the offer. But he didn't know Lilly. Even with her list of possible hiding places, he would have no idea where she would have tucked away the USB. "I should be the one who goes into the house while you stay back with Polly. We're here, anyway, so I might follow this lead to its logical conclusion. I'll be fine—I promise. It won't take long. A half hour, tops."

"Etta, after what happened before with the intruder, I don't think…" Steven's eyes were clouded with worry.

"I know you'd rather be the one to take the lead on this, but it has to be me. I can do this. I can be brave like you, or at least I can try." She reached out and touched his hand, holding his gaze for a moment, and then she was out the door.

She had to dig deep for an extra spot of courage as the hundred-yard trek to the house felt interminable. Every sound seemed amplified by the darkness. Her footsteps seemed too noticeable. Her breathing too loud. With trembling fingers, she inserted the key into the latch.

But the handle refused to turn. Had someone changed the locks? The blood that had already been pounding in her chest intensified in its beat.

She fumbled with the lock twice more, jigging the key and pressing down even harder on the handle. Her hammering heart slowed its frantic pulsing as the door swung open and she stepped inside.

Upstairs first. She'd save the kitchen for last. The memories of the attack there still lingered in her mind.

She flicked on her flashlight. With twenty minutes to go and counting, she took the steps two at a time.

She'd start in the bathroom. Lilly had always liked to hide things with her makeup. She opened the top drawer on the vanity and rolled the beam of light across a tangle of necklaces, but there was no sign of a thumb drive. Onto the bottom drawer, which contained only a half-dozen tubes of lipstick and mascara.

She continued to check off the hiding spots on her list, but she kept coming up short. A knot of frustration tightened in her chest as she realized that a quarter of an hour had passed, and all she had proven was how little she knew of her sister.

But she wasn't ready to give up yet. She headed down the steps into the kitchen, her eyes scanning the shelf above the sink and settling on an African violet, now parched and droopy, on the windowsill.

Suddenly, it clicked. The drawing Polly had shown them in the Airstream. Was it possible that she trying to show them where Lilly had stashed the USB?

She set the plant on the counter and began to dig, her heart pounding. The soil was dry, almost hardened by the lack of water, but she clawed and sifted through it with her fingers. She touched something hard, so she dug a little deeper. When she pulled her hand out of the dirt, clenched in her palm was a two-inch thumb drive. She brushed off the loose soil clinging to the case and slipped it into her pocket.

She pulled in a deep breath and enjoyed a moment of elation. But it was short-lived.

The click of the front door opening echoed through the hall and sent her senses into overdrive.

Was it Steven? Had he left Polly alone in the Airstream and headed to the house to see what was taking her so long? No. She had been gone for less than twenty minutes. Not enough time had passed to cause him to panic.

At least not yet.

Voices echoed in the hall. There seemed to be two—or maybe three—intruders. Too many for her to take on alone. Panic threatened to overwhelm her. How was it possible that the men had found her here alone?

But she refused to give in to the paralyzing fear engulfing her senses. She scanned the kitchen. Where were the knives? Or that cast-iron skillet? There had to be something—anything—she could use as a weapon. But the men in the hall were getting closer, and there wasn't time to reach the back door.

Her gaze landed on the broom closet a few feet away. It was barely wide enough to fit a pail of cleaning supplies and a dustpan. But if she stood on top of the bucket and held her breath, she might be able to squeeze inside. But what to do then? She'd be trapped with no chance of escape, and no idea at all about what was going on. But what was the alternative? She slipped inside and pulled the door closed in the nick of time.

Heavy footsteps sounded against the kitchen floor, followed by the slamming of cabinets and clattering of silverware in drawers. The intruders appeared to be looking for something, not someone. And considering the sounds drifting through the closet door, it was probably something small.

As small as a thumb drive? It was certainly possible that Greg had shared his concerns about Lilly's investigative work with Sam Colfax, who had, deliberately or accidentally, passed on the information to his colleagues at the firm. Well, even if the intruders found her, Etta wasn't going to make it easy for them to claim the USB. She twisted open the upper casing of her flashlight and dropped the small device inside, next to the bulb. Then she reassembled the mechanism and slipped it back into her pocket as she waited for the next shoe to drop.

The intruder's footsteps were closer now. Etta imagined him stopping inches from her hiding place, deciding whether or not to check the closet. She held the knob tight as he pulled and twisted, doing his part to win the tug-of-war. One final, hard yank, and she lost her grip, and a shaft of light flooded the closet, revealing the face of a burly man who had the presence of mind to reach inside and cuff her wrists.

"Well, this is a surprise. Hey, Mike," he called out. "Come and see what I found!"

Her heart plummeted in her chest as Mike appeared at the kitchen door. Even with his long gray beard masking most of his features, she could see the sly grin on his lips.

"Nice find, Pete." Mike—or Gray Beard, as she had been calling him—cackled with delight. "Henrietta Mitchell, I assume. Funny thing. We've been looking for you everywhere. Little did we know that if we had just waited, you would have come to us."

Gone was the chatty neighbor, concerned about her state of mind. In his place was an angry and formidable foe. "TJ's going to be pleased," he said in a voice that was laced with menace. "Get upstairs and tell Doug about the change of plans. We're looking for the kid, who's probably hiding somewhere in the house. Find her, and we've solved all our problems."

Mike gave her a menacing smile as Pete headed up the stairs. "You've caused us a great deal of trouble," he said in a threatening tone. She shrank away from her assailant, into the shadows, but only long enough to grab the first spray bottle she could reach on the shelf of cleaning supplies. She squirted it into the man's eyes. Mike stumbled backward, and she gave him a hard shove before skidding away through the patio door.

She had only a small head start. But it was dark and she knew the lay of the land. She knew she wouldn't make it to the gate in time, so she climbed inside the storage unit along the back patio wall, bending her knees until they were almost touching her face and pulling the lid closed on top.

The kitchen door slammed open, and the tread of heavy boots could be heard against the concrete patio. Then silence. Hardly daring to breathe, she imagined her pursuer looking to the right and the left, trying to decide which way she had gone.

An electric buzzing split the air, followed by a loud groan of pain.

"Are you there, Etta?" a voice whispered. "It's me. Steven."

With her free hand, she pushed aside the container's lid. "I'm here," she said. As she climbed out of the bin, her eyes were drawn to the spot where Gray Beard was lying, twitching on the patio floor.

Steven reached over and took her hand. "That Taser jolt I hit him with won't last long. We need to get out of here as fast as we can."

Chapter Twelve

The city lights of each passing town disappeared into a darkness broken only by the occasional green highway sign pointing bleakly to a crossroad ahead. Highway I-35 streamed like a smooth ribbon between Dallas and Oklahoma City, an easy drive if Steven could ignore the occasional twinge in his right leg. It would be nearly dawn before they reached Kansas and put the South behind them on their journey home.

But he was getting ahead of himself. They had miles to go before they reached South Dakota and the safety of his family's ranch. He exhaled in relief, reveling in the fact that they had made it this far and that Etta was okay.

He shot a glance at her. She was curled up on the passenger seat beside him. Was it his imagination, or was she looking extra beautiful with her hair all tousled and that flush in her cheeks?

"You sure you're not hurt in any way?"

"Absolutely," she said. "Thanks to you."

No. He had to give this one to God. He had been waiting in the Airstream, checking the time, when he was struck by a sudden conviction that he needed to see what was happening at the house. Polly was fast asleep, and even though Etta hadn't been gone long enough to cause him to worry, he couldn't shake the feeling that something was wrong. And grabbing the Taser from the glove compartment on his way out the door proved to be a key decision. As was the fact that Etta had been able to hide from the man pursuing her. Gray Beard, she called him, though they now knew his real name was Mike. She had gotten names and descriptions of another as well—Pete. She hadn't seen the one named Doug, or the man who hadn't been at the house but who seemed to be in charge of the operation, this mysterious TJ.

He snuck another glance at Etta. Maybe, after everything they had been through thus far on their journey, now would be a good time to have the talk they had been avoiding since he'd first arrived at Lilly and Greg's house. When he had taken her hand on their sprint toward the Airstream, in his instinct to protect her, he'd felt a jolt of a longing for what was once between them. And he had wondered...had Etta felt it, too?

It was hard to say. It seemed that she did want to talk tonight, but not about her feelings. She wanted to discuss what he thought the men had been doing at the house.

"They were looking for something, too. Do you think Greg told Sam Colfax that you visited him at the prison?"

He shrugged. "I asked him not to mention it, but at this point, we have no way of knowing what he said."

"But we have the evidence now, so we can find out for sure."

"We sure do. I can't believe the thumb drive was in the plant like the one Polly drew. Even so, it was touch and go there for a moment."

"Mmm-hmm," Etta agreed. Which seemed like a mild reaction to the fact that she had been moments away from being discovered hiding. And if she had been caught... He didn't even want to think about it. What he wanted to think about was the sensation of Etta's fingers entwined with his as they'd run toward the Airstream. "What do you think is on the USB?" she asked.

He shrugged again. "I'm not sure. Ideally,

it will be information that will lead us to Lilly's killer."

"Huh," Etta replied. Clearly, she was hoping for a more prolonged discussion.

But he wasn't willing to engage in idle speculation. They needed to wait until they reached the ranch and logged into a secure network. Then, there was a good chance that many of their questions would be answered.

"Are you getting tired? Want me to drive?" she asked.

"I'm good for at least another half hour or so. Is Polly still asleep?"

Etta craned her next to check the back of the Airstream. "Out like a light. She's really been a trooper, all things considered." She was quiet for a moment and then picked up a thread of an old conversation. "Do you think what Lilly was doing was on the up-and-up?"

What she meant was…do you think my sister got killed because she tried to blackmail the wrong person? But he wasn't going to touch that one with a ten-foot pole.

Etta continued. "Maybe she really was writing some sort of exposé. But if she was trying to extort money from whoever it was that she was investigating, it would have been a good motive for murder. And it would explain a lot about these people who are after us. But I have a hard time imagining that she would have risked the life she had made with Greg and Polly."

"Maybe she didn't see what she was doing as a risk. Maybe she felt like she had it all under control."

"Yeah. Jordan was right in what she said about Lilly. That she always tended to act like she was the smartest person in the room."

Steven nodded, surprised that Etta was able to recognize that about her sister. He hadn't known, until Greg mentioned it, that Lilly had spent time in juvie. But he wasn't at all surprised. "You said that she changed and became a great mother and wife, but I'm still kind of ticked off at her right now. Whether it was blackmail or some more legit scheme, she's the cause of this whole mess. No matter how you look at it, she should have taken her information to the police."

"But…"

He shook his head. "She should have been smart enough to know the risks. Now Greg's in jail and Lilly isn't talking. And you're on the run as a fugitive."

Etta shot a glance at him. "And you're impli-
cated for helping me and Polly."

"I'm not worried about that, Etta."

Etta shook her head. "You're right about Lilly
being jealous of the time you and I spent together. But, you know, despite all her faults,
she helped me sort through a lot of the anger I
felt toward my mother. She gave me a Bible and
taught me forgiveness and how to pray. Funny.
In most families, it's the other way around. The
older sister leading the younger one. But not for
us. It was all Lilly."

"Well, I'm glad to hear that. But that doesn't
take away from the fact that your sister got
caught up in something that was more than she
could control."

Etta nodded. "That's true. But she shouldn't
be blamed because things didn't work out between us."

"I agree," he said, tapping his brake as the
semi in front of him slowed for a turn.

"Good. Because it's important that you recognize that we broke up for reasons that have
nothing to do my sister's manipulations."

"Why do I need to realize that?" he wanted
to know.

"Because we're here now, on the way to the

ranch. I assume your family knows that we once dated. Or maybe they don't. I guess I shouldn't make assumptions."

"They know."

"Okay, then. So what if your mom asks what caused the break-up?"

"I guarantee that there is no way she is going to ask you that."

"But what if she does? What should I tell her? Should I mention that you thought my sister was a brat? Or, shall I describe the way you asked me to marry you?"

He glanced back at her. Were they really going to do this now? Apparently they were, since all of a sudden, Etta seemed extremely fired up by the subject.

"Okay, Etta. I give up. I can see you have a lot to say on this particular subject. Tell me, then. What was so awful about the way I proposed?"

"Let's just say that I wasn't thrilled to have such a private, romantic moment captured on the jumbotron at a Rangers game during the seventh-inning stretch."

"You said yes."

"Of course, I did. The entire stadium was applauding and shouting for me to take the ring. I had to smile and act like I was happy. Anything else would have been humiliating for both of us." Etta shook her head. "C'mon, Steven. I realize that at that point, we had only known each other for a short time, but, even so, you should have understood that kind of public spectacle wasn't my style."

Indignation pulsed through his veins. "I guess that explains why you changed your mind the next day."

She shrugged. "Well, that wasn't the only thing. It just caused me to realize that we didn't know each other well enough to make a lifelong commitment."

He scratched his head. His short haircut was just at the very beginning of growing in, and his scalp felt itchy and uncomfortable. Then again, maybe it was just the direction that the conversation seemed to be taking.

"So what was the real reason you had for turning me down? You better go ahead and tell me. Because, I've got to say, this stuff about you not liking my proposal is all coming as a complete surprise to me. When you handed me back my ring you claimed that you couldn't get married because you needed to care for Lilly until she finished high school and that you had plans to work as a traveling nurse. You claimed that was your dream, and I believed you."

"It *was* my dream." She turned toward him. "Obviously, since that was what I did after you left. And it's what I'm still doing today. Look, I admit that we left a lot of things unsaid when we broke up. The way it went down was so raw and filled with emotion. And even though I knew that our getting married at that point would be a big mistake, it didn't mean that I didn't care."

He shrugged. "So you cared about me, and once upon a time you even claimed that you loved me. But you didn't want to spend the rest of your life with me?"

Etta nodded.

"Wow. Okay, then. I guess I always thought that the way we felt about each other would be enough to get us through any rough patches along the way. But you know what, Etta? I'm actually glad I didn't know about any of this at the time. It might have been hard to deal with the fact that I was a complete dope to think that having twenty thousand people cheering at the idea of us tying to knot was romantic."

She let out a breath. "You are deliberately misconstruing what I've been trying to say. Let me try again. Do you remember telling me that you wanted to take me away from my 'dysfunctional life'?"

He shook his head. "I don't."

"Well, you did. And I knew that by that you meant Lilly. You thought I needed to be rescued. But I finally had my nursing degree and Lilly was almost old enough to be on her own. I told you. I had plans. Maybe they weren't as exciting as a bull-riding career, but they were mine."

"That's not fair." He glanced at her. "I never expected you to follow me around the country watching me compete. I knew you had your own career. I just thought that once we decided to get married, we'd have a conversation about how to make it all work out."

"You didn't say that, Steven." Etta's voice was low, almost a whisper. "Maybe you planned to mention it later, but there wasn't the chance. You walked away from me, and, until a few days ago, I never saw you again. I always thought that…" She trailed off.

He looked over again. Even in the darkness, he could see that she was crying.

"What, Etta? What did you think?" he asked.

She sniffled and took a moment to pull herself together. "I guess I thought that eventually, you'd reach out to talk. But you didn't. You just rode off into the sunset, and that was it. End of discussion. Case closed. It was hard for a while, knowing I had trusted you with my heart. But then I started to realize that it all worked out for the best. And even now, I really do believe that. Don't you?"

Etta waited for Steven to respond, but he didn't. He just kept his focus on the road ahead.

That realization about them had gotten her through a lot of hard times in the days and months after he left. It took time, but she had successfully convinced herself that their breakup had been a positive thing that had allowed her to keep moving ahead. Once in a while, she'd needed to remind herself of that, when she was feeling lonely or blue. But in time, she got to the point where months went by when she didn't even think about Steven or wonder what he was doing. So why, all of a sudden, was she baiting him into agreeing that he felt that way, too?

But if she had been expecting Steven to claim that he wished that they had done things differently, it didn't seem like it was going to happen. The firm set of his jaw and his hard stare out the window of the Airstream made it clear that he wasn't willing to go there. And how could she blame him? She had just come right out and claimed that their breakup was a good thing, and that she was better off alone.

But was she? She trusted Steven with her life. But it was a different story when it came to her heart.

She settled back against her seat and closed her eyes, determined to rest so that she would be alert for her turn behind the wheel. But sleep didn't come, no matter how hard she tried. She rolled on one side and pressed her head against the cool glass of the window. Two minutes later, she swung up her legs onto the seat, turning toward the front of the vehicle. When that didn't work, she shifted again, this time facing the driver's side. That was the death knell to any hope of slumber as she saw Steven's tense profile glaring straight ahead.

She cleared her throat. "Steven?"

"Yeah?" His tone was hard. Maybe he assumed that she wanted to continue their previous conversation, but he needn't worry about that. She had said all that she wanted to say. "What would you say to taking a break and letting me take a turn behind the wheel?"

A pause. "Okay" was his monosyllabic answer. He pulled off the highway at the next exit.

While he gassed up the RV, she headed inside the small convenience store, stopping to buy coffee at the kiosk by the counter. Returning to the Airstream, she climbed in the driver's side and set her cup in the holder. "I needed a jolt of caffeine to keep me awake. I assumed you wouldn't want any since this is your chance to sleep."

"That's fine," he said.

His response was two words this time. Maybe by the time they got to South Dakota, they'd be communicating in whole sentences again.

But, really, what had she been expecting when she'd steered the conversation into such difficult territory? A heavy sense of regret weighed down on her shoulders as she thought of something she had heard a long time ago. *Forget the mistake. Remember the lesson.*

That advice had proven to be extremely productive in her dealings with issues that cropped up at the hospital. The problem was that she wasn't exactly rational when it came to Steven. If caring for him was a mistake, then what was the lesson? She had loved him once, maybe a lot more than she cared to admit. And it was true that, in the days and months after he left, she had expected him to track her down at some point, if only just to talk and catch up. And when he hadn't, it had hurt her pride. Because, first and foremost, they had been friends. And it would have been fun to talk about his career, her travels, Lilly's wedding and the birth of Polly. Of course, there had been nothing stopping her from reaching out to him. He would have been easy enough to find with the schedule for the bull riding competition as close as a click away.

She hadn't done that, though. Probably pride, once again the logical culprit keeping them apart. The end result was that she and Steven had gone from a situation where they spent almost every day together to zero contact whatsoever. Okay, it was true that once or twice in those first few years, she had allowed herself to google his name to see how he was doing on the circuit, but that was it. And, as time passed, following his accomplishments began to seem slightly stalkerish, and she had forced herself to move on.

Which she had. How successful she had been with that was open to debate. It hadn't been easy. Over the years, she had gone on dates with doctors and men she had met through her co-workers. A lot of them had been nice, but there was no spark. Once or twice, she thought there was potential, but it never seemed to pan out.

She had to assume Steven had continued to date as well, though at present he didn't seem to be in a relationship. That was surprising. She had seen firsthand how beautiful women flocked to the top bull riders. And Steven was the best-looking and the nicest of the lot, at least when she'd known him. She snuck a glance at him in the passenger seat of the trailer. Still as handsome as ever.

That was his problem in a nutshell. He was too perfect. Starting with his idyllic childhood growing up on the ranch, and then, moving on to his success on the rodeo circuit, all the while presenting an image of Mr. No Worries or Cares. His ability to detach himself from stress and worry really was his superpower. She glanced over at him again and his eyes blinked open.

"What?" he asked.

"I didn't say anything," she said.

"Okay," he said.

"Well, I guess I did want to say something. I'm sorry for what I said before about your proposal." She blew out a long sigh. Did eating humble pie really have to be this hard?

"You're allowed to think whatever you want, Etta."

"I know, but I sounded meaner than I intended. It was just so unexpected, that's all. I mean, I had no clue you were going to pop the question, and then to see the two of us on the screen with the whole stadium cheering...well, it threw me for a loop."

"I got that from what you already said," he replied, covering his yawn.

"Sorry. Go back to sleep."

"We can discuss this if you want, but there doesn't seem to be a point to it. Or a whole lot more to say. I asked you to marry me, you said yes. Then you said no, and that was that. I'm really not up for analyzing how it all worked out for the best because we have no way of knowing whether or not that's true."

"Right," she answered instinctively. But then she thought about it. What did that even mean? That breaking up hadn't been the best option?

"I guess we both got what we wanted. I got to travel and see the country, and you got to be a major star on the PBR circuit, scoring in the top ten at most every event."

His lips bent into a sardonic grin. "I thought you didn't follow my career."

She felt heat spreading up her cheeks, though she was comforted by the fact that it was too dark inside the cab for Steven to see it. "I haven't lately. But I used to check in with the standings once in a while. I was pleased to see that you were doing so well."

"Thanks for that, Etta. And listen. All of this stuff is water under the bridge. I'm just glad I can help you find out what happened to Lilly. And don't waste one moment worrying about my mom or dad giving you the third degree. They're not like that. They've only heard good things about the beautiful nurse I met fifteen years ago while I was in the hospital in Texas. So they're not going to interrogate you about your reasons for not wanting to marry their son."

Chapter Thirteen

The fifteen-hour drive had taken a decided toll on Steven's leg. Although he had tried to hide his discomfort, Etta noticed his pronounced limp each time they stopped for gas, and she never hesitated to call him out for overextending his time behind the wheel. But he had been adamant about doing his share, and, with two drivers changing off every couple of hours and with a couple of long breaks for all of them to stretch their legs, they made great time getting through Kansas and Nebraska and were well ahead of schedule for a four-o'clock arrival at the ranch.

His parents were waiting on the porch when they pulled into the driveway, his gray-haired dad in his usual plaid shirt and worn jeans and his blonde mother, dressed up for the occasion in a long skirt and cotton blouse tied at the waist. As he drew his mom into a tight hug, Steven said a silent prayer that she'd resist the urge to ask too many questions about his current circumstances. Despite his earlier claim that his mother wouldn't pry, there remained just the tiniest chance she might, if the mood struck, pose a question or two about the reasons for their long-ago breakup. But all his worries dropped away as his folks welcomed their visitors with open arms.

"Etta and Polly," Steven said, stepping back to widen the circle. "These are my parents, Scott and Sandy Hunt. Mom, Dad, this is Etta and her niece, Polly."

"Nice to meet you, Mr. and Mrs. Hunt," Etta said.

"Please. Call us Scott and Sandy," his mom insisted.

"Scott and Sandy, then." Etta smiled. "I want to thank you for letting us hole up here for a bit while we figure things out."

"Wouldn't have it any other way," his dad said. "And we insist that you make yourself at home. We'll hold off on the grand tour for now, but I'm wondering if one of you might know something about horses."

Well done, Dad. Steven was glad he had prepped his father in advance.

There was a moment of silence as all eyes fixed on Polly, whose nod was hardly perceptible.

Scott clapped his hands. "I'm happy to meet a young'un who appreciates beautiful animals. I was just about to head to the barn to check on one of the mares who has been off her feed. I wonder if you'd like to come with me and see how she's doing."

Another small nod of the head, and off Polly went with Scott to the horse barn.

Sandy snaked an arm around Etta's waist and led her into the house. "I'll show you your room, and you can get settled. I put Polly right next door in an adjoining bedroom, but if need be, we can open the trundle bed and she can sleep next to you."

"Thanks, Sandy," Etta said as she followed his mom into the house.

Finding himself alone on the porch, Steven took a moment to breathe in a lungful of clean, fresh air. This truly was God's country, from the rolling hills to the fields of golden grasses. It was home, and he loved it more than any other place on earth. But despite the awesome grandeur of the landscape, he suddenly felt mentally and physically exhausted, a condition he aimed to keep hidden from his mom.

He should have known there was no chance of that.

"You look tired," she said without preamble the moment she returned to the porch. "And I can see that you haven't exactly been following the doctor's orders about avoiding too much stress on your leg."

"Aww, Ma." He shrugged, all of a sudden feeling like a ten-year-old kid allergic to advice. "I really am doing okay."

"I guess I'll have to believe you since you always tell the truth," she said, raising her brow. "In any event. I'm glad we can offer your friends a safe place to stay."

Of course. His mom had an enormous heart for helping others. She hadn't hesitated for even a second when he had called from the road and described their circumstances.

"But," she continued, her eyes sparkling with canny intelligence, "now that you're here, I'm going to stay on you about making good choices. You're not twenty-one anymore, Steven. Serious injuries like yours take longer to heal. Which means you need to listen to what your doctors say."

"Yeah, Ma. I know."

He pulled in another deep breath and resolved not to push back against his mom's unsolicited advice. All of the broken bones and dislocated shoulders he suffered in the ring had been hard on her as well. In fact, it was one of the reasons he had begged her not to visit him fifteen years ago when he ended up in the hospital in Texas. That had been the worst injury of his career, and he knew that it would've caused her untold distress to see him during his recuperation. Talking on the phone was easier. That way, she didn't have to deal with the reality of his bent and bruised body stretched on the bed.

He had often thought that his life was divided between things that had happened before and after he almost lost his life at that rodeo in Dallas. Up until that point in his career, he'd been just muddling along, enjoying the prestige of being part of the circuit. He'd finally become a contender, but he lacked the skills of a true champion. Then two things happened. He got hurt, and Etta rejected his proposal. The fire was in his belly then, and with that new resolve came a determination to be the best. And he'd succeeded beyond his wildest expectations. But that didn't make the risk he took every time he competed any easier on his family.

"I like your Etta," his mom said, pulling him back to the present. "She seems spunky."

He smiled at that, "spunky" being the highest compliment in his mom's vocabulary.

Still, he didn't need her throwing around phrases like "your Etta" and suggesting that the two of them were anything more than friends.

"Remember. We talked about this when I called you yesterday. Etta and I are not in a romantic relationship. I'm just doing what I can to keep her and Polly safe and help solve her sister's murder."

"Of course. It upsets me to think of a little child left without a mom, her dad in jail and her aunt on the run. I was going to say something to Etta when I showed her to her room, but I decided it might be best not to open up old wounds."

"It's not an old wound, Ma. The person who killed Etta's sister is still out there, and Polly won't be safe until he or she is brought to justice. That's why I brought them here, so that they'll be safe while we try to figure out what's going on. I can't begin to tell you how much I appreciate your willingness to offer them a calm haven from all the trouble."

"Your dad and I are glad to help in any way we can." Sandy pushed her hands into the pockets of her faded jeans and tilted her head toward the kitchen. "But right now, since I've exceeded my limit on lecturing, I'm going to go work on dinner. I know I don't need to tell you this, but you and Etta should feel free to use the office as a base of operations. The sooner you get some answers, the better it will be for Polly."

Steven followed his mom into the house and then headed up the stairs.

The guest-room door was open, and he could see that Etta had changed into jeans and a bright yellow T-shirt from their shopping spree at Walmart.

"I like your outfit." He grinned.

"Thanks," she said. She patted her pocket. "I have the thumb drive right here if you're ready to get down to business."

He was, though he wouldn't have minded spending a few more minutes admiring Etta's relaxed style.

He led the way down the stairs and along the first-floor hallway into the office. "I'll use my dad's tablet and see what I can dig up about the law firm representing Greg. You can use my mom's desk by the window. I assume her password is still John 3:16. She chose her favorite Bible verse so she won't forget."

Etta settled back into Sandy's ergonomic chair. "Wow, this is supercomfortable. I could work here forever." She tapped in the pass code and slipped the USB into the port.

"Let's hope that won't be necessary, though I have to admit to being intrigued at the thought of you and Polly staying here until she enters college. Would that be South Dakota State?" Steven smirked as he took a seat on the couch. Etta had been teasing when she made that suggestion, but he did wonder what she thought about his home state.

Tablet open, he began a search for information about the law firm of Thompson, Colfax and Bickler. There was a definite connection there, he was sure of it, but progress was slow going, as he waded through pages after page of laudatory claims, searching for a connection between Lilly and Matt Bickler.

He wondered if Etta was having some degree of success. Her eyes remained fixed on the screen.

A loud sigh followed by an exclamation of delight drew him across the room to join her.

"Look at this, Steven!" Her eyes shone with excitement as she pointed to the screen. "It's an old *People* magazine article about a group of radical college students from the seventies. They were known as the JIF8, or Justice in Full, and they were famous for using violence to advance their political agenda. They'd plant bombs at big events like parades and concerts. Dozens of people were hurt, and a handful died after one particular explosion at a soccer match in down-town Detroit."

"Serious stuff then," Steven said, leaning in for a closer look.

"So serious that the FBI eventually raided their headquarters, and seven of the eight orig-inal members were arrested, tried and sent to jail. But one member of the group, the actual bomb maker, managed to evade the authorities. Her name was Belinda Lee Caruso. And look at this! Lilly circled her picture on the thumb drive." She pulled up a photo of a twenty-year old woman, with wire-rimmed glasses and long hair pulled into a long, flowing braid. "Could she be the focus of the big score Lilly mentioned to Jordan Shapiro?"

★ ★ ★

Etta could barely contain her excitement as she settled back in the chair. "I'm trying to stay calm here, but this has to be a major clue, doesn't it?" She scrolled through a couple more pages until she came upon a letter to an agent, asking if there was any interest in a work of nonfiction about a seventies fugitive who had been hiding in plain sight. "And check this out! Lilly obviously felt confident enough to shop this idea around."

Steven's eyes narrowed as he took a moment to read what Etta had pulled up on the screen. "We seem to be getting ahead of ourselves here. Who's to say Lilly had either the evidence or the writing chops to get a deal from a publisher?"

But Steven's less-than-enthusiastic reaction failed to dampen Etta's eagerness. "Don't forget. Lilly was a reporter, so she wouldn't have gone chasing a story without securing the necessary proof. There could be information that she didn't load on the thumb drive."

He nodded. "True. And it's easy to imagine that Belinda Caruso wouldn't want to draw any attention from the FBI."

"I know, right." They were on to something. She knew it.

It seemed that Steven did, too, because he appeared more interested by the minute. "So, presumably, Lilly showed her hand while she was snooping around, and Belinda Caruso realized what she was up to."

An overwhelming feeling of sadness suddenly swamped Etta's senses. She could readily imagine her sister's excitement as she uncovered such a big scoop. Lilly had always been prone to jump in with both feet without recognizing the consequences. In her zeal, she might have gotten careless. And that was a fatal mistake.

"But even if we accept the fact that Belinda killed Lilly," Steven said, his voice interrupting her melancholy musing, "who are these men after Polly?"

That was the question. They had already zeroed in on the connection to the law firm, and there were other names and descriptions they had picked up along the way—like the man named TJ. But how did a radical fugitive from the seventies fit into the equation?

Steven pulled out his phone. "It's after five. Polly and my dad are probably back from the barn, which means that, any minute, my mom is going to be calling us for dinner."

Right on cue, Sandy Hunt's voice boomed out through the hall.

"Steven! Etta! Time for supper."

Steven grinned. "Ha! I told you. I don't know how it happens, but whenever I come home, my stomach resets to mom time."

The copies could wait, Etta decided. She followed Steven out of the office and into the dining room. Polly was already seated at the table, her smile hinting that she had enjoyed her time in the barn.

Steven counted aloud the places around the table. "Six?" He raised an eyebrow in his mother's direction.

"Seb's on his own tonight since Tacy has Bible study. He'll join us after work."

"Seb, huh?" Etta tucked in a secret smile. Since meeting Steven, she had been intrigued by the existence of his identical twin brother. "We're alike only in appearance," Steven had told her once with a mysterious wink. Perhaps tonight she'd find out what that meant.

Funny, though. When Seb ambled into the dining room midway through dinner, it was the twins' current physical differences that most surprised her.

Seb was broad and burly, so different than Steven's wiry physique. Then again, it might have been the uniform—the gray shirt tucked into creased black pants and the felted cowboy hat he quickly removed from his head—that made him appear taller and a lot more formidable.

"Nice hairstyle, little brother," Seb declared. Steven smiled, stood up and then allowed himself to be pulled into a tight bear hug by his brother. "And who are these beautiful ladies joining us for dinner?"

Steven was quick to make the introductions, though it seemed clear from the twinkle in his brother's eye that Seb already knew who they were. "Etta, Polly, you probably guessed that this is my brother, Seb. But you should call him Sebastian."

"Hey, hey, hey. Let's not go there. Otherwise, I might have to retaliate by mocking your new look."

"Boys! Enough!" Sandy's no-nonsense tone put an end to the good-natured bickering, and Seb slid into the open chair next to his brother.

"Say, Ma. I wouldn't say no to some of your famous roast beef."

Surreptitiously observing Seb from across the table, Etta began to revise her original assessment. She could see that while there were a number of differences in Seb and Steven's outward appearances, both men shared the same strong jaw, dark, intelligent eyes and crooked smile that made it obvious they were brothers.

"So," Seb said once the last piece of pie had disappeared from the dish. "I have some information that might be of interest."

Sandy picked up the cue and made a move to shepherd Polly from the table. "If you don't mind helping me load the dishwasher," she said to the little girl, "I'll tell you a story about that mare you met today in the barn and how she led Seb on a mighty chase for three miles into town."

When the kitchen door swung closed behind them, the mood of the dining room changed. Gone was the carefree atmosphere of the past hour, leaving in its place a mood of worried anticipation. Seb didn't waste any time getting to the gist of it.

"Dad started filling me in about what's going on with Etta. Which is interesting, since earlier today one of my deputies took a call from the desk clerk at the Bluebird Hotel. Apparently, a man checking in was asking about a woman and a little girl staying at the Hunt family ranch. The clerk was suspicious, especially after he caught sight of a fairly large handgun tucked in the waistband of the stranger's pants." Seb paused to rub a hand across his chin and then directed his words to his twin brother. "So I'm thinking that maybe this would be a good time for you to tell me the rest of the story."

Chapter Fourteen

"Where to start?" Steven mused, holding Etta's eyes. He shook his head.

"How about the beginning?" his brother suggested.

Easier said than done. Etta had killed a man in self-defense, not a crime in and of itself. But the leaving-the-scene part...that was different. Could he describe the situation without mentioning several of the salient facts?

"How much did Dad tell you about why we're here?"

Seb shrugged. "Not much. He said that you had gone to Texas to see a woman he described as the one who got away." He glanced at Etta, who shifted in her seat.

"Not sure why he said that, but whatever."

"He said that her sister had been murdered. I assume he was talking about you, Etta." He faced her again. "I'm sorry for your loss. And that's about it. I assume there's a lot he left out."

Steven sighed. "Well, the fact that this guy has turned up in town, asking questions, changes the dynamic. Polly's in danger because of something she might have seen or heard the day her mom was killed, and she hasn't been able to tell us what that is."

"Complicated." Seb shook his head.

"That's an understatement." Steven looked across the table at Etta. She had remained mum during the discussion, allowing him to decide how much to say. When neither of them spoke, Seb continued.

"Well, so far, the guy at the motel is just sniffing around. It seems likely that no one outside the family knows that Etta and Polly are here, and we can do our best to keep it that way. But just in case, I can have one of my deputies keep an eye on the motel and make sure there are no other unexpected visitors."

Steven exhaled a long sigh of relief. No matter how dire the circumstances, his family would always have his back. But that worked both ways. He needed to get Seb up to speed about what he might be getting into.

"All cards on the table here, bro. Back in

Texas, Etta used deadly force to defend herself when a man broke into her house and came for Polly. I know you won't approve, but we left the scene rather than reporting what had happened to the authorities. The original plan was to head for the ranch after a few quick stops to see what we could find out about what was going on. I thought I'd been able to stay off the radar, but given the number of cameras everywhere, it was probably just a matter of time before they sussed out my identity." And once they figured out who he was, it wouldn't have taken them long to figure out about his family's ranch and where they may be headed next.

Seb nodded. "I know I'm not telling you anything you haven't figured out already, but this seems a lot bigger than just a murder. First thing you learn as a cop or an investigator—follow the money. Someone is bankrolling this operation for reasons that at this point aren't completely clear."

Etta pulled in a short intake of breath, and both men turned to face her.

"Wow," she said. "It just suddenly hit me to hear it all broken down that way."

"I get it," Seb said. "But I take it you've made some progress in identifying your sister's killer."

"We think so," Etta agreed. She explained what they'd found on Lilly's USB. "It's just an assumption at this point, but we think Lilly discovered Belinda Lee Caruso living somewhere in Texas. Again, we're guessing here, but we think this woman got wind of what Lilly was up to and killed her to keep her secret from being exposed. That's our theory, anyway. At this point we don't have any evidence."

Seb pushed back his chair and stood up. "Okay, then. I'm thinking I should head over to the Bluebird and maybe see if our inquisitive visitor is still on his own or if anyone else has joined him."

"I'd like to come with you," Steven said.

"No." Seb shook his head. "It's best to keep things as low-key as possible. I'll just stroll by the office and look for a chance to ask a few questions. In the meantime, you two should dig up what you can about anyone and everyone who could be involved with this fugitive. Maybe her coconspirators? Most of them may have served their time and gotten out of jail. It's hard to understand why they'd be helping her since she was the one who escaped punishment, but you never know."

After Seb left, Etta took Polly upstairs to put

her to bed. Steven returned to the office to
check into the whereabouts of the other seven
members of the JIF8. But that task was proving to be nearly impossible without access to a
larger database. After an hour of searching, all
he knew for certain was that three of Belinda
Caruso's colleagues had died in prison and the
other four had served their time and eventually
been released from jail.

On a whim, he opened his billfold and pulled
out the license he had been using to support his
identity as Matt Bickler, along with that blue-
and-white sticker. It read, "Reelect TJ Bishop
for Texas AG."

TJ. Wasn't that the name Etta had heard mentioned by one of the men who'd broken into
the house? A quick search of the website of the
current attorney general revealed that he was a
former partner at the law firm of Thompson,
Colfax and Bickler.

"The plot thickens," he muttered to himself.

The office door opened, and Etta walked over
to join him.

"Did you find anything?" she asked.

"Still working on it." He looked up at her.
She was looking especially pretty with her cute

new haircut and her eyes so bright with anticipation. "Polly go down all right?"

"Yup. I tried to see if she had any reaction
to the name Belinda Caruso, but I didn't notice any change in her countenance. She just
seemed tired. And happy. Even after just a few
hours spent with your dad in the horse barn,
the change in her is amazing. Your parents are
both so kind."

Well, she wasn't going to get any argument
there.

Etta smiled and Steven's heart began to beat
harder in his chest. How had his dad described
her—the one who got away? He supposed that
was more than a little true as he had been slowly
coming to terms with the real reason he had
gone to Texas just a few days ago.

Maybe he should share that thought with
Etta. He glanced at her and held her gaze. "You
know all that personal stuff we discussed during the drive here from Texas? I feel like we
opened up some cold, hard truths about our relationship. But I realized that I really do need to
apologize for my proposal. I don't know what
I was thinking, arranging to have it shown on
the jumbotron, but I do remember praying that
you'd say yes."

Etta smiled again. "Well, in a way, it was successful, since that's what happened. But as long as we're clearing the air, I'm sorry, too. I shouldn't have hijacked the conversation so long about past grievances. My only excuse is that my adrenaline was still pumping after you rescued me at the house. And…" She shrugged. "I do tend to get caught up with ideas that get stuck in my head. But before I forget, I thought of something important when I was tucking Polly into bed. Remember when all of this started, and we were looking for Polly at the house?"

Steven nodded. Apparently, now wasn't the time to admit his real reason for his visit to Texas.

Etta continued. "When I went outside to see if Polly was in the yard, I ran into a neighbor who was taking pictures for the neighborhood-share app. And I had a thought. It's probably unlikely, but maybe if we went to the site, we could find a photo of someone who resembles Belinda Caruso."

"On it," he said. It only took a couple of minutes for him to pull up the app and then a few more to find the photos from the block party. "What do you think of her as a possibility?" He pointed to a picture of a tall, slender woman in a plaid sundress.

"I don't think so," Etta said, shaking her head. "Why don't I print the photo in the article, and we can see if we can look for similarities?"

A few minutes later, she returned to Steven's side with a grainy photo of a young Belinda Caruso. Lilly had circled the photo and written a question in the margin.

Birthmark?

"Do you have a magnifying glass?" she asked Steven.

He handed her one from the drawer, and she held it over the picture. Yup. Lilly was right. There was a small diamond-shaped birthmark on Belinda's neck.

She tacked the photo to the bulletin board above the desk as Steven scrolled through what seemed to be an endless file of block-party photos.

A shuffling sound outside the office caught their attention, and Etta walked across the room and opened the door. There stood Polly, her thumb in her mouth and her fingers wrapped around the bunny she was clutching to her chest.

"You okay, hon?" Etta asked.

Polly nodded.

"Can't sleep, huh? That's okay. I'm almost ready for bed myself."

Polly's eyes widened and her hand started to shake as her trembling finger pointed toward the photo frozen on the computer screen. On either side of the picture were kids holding Super Soakers, and in the center were a half-dozen adults caught in the crossfire, all with dripping-wet hair and sodden clothing. At the back of the group, barely discernable at first glance, was Lynn Weber. Lilly and Greg's next-door neighbor…and clearly the source of Polly's distress.

Two hours later, Etta was still wide-awake as the implications of their recent discovery played through her head.

She would have never suspected that Lilly's kindly neighbor was a wanted fugitive who had evaded the police for years. Even as she recognized the terror in her niece's eyes at Lynn's picture, it was still hard to imagine the gray-haired woman who wore a smile every morning as she walked her golden retriever down the block as a ruthless killer. A bomb maker with no respect for human life.

But once she had settled a greatly agitated Polly back into bed, she and Steven had compared the two photos side by side, they were able to notice some similarities. Lynn Weber and Belinda Caruso both had high cheekbones and sloped shoulders, but that was hardly enough to claim a definite match. Especially since there were plenty of differences as well, including eye color—"contacts," as Lilly had suggested—hair color and cut. Etta had pointed to her own red hair—"Almost too easy," she'd said. Unlike Lynn, Belinda had a pointy chin and thin lips, but those could have been changed or disguised with makeup or plastic surgery. The truth was that if hadn't been for Polly's reaction to the photo of her neighbor, Etta and Steven might never have made the connection.

Despite all the points of dispute, there was one key factor that convinced Etta and Steven that they had found Belinda Caruso's alter ego. In the block-party photo, Lynn's hair was wet and limp, having been doused with spray from the water guns. It was so limp, in fact, that it fell short of her neck and allowed for an excellent view of a diamond-shaped birthmark identical to Belinda Caruso's.

Had Lilly noticed that birthmark when she'd watched Lynn swimming in her backyard pool? Or was there something else that had caused her sister to realize that her neighbor bore a distinct resemblance to the seventies fugitive? Leave it to Lilly. How many other residents of Silver Creek remembered or, for that matter, ever knew the story about the JIF8 and the bomb-maker fugitive?

Etta sure hadn't. But now that she thought about it, other clues to Lynn's deception had been there all along. Like the unlikely coincidence of her neighbor showing up on the doorstep immediately after the break-in. And hadn't Greg told Steven that a neighbor had advised him to hire Sam Colfax to represent him in the case? What better way to subtly undermine Greg's defense.

Anger threaded through Etta's senses as she thought about what could have happened the day her sister was killed. The police who arrived at the murder scene had been quick to decide that it was a domestic dispute turned deadly, but her brother-in-law never wavered in his claim that his wife was alive when he left for work. No one suspected that a kindly neighbor might have dropped by the house that morning and waited until Lilly wasn't looking before slipping poison into the carafe and her mug.

It would have been almost too easy, casting

Greg into the role of the convenient scapegoat. But there was only one snag in that plan, and that was Polly.

Where was her little niece when all of that was going on? What had she heard, and what had she seen? The answers remained locked up inside of her. Maybe someday they'd find out the truth.

Around midnight, Etta finally drifted off to sleep. When she finally woke up, sunlight was already streaming through the window, and there was a message from Steven on her burner phone.

Decided to show Seb the photos of the SUV that followed us in Silver Creek. The driver with the moustache is definitely one of the staffers working for the Texas AG. More grist for the mill, right?

Etta sat up in bed as a sense of guilt pulsed through her. She'd been asleep while Steven had been working, following through on the information they'd discovered the night before.

Next to her on the trundle bed, Polly was waking up. Her tiny fingers reached out to squeeze Etta's hand, and Etta held on tight as she twisted around on her side for a better view of her little niece.

"You doing okay, Pol?" she asked, blinking back a tear.

The little girl's nod was slow and certain.

"Good. Now what do you say to heading downstairs to get something to eat?"

Breakfast was a feast of scrambled eggs and bacon, oatmeal and toast. Seb and Steven were still out, but as she and Polly ate, Scott filled in her niece on his plans for the day. "Any chance you'd like to join me when I check on the horses?" he asked, his eyes twinkling as he took in the little girl's delight. Five minutes later, they were out the door and headed for the stables.

"And then there were two," Sandy said with a smile. "What can I do to help you get settled in this morning? Really, Etta. Having you here is lovely. And Steven seems happier than he's been in a long time. And that's a wonderful gift for a mother's heart."

Etta's eyes went misty. After all the drama of the past few days, Sandy's kindness had somehow produced a wave of unexpected tears. She quickly turned her head to hide the wetness on her face.

"Would you mind if I did a wash?"

"Of course," Sandy said. "Come with me downstairs and I'll help you get started. If you have time, you may want to hang your stuff on the line. It's more work, but you can't beat that fresh scent."

Sandy was right, Etta decided a half hour later as she carried a load of T-shirts and jeans to the back of the ranch house. The morning sun warmed her shoulders as she pinned her clothes on the line. The air was fresh, and the landscape was breathtaking. No wonder Steven loved it here. Maybe if things had been different, she might have come to feel the same way.

She banished those thoughts with a shake of her head. She'd had her chance with Steven. And she had rejected his proposal and sent him on his way. So why was she focused on all of this now?

Perhaps it was the thoughtful way he had treated her and Polly. And others as well. Watching him talk to his parents and joke with Seb in such a fond way. Even the way he interacted with Kenny, the kid from the trailer park, who had seemed over the moon to receive the gift of a signed cowboy hat.

But Steven had always been kind. So what exactly explained her sudden change of heart? All along, had she been secretly hoping for a second chance? Was it even possible for their love story to have a different ending?

Maybe. But only if she put aside her stubborn pride and allowed herself to trust him again with her heart.

A sudden cool breeze from the west sent a shiver up her arms. She looked up and noticed that a few dark clouds had drifted across the now overcast sky. Her gaze flitted toward the still-wet clothes she had fixed to the line. If she didn't know better, she'd think that it was about to rain. But hadn't the sun been shining just minutes before?

She received her first lesson in the vagaries of South Dakota weather as the first drops landed on her head. What to do next? Should she pull down the clothing she'd just pinned up or rush to seek shelter inside the house?

The choice was made for her as the sky darkened even more and rain began to fall in thick sheets. As thunder rumbled, and a crack of lightning split the air, she began to run, abandoning the clothes on the line.

"Sandy?" she called out, rushing into the house and through the hall.

No answer, just the thudding of boots against the kitchen floor.

"Sandy?" she cried out a second time.

"I'm upstairs, hon. Be there in a second."

Two things happened, almost at once. A man bounded out of the kitchen, sprinting toward the front door, and Sandy appeared at the opposite end of the hallway, her head bent over a stack of folded sheets she was holding.

Etta opened her mouth, but she couldn't get out any words.

The front door slammed shut, and Sandy set down the sheets, looking concerned when she noticed Etta. "Oh, honey. Are you all right?"

Etta pressed against the older woman's shoulder, her face wet with tears. "You didn't see him?" she choked out.

Sandy's brow creased. "See who?"

"I was hanging clothes when it started to rain. But when I came inside… I heard someone in the kitchen. I thought it was you, but it was a man."

Sandy slipped her phone from the pocket of her apron and punched in a number. "Scott? We've had an intruder. Call Seb and Steven and tell them to get up here as fast as they can." As she talked, she grabbed a set of keys from the counter and walked across the room. It only took her a second to unlock the gun cabinet and insert a magazine into a formidable-looking pistol.

She pulled up a chair and faced the back door.

"Now, we wait." She remained in position until her husband and two sons had arrived at the ranch house. Only then did she eject the magazine from the pistol and lock it back in the cabinet.

"There's no trace of him. He's gone," Steven said after they'd searched the property. He sat down next to her at the kitchen table, and the others followed suit.

"Where's Polly?" Etta asked.

"I called my wife Tacy and she came over to get her. Our place is right next door," Seb assured her. "Take your time and describe what happened before and after you saw the intruder."

She was relieved to hear Polly was safe. "It's not much of a story," Etta admitted, but she explained what happened.

"Do you have a description?" Seb queried. "Tall? Short? Young? Old?"

Etta shook her head. "It all happened so fast. I'm sorry."

"No worries." Steven met and held her anxious glance. "I just wonder what he was doing inside the house. Was he looking for Polly and thought he might find her at the ranch?"

"Could be," Seb agreed. "Once we're through here, I'll head into the office and arrange for a couple of deputies to provide round-the-clock protection."

Steven pulled out his phone and scrolled down to a photo of a well-dressed man in a three-piece suit. He handed his cell to Etta. "Thought you might be interested in something I found this morning. The man in the picture is Terrance Joseph Bishop, also known as TJ, current attorney general for the state of Texas. Also, coincidentally, a former partner in the law firm of Thompson, Colfax and Bickler. Recognize the woman standing next to him?"

"Is that…?" She looked up at Steven. "Lynn Weber…aka Belinda Caruso?"

"Yup. She's wearing glasses and her hair's different, but I'm pretty sure that's our little terrorist, standing next to her son."

"Her son?" Etta gasped.

"Yeah." Steven nodded. "This is getting really complicated. But it gets us closer to figuring things out."

"Can I see that, too?" As Seb reached for the

phone, his gaze moved past Etta toward the back door. He stood up and paced across the room, moving slowly and taking his time dragging his fingers under the counters and below the cabinets along the wall. He stopped suddenly in front of a lamp and then tilted the base sideways to reveal a small button-shaped device affixed to the shade.

Then he raised his fingers to his lips and motioned that they should follow him outside.

Chapter Fifteen

"A bug!" Etta exclaimed. "That means they can listen to our private conversations. How can we ever feel safe?"

Sandy reached over and took her hand. "Don't fret, hon. Seb's the sheriff. If they come after you or Polly, he'll bring the force of the law down on their heads."

Etta nodded. She believed Seb—and Steven—would do everything possible to protect them.

Steven blew out a long sigh. "That's all true, Ma, but we've got to stop playing defense on this. We need to do something proactive, like lure Lynn to the ranch. With no evidence to link her to Lilly's murder, it could be our only chance of getting a confession."

It seemed a bit reckless—classic Steven—but he had a point. She was tired of running. She wanted to know what had happened to her sister.

"Would she be willing to come here?" Seb asked.

Steven shrugged. "Maybe she'd do it if she knew that we have evidence linking her to JIF8 and Belinda Caruso. That's our best bargaining chip to get her attention."

"But is the evidence all that solid? From what you told me, it's just a picture and article from an old magazine," Seb said.

"True," Steven admitted. "But I can't imagine Lynn would be pleased to have it out there. And, not only that, but we have the connection between the men who have been pursuing us and the office of the current AG. I assume Lynn has a stake in her son's political future. And with TJ Bishop currently in a tight race for reelection, neither of them would want even a whiff of scandal."

"Okay. Let's say she agrees to come to the ranch. What's the endgame? What can Etta ask for in trade for her silence?" Sandy asked.

Etta was quick to answer. "Polly's safety—guaranteed. That would be my main demand."

"But how could you trust a terrorist to keep to her part of the bargain?" Scott asked.

Steven shook his head. "We're getting too deep in the weeds here. There isn't actually going to be any sort of trade. We're just dangling the idea as a way to convince Lynn that we mean business."

"Hmm." Seb's lips twisted in a sly smile. "And this is where the listening device fits in. They don't know we found it, so we use it to our advantage."

"Lull them into a false sense of security," Steven declared.

"Right," Seb agreed. "If Etta can talk Lynn into coming to South Dakota, we use a wire in the hope of extracting a confession."

But first, they needed to head inside so Etta could call Lynn and issue the invitation. Etta's fingers shook as she tapped in the numbers to make the call.

"Hello." The sound of Lynn's voice sent shivers up Etta's spine, but she took a deep breath and forced herself to speak.

"Lynn, this is Etta Mitchell, Lilly Sanderson's sister. I'm staying at a friend's ranch in South Dakota, and I was hoping to persuade you to join me here."

"Now, why would I want to do that?" Lynn asked—she seemed to be feigning confusion.

Etta pulled in another deep breath and made a concerted effort to moderate her tone. This would be a lot harder if Lynn agreed to come for a visit, so she needed to get used to remaining calm under pressure.

"Because I know who you are…and I know what you did. But what I want is simple. You need to call off your lackeys and leave us alone. In return, I'll stay mum about what I know about Belinda Caruso and hand over what evidence I have. But we have to meet face-to-face, just you and me, and it has to be here in South Dakota."

There was a pause on the line. "Why can't we talk in Texas?"

Etta didn't answer.

"Cat got your tongue, eh? Seems like you're the one with all the secrets and lies. I suppose you may have some explaining to do about the body that was discovered on Dogwood Drive. Or about the fact that your fingerprints were all over the murder weapon," she said smoothly. "Really, Etta? Hitting someone in the head with a frying pan? How positively domestic of you. And here I was thinking that nurses are trained to save lives."

Deep breaths. Deep breaths. "I can explain my actions, Lynn. But can you? My sister dug up some very convincing evidence linking you to

JIF8. If anything happens to me or to Polly, I've made arrangements for everything to be sent to the FBI. I assume they'll be very interested in learning about your double life. And so will the reporters covering your son's campaign." She paused for a moment to let that sink in. "Shall I text you the address and plan on seeing you tomorrow?"

Lynn caved, as they'd hoped, and agreed to come to South Dakota. "Just the two of us women for a little exchange," Etta said as she wrapped up the call. But she had no expectation that would be the case.

She didn't think she'd to be able to settle down that night when she went to bed. But the sight of her little niece, curled up in the trundle bed with her bunny, reminded her that nothing had changed since Greg had been handcuffed and taken to jail. She had been charged with the duty of keeping Polly safe, and that was what she was going to do. It was that thought that allowed her to drift off to sleep.

The buzz of a text jolted her awake. Daylight was streaming into the room. Bleary-eyed, she read the message that Lynn's flight was on schedule to arrive at twelve o'clock sharp. Her eyes flashed down to the time on her phone—

7:00 a.m.—which meant she had only five hours to get ready for the meeting.

Treading lightly down the stairs, she poked her head into the kitchen. Steven was already awake, a stack of pancakes and a few sausages on the plate in front of him. He stood up to greet her with a smile.

"Morning," she said.

Her voice must have quavered because Steven walked over to where she was standing and pulled her in close. "You still hanging in there?"

She nodded, suddenly teary.

"You know you're wonderful, right?" He looked down at her with his warm, dark eyes, his arm still around her shoulders. "Smart and courageous and kind and…"

A blush of warmth bloomed on her cheeks. "Steven, no. I'm not any of those things. The truth is that I…"

He released her suddenly and pointed to the listening device on the lamp.

Message received. Anything said in this room would be heard by the person who had planted the bug.

This wasn't the time for emotional revelations. She had always known that the trip north might mark the beginning of the end of their relationship, that being home would cause Steven to yearn for a return to normal. And who could blame him? His actual life was pretty great—the ranch and the horses and the loving family who were always there to support him and welcome him home. Nothing remotely similar to what it had been like for her growing up, with an absent mother and a delinquent sister.

But for all her faults, Lilly had come to understand that she was worthy as a child of God, while Etta was the one who'd refused to change. She continued stubbornly pushing people away—Steven, her colleagues on the job, even Lilly, in the end. A wave of regret washed over her. How had she let this happen? Not only had she allowed a chasm to form between herself and her only sister, but she had also forfeited time they could have spent together, time she could never replace. Maybe she didn't deserve happiness. Clearly, she hadn't tried hard enough to be a sister, a fiancée, or a friend.

She pulled herself out of her funk and looked at Steven. He held her gaze and pointed to the door, then gestured that she should follow him outside.

Once they reached the lawn, he put an arm around her shoulders and pulled her close. "You looked worried. And who can blame you? This is going to be a hard day for you more than the rest of us. I realized this morning that there's one major disadvantage to being home that I hadn't anticipated. It's the fact that we haven't had much of a chance to talk."

She forced a smile. "It has been a big change to have so many people around all the time. Especially after we spent so long on the road, doing almost everything together, with very little time apart."

"You make it sound like that was a bad thing."

He raised an eyebrow, and her heart did a somersault in her chest. Maybe she had been wrong in her previous imaginings. Steven did not view their trip to the ranch as an end of their relationship. It seemed possible—dare she hope?—that he saw it as a kind of beginning.

"I didn't say it was a bad thing," she spluttered, all of a sudden nervous about the emotions crashing around in her brain. "I like hanging out with you. Even if it means that we're stuck in a car or a van or even in the Airstream."

"Good," he said. He reached for her hand and brought it to his lips. "I feel the same way. I didn't realize it at first, but that was what I was hoping for when I showed up on your doorstep in Silver Creek. Not the part about the men following after us and trying to hurt you and kidnap Polly, of course. But, as for spending so much time together, yeah, I liked that a lot."

The rest of the morning passed in a blur. Once Steven finished his breakfast, he showed her where Seb's team had set up a wire to record her conversation with Lynn. Then Seb himself arrived with a report that so far, all was proceeding according to plan. Lynn's plane had landed right on schedule at the Rapid City Regional Airport, and she had rented a car for the drive to the ranch.

"Is she traveling alone?" Etta asked.

Seb shook his head. "Not a chance. Separate cars. Got to keep up the pretense that she's here on her own. But we're expecting company. Don't worry about that."

An hour later, the rumble of tires along the driveway heralded the arrival of a visitor. Etta was watching through the window as a blue Mercedes SUV pulled into a space at the end of the drive. The driver's side door opened, and Lynn stepped out.

Go time.

Etta pulled in a breath and waited. She was as ready as she'd ever be. *Help me, Lord*, she pleaded in a whispered prayer. *Guide my words and rule my actions.* Then she closed her eyes and counted to five before she answered the knock at the door.

Short and wiry, with her midlength gray bob and oversize glasses, Lynn Weber looked just as Etta remembered. Then again, why would she have changed since the last time Etta had seen her, standing at her front door in Silver Creek with a plate of cookies?

Hmm. She had almost forgotten about those cookies. Good thing they had left them behind in the rush out the door. Given everything they now knew about Lynn, she wouldn't have been surprised if there had been some unusual ingredient included in the recipe.

"Hello, Etta." Lynn's artificial smile quickly faded from her lips. "I see that you changed your do. It looks nice. Different, but very stylish."

Etta instinctively ran her fingers through her cropped hair. "I thought we could talk outside on the patio."

She led the way down the hall and through the kitchen, then out the back door.

"Lovely home your friends have here," Lynn said.

Once again, Etta didn't acknowledge the compliment. As Lynn bent to admire the yellow-and-purple pansies on the patio. Etta's hand went to the listening device taped to her chest. Although it seemed unlikely that Lynn would bare her soul and confess to crimes old and new, Seb thought it was best to be prepared just in case. Whenever his team had the chance to act on an arrest, they'd take it.

Etta took a seat at the round patio table, motioning to Lynn that she should do the same. She had decided in advance not to offer refreshments. Why pretend this little get-together was something it wasn't?

"First, I want to thank you for coming here today. We do need to talk, and this didn't seem like a conversation we could have on the phone. What I am asking for is simple. I want your assurance that Polly will be safe. In return, I agree to destroy the evidence on Lilly's thumb drive connecting you to Belinda Caruso."

Lynn opened her mouth to respond, but Etta shut down whatever she intended to say.

"There's nothing you can say that will change the facts. My sister was an astute observer of people. And in the course of living next door to you, she somehow discovered your real identity. I'm not sure how you found out what she was working on, but once you did, you realized that she had enough information to blow your cover. So you killed her. Simple as that."

Lynn blew a short breath through her nose and shook her head.

"Dear, sweet, naive Etta. I think you've fixed on me as a convenient scapegoat to help you deal with to the loss of your sister. I'm sorry Lilly was killed. She was a nice person and a good neighbor, but you know as well as I do that she could be headstrong and willful, especially when she didn't get her way. I can't count the times that I heard her arguing with Greg on the patio or yelling at Polly for wandering into the yard."

Etta felt her whole body tense. "Lilly loved her family."

Lynn shrugged. "I'm glad you believe that, but she certainly had an odd way of showing it. And it's certainly your right to ignore the facts if it helps you cope."

A surge of anger pulsed through Etta's veins. She wanted to reach across the table and slap Lynn. But this was exactly the type of thing she had resolved to avoid. She looked down at her watch and checked the time. Twelve fifteen. It wouldn't be long now. She just needed to be patient in allowing Lynn to control the narrative.

★ ★ ★

Steven's heart drummed a staccato beat in his chest. Was it going to work? The plan had made sense when they had discussed it last night. But now, in the cold light of day, there seemed to be way too many variables at play.

A cold bead of sweat trickled down his back.

He hated leaving Etta at the house with Lynn. But this was the only way. And Seb had assured him that his men were watching the homestead. But still.

He'd never forgive himself if anything happened to Etta.

It had been dawning on him little by little over the last few days that she was a great deal more than just a friend. Obviously, she was beautiful, and time had only made her face softer and kinder. But her looks had never been the only attraction. He had discovered early on that she was made of deeper stuff.

Etta had accused him of trying to rescue her, of thinking that he could solve all her problems by whisking her away from her dysfunctional sister and into the bosom of his own traditional family. Well, maybe she'd had a point. He had imagined himself as a sort of knight in shining armor, offering his love and security. But what he'd viewed as romantic motivation, she seemed to have judged as some sort of misplaced machismo.

Hopefully, he and Etta had put all that behind them. It had taken a while, but they seemed to have landed in a pretty good place. Especially after their talk that morning. He hadn't realized what a toll all the planning and anticipation was taking on Etta. She had placed her life on hold to protect Polly, and circumstances had catapulted her into a hornet's nest of drama, danger and intrigue. But she had risen to the challenge. Through it all she had never once allowed herself to give up.

He still believed he and Etta should have been able to make it work. And he suspected that she felt the same way, too. He had seen the look in her eyes when they were standing outside on the patio. Maybe their timing hadn't been right fifteen years ago. Maybe he hadn't fought for her hard enough. It didn't matter. That was in the past. It was the future that he cared about now. And he wanted a future that included Etta. He loved her. He'd always loved her. Tomorrow, when all of this was over, he was going to tell her how he felt. And if she tried to walk away again, well, this time, he wouldn't let pride get in his way. He'd just follow her back to Texas.

But first, they had to deal with Lynn and her minions. Impatience threaded through his limbs. The hay was tickling his nose where he was lying crouched in the loft, and his leg twinged from inactivity. He felt a strong desire to crack his knuckles. Anything to keep his mind off the waiting.

But they were as ready as they would ever be for what would happen next.

He glanced down at the scene below him in the hayloft. Cameras and listening devices had been installed out of sight on the beams around the stable. And there was his father looking completely at ease as he groomed Sandstorm, his favorite horse, and chatted with the little girl standing by his side. Steven took a deep breath and tried to stem his growing anxiety. This was crazy. He was usually the reckless one. But this involved Etta and his family and Polly. And there was no denying the level of risk. He closed his eyes and offered a silent prayer. *Please, God. Grant Your protection and wisdom.* The tenseness around his shoulders eased a bit, but his heart continued to thud.

He opened his eyes as the crunch of gravel

announced the arrival of an approaching vehicle. This was it then, the moment they had been waiting for. His mind registered the sunlight penetrating the gloomy space as the barn door slowly slid open and the hinges made a creaking sound, followed by the thudding of footsteps against the wood plank floor. He could see his father's back stiffen as he slowly turned around. Three men stood framed by the open doorway, each holding a pistol.

Steven clenched his fingers. He wished he had a weapon. But Seb had only agreed that he could come along if he promised to stay out of the action, claiming he was too much a liability as a civilian, and an injured one at that. In truth, he suspected that his brother had allowed him a place in the hayloft to keep him as far away from Etta as he possibly could.

"Who are you? And what do you want?" his dad asked the strangers.

"Never mind who we are. We're here for the girl."

"And you think I'm just going to let you take her?" Scott sneered.

"Actually, we do. We can be pretty persuasive."

His father reached for a short plank, which

had been propped against the stall. "So can I. You're not going to shoot me in my own barn. Why don't you put those guns away, and we can talk?"

Scott Hunt had been instructed to draw out the conversation as long as possible. But knowing what the plan was and watching it play out were two totally different things.

One of the men chuckled. Steven realized with a start that it was Matt Bickler.

"Look. We don't want any trouble. We won't touch the aunt. But we need the kid." He waved his gun toward the girl. She hadn't turned around, but his father had thrown a protective arm on her shoulder.

"Look," Scott continued, "my son is the sheriff. He won't rest if you do anything to hurt me or the girl. So you might as well recognize that you're not going to get away with this. Leave us alone, and we won't report you for trespassing on our property."

"Ha!" one of them laughed bitterly. "Trespassing is the least of your problems, old man. Our demands are nonnegotiable. Give us the girl, and we'll be on our way."

"What are you going to do? Kill her? If you try to take her, you'll have to go through me first."

What was his dad doing? He wasn't supposed to threaten the intruders in any way. Steven squinted down at the men. They seemed to be shrugging their shoulders.

"Look, we prefer to keep things clean and simple. Too many bodies are messy and hard to deal with." Bickler shrugged. "But hey, it's your call. If you want to go down fighting, we can do it that way as well. I've never been afraid to pull the trigger."

There! That was what they needed! But would that vague threat hold up in court? It didn't matter at that point since the man had threatened to kidnap Polly. This was the moment when Seb and his deputies were supposed to reveal themselves and grab the criminals. But no one seemed to be moving. His father was staring at the intruders, his hand still across her shoulders as he protected the girl.

"Well, I guess we're going to have to do this the hard way then," the man with the gray beard said as he lifted up his gun and pointed it at Scott. The other two did the same.

Steven raised his head, uncaring if he drew attention to himself up in the loft. Where was Seb? Why weren't they stopping this?

There! Two deputies seemed to have materialized behind the intruders. But they were too late.

Bang! Bang! Bang!

"No!" Steven couldn't stop the scream that escaped from his lips as he watched two bodies crumple to the ground.

Chapter Sixteen

"No!" Steven screamed again as he leaped from the hayloft. He needed to do something, since obviously the plan had gone dreadfully wrong.

Too late, he realized the folly of his action. It was a twenty-foot drop from the loft to the floor. Sure, he and Seb had made the jump when they were kids. But it had hurt even then, with a pile of hay to lessen the impact.

His body crashed into another person, but it wasn't one of the intruders, unfortunately. It was Seb, who seemed to have appeared from nowhere, wrapping his arms around Steven and staggering backward as he absorbed the impact of the fall.

"What are you trying to do? Get all of us killed?" Seb's anger was palpable.

"Me?" Steven pulled away from his twin. "What about you? You let them shoot Dad!"

Seb choked out a scoffing snort. "I used to

think you'd make a good cop because of that staggering courage of yours. But I forgot about your mile-wide reckless streak. Look around you, brother. Everything worked out just like we planned."

Steven turned to survey the scene. His dad was standing upright, grinning as he unbuckled the Kevlar vest from beneath his flannel shirt. The diminutive female deputy who had spent the last twenty minutes kneeling on the ground, with the bottom of her legs covered with hay, had also shed her long, brightly colored raincoat to reveal her own bulletproof vest. All three of the intruders were now in handcuffs and surrounded by a half-dozen deputies. A feeling of chagrin crept up Steven's spine as his cheeks burned with embarrassment.

"Right. Well, thanks for catching me." He paused, then said, "I guess we did it then."

"We?" His brother's voice held just a bit of mockery. "You nearly blew the whole thing. Good thing Dad was able to follow the plan. Hopefully, once we examine their phones, we'll have enough evidence to convict them of attempted kidnapping and murder."

"So it's over?" Steven still couldn't quite believe what had just happened.

"Well, for me, it's just the beginning. I'm going to have to write a whole bunch of reports, explaining how I let a fugitive hide in my jurisdiction. Probably the FBI will want to take this one over. But, yeah, I get your meaning. It's over."

Steven closed his eyes and sighed, relief pouring through body. *Thank You, God.* He sidled over to his father. "You okay, Dad?"

"I might be a bit sore for a few days, but I'm fine." Scott was still brushing hay off his shirt, but a smirk was playing on his lips. "Nice to know that you've got my back although I'm still not quite certain what you thought you were doing when you catapulted off the loft."

"Right. Well, I figured I'd come up with a plan by the time I landed. I usually do."

"True enough," Scott agreed.

"I just radioed the sniper," Seb interrupted. "Etta and Lynn are still on the patio. We'll head up there and take Lynn in. Who knows, we might even be able to get her to turn on her son. Wouldn't that be the cherry on the top of the cake? Connecting the Texas attorney general to a kidnapping plot instigated at his mother's behest."

Steven shook his head. Trust his brother to be thinking about the case.

He quickly stepped beside his brother and another deputy as they started walking toward the house.

"Now, don't pull another stunt like you did in the barn," Seb said.

Steven nodded. It was a fair warning. Still, with her network of support gone, he didn't see Lynn putting up too much of a fight. And the two armed deputies who, along with the sniper, had been watching the house would be on hand just in case.

As they crested the hill, his parents' house came into view. He couldn't see Etta, but once again he felt a pounding in his chest.

It took only two minutes for them to cover the remaining distance. Steven felt an immediate urge to run over to Etta and pull her into his arms. But Seb placed a warning hand on his shoulder. "Let it play out according to the plan."

Steven grunted his assent as they continued their stealthy approach, waiting until they were less than five feet away from the women.

"Lynn Weber," Seb stated in a calm voice. "You are under arrest for your role in the attempted kidnapping of Polly Sanderson. You have the right to remain silent. You have the right to an attorney—"

Seb's words were cut short as Lynn seemed to crumple downward, only to lurch back upright a half a second later clutching a six-inch knife she'd clearly hidden under the leg of her pants.

With her free hand, she twisted an arm around Etta while holding the blade against her throat. "Take another step, and your girlfriend will die."

Steven stopped in his tracks. This was definitely not part of the plan. He glanced at Seb. The creases on his brother's forehead were not reassuring. He glanced upward, toward the roof of the shed. He could see the glint of the sniper's rifle, but with Lynn holding Etta in front of her, there was no way to make a clean shot.

"Don't move," Lynn screeched, her eyes flashing with rage. "I haven't survived for forty years to be taken down by a couple of no-account hillbillies from flyover country. I've disappeared once before, and I can do it again."

"Etta..." Steven began.

"It's okay, Steven," Etta insisted. "Polly is safe. That's the important thing. And you were the one who made that happen. I don't know what I would have done without you."

"Etta, no. This isn't over. I love you." Steven could hear his voice break. He couldn't let it end this way.

"You…love me?" Her eyes softened. "But I thought… Well, it doesn't matter. Because I love you, too." Tears were streaming down her face.

"Oh, shut up!" Lynn began to walk backward, the blade of her knife pressed against Etta's throat. "You—" She gestured toward Steven. "You can be our driver since this woman is so precious to you. Get the keys out of my purse. Stop stalling. Let's do this now." She let out a laugh tinged with hysteria.

"No, Steven. You stay here. Let me go alone," Etta said.

Steven walked over to the table and fished his hand inside Lynn's navy purse. Keys in hand, he headed toward the Mercedes parked thirty feet away.

"Don't try to follow us—" Lynn told Seb and the other deputies "—or she goes bye-bye." Lynn cackled. "Move it," she said, pushing Etta forward. They headed around the house and toward her car before Lynn shoved Etta into the back seat. Lynn climbed in next to her.

Steven slid into the front and started the car. The sinking feeling that had been turning his stomach for the last several minutes suddenly gave way. He knew what he had to do. He just needed to wait until the moment was right.

"Put on your seat belts," he said, snapping his own quickly in place. He pressed down on the accelerator and pulled out of the driveway. He glanced at the rearview mirror and saw that Lynn had lowered the knife and was fumbling for something in her purse.

This was it then. Up ahead, a gnarled oak marked the turn-off to the main road. That tree had always been there to welcome him home, even when he was bruised and broken from the rodeo. His breath caught in his throat as he yanked the wheel to the right and pressed down hard on the accelerator.

The last thing he remembered was the crunch of metal shattering against wood.

Etta bit back a scream.

The crash seemed to happen in slow motion—and fast forward—at the same time. One second, she was sitting in the back

seat with Lynn beside her. The next, she was pinned by the impact of an air bag pressed against her chest. And yet, somehow, she had known that Steven was planning something and that there was nothing she could do or say to stop him. From his hunched shoulders to his grim expression, he was going to save her, no matter the consequences. As the car veered toward the tree, she knew had done her part to forestall the inevitable. Latching her fingers around Lynn's wrist, she struggled to grasp the handle of the knife. For a woman in her seventies, Lynn was surprisingly strong. But righteous anger fueled Etta's determination. In the seconds before the SUV hit the tree, she had managed to knock the weapon to the floor.

But her success came seconds too late as the air bags inside the car deployed, and she felt the impact of the seat belt pulled taut against her chest. For several heartbeats, everything was calm, as if she had been enveloped by a large white cocoon. But then reality came charging back, with the sounds and scents of danger.

Sirens were blaring behind them, and the acrid smell of smoke assailed her nostrils.

She was having trouble thinking straight or functioning in a logical way. But one thing she knew for sure was that she needed to find Steven. As the driver, he had taken the brunt of the collision. She needed to reach him to make sure he was okay.

She unclicked her seat belt. The inside of the once large and comfortable vehicle suddenly felt dark and cramped. With a start, she realized that the car was bowed in the center, the passenger door bent inward on the twisted frame. She pulled against the door handle while kicking the inside panel with her feet.

It didn't open.

Summoning her last reserves of strength, she gave a hard thrust and the door gave way, a few inches at first, but then wide enough to allow her to escape.

Tumbling onto the ground, she was surprised to find all her limbs in working order. She had survived the crash unscathed. But what about Steven? She turned back toward the car, but strong arms reached out to stop her.

Scott.

"It's okay, Etta. I've got you. Don't worry."

That's when she realized she was crying. "I need to help Steven. Where is he? Is he okay?"

Scott shook his head. "They're working on getting him out now. Ambulances are already here, and the paramedics will do everything they can. They pulled Lynn from the back seat. She was knocked unconscious by the crash, so she's on her way to the hospital. Handcuffed to the gurney."

Etta gulped in a breath of air. She hadn't even thought about Lynn, only Steven. "I'm so sorry. This is all my fault."

"Shush." Scott led her away from the car. "How could that even be true? None of this is your doing. But let's get you checked out as well."

Etta allowed the paramedics to assess her vitals even though she knew she was fine. Scott looked at his phone and then sat beside her as they watched the firefighters working to open the door on the driver's side of the vehicle.

"Sandy just texted that she and Polly are going to stay with Tacy for a bit longer. They'll head for home once everything's okay."

"Thank God everyone else is okay. Scott?" Etta's throat felt like sandpaper. "Can we ask the Lord to save Steven?"

"Of course." He closed his eyes and began to pray. "Heavenly Lord, please give Steven strength. Be with him and with the brave men and women working to save his life. We know that You never fail us, even in times of trial. Please give us the courage and faith to trust in You. How great Thou art. Amen."

Etta looked at Scott. He didn't know—how could he?—that he had chosen the perfect words to sustain her through this trial. She reached over and squeezed his hand.

They both sat in silence, watching the activity around the Mercedes. Suddenly, there was an exclamation as one of the men shouted, "We got it open." The driver's side door was removed, and two paramedics climbed inside. Etta held her breath. Her insides felt wound tighter than a taut coil. The minutes felt like hours as they waited to see what would happen next.

Finally, Stephen's body was pulled out and laid on the waiting gurney. He was surrounded by paramedics, so she couldn't see much of what was going on. She and Scott stood up as Seb walked over to them, his face weary and tired. But there was a brightness in his eyes that was reassuring.

"He's unconscious, but his vitals look good. And he may have rebroken a few of his ribs. They're taking him to Mercy Hospital to see if he needs surgery. You two can ride with me."

Etta closed her eyes. Steven was okay. *Amen* silently echoed in her heart. Nothing else really mattered.

She climbed into the back seat of Seb's truck, glad for some time alone with her thoughts.

Then again, maybe those thoughts were too confusing to even contemplate. Steven had said that he loved her. And she loved him. But that had been true fifteen years ago, and things hadn't worked out. Who could say it wasn't even more complicated this time around? Switch out her role as her sister's guardian for her responsibilities to the child who had been left in her care. And while it was true that it wouldn't be long before Greg was released from prison, she was now even more determined to remain a part of their lives. Polly needed stability, and that meant more than occasional visits at Christmas and birthdays. It meant an aunt who lived nearby. And Steven's family was in South Dakota, which, as she well knew, was almost thirteen hundred miles away.

Etta sighed. Just a few minutes ago she had been basking in Steven's declaration of love. But already she was putting up roadblocks to any future entanglements.

Seb kept to the speed limit on the drive to the hospital, so it was thirty minutes before they pulled in front of the emergency-room entrance. But Etta wasn't going to complain. It had given her time to think about her relationship with Steven, though ultimately she had reached no resolution. She rolled her shoulders up and down, trying to ease the tension. How could they ever make things work?

"Just got a message from my dispatcher," Seb said. "Steven doesn't need surgery, but they want to keep him overnight. He's asking for you, so why don't you head up to see him while Dad and I park the car. He's in room 203. We'll join you in a bit."

"Thanks," Etta said, forcing a tight smile.

She passed through the automated doors and entered the lobby, where she filled out a form for a visitor badge. Steven's room was on the second floor, but as she counted the number plates along the corridor, the tighter the knot in her stomach seemed to clench. She stopped when she reached room 203. This was it. The moment of reckoning.

But as she stepped inside, all the worry and anxiety disappeared in a flash. There was Steven, lying in a bed. He had bandages across his face and his chest, but when he saw her, his face broke out into its familiar smile. He didn't say a word but held out his arms.

She didn't hesitate. She walked straight toward him, stopping short to press his fingers to her lips. But just that quickly, she released his hand, her wide smile transformed into an anxious frown.

"What did you think you were doing back there, running like a wild man into that tree? You could have died, and then what? Seriously, Steven. If I wasn't so grateful to see you, I'd probably stop talking to you for at least a couple of days."

"I wasn't really thinking of the ramifications. When I saw Lynn lower the knife for a moment, I knew that was my chance."

"Well, I'm thankful for that crazy move of yours, which probably saved my life."

"Ah, shucks, Etta, I don't want your thanks. You know that." His voice sounded thick with emotion.

She looked at him and shook her head. "Now why does this seem so familiar? Blood-pressure cuff. Hospital bed. Feisty patient with a sweet, crooked smile."

Steven started to chuckle before clutching at his side. "Don't make me laugh." He paused, a serious look on his face. "But you know, this isn't at all like before. Last time, I was stuck in the hospital for weeks. And I had to woo you as an invalid. This time, the doctor says I'll be out in a day, so you'll be up against the full force of my charm. But, do you wanna know the real difference?"

Etta nodded. The look in Stephen's eyes made her heart drum even faster in her chest.

"This time, I have no intention of letting you go."

Well. That settled that. If Steven wasn't giving up, then neither was she. It was simple really. She just needed to push aside all the obstacles and open her heart to love.

He drew her toward him and then paused with his lips a mere breath away from her. "Does trying again sound like something you'd be interested in?"

He didn't wait for an answer as he pulled her closer for a long, deep kiss.

Epilogue

Three months later

It was the perfect day for a ball game. Cloudless blue sky, and the temperature was cool enough by Texas standards. And the Rangers started the series with a winning record. Just barely, but Etta wasn't going to complain.

She and Steven had come to the ballpark on a date.

Her mind flashed back to those days after the showdown at the ranch. She hadn't known then—how could she have?—that a deep, abiding kind of happiness was just around the corner, that all she needed to do was reach for it and hold fast. Despite everything Steven had said that last day at the ranch, she had still half expected that once Belinda and her accomplices were arrested, she and Steven would part company, recognizing the impossibility of making things work. But that wasn't how it had ended, not by a long shot. Instead, there had been a kiss, and not just any kiss. It was a kiss that promised a solution to any and all dilemmas, and many good things to come.

But before all of that, there were countless details to be ironed out. The case against Greg was dismissed, but Polly was still not talking. And though Greg had arranged for her to visit a therapist, she was clearly having difficulties dealing with her mother's death. Etta had charges of her own to face in Texas. Even with Steven backing up her self-defense plea, there was still the issue of fleeing the scene, which, to her great relief, ended up being resolved with a suspended sentence and a judge's order that she perform one hundred hours of community service.

So given all that, it made sense for her and Steven to take things slow and easy. Their time on the run had set a high bar in terms of excitement, but not so much in romance. But gradually, all that had begun to change. She found a less demanding job at a hospital near Dallas, which allowed her to spend evenings and weekends with Polly. And, over time, her short bob had grown out, and after a couple visits to a good hairdresser, her hair was almost back to its natural color.

Of course, given all the travel requirements of a long-distance relationship, she had been asked more than once if her return to Texas was permanent. Her answer was always the same—time would tell, but she was committed to maintaining a close relationship with her niece.

And when Steven arrived in town for a visit with a couple of tickets to the Rangers game, it was hard not to think about what had happened the last time they had been at a game together. But she had managed to shake off any misgivings. After all, Steven knew how she felt about his public proposal since she complained about it at great length, and quite shrewishly, she might add.

The visiting pitcher was warming up when Steven appeared at the end of the row, clutching a box of popcorn and two bottles of water in his hands.

"Long line," he explained, sliding in next to her in his seat. "Glad I didn't miss the start of the game. Hope it's a good one." He reached over to squeeze her hand.

And it was, though maybe a bit too tense for her liking. The Rangers' shortstop ended up

driving in the winning run during the last in-
ning of the game, causing a good deal of rejoic-
ing in the stands. As she and Steven joined the
jubilant crowd flooding out of the stadium, he
looped an arm around her waist to guide her
toward the exit.

"How did it go with the interview you had
with that reporter?" he asked.

"Okay, I guess." Etta had been surprised by
how quickly the conversation had turned toward
her reactions to the upcoming trial. But what
could she say beyond the fact that she was glad
that Belinda Caruso was being held account-
able for her past and present crimes. There were
so many questions waiting for answers, but it
would be up to the DA to prove how much all
the parties involved had known about the scope
of Belinda's plan. With plausible deniability, her
son, the attorney general, had remained above
the fray, though he had decided to pause his
campaign for reelection. Etta wasn't sure she
believed his story that he was unaware of his
mother's deception and her true identity, but
so far Belinda had resisted throwing him under
the bus in any way. As for the fate of the rest of
her henchmen, there had been quite a few legal
shenanigans on the part of their defense. It re-

mained to be seen if they'd pay the price for their role in covering up the murder.

"Finally, there will be justice for Lilly," the reporter had said, snapping her notebook shut to signal the end of the interview. And Etta had nodded, though she doubted that it would be as simple as that. Her sister was never coming back. Greg would do his best as a single dad, but Polly would grow up without a mother. For all of them, nothing would ever be the same. But, with God's help and mercy, they'd learn to deal with their loss and find a way to keep Lilly's memory alive.

"Hey." Steven looked down into the box of popcorn he was still holding his hand. "There's not much left, but do you want the last bits before I toss it in the trash?"

She was about to say no when something sly in his smile made her change her mind. As she reached into the box for a last piece of popcorn, her fingers closed around a something on the bottom, something square and hard, which she grasped in her hand.

"What's this?" Her voice came out as a high-pitched squeak.

One look at Steven's crooked grin, and she had her answer. As she flipped opened the lid of the red velvet box to reveal a sparkling diamond ring, he dropped to bended knee. "Henrietta Louise Mitchell, I got it wrong the last time, and that's on me. But I never stopped loving you, and I am hoping now that you will do me the honor of agreeing to be my wife."

"Of course, I will. But wait…"

The smile slipped from his face. "What?"

"Don't you think we should figure out where we want to live before we make a permanent commitment?"

"I actually thought about that. How about nine months in Dallas and summers at the ranch? It's not a long-term solution by any means, but it will work until Polly is talking again and we have a chance to figure the rest of the stuff out."

"Okay," she said. Even she knew her voice sounded tentative.

"Listen, Etta. Things are never going to be perfect. Our future is in God's hands, and we need to trust that our love will be strong enough to make it all work."

Love filled her heart, and she knew that with him, it would all turn out okay. "You really are one very smart cowboy," she said as her eyes filled with tears.

Steven slipped the ring on her finger and then

stood to pull her into a tight embrace. A small crowd outside the stadium stopped and stared, but she didn't care. She, Etta Mitchell, loved Steven Hunt, and this time, she was happy to share their moment with the world.

Undercover Colorado Conspiracy

Jodie Bailey

MILLS & BOON

Jodie Bailey writes novels about freedom and the heroes who fight for it. Her novel *Crossfire* won a 2015 RT Reviewers' Choice Best Book Award. She is convinced a camping trip to the beach with her family, a good cup of coffee and a great book can cure all ills. Jodie lives in North Carolina with her husband, her daughter and two dogs.

Visit the Author Profile page
at millsandboon.com.au.

Fear not: for I have redeemed thee,
I have called thee by thy name; thou art mine.
—*Isaiah* 43:1

DEDICATION

To Shannon,

You are amazing and strong and wonderful.

Thank you for reading my first manuscript
from cover to cover *in front of me*
and for believing in me right from the start.

I'll always love you, my sweet Georgia friend!

Chapter One

There was no way her cover had been blown this quickly.

Army Special Agent Thalia Renner pushed herself faster down the wooded trail of the high-end ski resort where she and her partner were undercover investigating a possible crime ring. The thin layer of snow that had drifted through the tree branches crunching under her running shoes. She'd been blindsided by a man wearing a mask. He'd stepped out of the early-morning shadows and landed a blow before she could react.

The kick to his solar plexus ought to slow him down.

But he'd be back, and he'd be angry when he caught his breath.

A warm trickle of blood coursed down Thalia's cheek from a stinging cut beneath her eye, though she didn't dare risk losing momentum by swiping at the spot where her attacker's fist had landed.

Behind her, heavy footsteps crunched through twigs and leaves and snow, but as near as she could judge, the man wasn't gaining on her.

Her foot caught the side of a rock as the trail narrowed and curved around a bend in the mountain. She stumbled and managed not to fall, forcing herself to run faster.

The light of dawn grew brighter with every step. Surely she'd reach the end of the trail at the resort soon. How far had she run?

The January Colorado cold burned her face and lungs. Her leg muscles protested.

This was the stuff of nightmares. In reality, she stood her ground and fought. In nightmares, she ran.

Unfortunately, the personality of her undercover persona dictated she run. If she made a stand and announced her true status as a federal agent, an operation that had taken a year to plan and execute would die a sudden death on this very mountainside.

Shoving a tree branch aside, Thalia tried to focus on the trail in front of her and not on the heavy footsteps dogging her down the mountain. Somehow, the brute chasing her had gotten the jump on her as she'd rounded a bend in the trail about fifteen minutes into her predawn run.

That never should have happened. She was too highly trained for some thug to surprise her.

But it *had* happened.

She tapped into the anger with her failings and used it to fuel her footsteps. While she'd love to turn and fight, a knock-down, drag-out would only end with few answers and more questions than her undercover persona could ever admit to.

If her cover wasn't already blown.

Either the guy breathing down her neck had been sent to take her out, or she'd unhappily fallen victim to a random sicko lying in wait for any lone female who came running along the trail.

The footsteps behind her stopped and the sound of her pursuer's breathing faded away.

Finally, she'd worn him out. She'd pause for a sigh of relief, but there was no way she was slowing down now. No, Thalia ran harder, eager to put more distance between them before he caught a second wind and—

Her foot landed awkwardly on a jutting root in the trail and she pitched to the side. Her ankle rolled under her weight. Her body hit the ground hard, her shoulder bearing the brunt of the impact. She tumbled down the hill with the momentum, ducking her chin to protect her head.

A loud *pop* rang in the morning stillness.

Was that her arm?

No. There was no pain.

Was it—

Another crack, and the bark on the tree beside her splintered.

For real? He had a silencer? It made enough noise for her to hear yet it wasn't loud enough to alert anyone at the resort. And the guy was playing dirty, shooting at her while she was down.

If only she had her sidearm to return fire. Leaving her suite without it had been foolish, but she'd been afraid of shattering her cover.

Another shot rang out and Thalia rolled deeper into the thick underbrush, her shoulder and ankle aching. This low on the mountain, the trees and shrubs grew thick, hopefully providing enough cover to hide her in the ever-increasing morning light.

Thalia eyed the trail a few feet above her then scanned the forest around her. She might get hopelessly lost if she went too far off the path, but lost was better than dead from a bullet to the back of the skull. Pushing deeper into the trees, she ducked behind a tall pine and judged the size of the tree trunks around her, looking for the largest to run to next.

There.

No footsteps or breathing sounded above her, so she headed for the larger tree, the pain in her ankle easing with each step.

Another shot. Another bullet zipped through the forest growth several feet away. He was firing blind, aiming for the sound of movement.

Hopefully he'd stay on the trail or give up. Or maybe the cavalry would arrive.

She hated calling for help. With her level of training, she should be able to handle an attacker on her own.

She had no choice though. Thalia Atkins, investment banker and military wife, would never have the skills Thalia Renner, undercover investigator, possessed, even if her hobby was kickboxing. Until she knew for certain her cover had been blown, she had to play the part to the hilt, and that meant not defending herself unless it was absolutely necessary.

After a slow swipe at the oozing blood on her cheek, she eased her hand to the thigh pocket on her leggings, trying not to move enough for trigger-happy Pistol Boy to notice. A quick text to her partner would have backup here in minutes.

The phone snagged on Lycra and a sharp sting cut into her finger.

Oh, come on.

The screen was shattered, either from her fall on the trail or the earlier scuffle with her assailant.

The sounds above her changed. Underbrush snapped as the man moved down the hill, heading directly toward her.

The only way out was a direct charge. No more running. She'd have to stand her ground and fight, whether she wanted to or not.

This time, though, she had the element of surprise. It was clear he wasn't exactly sure where she'd taken cover. That was her biggest advantage.

Glancing around, she found a broken tree branch about the size of a baseball bat. Slowly, Thalia hefted the wood that wasn't too heavy and would serve her purpose. She firmed up her stance and waited.

Heavy breathing drew nearer. *See? This is what happens when you focus too much on weights and skip cardio.* Guys like this were big and scary-looking, but they were all muscle. No endurance. The way he was sucking oxygen, he might be able to best her with brute strength for a moment, but she'd outlast him in the fight.

She hadn't been beaten in a fistfight yet.

A shadow moved to her right.

Thalia held her breath, and as the man passed beside her, she swung.

The branch shattered as it caught Brute Boy square in the face mask. It did the job. He howled in pain, stumbling backward, the gun slipping to the ground as he grabbed for his nose. Blood smeared his fingers when he whirled toward her.

Dive for the gun and risk getting pinned? Or stick with her training and go hand-to-hand?

He made the decision for her. With a roar that seemed to rattle the trees, the man charged.

Thalia was ready. She sidestepped, throwing her elbow up to catch him in the jaw.

Her strength and his momentum combined to whip his head back in an uppercut that dropped him like a limp rag.

Thalia bent at the waist, hands braced on her knees, weak from the sudden drop in adrenaline. The guy wouldn't stay out more than a minute, which should be enough time for her to get away. Working quickly, she dug through his coat pockets until she found his wallet and phone. She shoved the phone into the left thigh pocket of her leggings and the wallet into her jacket pocket, then scrabbled through the leaves and found the pistol. After slipping the magazine into the other jacket pocket, she checked the chamber then zipped the weapon in with the wallet.

She reached for the bottom of his mask to lift it and get a good suspect description, but he stirred and moaned. He'd come to soon, and she needed distance between them when he did. She didn't dare hang around any longer.

Thalia turned and bolted up the hill, her ankle aching but not enough to keep her from running. She was desperate to get to the hotel suite.

Desperate to know she hadn't somehow blown a mission that had already become too personal.

Army Special Agent Phillip Campbell tugged a gray sweater over his black T-shirt and wiped the condensation from the bathroom mirror. Until this mission was over, these would be the few moments of peace he got every day. While his partner went on a morning run, he squeezed in a shower before she trashed the bathroom. Since he was bunking on the couch in the living room of their suite and Thalia had taken the bedroom, the alone time he needed to reset and recharge was scarce.

No one had ever accused him of being an extrovert. This mission severely challenged every iota of people-person inside him.

Phillip scrubbed a hand over his damp brown hair, roughing it up. Good enough. It would dry before they had to show at breakfast and start charming the other lodgers at the Rocky Mountain Summit Resort.

His blue eyes hardened in the reflection. There was a grand total of ten married couples on the property, all who'd recently signed with Stardust Adoptions in the hopes of starting a family. Several times a year, the agency hosted a weeklong retreat where potential parents bonded with other couples and met with Stardust counselors who worked to partner them with birth mothers.

To provide this weeklong parental training retreat and "babymoon," Stardust had partnered with Rocky Mountain Summit, an all-inclusive resort designed to provide a vacation atmosphere that kept the guests corralled together for the week.

Easy to watch. Easy to be watched.

The agency had come to the attention of their military investigative unit, Overwatch, over a year earlier. The adoption agency's owner, Serena Turner, was suspected of matching adoptive families with "birth mothers" who weren't actually pregnant. It appeared the waiting parents would hand over money to care for the mothers only to be told that, at the last minute, the mother had changed her mind and was keeping the baby. Because the agency's contract stated there were no guarantees, refunds or reimbursements, some waiting parents had lost thousands of dollars.

In what was billed as an altruistic move, the Turners footed the bill for two military couples to join each retreat, and at least three of those couples over the past decade had seen their dreams dashed and their accounts drained. That was enough to bring Overwatch into play. While the unit typically investigated deep within the military system, they'd been called in due to the complexity of the operation and the amount of time it would require two investigators to remain undercover as a married couple.

Several teams had applied in the hope an Overwatch team would make the cut.

Phillip and Thalia had received the call.

The thought of someone playing on the emotions of hopeful parents soured Phillip's stomach. He hoped their intel was wrong, but at the same time, his driving motivator was to bring the agency to justice if the accusations were true.

It had taken time to build their undercover profiles and to set up housing on Fort Carson in Colorado, where he and Thalia had been posing as a married couple for several months. Only they knew they shared a house but not a bedroom. Overwatch's team had done a fabulous job of building a foolproof backstory for them, though it had taken time to apply and to be accepted to a retreat. Now they needed evidence.

It was a tall order for one week, but they'd faced worse.

Phillip ran his toothbrush under the water that poured into a polished marble sink and started scrubbing. Despite the gravity of the situation, he had to smile. He'd roughed it in places the American public would never know about. For now, he'd soak in a little luxury. Their next mission could find them in the darkest regions of a foreign country, wrapped in poncho liners and sleeping in the dirt, with organic cotton sheets only a distant memory.

He rinsed his mouth then swiped his face with the kind of towel he'd never imagined existed. His own were thin brown Army issue. Maybe when this mission was over, he'd spring for something a little softer.

This mission had the potential to spoil him.

The suite door banged against the wall in the living area and Phillip froze. It was too early for housekeeping. Too soon for Thalia to have finished her run.

Quietly, he reached for the pistol he'd laid on the back of the toilet. It was never far away. He inched toward the door, holding the weapon low in both hands as he glanced through the crack into the bedroom.

All was still. Whoever had entered was still in the living area.

Grateful for the plush carpet that muffled his bare footsteps, he sidestepped to the bedroom door and pressed against the wall, then peeked out.

Thalia stood with her back to him at the kitchenette's sink, water running into the copper basin. She splashed her face then reached for one of the dish towels on the counter.

Exhaling slowly, Phillip tucked his SIG into the concealed holster at his waist. All was well. *Maybe.* They'd been partners for nearly three years. From past missions, he knew she typically ran for an hour, so her early return was notable. "Cold get to you?"

Thalia's head jerked up and she grabbed the counter with both hands, the cloth she'd used to wipe her face falling silently to the dark hardwood.

"Yes." She spoke the word in her typical no-nonsense tone, but beneath her blue windbreaker, her shoulders shook.

"Not buying it." While their team was one of the youngest in the Overwatch program, they'd already been on nearly a dozen missions, from investigating attacks on an infantry captain and his young daughter to protecting a potential Overwatch recruit from a criminal seeking revenge.

His footsteps thudded softly on the hardwood that marked the living areas of their suite. The wood was cool beneath his feet. Nonetheless, that coolness did nothing to quell the rising heat of warning in his belly.

Thalia Renner didn't shudder.

When he reached her, he stopped short of

grabbing her shoulder and turning her to face him. He'd have to pull the truth out of her slowly by being her sarcastic teammate, not behaving like a friend. As close as they were, she still tended to view concern as intrusive.

Phillip leaned against the counter beside her and crossed his arms over his chest. "What gives? You take on a bear out there?"

She had turned her face so all he could see was her profile. Her jaw worked from side to side before she spoke. "You could say that." With a deep inhale, she looked him full in the face.

Phillip's hands dropped to his sides. "What happened?" He reached for her despite knowing it wasn't the wisest idea, gently turning her to face him.

Beneath her left eye, blood oozed from a cut, blazing a trail to her chin. Small drops stained the front of her jacket, which was smeared with mud. A bruise was forming around the edges of the cut, an angry red against her olive skin. The black headband she'd used to pull her hair back was gone and brown shoulder-length waves tumbled in every direction, leaves and twigs tangled in the strands.

"Did you fall off the mountain?" He backed away and surveyed her from head to toe, but other than the injuries he'd already cataloged, she appeared to be unharmed.

"Not exactly." She sighed heavily then pulled her shoulders back, seeming to find the inner strength Phillip knew well. "A freakishly huge Neanderthal attacked me on the trail." The statement was so calm that it took a second to register.

"Wait. What?" Nobody got the jump on Thalia.

"I handled him." She backed away and walked to the island separating the kitchen from the living room. She was in investigator mode, relating the facts. Reaching into her pockets, she slid a cell phone, a wallet, a pistol and a clip onto the gray granite. "Got these off of him."

"You *handled* him? What does that mean?"

"It means he was coming to when I left." She grabbed the wallet and flipped it open. "We just arrived last night. There's no way our cover is blown already, is there?"

Phillip walked to the floor-to-ceiling windows overlooking thick forest that sloped away from the lodge. A thin layer of snow blanketed everything. It all looked so peaceful.

Peace was always deceiving.

He turned and walked into the middle of the

living room, skirting a large live-edge wooden coffee table. "Unless you have evidence to the contrary, I doubt it. It's more likely he was an opportunist who saw a female and took his chances."

Chances that could have killed his partner.

Thalia nodded as she slipped a card from the wallet. "He didn't act like a pro. He came out of nowhere, but he confronted me head-on and lost the element of surprise. Although he did have a silencer." She pressed her cheek with the pad of her finger.

"He shot at you?" She could not be serious.

"A couple of times." Dropping the wallet and the license to the counter, she lifted her brown eyes to his. "Regardless, you're right. We can't assume someone has already made us. It took way too long to get here. But this does lead to a bigger problem."

"What could possibly be bigger?"

"How about the fact that we're supposed to be a lovey-dovey husband and wife who are in the process of adopting a child, and now I have this?" She aimed a finger at her cheek. "We're out of here in a heartbeat if someone decides Staff Sergeant Phillip Atkins, working in military intelligence, is smacking his wife in the face when no one's watching. We have to report what happened to the resort's security team."

She couldn't be more right. They were supposed to be deep undercover, so deep that if someone was concerned and called the police, they'd have to play their roles through until the investigation was over. There was no "get out of jail free" card on this op.

There was a way out of this. "So, job one is making sure no one thinks I did this to you. Did anyone see you when you came in?"

Her eyes caught the spark that said she'd followed his train of thought. "I came through the lobby. Don't know if anyone saw me, but they'll have cameras." Rounding the island, she strode into the living room. "Call the front desk. Tell them your wife was attacked on the trail, but don't say by who or what." Dropping to the couch, Thalia rested her hands on her knees and stared out the French doors, her face clouding.

Concern blipped across Phillip's radar. Was she hurt worse than she'd let on? Internal injuries could—

Thalia's head jerked up, her expression hard. "Phone call. Now."

Nah, she was fine. Just getting into character as the terrified victim. Thalia could fight with the best of them. Eight years earlier, one of her first undercover ops, before she'd joined Overwatch, had been as a female MMA fighter busting up a drug ring. She'd briefly revisited that persona a few months earlier when she'd stepped into the cage for a week to determine who the key player was in another drug ring.

He'd hated that op. Watching her step into the octagon for a no-holds-barred fight had been… Well, it had been rough.

This had the potential to get rougher.

Reaching for the phone, Phillip shot up a quick prayer. As soon as he dialed, their cover personas were under scrutiny in ways they hadn't calculated or practiced.

If they failed to sell the ruse, then the entire op could explode in their faces.

Chapter Two

"Nothing like this has ever happened on our property before." The resort's manager, Dale Carmichael, was a slender man who was taller than Phillip. He wore khakis and a button-down shirt sporting the Rocky Mountain Summit logo. Settling on the edge of the recliner at an angle to the couch, he looked over his shoulder at the head of security.

Phillip let his focus drift to the other man as well. Chase Westin was most definitely prior service. His stance and haircut gave him away. He shook his head, though he never looked away from Phillip. "Not as long as I've been here." The words were laced with suspicion.

There was no doubt this looked bad. A random attack on a resort with private security and ringed by fences? The more likely scenario was a domestic altercation, and Westin clearly had those thoughts.

Being on the other side of accusatory scrutiny was unnerving. Phillip was telling the truth. When it came to his partner's safety, he wouldn't lie.

The unspoken implication that he was being dishonest bristled under his skin. It brought back too many painful memories, reminders that telling the truth didn't always bring help. Sometimes, it brought pain.

But this wasn't about him. It was about Thalia and their investigation. He shifted on the couch and rested his hand on her lower back. He was supposed to be a soldier concerned about his wife, not an investigator digging for information. For two people who should be flying under the radar, this was a terrible situation.

Terrible and potentially dangerous. Serena Turner was present, as well, and if she was truly guilty of bilking families out of money, there was no telling what she might do to protect her interests if she caught wind of an investigation.

Thalia flinched as the resort's on-site nurse practitioner, who was seated on the other side of her, cleaned the cut beneath her eye.

The medic winced, as well, and her dark ponytail bobbed. "Sorry. I should have warned you it was going to sting. What did that guy hit you with?"

"His fist? Maybe? It was still kind of dark…" There was no doubt Thalia could provide every detail of the encounter, yet she was holding back to play the part. "Everything happened so fast." She ran her hands along her thighs and gripped her knees. "I'm used to cuts. I trained in mixed martial arts for a while. But that's all controlled, not out in the woods where…" She trailed off as though it was too frightening to talk about.

Phillip carefully watched Thalia, seemingly afraid of letting her out of his sight. If he was truly her husband, he'd be kicking himself over not accompanying her on a predawn run along deserted trails. "I should have gone with her. This wouldn't have happened if I'd been there."

The regret in his tone was real. Maybe he really *should* have accompanied her.

She'd have never let him. He hated running and had never joined her before.

It wasn't as if Thalia was helpless. She'd handled herself in more dangerous situations than this, and adding the past boxing experience to her résumé allowed her to defend herself to an extent without raising too many questions.

Still, sitting beside her acting as her husband,

the feelings were different. Pain gripped his heart at the thought of her fighting for her life alone in the semidarkness. If something had happened to her out there...

His fingers tightened slightly against her shirt.

Beneath his palm, her back muscles tensed. The role of victim was difficult for her, and his overprotective gesture added fuel to the fire. While she was a chameleon when it came to undercover work, anyone who knew her well could see the truth in her posture.

Beside the couch, Serena Turner stood with another security guard, watching the proceedings. The owner of Stardust Adoptions hadn't said much since the group had entered the suite ten minutes earlier. She'd quietly observed, her eyes scanning the room, presumably searching for clues.

Like Westin, she probably wondered if Phillip had injured Thalia. His stomach clenched at the thought.

As if she could read his mind, Thalia leaned closer to him as though he was her safe place, projecting a wife who trusted her husband.

Westin looked away.

Phillip wanted to high-five his fake wife. *Good job, partner.*

Just as quickly, the security chief pinned Phillip's gaze again. "Mrs. Atkins, I'd like to hear your story from beginning to end." It was a challenge. The way he scrutinized Phillip's reaction spoke a whole lot of volumes. "Mr. Atkins, if you don't mind, I'd like you to answer a few questions for Mr. Simms in the hallway."

Separating the two of them was a clear tactic, providing the ideal time for an abused spouse to speak up.

Every step they took in the next ten seconds could affect the future of their investigation. They were already too bright on the radar. If Stardust thought there were domestic issues, the company would either watch the two of them closely or ask them to leave.

What Thalia did next was critical.

She backed away from the medic and turned her face into Phillip's shoulder. "No. I'd rather forget it happened."

Phillip pulled her closer, the urge to protect her surging through him. Even though he knew this was an act, there was something about her vulnerability that spoke to his heart.

He placed a kiss on the top of her head. It felt more natural than it should. "I'll be right outside. You're safe with these people." He made a point of looking at the female medic, who had been nothing but caring and concerned. "You'll stay with her?"

The woman nodded and seemed to relax. Phillip's apparent lack of concern about what Thalia might say had eased the posture of the onlookers.

Except Westin.

Investigator to investigator, Phillip admired the man's eagerness to protect the victim, something near to his own heart.

But sitting on the other side of that stare, having his character silently questioned and his story doubted…

The stinging pain it shot through him was almost more than he could hide.

Thalia pulled away and lifted her chin toward his. For the first time since this entire cadre of people had invaded their space, he looked her full in the face.

The slight sheen of tears in her brown eyes almost slapped him sideways. For a split second, this moment was real, and she needed him.

Then she straightened as though drawing on inner bravery. "Okay."

When Phillip stood and headed for the door, she squeezed his hand before letting go.

He let the security guard, Simms, usher him out without looking back.

He was too afraid of what he'd do if he did.

Simms shut the door behind them and leaned against the wall, watching Phillip. He was probably in his late thirties, and he wore the air of cynicism that came from seeing too much too fast.

Phillip wanted to ask if he was a former cop, but he kept his mouth shut. That would be a bit too intuitive. Instead, he shoved his hands into his pockets and waited for Simms to break the silence.

He didn't have to wait long. "Your wife came back from the trail like that?"

"She did." He let his anger stoked by the reminders of his past bubble to the surface and channeled it to its best use. Pulling his hands from his pockets, he balled his fists. "I don't understand how this happened. This is supposed to be a safe place. I would never have let her go alone if I thought it wasn't. You haven't done your job when—"

Simms held up a hand. "Settle down. I'd be pretty angry if I was in your position too."

"Westin thinks I hit my wife." Phillip didn't

bother to hide his disgust at the very idea. "I would never—"

"I believe you." If that was the case, then why did the man still seem skeptical?

"Thank you."

"The person I don't believe is your wife."

The matter-of-fact statement almost rocked Phillip right out of character. He tensed his jaw to keep it from dropping. "What are you saying?"

Simms shrugged, all nonchalance and arrogance. "What they said in there was true. There's never been an assault on the property. That's a secluded trail. Nobody would go up there in the dark in this weather and wait around hoping a victim would happen along."

A charge ran through Phillip's veins. Simms suspected something. Somehow, they'd let their cover slip. A year of planning and practice could unravel in the next breath if he didn't meticulously play his role. "My wife is not a liar."

"Not on purpose, maybe." Simms sniffed and picked the cuticle on his right thumb. "But she's been through a lot, I'm guessing. You're here to adopt a kid. That's emotional. Stressful. Maybe she fell. Maybe she hit a low-hanging branch in the dark and thought someone was after her. Maybe—"

"Stop talking. Now." Phillip stepped closer to the man until their toes practically touched. The words shot fire through him like he hadn't felt in years. To not believe someone who was telling the truth was unthinkable. It stung. It hit way too close to his own experience.

You're lying.

That would never happen.

You're paranoid.

Words from the past bled into the air between them, filling the space until Phillip thought he might choke on them. Voices of authority who should have helped had dismissed him. Had shattered lives.

He'd dealt with this pain. Had put it away and vowed it would never rise again.

It could not show up now, when this investigation depended on them maintaining their identities as a happily married couple. Nothing could interfere with his job.

Simms straightened, his hands falling to his sides as the arrogance leaked from his posture.

Phillip backed away before he did something he'd regret. "Thalia doesn't lie." He ground out the words slowly. "She's not hysterical. The cut on her face ought to tell you that. For you to dismiss a woman's experience because she's a woman is—" The words wouldn't come. Anger flared for Thalia, for himself, and for everyone who'd ever been doubted. "Unless you have a question that might lead to something productive when it comes to protecting the guests on this property, we're done here."

Looking up the hall, Simms said nothing.

Good.

If he had, it could have led to trouble. Maintaining his cover under the strength of these emotions was impossible.

If Phillip wasn't careful, his past could wreck everything.

"Thank you all. We appreciate your concern." The door clicked softly as Phillip closed it behind Serena Turner and the security team.

Thalia sagged against the couch and pressed her fingertips to her forehead. Playing the terrified victim had sapped her more than the earlier fight with Trail Boy. Shivering and trembling against Phillip's shoulder had taken every inch of her skills. She needed a shower, not just to wash off the blood and mud but to rinse away the sense of weakness crawling up her spine.

There was one more thing she'd like to shake

off. Leaning into Phillip's shoulder while his arm was warm around her had felt a little too… comfortable. Most likely, her adrenaline had ebbed at the same time Phillip had taken a seat beside her, dropping her muscles into an odd state of flux.

At any rate, a shower would have to wait. Drawing on her reserves, Thalia stood. They had work to do, and with their first group activity scheduled immediately after lunch, they had precious little time.

At the counter, Phillip shoveled in pancakes, bacon and eggs ordered in by the resort manager. He pointed a fork at the silver dome over her plate. "Fuel up, Thal. It's going to be a long day."

"Mmm-hmm." She was more interested in diving into the contents of the wallet and phone she'd stashed in one of the kitchenette drawers, but she lifted the cover from her food instead.

The buttery scent of pancakes and the salty aroma of bacon hit her stomach where it counted. Fighting for her life made a girl hungry. Acting helpless made her ravenous.

She grabbed a slice of bacon and retrieved the wallet and cell phone as she took the first bite. The taste paused her hand midreach. "Wow."

Brown sugar and maple syrup and salt played very nicely together. This deserved a second to be savored.

"I know." Phillip's grin was contagious. "The food alone is going to make this week worth it."

"So is finding proof that Stardust is stealing from innocent victims." She swallowed the bite and forced herself to remember why they were there.

The sweetly brined bacon turned bitter. Their first objective wasn't settling into the lap of luxury. It was discovering whether or not Brantley and Serena Turner were lying to prospective parents and stealing money from them.

No, their *first* objective was figuring out why she had been attacked. If someone knew their true identities, then the investigation was shot and their lives were in danger.

Covering her plate, Thalia wiped her hands on her leggings. She slid the cell phone to Phillip then lifted the wallet and once again removed the driver's license. "I'll start with the ID. See if you can get into the phone." Of the two of them, he was the more technology-minded. Their unit's computer and cyber expert, Dana Richardson, had entrusted Phillip with a hefty pile of equipment that would aid them in their investigation. "Did Dana give you a password cracker?"

"Been dying to see if it works. She designed it herself." He left the phone on the counter and headed for the locked case where he'd stashed their more sensitive equipment.

Of course she did. Dana breathed technology. If she couldn't find what she needed, she created it. She'd left WITSEC a few years prior to consult with Overwatch, and she'd never been happier.

The fact that the unit's second-in-command, Alex "Rich" Richardson, was Dana's husband didn't hurt.

Phillip returned, carrying two laptops. He set one by her hand and opened the other, then created a secure connection with his phone and started typing. "I'm updating Rachel first."

He was right. Their team leader should know what had happened. Thalia held up the license. "This is likely a fake, but the name is Hudson Macy." The guy on the trail had been built nothing like she'd picture a *Hudson*. His license photo showed the same general face shape as the man in the mask and the same broad shoulders, but the smile and the tie were a bit disconcerting given the menacing chill in his eyes earlier.

"Address is Colorado Springs. That's less than two hours away, so we could be dealing with a local."

"Colorado Springs is practically at Fort Carson." Where they were supposedly living. It bore looking into. "Think there are prints?"

"Doubtful. I contaminated everything in my rush to get out of there, but you can try. Best chance is on one of the cards in the wallet or a bullet in the magazine."

"Well, this phone should tell us all his secrets and can tell us if he's an assassin or an opportunist."

For their sakes, she hoped it was option two. For the resort? If a man was targeting women, then there were innocent lives to worry about. She opened the laptop and surfed to the app they used to run background checks. "Management wasn't too happy about me being attacked."

"It's not good for their image, but hey, we'll get the star treatment now."

"You're way too obsessed with the luxury side of this op."

"Two words. *Powdered. Eggs.* Those don't exist here." He flashed a quick grin then went to work on the phone.

His smile skittered along her stomach, tightening her muscles. Thalia dug her teeth into her lip. That particular reaction had happened more than once lately when she'd caught sight of him or found herself noticing he had intensely blue eyes.

She needed a break. They'd spent too much time together pretending to be a couple, so it was naturally seeping into her subconscious.

She scrubbed her hand over her mouth. "Powdered eggs? You're right." Several months earlier, they'd tracked a suspected smuggler through the mountains of West Virginia, sleeping in the elements and eating MREs because they didn't dare light a fire and risk calling attention to themselves. Powdered eggs had earned the top spot on her *never again* list. "I guess we're due a little brown sugar maple bacon."

"Which you should be eating."

Oh, how she wanted to argue that she could take care of herself, but frankly, he was right. There was no telling what the rest of the day would bring.

"Here." Phillip slid her laptop next to his and hip-checked her out of the way. "I'll run the background check. You eat and get a shower. It could take hours for Dana's program to crack the phone's password."

"I'm fine." She wasn't incapable or weak or even rattled. He didn't need to act like she was. *Immovable object, meet unstoppable force.*

When she shoved back, he widened his stance and barely wavered. "All I'm saying is I've already had a shower and you need one." He glanced at the huge dive watch he always wore, even though he hadn't strapped on scuba gear in several years. "Lunch isn't as far away as you think."

"Fine." She reached into her pocket and retrieved her busted phone. "Do you think you can transfer the data to one of the spare devices Dana sent with us?" They always traveled with backup phones, in case they needed a burner or, like today, one met its demise. She was infamous for being hard on her equipment.

Phillip held out his hand and raised an eyebrow as she dropped it into his palm. "Wow. You killed this one deader than usual, but yeah, I can handle it. Oh, and when you come out, we should probably go over the finer points of our backstory one more time."

They knew it by heart. Had been rehearsing it since the moment they'd opened the files for their undercover identities several months earlier. Had lived in separate bedrooms in the same house for months and had been in countless social situations in character.

Still, arguing would be a waste of energy. Phillip felt better after rehearsal, although he was stellar at winging it.

Thalia kicked off her running shoes and padded toward the bedroom.

"You going to leave those there? In the kitchen? Really?"

She smiled and kept walking. Phillip was a neat freak too. She shut the bedroom door on his sigh. Her shoes would be sitting neatly by the main door to the suite by the time she returned.

Goading him was childish and she had no idea why she did it. It just made ops with him a little more interesting.

By way of making amends, she hung her towel after her shower and tucked her toiletries away so he wouldn't have to do it later.

Just this once.

When she walked into the living area, Phillip was still at the island, reading her computer screen. "I ate your eggs."

They were probably cold anyway. "Did you leave the bacon?"

"Put it between two pieces of toast for you."

She took the makeshift sandwich and started

reading the screen aloud. "Hudson Macy. Address matches the ID card. Couple of speeding tickets. No misdemeanors or felonies."

Phillip swallowed a sip of orange juice. "Works as a government contractor outside of Colorado Springs. Guy has nothing in his background to suggest he'd body-slam a woman on a secluded running trail."

"He didn't body-slam me." Thalia spoke around bread and bacon, then wiped her mouth with the back of her hand. She'd have to remember her manners if she was going to make her cover story work. "Either Hudson Macy has a secret life—"

"Or someone stole his identity."

"Why would someone carry a fake ID to attack me on the trail?"

"Maybe he was headed elsewhere afterwards and needed it? He didn't expect you to take him down and pick his pocket, after all."

"True." Tapping her finger on the granite, Thalia considered their options. "Let's have Gabe do a deep search on his background and run a profile, dig into his social media, see if any of his other photos match this one." Their profiler was one of the best out there. Gabe would have something back to them quickly.

"And we'll see if someone can do a drive-by of his house. If he's there, they can let us know how badly damaged his nose is. Pretty sure I broke it."

Phillip arched an eyebrow, waiting for the rest of the story.

"With a tree branch."

"Okay, then."

Thalia crammed in the rest of her toast and bacon then wiped her hands on a linen napkin. She gently smoothed the front of her thin black sweater and pulled the hem down over pale beige linen pants. This outfit was not her typical comfy jeans and soft tee. It was a good thing these had come with the price tags already cut off. This outfit would probably pay her electric bill for a month.

"You're certain your cover's not blown?" There was Phillip again, looking to make sure the plan was still good.

"He didn't call me by name or make any indication he knew who I was. Given that we arrived late yesterday evening and we've got Dana's little machine that constantly pings for bugs in the room, I don't see how we'd have been made."

The statement held more bravado than she felt, because if she was wrong, then they were both walking into a trap.

Chapter Three

"I feel like we're at a time-share resort and I've spent half of my life listening to a sales pitch." Thalia shoved her hands into the pockets of her red ski jacket, her expression a blend of amusement and skepticism.

Phillip walked beside her toward the ski lodge on the resort property, their feet crunching in the thin layer of snow as they kept pace with one another. The weather was warmer than normal and the snowfall had been light for January, but the resort had been making snow to keep the slopes running at capacity.

Thalia wasn't wrong about the sales pitch. Their initial meeting over lunch had been nothing but praises and testimonials for Stardust, even though the couples present had already signed on the dotted line. Maybe the Turners wanted to reassure everyone they'd made the right choice, yet still… It had felt like a hard sell.

Beside him, Thalia tensed and scanned the area as though she was searching for something.

His emotions still running high after the veiled accusations of the morning, he followed her gaze but saw nothing. She was a sharp investigator, so it was possible she'd spotted something he hadn't.

Or, like him, she was rattled, though it would be the first time a fight had left her out of sorts. He glanced at her as they walked. While a casual observer would think she was a normal wife headed for an afternoon of skiing with her husband, the way her hands fidgeted in her pockets spoke of an edginess she didn't normally display. "Do you see something?"

She shook her head. "No, but I feel like a walking target. The only thing more visible than this ski jacket would be the Day-Glo orange vests deer hunters wear." She raised her hands in mock surrender. "Don't shoot. I'm a human, not a twenty-point buck."

"Twenty? That'd be a seriously hefty buck."

"You know what I mean."

"Point taken." He'd never seen her wear red before. She tended to dress in dark colors, a habit born out of their job, where *inconspicuous* was vital to their survival. At least his jacket was a dark royal blue.

He leaned away and looked her up and down as they reached the porch at the back of the lodge. Several other couples milled around, some from their group and some who were simply vacationing at the resort. "It's different but it…it looks good on you. The color, I mean." It really did. Red seemed to work with her dark hair and olive skin. The color changed her look somehow. He couldn't really explain why.

"Why, Mr. Atkins, are you calling me beautiful?" Just like that, as they drew near other people, she slipped into her role as his wife.

That meant it was time to be on his A game as well. He rested his hands at her waist and drew her closer, then planted a kiss on her forehead. The absolute naturalness of the gesture settled into his chest.

Then it rattled like a sudden earthquake. Kissing Thalia should never feel right. It should feel…

Well, it shouldn't feel like *that*.

And he'd long ago learned that relationships were to be avoided. When you loved someone, they had the potential to turn on you in ways you never saw coming.

Dangerous ways.

"Are you two still newlyweds or something?" A laughing male voice from behind shook Phillip out of the moment.

Before he turned, Thalia wrinkled her nose and batted her eyes, the very definition of *adorable*.

Thalia was never *adorable*. Rugged maybe. Tough. Unconventionally beautiful at times. But never *adorable*.

She was flirting with him. He'd watched her pull that move on men she wanted to charm into thinking she wasn't a threat, but he'd never had that look directed at him.

For the first time, he understood why the ruse worked. It almost made him want to forget about surreptitiously interviewing other couples, to sit down with her and to talk about everything and nothing for the rest of the day.

They'd done that before, as partners and friends, but right now—

A woman's laugh drifted to him. "Definitely newlyweds."

Oh, yeah. Somebody had spoken to him.

And he'd do well to remember this relationship was all pretend.

He tapped Thalia's nose with his index finger and forced himself to turn away.

A couple he'd seen at lunch stood nearby. The woman was average height and had blond hair cut to chin length, with deep brown eyes and cheeks pinked by the cold. She somehow looked both elegant and approachable.

Her husband had his arm around her waist. He was a couple of inches taller than Phillip and was rail thin, with short brown hair and a ready smile. He extended his free hand. "You must be the other military couple they invited to this thing. I'm Drew Hubbard." As he shook Phillip's hand, he glanced at Thalia. His gaze lingered.

A surge of jealousy wavered through Phillip, but then Drew turned to him with a question in his eyes.

Phillip bristled, waiting for the accusations to fly. Drew must have noticed the cut beneath her eye. Although the resort's nurse practitioner had tended it, it was still red and angry. No amount of Thalia's makeup had been able to cover it.

Drew said nothing.

The woman with him didn't seem to notice. "I'm Gabrielle. Drew belongs to me."

Thalia laughed and reached for Phillip's hand, lacing her gloved fingers with his. "Well, I guess

Phillip belongs to me, then. And I'm Thalia Atkins. Also, how did you know we were military?"

"We're not exactly newlyweds. Been married four years." Phillip ignored Drew's concern and cut off Thalia's question as he squeezed her fingers. "You've been married to me long enough to know soldiers can sniff each other out from a mile away." His cover was an intelligence analyst newly stationed at Fort Carson. He'd been living and working the part for months, but he'd still have to be careful about what he said regarding previous duty stations. If he mentioned a unit Drew Hubbard had once been attached to, the guy would know in a heartbeat Phillip wasn't who he claimed to be. "Where are you stationed?"

"We're at Schriever." Drew glanced away and then back. "Got there about a year ago. Moved in during a snowstorm."

Phillip didn't ask anything further. Schriever Air Force Base had transitioned to Schriever Space Force Base. Like most posts, there were classified operations ongoing, and when Drew didn't offer up specifics about his unit, it wasn't hard to read between the lines. There were many in Space Force who focused on satellite intel and security. Drew was likely one of them.

"We came from Florida, and I'm still getting used to the cold." Gabrielle looked at Thalia for the first time, then tilted her head in question and leaned closer. "What happened to you?" Immediately, her eyes widened and she backed away. "Sorry. I… That was rude." She winced.

"Don't worry about it. I tried to cover it up, but it didn't work. People are going to wonder." Thalia slipped into the timid posture a recent assault victim might carry. "I had an incident while I was running on the trails this morning."

"That was you?" Gabrielle slipped away from her husband to lay a hand on Thalia's arm. "The one they were talking about at lunch when they announced they were closing the hiking trails for a few days?"

"That was me. And, honestly, I really don't want to talk about it." She eased closer to Phillip as though she needed his support. "I'd rather forget it happened."

He let go of her hand and slipped his arm around her shoulders. "Do you want to go to the room?" Not that they should when they were investigating, but it sold the act.

"No. I need to be out with people, not sitting

around getting into my own head. But I'm not really up to skiing." She turned to Gabrielle. "It looks like you aren't either."

Gabrielle extended her right leg and looked down. A soft walking boot Phillip hadn't noticed encased her foot and went halfway up her calf. She lifted a wry smile. "I fractured it a couple of weeks ago. We had a formal and I was wearing heels. Stepped off our bottom step and right off the side of my shoe. It was not pretty."

"But like the *hooah* wife she is, she didn't say a word about how bad it hurt until after we got home." Drew gave Phillip a knowing look. "You know how milspouses can be sometimes."

"I do." Although she was a soldier and not a military spouse, Thalia was the same way, working through adversity without a complaint. She'd sprained her wrist once on an op and hadn't said a word until they were safely at headquarters. She compartmentalized pain, even the internal kind from being blindsided on the trail. It was tough to tell how much of her silence and hesitancy was an act and how much of it was the trauma of battle. She might be a hardened undercover agent, but she was also human.

Even Phillip was struggling a little, wrestling

with his own issues over the incident and the aftermath. He hadn't been with her to keep an eye on threats from behind.

And he'd been silently accused of inflicting pain on her. The accusations settled in his stomach like a rock, and the pain rested on a bed of buried fear. Danger could come from the most innocent of places.

What if it was coming after Thalia now? After him?

As though the memory of the morning's interrogation had conjured him out of thin air, Chase Westin stepped around the corner of the building, surveying the guests. When he spotted Phillip, he tipped his head in greeting, but the gesture held an air of arrogance and cynicism.

Phillip looked away, as though he hadn't seen the head of security. He struggled to keep his expression passive. Westin reminded him too much of the coaches and authority figures in his past who'd called him a liar and had dismissed his concerns until it was too late. That was a mental and emotional room he needed to keep locked up tightly.

Westin represented a bigger problem.

Something had raised the man's suspicions. They needed to be careful. If he started digging, he could blow an operation that had taken much too long to set into motion.

And that might make him the biggest threat of all.

Westin was eyeing Phillip, but it was tough to discern why.

Thalia had to walk a fine line since they'd garnered additional scrutiny from the resort's head of security. Too much affection would look fake. Too little would make it seem there was trouble in their paradise.

Something about the glint in Westin's gaze sent a shiver through her. Given the strength of intuition honed by years as an investigator, that wasn't a good thing.

Phillip noticed. He tightened his grip momentarily then kissed her temple. "You okay?" His warm whisper brushed her ear and sent another kind of shiver down her spine. One that shouldn't be there. It was tough to tell if he was asking investigator Thalia Renner or if he was asking wife Thalia Atkins.

She opted to believe it was the undercover persona talking. "I'll be fine. How about you two go skiing while Gabrielle and I keep each other company with something warm to drink?"

A flicker of disappointment crossed Phillip's features. "So you were serious? No skiing for you?"

"Tomorrow." She loved skiing, yet, for some reason, standing close to him under the awning of the ski lodge, the line between reality and undercover was blurring.

She was not a fan.

She needed a moment away from him. It would also give her time to dig into the Hubbards and to discern if they were targets of Stardust's suspected schemes.

"You don't have to keep me company. I'd planned to read." Gabrielle held up a book. "But I won't argue if you want to spend some girl time together. We've been at our duty station for a year, but I haven't made any close friends."

"Coffee sounds great, and so does girl time." Nothing about that line was her. Thalia would a million times rather be flying down the mountain and pushing herself to her physical limits. *Girl time* was not her thing. The only real friend she had was Phillip, though she'd gotten closer to a couple of women in the unit recently. In their line of work, people moved too often to invest time in relationships. She kept her circle small.

They had work to do, and part of that work involved ferreting out what was happening to military couples who were involved with Stardust. The job required sacrifices, and she'd be sure Phillip heard all about how she had to sit inside while he enjoyed perfect skiing weather.

Thalia gave Phillip a shove toward the ski rentals and glanced at Westin again. He'd vanished, either into the lodge or around the corner of the building.

At least he'd stopped watching...for now. His questions after Phillip had left the room earlier had been pointed. It was clear he thought Phillip had inflicted her injuries. She'd had to be careful to answer without growing defensive. Her partner protected others. He didn't victimize them. She resented the implication that Phillip was less than honorable.

The head of security had finally backed off when she'd suggested he check the lobby cameras, which should clearly show her leaving uninjured and returning with a bloody cheek.

It was likely he'd done exactly that. So, if Phillip was cleared, why was Westin still behaving as though he was guilty?

Thalia and Gabrielle said their goodbyes to the men then walked into the lodge. The warmth was nearly too much after the chilled mountain air.

Thalia unzipped her jacket and pulled her knit cap from her head, not even bothering to smooth down the static frizzies left behind. "You'd think they could tone the heat down a little."

"No kidding." Gabrielle shed her parka and pointed to a table near a window overlooking the foot of the hill. "We'll watch for them to come down."

"Grab the seats, and I'll grab the drinks. Hot chocolate or coffee?" Thalia drank so much black coffee on missions that, when the treat was available, she preferred her caffeine to come with a sugar rush. Especially after this morning.

"Latte. No syrup."

With a thumbs-up, Thalia headed for the coffee bar in the corner. She scanned the faces in the crowded building, which was essentially one large gathering space with couches, tables and chairs arranged in comfortable seating areas. The walls were traditional logs, built to look like the place was rustic and old, though it had been constructed in the early 2000s. Large windows on both sides of the long room looked out over the landscape, one side down the mountain to the main resort and the other up to the ski slopes.

None of the faces in the room resembled the photo of Hudson Macy or the build of the man who'd come at her. If her attacker was mingling with the resort guests, he hadn't made it to the ski lodge.

The line was about five people deep, so she took her place at the end of it and watched the baristas work. A younger woman with brown hair and sun-darkened skin took orders at the register. A dark-haired man was steaming milk, while a woman wearing a stocking cap stood facing the coffee machines, pulling a shot of espresso.

All of them looked as though they spent their time outdoors and only worked to pay the bills that allowed them to get back into nature. She could understand that kind of lifestyle. Had she not joined the Army, it would have been her own.

As the line advanced, she gave a longing look out the window at the ski slope. *Tomorrow.*

When she stepped up to make her order, the female barista had disappeared and the dark-haired man was working double duty with a scowl on his face. Given that the line behind her was growing, she couldn't blame the guy. After she ordered, she stepped down the bar and looked at the frowning worker. "Bad time for your coworker to step out."

"Mandatory break time." Shoving the drinks toward her, he frowned and went to work.

Okay, then.

Thalia grabbed their order and returned to the table, where Gabrielle was scrolling on her phone, her forehead creased. Tough to say if it was concern or anger. She laid the device face-down on the table as Thalia approached and looked up, forcing a smile.

"Everything okay?" Nosy was the only way to go in this job. She slid Gabrielle's drink across the table as she sat.

"It's fine. Just an email about another job I didn't get."

"I'm sorry. What do you do?" Part of the investigation was discovering why Stardust footed active-duty couples' bills for coveted re-treat spots. While the motive could be patrio-tism, Overwatch's suspicions said it likely wasn't. Getting to know Gabrielle would help her de-termine if there was an obvious target on their backs.

"I work in marketing for art museums. It's a

specialized career. There aren't a lot of openings around military bases." The statement was matter-of-fact, but her tone held an edge. "I'm from Chicago, and I worked for an art museum there. It was my dream job, but I had to go and fall for the guy my soldier brother brought home for Christmas. Drew's parents died a few years ago, so he didn't have a family to go home to. I met him on Christmas Eve and he'd won me over by New Year's."

A lot of soldiers married quickly, so that wasn't abnormal. "Army life can be hard on spouses. All the moving makes it tough to build a career." Moving between assignments every two to three years could take its toll, financially and relationally. She'd met plenty of nurses, lawyers and others who couldn't work in their chosen fields because they were following their spouses around the world, making a new home everywhere they landed. Licenses didn't always transfer between states or countries, and the constant moving made some employers gun-shy about hiring spouses.

She was grateful she only had to worry about herself.

"Drew's worth it… Most of the time." Gabrielle grinned then sobered. "When we adopt,

I can stay home and not have to worry about working until after he retires. That's the deal. I follow him while he's in, then I call the shots on where we live when he gets out."

"Sounds fair." Sipping her coffee, Thalia glanced around the room. There was still no one who piqued her interest, though the line for drinks was growing longer. "What brought you guys to Stardust?" Time to dig for answers.

"That's a hard one. I really don't want to get into it. I'm sorry." Pursing her lips, Gabrielle lifted her mug. She didn't drink, just simply stared at the contents. "I'm hoping we can adopt soon. I spoke to Serena this morning. She thinks we can find a birth mother to partner with quickly."

"Really?" Thalia let her eagerness show. The other woman would think it was because she was hoping for a fast process, as well, not because there might be something slightly off about Serena making a promise to a couple who had just signed up for their services. The back of her neck tingled like it always did when information was near. "What makes her think—" Her phone hummed in her pocket, the three repeated buzzes indicating a call from her team leader, Captain Rachel Slater. Horrible timing, but she dare not ignore it.

With a frown, she withdrew the phone and held it up. "I'm sorry. Real estate agent." She hated to leave at a time like this, yet she had no choice. Rachel would only call if she had news. Routine messages came through text. "I'll be right back."

Gabrielle nodded and flipped her phone over, pressing the screen to light it up. A dark photo appeared, with some sort of white shadow on it, but the angle wasn't right for Thalia to discern what it was.

She moved away from the table, holding her phone to her ear. "Hang on. It's crowded in here." When Rachel didn't answer, she hustled for the door and stepped out, rounding the corner of the building away from the slopes. It was quieter there, and she didn't want to chance being overheard.

"Okay." She leaned against the building, the only sound the low hum of a nearby heating unit. "What's up?"

"I have intel on your attacker. Can you grab Phillip and head to your suite? I want you together in a secure location, so we aren't overheard."

"It'll take me a second. He's skiing."

Rachel chuckled. "And you're not?"

"He won the coin toss."

"And you're going to make him pay."

"You know me so well." Rachel was one of the few Thalia could relate to with ease. "Give me a few minutes, and I'll catch him at the end of his run."

"Yell when you're ready." Rachel killed the call.

Thalia pocketed her phone. She'd tell Gabrielle there was a call she and Phillip needed to take together. Their cover story said they were living on post but trying to purchase a house on the civilian market, so news from their Realtor would do the trick.

Something crunched beside the heating unit and Thalia saw a shadow before a force slammed against her, shoving her body chest-first against the log wall.

The air left her lungs. She dropped to one knee and tried to rise, but a kick to her lower back thrust her onto her face in the snow.

Voices came near around the corner. There was a muffled curse above her before footsteps bolted away.

Thalia struggled to her feet and whirled. Whoever had blindsided her was long gone.

She sagged against the building, trying to catch her breath.

The only thing her attacker had left behind was the truth...

What had happened on the trail was planned.

And Thalia was the one wearing the target.

Chapter Four

"I hope Rachel's got good intel. Pulling me off of the slopes before my second run in was cruel." Phillip tossed the quip out there and waited for Thalia to catch it.

She let it fall. If it had been a ball, it would have thudded to the plush hallway carpet.

Something was wrong. When Thalia had told him they'd had a call from their Realtor, their code for a message from their team leader, her demeanor had been off. It was as though she had turned in on herself, even though she stood tall.

She'd also developed a limp he hadn't noticed before.

Now there wasn't a single sarcastic remark about him skiing while she worked?

Hmm.

Phillip stepped ahead of Thalia and opened the door to their suite. He ushered her inside, resting his hand on her lower back as she passed.

She inhaled sharply with a gasp of pain.

Enough was enough. He needed the whole story as soon as he'd closed the door and they knew no one was listening. Otherwise, his mind would start spinning tall tales born out of past paranoia. He recognized the tendency, but he couldn't always stem the tide of intrusive thoughts.

While he secured the door, Thalia went to the counter and emptied her pockets. She bent as if to take her pistol from its ankle holster then straightened and left it in place.

That was a sure sign she was on edge. "Thal, what's going on?" What had Rachel told her? Was the op in trouble?

"Nothing." She faced him, her back straight as though her spine had been replaced with one of his skis. "We have a video call. Rachel has intel she wants both of us to hear."

A narrow line of pain had etched between her eyebrows since he'd left her to board the chairlift. "You're not telling the truth." It grated every nerve ending in his body to say that. Thalia had never lied to him. If she was being dishonest now…

Their partnership required trust. It kept them

alive when the stakes were high. Without that, he could lose his life.

He could lose her…and so much more.

Thalia's glare was red-hot. She nearly spoke, but then she stalked into the bedroom, returning with a laptop from the locked security bag their equipment was stored in. Resting it on the counter, she addressed the device instead of him. "Rachel's waiting, then we need to get out there. There's a story when it comes to the Hubbards. Stardust has essentially told them they can fast-track an adoption. That sounds wrong to me. And by her own admission, Gabrielle's not telling me everything."

"That makes two people keeping secrets." Phillip snapped the words as he crossed the room to stand behind her. He rested his hands on her shoulders. Touching her like this was something he'd never done outside of his undercover persona. "Talk to me." The words were raw, the kind of plea he rarely made, but something was shifting, inching her away from him.

They were too close for her to keep things from him. She was his closest friend. He relied on her to be the rock in their partnership.

He expected her to pull away from his touch.

Instead, she sagged slightly, leaning into him, her back resting against his chest. It was as though she needed his support.

Thalia was strong, yet the need to comfort and protect her raced through him. The past few days, the urge to pull her into the circle of his arms and to shield her had been growing. Was it real? Or was it because that's what spouses did for one another?

His brain was as scrambled as his breakfast eggs, unable to separate fact from fiction.

As though she read his mind, Thalia straightened. "I'm dealing with the adrenaline crash from this morning." She opened the laptop, inserted her CAC card into the chip reader and punched in her password.

Phillip let his hands fall to his thighs. Thalia was lying. He knew her too well to believe otherwise. Stressed Thalia was all snark and attitude, not coldness and evasion.

He nearly reached around her to shut the computer so they could have this confrontation head-on, but Rachel answered before he could.

"You two look like somebody replaced your coffee with decaf." On the screen, Captain Rachel Slater cocked one eyebrow and studied them across the miles. Dark-haired and fit, Rachel had been their team leader for several years. They'd all grown particularly close after working together to protect Captain Marshall Slater and his young daughter from a stalker.

Rachel had bonded with Marshall over the pain in their pasts, and the two had married the year prior.

Having adopted Marshall's daughter, Emma, Rachel was particularly invested in the Stardust op. So was Thalia, who had been adopted from overseas as a toddler.

Thalia smiled. "No decaf here. The coffee is top-notch. So is the food. We could get used to this."

It was an act. Thalia was never what anyone would call *chipper*.

When Rachel clearly picked up on the vibe, Phillip stepped next to Thalia to deflect. Whatever was happening, it was inside him and between the two of them. "Three words, Rach." Phillip held up three fingers and counted off. *"Maple. Crusted. Bacon."*

"One word. *Jealous*." Rachel glanced behind her then lowered her voice. "I'm working from home because snow closed school, but Marshall had to go to post. My breakfast was frozen French toast sticks dipped in honey because we're out of syrup."

This time, Phillip's smile was genuine. Rachel enjoyed being a wife and mother, but she'd been vocal that grocery shopping was Marshall's thing, not hers. Clearly, someone had missed a trip.

Thalia chuckled. "Never thought I'd see you go domestic, *ma'am*." Their team never used formal titles. Thalia only did it when she wanted to poke under someone's skin.

This was the partner he knew. Maybe she'd been telling the truth when she'd said the morning's attack had rattled her cage.

Though even that would be out of character.

"Down to business." From the laptop, Rachel's tone drew him into the reason for their call. He should focus on the investigation, not on the weird undercurrent in the room. "I have intel on the driver's license you took off your attacker." She clicked something and half of the screen changed.

A photo cropped from a government-issued ID popped up. The man had a slim face and dark hair in need of a trim. His smile was genuine and his expression was open.

Thalia glanced at Phillip. "That's not the guy from the trail or from the driver's license."

"So we're dealing with a case of stolen identity."

"Yep." Rachel closed the photo. "Dana's working on the identity of the guy in your license photo, but it will take time."

Television made it seem like facial recognition was faster than microwaving popcorn. In reality, it was a complicated process regulated by privacy laws and hampered by scattered databases. A positive ID could take days, if they ever got one.

"What do we know about the real Hudson Macy?" Thalia stepped to the left so Phillip could get closer to the screen.

"That's where the fun begins. The real Mr. Macy works for ACE Icon. They're a high-tech security firm that installs and maintains alarm systems for government buildings, including some on Fort Carson."

This was bad. "It's possible someone stole Macy's identity in order to access those buildings."

"It's also possible he's just a guy who had his identity 'jacked, though we haven't found anything unusual in his finances so far." Given the tension that threaded through Rachel's voice, there was more news coming.

Thalia heard it too. "What else?"

"Nine months ago, Hudson and his wife, Camryn, attended a Stardust retreat at the resort. Six months ago, they adopted a little boy."

"Whoa." Phillip hadn't seen that one coming. "Do we think the identity theft is tied to the agency? The resort? Or is it an unhappy accident?"

"Given I was attacked on the property by a guy carrying the identity of a former Stardust guest?" Thalia's snark had returned. "I don't believe in coincidence."

"Mama Rachel!" A little girl's voice drifted through the speakers. "I dropped Mr. Whiskers in the toilet!"

Phillip snorted as Rachel jumped up. She leaned close to the camera. "Gotta go. I have Dana searching for other guests who might have had their identities stolen. I'll get back to you. There's no evidence your cover is compromised, but be careful."

When the screen went dark, Thalia faced Phillip. The mask she'd been wearing during the call stayed firmly in place.

She made no sarcastic comments about motherhood or stuffed animals in toilets.

Yep. She was hiding something. "Thalia, I need you to tell—"

"I have a headache." Without looking at him, she stalked into the bedroom and shut the door.

Lies. All of it. He strode to the bedroom door and reached for the handle, then stopped.

Although he was her friend and her partner, he wasn't truly her husband. There were lines between them that he couldn't cross and one of them was demanding to know her innermost thoughts. No matter how much he wanted to, it wasn't his place.

But if she wasn't honest with him, how could he protect her?

Did she even need his protection?

He'd missed the signs once and it had made him the brunt of accusations that were untrue. The same kinds of accusations that had been silently lobbed at him today.

No one had believed his innocence until it was too late. He'd nearly lost his family.

The air thickened, sticking like glue in his lungs.

His breaths came faster. His heart pounded. He needed air.

He headed for the French doors, twisted the lock and pushed out onto the patio, which overlooked a gentle slope down to a stand of trees that ringed a pond.

It didn't matter the trail to the pond was closed in the wake of Thalia's attack, he had to get away from the memories.

He jogged down the hill and along the path through the trees until he reached the edge of the thinly iced pond. He bent double, hands on his knees, heaving air. *God, why? We were past this pain. This fear.*

He hadn't had a panic attack in over a decade. Had fought physical battles and literally faced death without emotions choking him.

Yet here was his past rearing—

Something slammed into the back of his legs.

His knees crashed to the ice, cracking through. He sank into water to his thighs, deeper than he would have expected. Thrown off balance, he struggled to stand, but his hands landed on the slick ice and slid forward, breaking through. He couldn't pull his legs free.

A blow to his upper back shoved him farther onto thin ice. His shoulder broke through, plunging his head under water. His forehead hit bottom.

Something heavy—someone heavy—threw their full weight on top of him, holding him under.

He struggled, the frigid water numbing his cheeks and stinging his eyes. His lungs burned, already aching from the earlier panic. The harder he fought, the more he wanted to inhale, but there was no air. No light. No nothing.

All of the advantage went to his opponent. He had no leverage. No way to push himself up, not with the full weight of a human being pinning him against the mucky bottom of the pond.

The person shifted and hauled him to the surface.

Phillip gasped in air.

A muffled voice broke through the roar in his ears. "She doesn't get to have you. It's not fair."

Before he could react, he was plunged beneath the water again, buried in icy pain and darkness.

Thalia flinched when the door in the living room slammed shut. She balled her fists, staring at the log wall.

There was nowhere for the frustration to go. She couldn't even slip on her running shoes and force the pressure out through a blistering run up the mountain. There was a small gym in the building, but hefting weights had never provided the same release as exercise in the outdoors.

Not coming clean with Phillip about the second attack gnawed at her. She never kept anything from her partner. Doing so while on a mission could be dangerous.

But she was angry at herself. Ashamed, even. It wasn't like her to be caught by surprise twice. The pressure inside her needed a way out.

Telling Phillip might open a valve.

Telling him might also drive him to pull the plug on this op. If Serena Turner and her husband were using Stardust to line their pockets at the expense of hopeful parents and children, then they needed to be stopped. Her own past demanded it.

She'd been the unwanted. The lost. Just a toddler when she'd been adopted from an orphanage in Eastern Europe.

Other children deserved the same chance to be found.

Uncurling her fingers, she shook the tension from her hands and paced to the bedroom door. She'd never felt so emotionally raw. It was like someone had scraped her skin off and the air burned the open wound. Maybe it was because the case hit too close to home. Maybe it was because she'd been blindsided twice. Maybe it was because she had to pretend she was weak.

The act was getting under her skin. When she went undercover, she typically played the role of someone who made things happen, the cocky newcomer who brought something valuable to the table. Never was she the one who had to depend on others to protect her.

She'd been scrapping since birth, and behaving differently made her feel as though she no longer recognized herself in the mirror.

But there was something more disconcerting. Something she didn't want to acknowledge.

She'd never found comfort in another person before. Had never wanted to have her hand held or to nestle into a man's arms. Today, when she'd leaned against Phillip's chest, she'd wanted to stay there forever. She'd felt safe.

That should never be. She didn't need someone else to protect her. She could take care of herself.

Why now? Why was Phillip's touch suddenly…different? And why did she care he was clearly upset with her? They'd argued a thousand times in the past. It was part of their dynamic.

Never before had she wanted to follow him

when he walked out. She'd always known he'd return and they'd pick up right where the argument had blown up. He was her partner. Her constant.

So why did his storming out and slamming the door make her feel empty...and scared?

Scared was a word she'd excised from her vocabulary decades earlier.

Now was not the time to allow it in again.

She'd face this directly. With a deep breath, she turned the knob and stepped into the living room. Phillip was likely sitting on the patio, letting the winter air cool his anger.

But when she stepped outside, the chaises were empty. A single set of footprints marred the dusting of snow, headed in the direction of a wooded trail at the foot of the hill. Overhead, the blue sky was dotted with increasing clouds, indicating a change in the weather.

Thalia tapped her fingernail against her thigh. Follow him? Or wait for him to return in a calmer state of mind?

The need to defeat her fears urged her forward. No matter the consequences, she needed to tell him the truth and clear the air. Maybe confessing would allow her emotions to stop this tug-of-war.

Thalia shivered against the cold, hesitating before ultimately deciding not to go inside for her jacket. Following Phillip's footsteps down the hill, she considered praying, but that had never gotten her anywhere. Phillip talked often about God. So did Rachel and her new husband, Marshall.

On their last mission with temporary team leader Hannah Austin, Thalia had practically been preached a sermon more than once.

She'd kept her rebuttals to herself. If God cared what Thalia had to say, He wouldn't have let her be abandoned as a toddler. At the very least, He'd have let her know where she'd come from, what her history was. He hadn't taken care of little Thalia, so why in the world would He care about the adult who'd been trained to take care of herself and others?

She was ten feet into the woods when a crash stopped her. She tilted her head, listening. It sounded like a splash farther up the trail. From their review of the resort's property maps, she knew there was a pond ahead. It was deep, dug when the resort was built and they'd needed fill dirt for landscaping. The water had to be partially frozen, but...

Phillip was too smart to walk across thin ice, wasn't he?

That didn't sound like someone drowning. It sounded like a fight.

For the second time in one day, she took off running down a trail, her heart pounding with adrenaline.

When she reached a break in the trees, she stopped so fast that momentum nearly pitched her body forward. A person wearing bulky ski pants and a thick jacket stood in knee-deep water, holding someone's head under the broken ice.

Phillip's blue coat was submerged as he struggled against the weight of his assailant.

Thalia nearly screamed she was a federal agent. Just in time, she remembered her cover. "Hey!"

Phillip's aggressor straightened.

Thalia navigated the slope as quickly as she dared, trying to keep her eyes on Phillip and the steep trail at the same time. She briefly lost sight of the pond as she rounded a stand of trees at the base of the hill.

By the time she reached the water's edge, Phillip's attacker was gone.

Phillip struggled to stand in the frigid water.

When Thalia raced to the edge, he held up a hand. "Don't." He was panting for air and shivering in water up to his knees, and he was soaked from head to toe. His face was white. His lips were pale and nearly blue from oxygen deprivation and cold. "No need…for both…of us…to…freeze…to death." Chattering teeth bit the words into chunks.

"You need to get out of there." He was no longer submerged, but he wasn't out of danger. They had to get up the hill and into the suite so he could warm up before the consequences of his polar plunge grew catastrophic.

"I know." He fired off the words and made his way out of the water. "We both…had… same training."

If he was snapping at her, he might be okay. She almost smiled. "You going to make it up the hill?" It wasn't incredibly steep, but the way he was shivering, the slope might as well be Mount Everest.

"Try…and stop me."

He made his way out of the water and brushed away the hand she offered, even though he was shaking violently. His forward motion never stopped as he headed around the trees and started upward on the trail.

Pride and anger would keep him moving, but Thalia stayed close behind, ready to offer a hand if needed.

When they reached the top of the hill, he stopped and eyed the resort in front of them. "Don't need any witnesses."

He was right. If anyone spotted Phillip coming off a closed trail in his current condition, it would only invite more scrutiny.

She felt like she once had at summer camp when she'd acted out one too many times. *One more incident and we're sending you home.*

They hurried across the open lawn to their door and slipped inside.

Thalia headed for the kitchen, pausing only to flip the wall switch to activate the gas logs. "Get into dry clothes. I'll make coffee."

At the bedroom door, Phillip turned. "You should have chased down…" He shook his head and his eyes clouded. He went into the room and shut the door.

The admonition burned. Maybe she should have gone after the bad guy, but the person had vanished by the time she'd reached Phillip. His safety had been her first priority.

She'd deal with who was behind the attacks

later, after she knew Phillip hadn't suffered any serious injury.

By the time he returned, wearing a blue Army sweatshirt, jeans and thick socks, the coffee was ready and the room felt like an oven. He took the mug from her and sat on the end of the coffee table closest to the fire. "Thanks."

The word sounded as flat and cold as the ice on the pond. He scrubbed the top of his damp hair with one hand, mussing it even more, then stared at the gas-fueled flames, brooding.

Phillip never *brooded*. He was the laughing one. The one who knew how to be serious without absorbing the pain and pressure. The one who diffused her sarcasm.

Thalia's earlier fear blazed hotter than the flames. She sat on the hearth to the left of the fire, trying to catch Phillip's eye. "Are you really okay?" Given how well they were trained, being blindsided could rattle a person.

She should know.

He sipped the coffee, his blue eyes icy as he stared at her over the rim of the mug. It was a long sip, almost as though he was weighing his words. When he lowered the mug, he lifted an eyebrow. "Do you expect me to answer? Like you answered me when I asked you earlier?"

Thalia winced against the sting. The words that almost burst out of her would have done nothing but reignite the argument that had started this whole mess. The argument she'd already admitted he was right about.

She kept her gaze on his, knowing she needed to speak the truth without shrinking. "Someone came at me while you were skiing." She laid out a quick version of the attack.

Phillip stood, looking down at her. "And you didn't tell me?"

Rising to balance the power difference, Thalia looked up into his eyes. "I'm telling you now."

Reaching around her, he set the mug on the mantel above the fireplace, the move nearly pressing her face into his shoulder. When he stepped back, he rested his hands on her biceps. "Are you hurt?"

He was so close. His hands were cold through her shirt, but he was definitely warming up. She could feel the heat of his chest. Again, she wanted to close the gap and—

And what, exactly? There was no way she'd allow her imagination to finish that line of thinking.

She stepped to the side, grabbed his mug and

held it out to him. "Are *you*? Seems you went through a lot worse than I did."

It was a long moment before he took the drink. With a lingering look, he sat on the coffee table. "I'll be fine, but we need to determine why this is happening."

They needed to do it soon too. Because now that Phillip had been attacked, it was clear both of them were in the crosshairs of a killer.

Chapter Five

It was too dark.

Something closed in on him. Enveloped him. Breathed hot down his neck.

He couldn't run. Couldn't escape. His muscles were frozen. Darkness and heat smothered him.

He tried to fight. Was too weak. Couldn't save himself.

"Phillip?" His name came from far away. Drawing him. Calming him. Carrying peace. If he could just reach—

A tap on his shoulder jerked him upright so fast he nearly cracked heads with Thalia.

She sat back just in time.

It was *her* voice that had pulled him out of the fear. *Her* voice that spoke of peace.

He didn't want to consider what that might mean.

Gradually, the room shifted into focus. Thalia sat on the coffee table beside the couch, where he'd fallen asleep. Her forehead was creased with concern. "I think you were having a nightmare."

"Maybe?" The emotions of the dream clung to him, yet he couldn't recall any clear images.

It wasn't hard to guess what chased him though. The evidence said his past had somehow found him. This was more than he could handle alone.

She doesn't get to have you. It's not fair. Had he put Thalia in danger? Was this all his fault? But…how? The person who had threatened him over a decade ago was no longer in his life. None of this made sense.

"Want to talk about it?" Thalia watched him, probably cataloging his facial expressions and trying to discern his thoughts.

He did…and he didn't. For their entire partnership, he'd kept that horrible season locked away. He wasn't going to release it into the open now. Giving it air gave it life. "It's ridiculously hot in here. If I was having nightmares, it's because I felt like I was being suffocated."

"You're telling me." Thalia stood and flipped the switch to shut off the gas logs. "I was in the bedroom reading background checks and forgot to shut the fireplace off after you fell asleep. You started moving around, so I thought I'd check on you." She went to the kitchen and shoved her phone into her pocket. "It's almost dinnertime."

Phillip dragged his hands down his cheeks, grateful she'd given him a minute to compose himself.

There would be no peace until he had facts. He needed to know the past hadn't returned to haunt him or to harm her. "What did you see when you came down the hill to the pond? Who was there?" He prayed the answer would silence the *She doesn't get to have you* echoing in his head.

Words very similar to those had appeared on a note in his girlfriend's locker in high school. *You shouldn't have gone out with him. He's mine.*

Phillip shuddered, still able to see the letters scrawled on a yellow sticky note. "Was it a man or a woman?" He steeled himself against the answer.

When Thalia turned, her gaze was shadowed. "I couldn't tell. They were wearing bulky clothing. By the time I got close, they were gone." She looked at her watch. "Look, we need to go to dinner. We can't risk drawing more attention to ourselves by hiding in our suite."

As much as he wanted to stay right where he was, she was right. They had a job to do. From experience, he knew keeping busy would prevent the memories from igniting nightmares he hadn't had since high school.

He had to set aside the wild, paranoid idea that a would-be killer from his past had inexplicably reappeared. It was impossible.

Wasn't it?

Phillip stood and tilted his head to stretch his neck, trying to convince his body a headache wasn't in the works. Fear didn't deserve to rule the day. The motion directed his gaze toward Thalia, and he realized for the first time she'd changed into fancier clothes.

A black one-piece pantsuit gathered like a halter top around her neck and then fell in loose folds to her waist. The legs were wider at the ankles, and she wore heels so high she could probably look him in the eye despite the fact he was three inches taller. Her hair tumbled in slight waves to her bare shoulders, and she wore smoky eye makeup.

He'd seen her dressed up before, but he was used to Thalia on missions, when she was in practical clothing.

Tonight, she was...

Wow.

Everything about the look made him forget

about the past. His stomach swirled in a way that had nothing to do with fear.

This was scarier.

Clearly, this day had made his head wonky.

Yes, Thalia was beautiful. Any man could see that.

No, that didn't mean he suddenly felt...*things* for her.

In fact, she was safer if he didn't.

Phillip stalked to the bedroom to change into something appropriate for dinner. Most of the meals would be casual, but this first night was to be a bit dressier.

He put on a dark gray suit, made quick work of his hair, then escorted Thalia into the hall, slipping into the role of loving husband while trying not to let his overwrought emotions take the wheel.

Halfway to the dining room, he caught her looking at him. Her expression mirrored what he imagined his had looked like when he'd felt that odd pull toward her earlier.

Needing to force some comedy into a moment he didn't understand, Phillip stopped walking. "You like what you see?" He held both arms out slightly and walked ahead of her like a model on the runway, arms and hips swinging. When he was a few feet away, he pivoted, tipped his head and winked at her, then sashayed back. "I clean up good, right?"

Lips pressed together and eyes turned to the ceiling, Thalia waited a beat before answering. She cleared her throat. "Yeah. Real good."

It sounded like she choked on her own laughter.

Mission accomplished.

Grabbing his wrist, she dragged him up the hall. "Let's go before I'm trampled by a mob of your adoring fans."

As they neared the dining room, more guests joined them. He reached for Thalia's hand and laced his fingers through hers, playing the part, praying *the part* didn't get her killed.

When she tightened her grip, it felt as though the tender possessiveness between them was natural. She was somehow his and he was somehow hers.

Rattled by the lightning bolt that struck him, he nearly dropped her hand.

But he couldn't. They were entering the dining room and their A game had to be in full play.

He scanned the room, praying he wouldn't see a familiar face watching Thalia with murder in her eyes.

Leaning closer, Thalia slipped her hand from his and pointed to a table in the corner. "There's Gabrielle. She left me with some unanswered questions earlier." Her whisper was warm against his ear, sending another bolt through him.

Was he being secretly electrocuted? Because this was weird.

It took a second to find his voice. "See if we can sit with them." Why did the words wobble? Taking a deep breath, he nodded toward the bar. While he didn't want her out of reach, he could keep an eye on her from there. "Cherry Cokes all around?" Phillip hadn't touched alcohol since high school, when he'd caught himself swamping himself to drown the fear. Thalia had never started, claiming she didn't like to have her thoughts and emotions compromised.

She never turned down a fountain Coke loaded with maraschino cherries and syrup.

Wrinkling her nose in the cutest of smiles, she dropped a kiss on his cheek and swept across the room to talk to Gabrielle. There was a grace about the character she was playing. It was a stark contrast given she'd been undercover as a fighter only a couple of months prior.

He both liked and disliked this softer side of her personality. Seeing this side of her was—

"You're newlyweds, aren't you?" A female voice jerked his gaze from where Thalia was crossing the room.

When had he walked to the bar?

He closed the remaining few feet to the counter and focused on the woman behind it, forcing himself into his role.

She watched him with a raised eyebrow and a tilted lip. She was probably in her early thirties, though the way she'd done her makeup and hair made her appear younger. Her straight auburn hair was cut bluntly at chin length, easy to care for on the go. Based on that and the winter tan, he'd guess she was an athlete or the outdoorsy type.

Phillip offered what he hoped was a friendly smile. "Everyone keeps asking that." He looked toward Thalia, but from this end of the bar, a large decorative pillar blocked his view.

"Well, I'm not sure how you made it over here without tripping over something, because you never took your eyes off her." The woman turned and reached for a glass. "What can I get you?"

Phillip ordered two Cokes—one with extra cherries—and leaned against the bar, wishing he could get a glimpse of Thalia. With all that had happened, he didn't like having her out of his sight.

"Yeah, y'all are still in the honeymoon period."

Phillip turned to the woman and read her name tag. "Claire, you're very observant." Maybe too observant.

"I was a paramedic in Denver for a decade." She slid the sodas to him. "I learned a lot about human nature."

"I'm sure. What made you walk away?" If Claire had worked here long, she likely knew quite a bit about Stardust.

"Saw more than I wanted to." Claire fiddled with a napkin as a shadow crossed her features. When she looked up, her expression lightened. "Remember that Patrick Swayze and Keanu Reeves movie where the guys robbed banks to fund their surfing?"

"Yeah?" Who didn't? It was a '90s action-movie classic.

"I decided I'd rather ski than work a day job, so I found a way to make the money that lets me."

"Not robbing banks though." He couldn't resist the joke, though it wasn't entirely funny. Anyone was capable of heinous crimes.

"No robbing banks."

"So you work here to fund your outdoor addiction?" The service staff tended to know a lot of behind-the-scenes information. He could draw intel about the Turners and Stardust out of her.

"I work the coffee bar at the ski lodge during the day and here at night. Pay's not great, but the job comes with a room and use of the lodge's amenities."

"And these adoption groups?"

"I figured you were with them." Claire swiped a spot on the bar. "Everyone's nice. They tip well." She smiled. "The Turners leave extra at the end of the week for us. They helped one of our cleaners pay for surgery after she broke her leg. They go way back with the resort owners, and they're all nice people."

Interesting. It didn't sound like the behavior of criminals, though it could be a cover.

Claire tipped her head in the direction Thalia had disappeared. "How did you meet your wife?"

The line at the bar was growing, and he needed to get eyes on Thalia. He shoved some bills into the tip jar and grabbed the sodas. "Long story."

"But an interesting one, I'm sure." Claire nodded toward the door. "You've got someone watching you too."

His heart stopped. He hadn't been imagining things. After all this time, she'd found him.

Slowly, he turned, prepared to see the face he could never forget, no matter how hard he tried.

Instead, he spotted Chase Westin standing by the entrance.

When Phillip met his gaze, the head of security turned and walked out the door.

Thalia surveyed the formal dining room as she made her way to Gabrielle's table. The large pillars supporting the ceiling were heavy, dark wood. The carpet was a deep green, and the overall vibe was more old-school men's smoking parlor than ski resort.

The rich colors and deep textures were comforting, although the dim lighting made it hard to see into the shadows at the corners of the room. Those dark places kept her guard up as she waved to Gabrielle, who motioned to two empty seats to her right.

But the prickles at the back of her neck were about more than dark corners. She could feel someone watching her.

Not just someone… Phillip. She didn't have to turn around to be certain. Something in her just knew.

Was the swirl in her stomach a good thing or a very, very bad thing?

In the hall earlier, when he'd pulled that supermodel stunt, she'd had to turn her eyes to the ceiling to keep from staring at him. He cut a dashing figure in his suit. It wasn't a look she saw on him often, and it worked too well. He'd stolen her voice, though he probably assumed she'd choked on laughter and not on bewildering attraction.

It was all disconcerting. Every bit of it.

There wasn't time to consider the strange sensation. In a few seconds, she'd reach Gabrielle and she needed to be wearing her Thalia Atkins face.

Another couple sat on the other side of the large round table, and there was one empty seat to Gabrielle's left. Probably, like Phillip, Drew was securing drinks while they waited for dinner.

"Mrs. Atkins?" At the sound of her "married" name, Thalia stopped and turned.

Serena Turner approached. With her dark hair hanging loosely to her shoulders and an elegant burgundy pantsuit tailored to her slim frame, the founder of Stardust Adoptions looked more like a model walking the runway than a woman who aided couples in building families. Serena rested a hand on Thalia's wrist. "I wanted to see how you're doing after the events of this morning."

Thalia wanted to launch into a thousand questions, starting with how the agency could promise Drew and Gabrielle Hubbard a quick adoption, but she bit her tongue. She was here to play wife and victim, not investigator.

It was the toughest role she'd ever played.

Closing her eyes, she swallowed her questions. "I'm fine. Thank you for asking."

"Glad to hear it." Serena withdrew her hand and tipped her head toward the table where Gabrielle chatted with the other couple. "I see you've made some friends. I hope that helped to ease your anxiety."

It was so hard not to ask how Serena knew she'd been chatting with Gabrielle. Who reported to Stardust's owners and why? Thalia exhaled slowly through pursed lips. "We have. The Hubbards are nice people. Our husbands are both in the military."

Serena smiled. "I understand that can forge a quick bond. I'm glad you ran into each other already." She glanced around the room then paused and raised her hand in greeting to someone behind Thalia. "I have to go, but we'll talk soon. I'm looking forward to hearing how your meeting with our counselors goes on Wednesday." With a quick pat to Thalia's biceps, Serena headed for a table where she slipped her arm around her husband's waist and accepted an introduction to another couple. She'd be at home schmoozing at a high-end fundraiser.

Something piqued Thalia's suspicions. Serena Turner was almost too kind, and unlike her promise to the Hubbards, she'd made no mention of a quick adoption to Thalia.

Maybe the Turners were suspicious of Phillip and of her. They could simply be watching, leery of any whiff of trouble in their marriage.

Thalia was still mulling when she slid into the seat next to Gabrielle, who was studying a card cut from thick, creamy paper.

Gabrielle held the page up as soon as Thalia was settled. "Dinner is classy tonight."

Taking the menu, Thalia skimmed it. Yeah, they were a long way from powdered eggs. Between the duck and a French dish she couldn't pronounce, the food choices promised to be rich. She passed the page to Gabrielle. "What does a girl have to do to get a burger and fries?"

"Break out after curfew and sneak into town? This place makes me feel like I'm at summer camp." Gabrielle grinned and laid the card aside. "Where's your husband?"

"Drinks." Thalia looked over her shoulder, but her view of Phillip was blocked by a pillar. She turned to the table, where the other couple were now talking to someone behind them.

Gabrielle followed her gaze and wrinkled her nose as if to say the pair wasn't overly friendly. "Drew's running late. He skied until the last second, then took forever to decide what to wear. He sent me ahead to see if I could find you two and a table. He liked hanging out with Phillip." She smiled. "Did your Realtor have good news?"

The practiced answer rolled off of Thalia's tongue. "She thought she did, but we're picky, especially when it comes to outdoor space. Right now, we live on post, and that tiny yard isn't enough for future kids to run around in, although we aren't far from one of the neighborhood parks." Playgrounds dotted the housing areas on Fort Carson, giving children places to run and parents opportunities to bond. She and Phillip had lived in a two-bedroom duplex for nearly three months, cementing their cover story as newcomers to the post.

"Yeah. That's why we bought off post, even though the market was running high at the time. We needed more space for our..." Gabrielle trailed off, pulling her phone closer and running her finger along the edge of its case.

The sadness radiating from the gesture washed a wave of melancholy over Thalia. "Is something wrong?" Normally, she'd be asking as an investigator. Not this time. This felt personal.

Offering a small smile, Gabrielle nodded and withdrew her phone from the table, holding it in her lap. "Most days."

As much as Gabrielle Hubbard smiled and chatted, sadness had hovered around the other woman all day. If Thalia could be her real self, she'd make a snarky comment about the dangers of keeping secrets. Instead, she swallowed her natural bent toward sarcasm and leaned closer to Gabrielle. "Seriously. I know you just met me, but is there something you want to talk about?" Although she hadn't picked up on any weird vibes, maybe the Hubbards were dealing with marital issues.

"This week is...hard." Gabrielle flicked her

phone and the screen lit up. The black-and-white image that had caught Thalia's attention earlier appeared.

This time she could clearly see it was an ultrasound. The image was grainy, but the photo showed the tiniest of babies, just beginning to develop features.

For the first time in years, Thalia knew what it felt like to have her heart sink. Given Gabrielle's demeanor, the tragedy in her life was obvious. "Gabrielle, I'm so sorry." While Thalia had never lost a child, her adoptive parents had survived several miscarriages and a stillbirth. They'd approached those anniversaries both with sadness and with love for their children, celebrating their lives while grieving their losses.

Running her thumb along the screen, Gabrielle stared at the image. "I've been pregnant three times. This is the only child I have an ultrasound of. The other two were still precious little peanuts. Dakota Jordan and Peyton Hudson."

"I love those names." It was clear the Hubbards had loved their children, even before they'd known what gender they would be. Thalia lightly touched the edge of the phone. "And who is this?"

"Alexandra Elizabeth." Tapping the side button to darken the screen, Gabrielle slid the phone onto the table and lifted her head to look at Thalia. Tears shone in her eyes, though none fell. "Thank you."

"For?"

"For asking her name. For acknowledging she was a tiny little person whose life had meaning. For understanding she was—is—very much my daughter."

Thalia's chin jerked up before she could stop it. "Of course she is. They're all your children." She'd been raised knowing she had siblings who hadn't survived. Had, at times, been jealous of them. They'd have known where they'd come from, while her history started at her adoption.

Gabrielle sniffed. "You'd be surprised how many people don't talk about them. Even my own family can't believe we named the babies and celebrate them each year."

"I can't imagine…" Thalia had witnessed her mother's pain and had thought often about her birth parents in Moldova, wondering who they were and why they'd let her go, why they hadn't wanted her.

Beside her sat a mother who'd lost three children she'd have given anything to raise. Who now, like Thalia's adoptive parents, longed to parent a child whose biological parents were either unwilling or unable to care for them.

Some things didn't make sense.

Thalia nearly spilled her mother's story, but she stopped herself. The key to undercover work was to share as little of her real self as possible, even in a situation like this one.

No matter how much it hurt to hold her tongue.

Gabrielle didn't notice her inner struggle. "Losing our children was the hardest thing Drew and I ever endured. Every day there's some measure of grief. Some days it wrecks me. Others, it's simply a stillness. Right now, being so close to adoption and being around so many other hopeful parents, it's all a little closer to the surface, I guess."

Thalia wanted to say something to take away the ripples of pain hovering in the words, but there was nothing. For one of the first times in her life, she was speechless.

"You know…" Gabrielle sighed and looked around the room as though she was searching for something, then she met Thalia's gaze. Where the tears had been, there was now only fierce love. "My children may never have breathed the air of this earth, but they lived. They existed. They changed the world."

Thalia tilted her head, intrigued.

"I know it's a little confusing if you aren't sitting in my chair." Gabrielle actually smiled. "They changed the world because they changed me. They changed Drew. We're different than we would have been had they not existed. They made us better people. A better couple. I... I know God differently, and I love people differently. I see how God made everyone as an individual and..." Her smile grew. "I'm not the same because of three little lives."

"You make me wish I'd known them." Thalia's words squeezed out past a lump in her throat. It wasn't what she'd normally say or how she'd normally feel, yet something about Gabrielle Hubbard's story and her faith in the midst of pain grabbed her in the throat and refused to let go.

Thalia squeezed Gabrielle's hand but released it quickly. She'd never been one to have close female friends. She'd always preferred to hang out with the boys, roughhousing and skimming over emotional conversations.

But something about Gabrielle's graceful spirit

made Thalia wish she'd cultivated the ability to form deeper friendships.

It also solidified her resolve when it came to the case. As Phillip and Drew approached the table, she knew...

They couldn't walk away, no matter what the danger. These were real people with real dreams, possibly being preyed upon and wounded. She wouldn't let that happen. She couldn't.

She would do what it took to protect Gabrielle and others like her, others like her parents, even if she had to die trying.

Chapter Six

"You're eerily quiet." Phillip held the door to the dining room open and swept his hand for Thalia to step out. He studied each person in the main lobby, looking for someone familiar, someone threatening.

Nothing.

"Eerily? Interesting choice of words." The sentence was light, the tone was not. She stepped past him into the large room with hardwood floors, leather furniture grouped into seating areas and soaring ceilings braced by wood beams. Through the windows fronting the building, falling snow swirled in a violent wind ahead of a front that promised colder weather.

Phillip tried to read Thalia's expression, but only her profile was visible as she swept past. She'd kept up their act during dinner, though the weary lines around her eyes had told him she was struggling with something.

Phillip slipped his arm around her waist. It was the kind of thing a loving husband would do, one of the gestures they'd practiced to appear natural. But now, it wasn't about the act. He wanted her close and safe.

Plus, it was unsettling to be out of step with her when they were typically so in sync.

Thalia slowed but didn't pull away. "What?" She leaned her forehead against his cheek to whisper the question, as though they were sharing an emotional moment.

They didn't share emotions... *Did they?*

And what would happen if they did?

He dipped his head so her forehead rested against his temple, and their breaths merged. They'd stopped walking and stood quietly breathing the same air, possibly even...

Thinking the same thoughts?

Likely not. Because his thoughts had run completely off the rails and were barreling straight for her.

"Phillip?" Thalia angled toward him. She nestled against his chest in a way she never had before, as though this was the most natural posture in the world.

If he turned... If she tipped her chin, then... *Then everything would change.*

Frankly, he no longer cared if it did. He had a feeling Thalia might be able to erase the horrors of his past.

Phillip slipped his hand up her side to her shoulder, easing her to face him.

When her brown eyes found his, they were full of questions tempered by an unfamiliar softness.

He wanted to drown in that gaze.

Sliding his hands up her arms, he let his fingertips graze her neck then cupped her cheeks in his palms, searching her face, trying to puzzle out what was happening.

He could kiss her. Could let himself believe this was real. That love wasn't something twisted and painful.

The fire in his heart went dark.

No. He'd been burned before, and he suspected the fire was raging close to all he held dear once again.

He couldn't take the risk, not when his actions could put Thalia in jeopardy.

Still, she drew him as she never had before. Made him want something different. Something more substantial. Something more like the roles they were playing.

Surely it was the fog of undercover work messing with his head.

As though she could read his thoughts, Thalia cleared her throat and looked around the lobby, avoiding his eyes. "We need to get to work."

That wasn't subtle. He'd crossed a line and she was letting him know.

It wouldn't happen again. "You're right. We have way too many questions needing answers."

She smiled brightly, a contrast to the tension between them, a show for onlookers.

So much between them was for show.

And with his past rearing its vengeful head, the subterfuge was taking a toll.

Thalia took his hand, turned and headed for the hallway. As soon as they were alone, she let go. The air tightened, same as it had at dinner.

Phillip couldn't go another second without knowing why because, frankly, she was scaring him as much as the threats to their lives were. "Do you want to talk about what's bothering you?"

She sniffed and shrugged one bare shoulder. It was dismissive. Hurtful.

The silence was so thick, he could hear the wind howling, even though they walked along an interior hallway on the first floor.

"Talk to me, Thal." He tried to keep his voice steady, though her behavior tweaked on old fears. How could he explain in a way she'd understand?

Thalia narrowed her eyebrows. "We can't drop this mission, no matter what happens."

As far as he was concerned, walking away was still on the table, especially if his suspicions proved true and they were in danger. "I don't—"

"I was a terror to my parents." Thalia stared straight ahead as she walked. "I was angry."

It took all he had not to stare. Thalia rarely talked about her past. For her to abruptly and deliberately release a full sentence was shocking. His fears evaporated, replaced by concern. "Want to talk about it?"

A gust shook the building. If this was the beginning of the coming storm, they were in for a rough night.

Thalia exhaled, the breath ruffling her hair. "I hope this passes quickly. The team will be pretty upset if we put them through so much work just to…you know, die at the hands of nature."

Her sarcasm was in full force, which meant personal story time was over.

For now.

Silently, Phillip slipped his hand into hers as

they walked the last few feet to their room, both offering and seeking support.

Swiping the key card, he shoved the door open. Maybe he could see her safely inside then head to the gym to—

Something dropped to the floor at Thalia's feet.

Phillip reached to his hip where his gun normally was, but he'd moved it to his ankle holster, where it was less likely to be seen.

Thalia bent to look at the object, then eased it closer with the toe of her black shoe.

A matchbox with tape on it. On the doorframe, a single match hung askew. It was a crude but potentially effective bomb trigger.

Thalia drew her weapon then gently pushed the door open, peering around the frame.

Heart beating triple-time, Phillip stepped in front of her. Normally, he wouldn't think twice about letting her take lead, but the need to shield her was greater than it had ever been.

He stepped deeper into the room.

The odor of gas intensified near the fireplace. "Gas is on. The pilot is likely out." He bent and reached into the fireplace to close the main valve. Nausea overwhelmed him at the rush of thoughts. This was too familiar. This was his worst nightmare.

This was how he'd nearly lost his parents.

Thalia started toward the French doors then hesitated. "Is there enough built up to call for an evacuation?"

If gas had accumulated, a spark, even one caused by opening the doors, could blow out this entire wing of the hotel.

It took a moment to force himself into the present and to find his voice. "It seems to be isolated. You're safe to open those."

Thalia peeked out to survey the area before she opened both doors wide.

Cold wind rushed into the room, ruffling her hair and the blinds.

Whoever had turned on the gas and taped those matches to the door hadn't hung around to become collateral damage.

Just like the first time.

Phillip swallowed his fear and tried to focus on his job. He should dust for prints, but whoever had set this up had merely blown out the pilot. There might be prints on the wall switch or the door... He doubted it. Their best chance for something usable would be the matchbox, but that wouldn't give them much. He'd seen similar matchboxes around the resort, a throwback to a different era. The cardboard likely held fingerprints from dozens of guests and staff.

Answers wouldn't change the facts. Someone had been here. Someone who hadn't cared if they killed innocent bystanders or destroyed the resort. If gas had built up and the crude trigger had worked, the resulting explosion would have obliterated the adjoining rooms and collapsed the floors above.

Someone had banked on a catastrophic blast.

Or they'd known the plan would fail and wanted to send a message. *I'm here and you can't stop me.*

Fear soured his stomach. Two plus two was adding up to four.

Almost fifteen years later, she'd found him.

How?

Panic surged through his veins, blasting his thoughts, releasing a firestorm of words he'd locked away since high school.

She's harmless.

You should be flattered a girl like that wants you.

You're paranoid…

Liar…

He'd clanged the alarm as the fire had raged closer.

No one had responded until it was too late.

He was helpless then and he was helpless now. The hits kept coming. The danger was real. Now—

A roar from the kitchen rocketed him to his feet. He whipped around, prepared to die.

Thalia watched from in front of the small stove as the whir of the exhaust fan filled the space between them.

"Turn that off." He stalked to the bar, helpless fear overflowing into anger and the need for control. "Have you bagged that matchbox? Or have you been doing nothing?"

Her eyes widened. His snap had been hot enough to ignite her fury. "You might want to rephrase what you just said, because I'm not your servant, *partner.*"

The word slammed into him with all of the force she'd intended.

Phillip bit back a fiery retort. He had to keep control, to find a way to go on the offensive. They'd get nowhere if he snapped.

But pride and anxiety wouldn't let him back down. With a pointed look, he walked around the counter and reached into a drawer where he'd seen some zip-top bags earlier. With his evidence kit hidden in a vent in the bathroom, he needed something more expedient. Snapping the bag open, he headed for the door to retrieve the matchbox.

It wasn't there.

When he turned, Thalia shifted her gaze to the counter.

The matchbox rested there, sealed in a plastic bag.

Thalia ran her tongue along her top teeth, something she did when she was taking time to think before she spoke. "I don't know what other world you went to for a little while, but you weren't in this room. I've bagged the evidence. I've texted Rachel." She walked to the bar, resting her palms on the surface. "The one thing I have *not* done is yell at you for letting your brain vacate the premises." She leaned forward. "You're welcome."

Phillip's ire cooled. He deserved every ounce of the sarcasm she'd lobbed at him.

His anger wasn't with her. His fear wasn't about her.

Thalia deserved better than to be burned by flames that should be directed elsewhere. Somewhere productive. Somewhere that might save them.

With a heavy sigh, Phillip walked to the counter and laid the unused bag on the granite then pushed it toward her as though it was a peace offering.

It was time to come clean. It was the only way to protect them both. "Thal, there's something you don't know about me."

"Like you have a death wish talking to me that way?" The heated words revealed more than she'd likely wanted. She wasn't angry. She was hurt.

"No. And…" He wanted to apologize, but the words wouldn't form. He'd hidden his past from her and then been upset when she'd hidden her present from him. He was a hypocrite. A terrified, helpless hypocrite.

Thalia grunted then went to the fireplace, where she inhaled deeply. The wind ruffled her hair. "We should shut the doors and call it a night. I don't smell—"

"It's about high school."

She faced him, her forehead wrinkled. Clearly, she hadn't expected him to say *that*.

"Thal, I was stalked, and it nearly ended with my family murdered."

What was he talking about?

Thalia sank to the raised stone hearth and balled her fists. Her thoughts spun. Too much was happening too fast. She was losing count of the ways both of them could have died today… and then there was that moment in the lobby…

It had seemed Phillip was going to kiss her. Everything had focused on her, as though she was his whole world.

Then…nothing.

As it should be.

So why had pulling away from him left her feeling empty?

The affection they were practicing to sell their story was becoming too comfortable. It was shaking up things she knew to be true, heightening the emotions of their friendship until everything felt like more.

Today had been all about shake-ups and the aftershocks kept rumbling.

Now this. In all of the years she'd worked with Phillip, he'd never hinted he'd been the victim of a crime, let alone one so intrusive and horrifying. As pale as his face was, it was clear the incidents of his past had demanded a cost he hadn't fully counted until today.

But why was he telling her this now?

Were her hands really shaking? She pressed them between her knees as Phillip sat on the coffee table and let his chin fall to his chest.

She looked at the top of his head, where his dark hair held a slight spiky wave. "I'm not following any of this." As much as her tactical mind tried, she couldn't put anything together.

Phillip had rested his hands on his knees and was focused on the floor between his shoes, which he'd complained at dinner were too tight.

That moment felt like a lifetime ago.

With a deep inhale, Phillip lifted his head and met her gaze briefly before focusing on the stone fireplace behind her. "I was stalked and no one believed me."

There was so much Thalia wanted to say, but this was a moment when her mouth needed to remain shut, even though it went against every ounce of her personality. Questions created physical pressure in her chest. She swallowed them and simply waited.

The effort nearly choked her.

Phillip cleared his throat. "She was a cheerleader. Tall. Blonde. Gorgeous. Literally the most popular girl in school. Had that All-American thing going on, like you see in all of the old movies about high school."

So, they were taking this detour into his past.

Okay. She'd follow, though she had no idea where this was leading.

Thalia could almost picture the young woman. She was everything Thalia wasn't but had once thought she wanted to be. With her shorter stature and unruly dark waves, she'd felt *less than* around those girls. Had always imagined they were laughing at her.

It had taken maturity and life experience to show her she had value.

But this wasn't about her. "What happened?"

"All of the guys were into her, even me, but from a distance. She was a junior. I was a freshman. She never noticed me… Until she did."

It wasn't hard to see where this was headed. One day, beautiful eyes had seen him. Yet the dream hadn't turned out the way he'd expected. Because she was gorgeous and sought-after… no one had believed him when it all went horribly wrong.

She wanted to stop him, to say she'd picked up the gist of it. The thought of Phillip in pain was more than she could take.

But he needed to see this through to the end.

"I played baseball, and in spring of my freshman year, I hit a grand slam in our second game. After that, she spoke to me when she saw me in the hall. Called me over the summer to ask me to a party, but I was grounded and couldn't."

He sniffed. "That's when things got weird. I don't think she'd ever been turned down before. Suddenly, she was everywhere. Showed up at a youth thing at my church. Turned up in one of my elective classes in the fall. If I'd been smarter, I'd have seen it coming." His voice was flat. Remembering was taking its toll. "Instead, I saw it as…meant to be. We started dating."

"You couldn't have *seen it coming*. How could a kid know what was happening? You behaved like a regular—"

"Don't." He snapped the word without looking up. "Early on, a football player warned me. The quarterback. He saw me talking to her in the hall. Told me she was trouble. I blew it off because, by then, we'd been dating for a few weeks, and she was perfect. Gorgeous. Friendly. Funny. I figured the guy was jealous because she was paying attention to me and not him. So, yeah, I should have listened. I should have known."

He was blaming himself. How? It wasn't his fault. After years as an investigator, he should know this.

Then again, she'd seen this happen so often in victims of violence. The misplaced guilt and shame were real and horrible. To think Phillip had been battling such things alone...

She wanted to touch him, to remind him he was an amazing person who didn't deserve what had happened to him.

But he didn't need consolation. He needed to let the memories bleed, likely for the first time since they'd happened. He'd never heal any other way.

"After we'd been dating for a couple of months, she... Wow." He sat back and dragged his hands down his face as though he could scrub away the memories. "She got controlling over who I hung out with, and then she started coming on strong, probably in an attempt to control me. She wanted to go past where I wanted to go. It was drilled into me early on to respect myself and whoever I was dating. I didn't take her up on any of her offers, and eventually, after a heart-to-heart with my dad, I broke it off."

"She didn't take it well?" Thalia couldn't keep silent any longer. She needed to do something, but there was no way to travel back in time and keep young Phillip safe.

"It was horrible. Notes showed up in my locker. She loved me. We belonged together.

When I started dating someone else, she became a target. My girlfriend got wild phone calls from random numbers. There were scratches on her car. Notes that said things like 'You don't get to have him. He's mine.'" Phillip stood, walked to the French doors and closed them, then shut the plantation blinds, eliminating any outside lines of sight.

How had he been in this much pain for this many years and she'd never known? It was taking all Thalia had not to go to him and…

And what? There was no way to fix this.

"I tried to explain to anyone who would listen. The guys on the team all said I should be flattered a girl 'that hot' wanted me, and I should give her what she wanted. They couldn't understand a guy trying to walk what he talked as a Christian. I went to teachers, the principal… Nobody took it seriously. Said she'd already come to them about me, telling them she'd broken up with me because I was abusive and I was trying to get her into trouble. Said she was afraid of me."

This was the source of the anger she'd sensed in him earlier, when they'd reported her assault and all eyes had turned to him, even though he was innocent.

"Even when things started happening to my girlfriend... I had one counselor accuse me of doing those things to make her dependent on me, like I was the issue. Like I was a sadistic abuser."

"This is why you're so good at working through motives for people, why you're inherently suspicious." So much about who Phillip was suddenly made sense. "And why you're always advocating for the victim."

"I know how it feels to be on the other side." His expression grew impossibly more grim. "Whoever tried to drown me today, the only thing they said was... 'She doesn't get to have you.'"

Oh, boy. She rocketed to her feet. That wording was way too close to what his stalker had written. No wonder he was riding an emotional tidal wave.

"It gets worse." He sniffed and turned to her, his forehead etched in deep lines. "Our team played an out-of-town tournament and my parents couldn't come. She broke into the house while they were sleeping and turned on the gas logs. Thankfully, a neighbor happened to see her leaving. He called my parents, thinking I was home and had snuck a girl in. If he hadn't been coming in late from a movie..."

His parents might have died. No wonder he was unraveling. Between the threats and the gas in their room, he was reliving his worst nightmare. "That's why you're wondering—"

"If, impossibly, Ashlyn is here. Especially since my supposed wife has been attacked twice. If she came after a girlfriend, she'd go ballistic on my wife."

"But at least one of those attacks was a man. I doubt she has an accomplice."

"True." Phillip shoved his hands into his pockets. "Could we be dealing with two different people? Two different motives?"

That would be a wild coincidence. She started to say so then stopped. Phillip had been dismissed enough. He didn't need her piling onto past pain. "We'll keep our eyes open, but we can't stop. These are real people, with real pain and real hopes. They need us to protect them from predators."

"I know." He shook his head. "And I need to get my head out of the past and into the present."

"You should have told me sooner."

"So you could judge me too?" He fired the

question then waved his hand as though he could erase the words.

Thalia flinched. He was so rarely angry, in spite of this pain he'd been holding in all of these years.

Despite the distance between them, he must have noticed her reaction, because he abandoned his post by the doors and returned to sit on the coffee table. "I'm sorry I've snapped at you so much. This is a lot at once. I thought I'd already dealt with it, but I also never thought I'd have to face Ashlyn again. I'm wondering if she's here." He reached over and brushed the hair from her forehead, then dropped his hand to his knee. "I shouldn't take it out on you. It's just you're... safe. And I'm scared she'll hurt you."

Safe. And yet today she'd hidden things from him. That had to be a trigger.

"Nobody wants their past rising up, especially when it's violent. Yours nearly cost you everything." She laid her hand on his knee and he covered it with his own. "I'll text Rich and have him see if he can trace where Ashlyn is right now. That will tell us all we need to know."

He nodded as his thumb trailed along the side of her hand. He looked up as though he was considering something, then he stood abruptly, severing the connection. "I need to do something constructive while we wait to hear though." He walked to the kitchen, opened a drawer and held up the master key card Rachel had obtained for them, his demeanor speaking of rigid control. "It's time to do some digging."

He was burying the fear, trying to beat it into submission by sheer willpower. It would never work, but Thalia had no idea how to stop him.

Chapter Seven

Honestly, he'd rather pack his stuff and go home. It might actually be safe there.

Although, if Ashlyn Moynihan truly was involved in the attacks on Thalia and on him, then nowhere was safe.

Phillip put one foot in front of the other on the walk to the Turners' suite only because Thalia was right. The Hubbards and other hopeful couples like them deserved to be treated fairly. Children who were waiting for adoption should have advocates. Birth mothers who had no choice but to surrender their children should receive compassionate treatment. This wasn't about the law and stolen money. It was about real lives and real dreams.

This op was too emotionally charged for many reasons, and the last thing he could do was give in to those emotions.

He offered a quick smile to a man headed

toward the lobby, chatting on his cell phone about the lighted hill for night skiing. The man laughed as he neared them. "Are you going to wimp out because of the weather, Ty? Really?"

Phillip's spine stiffened. That was the other reason he kept moving forward. He'd battled fear in high school after the dust settled. Had suffered from panic attacks that had locked him in his room and made him contemplate things he'd never dreamed he'd contemplate. Counseling and medication and a renewed relationship with Jesus had gotten him through those dark months, but he'd learned to recognize when his emotions threatened to swamp him.

From experience, the way to defeat the monster was to not give in to it. Running for safety only made it twice as hard to stand firm next time. Like a great white shark who'd suffocate without forward motion, the only way to survive was to keep moving.

Besides, he was now a decorated soldier and respected federal agent. A man who'd faced death and lived to tell the tale on more than one occasion. He stood in the line of fire for the defenseless. He advocated for the victim.

That hadn't stopped him from scanning the crowded lobby as they crossed it, looking for

Ashlyn. Likely, this was all coincidence and something else was going on at Rocky Mountain Summit. Something related to their investigation. Job-related danger he could handle. He was prepared for it. But a personal attack? From his worst nightmares? That would be—

"He's in for a world of disappointment if he thinks they're going to open the hill in this weather." Thalia chuckled then sobered. "The Turners' suite is two doors up on the right."

"Dana took care of the cameras?" He sure hoped their tech whiz had managed to shut them off. The last thing they needed was for one of Chase Westin's minions to see them waltzing into the Stardust owners' private rooms. While they had all of the documentation they needed for a legal search, producing it would put an end to the operation.

"She looped the feed." Behaving as though she had total authority to be where she was, Thalia pulled the key card from her pocket, swiped it and stepped into the suite.

The other couple were leading a seminar on introducing a new child to siblings and would be tied up for another hour, so there was little danger of being caught.

Still, they'd have to move fast. Surprises happened all the time.

As soon as the door closed behind them, Thalia whistled low. "I thought our digs were prime. I was very, very wrong."

He followed her as she stepped from a flagstone entry foyer into a large room with plush carpeting. The living area was twice the size of their own suite and featured upgraded furnishings and a full kitchen. The river rock fireplace was enormous, and the large windows and doors facing the mountains probably offered a spectacular view when the heavy curtains were open. From floor to ceiling, the entire room spoke of luxury and money.

Pulling on gloves, Thalia stepped deeper into the living area. "I'm complaining to Rachel."

"No you're not." For the first time in hours, Phillip's shoulders relaxed. This was the job he was trained to do. This was the partner he was meant to work with. She had a way of making him smile simply by being herself. "This morning you were happy with real eggs."

"What can I say? I'm spoiled now. All it took was a bite of candied bacon. I can no longer return to my paltry existence." She walked to the large dining room table adjacent to the kitchen.

Phillip tugged on his gloves and followed her, still smiling. The idea of a spoiled Thalia who preferred silk sheets to a canvas tent was hilarious.

She stopped at the table and studied the papers scattered across the dark wood surface. A laptop sat open at one end and another sat closed nearby.

Phillip lifted a folder from the top of a stack near the center of the table. "Looks like we found the nerve center of Stardust Adoptions."

He flipped open the folder and read the contents, recognizing the format immediately. It was the handwritten application they'd been required to fill out. This one was from a couple named Cade and Taylor Watkins. He'd met the two of them briefly while waiting for the ski lift. They were in their midthirties, hoping to adopt a second child through Stardust.

He flipped through the pages, trying not to pry deeper than was necessary. Behind the application were copies of the handwritten essays and letters Stardust included in packets to potential birth mothers. Rather than deal with online documents, the agency felt the handwritten touch was more personal.

It had been. As he'd worked with Thalia to craft their application, he'd definitely felt differently about the handwritten portions than he would have had they been working on their laptops. There was something emotional about pen and paper, and he'd worded things differently than he would have typed them.

That had been the hardest part of putting their backstory together because, at times, the dreams and plans they'd worked together to develop for their undercover personas had started to hit a little too close to things he'd always wanted but had never really verbalized.

"Anything interesting in those files?" Thalia sifted carefully through the loose papers, setting them back exactly as she'd found them. "All I have is receipts and travel expenses, probably because someone was entering them into their laptop earlier. Nothing out of the ordinary."

Phillip flipped past the initial application. "Background check. Credit report. Nothing that wasn't disclosed to us from the start." There were a few notes written on the inside of the front cover, first impressions about the lawyer and his elementary schoolteacher wife. None of the notations stood out as unusual.

So what was in the file on Phillip and Thalia Atkins?

He flipped through the stack, searching for

theirs. He passed the Hubbard file to Thalia when he came to it. "See if there's anything to indicate why they promised Gabrielle a child so quickly."

Thalia took the file and looked at the outside, then leaned closer to look over his shoulder at the folders he held. "Do you see any others with highlighted names?"

"What?" Phillip looked up then stepped to the side when Thalia was closer than he realized. In no way did he need a repeat of any earlier feelings he'd had when she'd stood close to him.

It was already too late. Lightning shot down his spine again, starting where her shoulder brushed his triceps.

Outside, the wind howled with a sudden gust, as though it had picked up on the volatility between them.

Thalia seemed oblivious. She held up the Hubbard file. "Their name on the tab is highlighted in orange." She planted a finger on the top file. "No highlight here."

"Maybe they already have adoptive parents looking at them?" He scanned the table and the rest of the room. "Remember how we made photo books that told our stories? I don't see them. They could be with potential birth parents, along with copies of the applications."

"Maybe?"

Phillip flipped through the rest of the folders. "I've got another one highlighted. Finn and Valerie Quinones." He stopped when the next flash of orange caught his eye. "Hey, Thal?" Sliding the folder from the stack, he held it up. "We're in the orange club too."

"We are?" She looked up from the Hubbard file. "Are there any others?"

"Just those three." Phillip opened their file and read the notes on the inside cover. There was only one. *Wife attacked on trail run. See RMSR incident report.* Nothing else in the folder was highlighted and there were no other notes. "Well, nothing has been put in writing to indicate any suspicions about us or our marriage."

"Good." Her voice was distracted as she flipped through pages. "I don't see anything out of the ordinary in the Hubbard papers. Nothing to say why Serena would tell Gabrielle this would move quickly."

"The resort filed an incident report on us. We may want to get a look at that. I'll talk to security about it. Not sure what reason I'll give for wanting to see it though."

"Have fun. Your buddy Chase will love chatting with you." She smirked, closed her file, placed it into the stack and then held out her hand. "I'll check out the Quinones file. Maybe they're military and that's why we're all highlighted. You want to make a sweep of the room?"

It was a command, not a question, but Phillip didn't take offense. They traded lead as they worked, and with his current spun-up state, he had no issues with her taking point.

He handed her the file and walked through the living area, surveying without touching anything. Two empty mugs sat on an end table. A romance novel lay on the sofa. A pair of slippers rested under the coffee table. Everything said a working married couple occupied the room.

He walked into the bedroom, which was lit by a bedside lamp. Outside, the wind roared as the predicted storm drew closer. He glanced toward the French doors, over which heavy curtains were drawn, then surveyed the space.

On the far side of the room, the closet door

stood open. If he was going to hide something, that would be his first choice.

Phillip went to the safe in the walk-in closet. It was closed and locked. Crouching, he inspected the shoes lined up in a row.

Bingo.

A canvas bag had been tucked into the corner behind a pair of blue stilettos.

Gently setting the heels aside, he lifted the bag, which was heavier than he'd expected, and peeked into it.

Three prepaid cell phones were inside, along with their packaging. Clearly, they'd been recently purchased and activated.

He pulled his phone from his pocket and texted Thalia. Found something. Texting kept anyone from hearing his voice inside the supposedly empty room.

Thalia appeared in the doorway immediately. "Is it enough to put this case to bed?"

"Not yet." He rocked onto his heels and pulled a phone from the bag, holding it up for her to see. "Three burners. Brand-new."

"Interesting. Have you powered one up?"

"No. I thought I'd wait for you. Why should I have all the fun?"

"Maybe we can—" A sound from the living

area jerked her attention from the phone. She looked at him, lips tight.

The door to the suite opened and someone stepped inside.

Thalia eased the closet door to almost shut and flipped off the light as Phillip slid the bag into its spot behind the shoes. If she believed prayer changed things, she'd ask God to make sure whoever had entered the suite would leave quickly so they could escape without detection.

If the newcomer settled in for the night, then they were trapped and their investigation was over.

Lord, if You're listening... The prayer was unbidden but one hundred percent heartfelt.

The person walked farther into the suite, their footsteps heavy on the stone entryway. Definitely not high heels. Probably a man. The carpet silenced further footfalls as the newcomer made their way into the living area.

Instinctively, Thalia and Phillip ducked farther into the closet.

Outside, the wind's roar increased. The lights flickered. The noise would cover their breathing, but it also kept Thalia from tracking movement in the other room. Without the ability to hear, she had nothing.

Another gust shook the building. The power blinked, plunging the suite into darkness for several seconds before the lights popped on again.

Thalia raised an eyebrow in the semidark closet and looked at Phillip, who had his back pressed against the wall by the door. A power outage would definitely work to their advantage. It would either drive the other person out of the room or would give them the cover of darkness to make their escape.

Although what would happen if they only made it halfway to the door before the lights came on?

She inhaled slowly. *One thing at a time. No sense in borrowing trouble.* They were trapped and already had enough to deal with.

Where was the person who'd entered the suite? Silence reigned, as though they'd heard Thalia's thoughts.

Gently, she slid closer to Phillip, trying to see through the small gap between the frame and the door. She couldn't hear anything over Phillip's breathing and the wind whipping the exterior walls.

The tiniest sliver of the bedroom was visible

through the gap, though there was no way to see the door or into the living area. Only the edge of the dresser was visible.

If they were caught, how could they explain what they were doing in the Turners' private living space? She could always say they were desperate and looking for something to help them get a placement quicker, but at the very least, they'd be booted off of the property.

At the worst? If something nefarious was going on in the agency, then they could easily be killed before they got the chance to offer a fake explanation.

She tried to see more, pressing her shoulder into Phillip's chest. Standing this close, the air between them was growing warm. She wanted out of the stupid closet into cooler air and roomier quarters.

Phillip's heart beat against her shoulder, the pace accelerating to match her own. It was stress, surely, brought on by their situation. It had nothing to do with their proximity. With the fact that, over the past few days, being close to Phillip had started to distract her more than it should, especially—

A figure passed the dresser.

Thalia fought a sharp inhale. It looked like

a man, most likely Brantley Turner. He was in the bedroom, only a few feet away.

Her heart pounded harder. She forced herself to breathe shallow, regular breaths. *Please don't let him open the closet door.*

Beside her, she could feel the identical rhythm in Phillip's chest. This time, she knew he was thinking the same things as she was, acting on instinct, following their training.

This wasn't the first time they'd been in dire straits. It wouldn't be the last. They'd get out of this, even if the *how* currently eluded her.

The wind seemed to hold its breath, as well, giving her the ability to hear more clearly.

It also increased the chance they would be heard.

A dresser drawer opened and shut, then there was a rustle of movement. The bathroom door closed.

Phillip nudged her. "Go."

Quickly and quietly, they slipped out of the closet and made their way across the bedroom into the living room.

When they were halfway to the door, voices drifted in from the hall.

Thalia stopped so suddenly that Phillip bumped into her, wrapping his arms around her waist and pulling her against his chest to keep them both from crashing to the floor.

A female voice gradually grew more distinct and stopped in front of the door. "Thank you for walking me to the room. I'm not sure where Brantley disappeared to."

Serena Turner. Right outside. Getting ready to enter.

Phillip released Thalia and shoved her toward the French doors behind the dining room table.

Outside, the wind renewed its howl, whistling around the doors.

Thalia bolted, praying Serena wouldn't hear and Brantley wouldn't suddenly appear.

At the exterior door, she slipped behind the curtain and unlocked the dead bolt, stepping out onto the patio as the main suite door opened.

Phillip was right behind her. He gently shut the door behind them.

They didn't wait to see if they'd been spotted. Thalia kicked off her heels and scooped them up in one motion. They ran through heavy, wind-driven snow, sliding on the slick ground, making their way along the back of the hotel by staying as close to the building as they could get.

But nothing blocked the icy wind.

Her bare toes were numb. Her hair and jumpsuit were soaked. Her exposed arms were wet and frozen.

She didn't dare slow the pace.

Hopefully, the snow was too heavy to allow the outdoor security cameras to get a clear view of their flight.

They didn't stop running and sliding until they reached the front corner of the building.

Phillip grabbed her arm and pulled her to a stop. "Wait."

His hand was warm on her frigid arm. "No. Freezing." They'd only been outside for a minute, but the wind and the wet snow had her feeling as though she'd plunged beneath the ice on the frozen pond alongside Phillip.

"I know." He turned her toward him and ran his hands up and down her arms from shoulder to wrist. "We can't come around the corner looking like we were fired out of a cannon. We have to look as though we were out walking and got caught in the storm."

"Out w-walking?" Her teeth knocked together. It was impossible to stop them. "Wi-with n-no coats? In a b-blizzard?"

"It's not a blizzard. And everybody thinks we act like newlyweds, remember? We get a pass for a lot of unexplainable things." Dropping his arm around her shoulders, he pulled her close and guided her around the corner, where the lights from the overhang by the main lobby lit the night like an airport runway.

An airport runway to hot coffee, a warm shower and dry clothes.

Thalia leaned deeper into Phillip's side, absorbing his warmth…

And trying not to acknowledge that being next to him was easily the place where she was in the most danger.

Chapter Eight

Phillip sat on the sofa and stared at the fireplace that had nearly been a weapon of untold destruction only an hour earlier.

The flames danced, warming the room cheerily as though the room hadn't been turned into a bomb and no one had tried to murder them. As though his mind hadn't spent the better part of the evening trying to decide if he was paranoid or if his stalker had returned.

He pressed his index finger between his eyebrows, pushing against a headache. The pain probably came from the hot and cold whiplash his body had endured too many times today.

This second near-freezing go-round, Thalia had borne the bulk of the pain. When they'd returned to their suite, she'd disappeared into the bedroom, her bare arms and shoulders red from wind and snow. The last thing he'd heard was her voice declaring she wanted dry hair, warm pants and a heavy sweatshirt.

On the other side of the closed door, her hair dryer fired up.

He smiled. It was almost like she'd known what he was thinking about.

He'd hastily changed into the sweatshirt he'd worn earlier and fleece pajama pants, then cranked up the fireplace after making certain it wouldn't blow him straight into the afterlife.

Despite the headache, he felt rational and calm. Their flight out of the Turners' suite had reset his thinking, forcing him into the job and out of his past. He'd also received word from the team that a quick check revealed Ashlyn Moynihan was at home near Nashville with her family.

His thoughts were his own again.

He'd been foolish to believe Ashlyn had traveled to Colorado just to make his life miserable this many years later. She had completed court-mandated counseling and was currently living the average-mom life. Her behavior toward him had been the result of a number of emotional and physical factors that medical intervention had helped her overcome.

She'd never reached out to him. Had never

indicated a desire for revenge. If she was going to come after him, there would have been indicators and it would have happened before now.

Did knowing she was in Tennessee really make things better though? The fact was, someone had tried multiple times to harm them, even kill them. They were in danger whether or not Ashlyn was safely tucked away in her home with her husband and two children.

In the bedroom, the hair dryer shut off. A few seconds later, Thalia opened the door. She was bundled up, as promised, in her heaviest sweatshirt over fleece-lined leggings. Thick wool socks covered her feet. Her hair was tousled from the hair dryer, hanging in wild waves to her shoulders, almost as though it had been styled by the gale outside.

She nearly took his breath away. The hammering in his chest was worse than it had been all day. Given he'd nearly been murdered, that was saying a lot.

There was something about her. Something new and different. Something that made him want to take all of their pretend moments and make them real.

If they were truly a married couple, he'd take her hand and pull her down beside him on the couch just to be close to her. Just to feel even a fraction of what he'd felt when they were tucked in that closet. So close, he could hear her breathe.

So close, she had to have felt the change in his heartbeat.

This was all wonky and weird. He looked away. What he needed was rest. Tomorrow, he'd feel more like himself and less like his partner was…was somehow something more than his partner.

She dropped into the armchair at an angle to the couch and flopped her arms over the sides like an abandoned rag doll. Dropping her head onto the chair's back, she stared at the ceiling. "What are you out here contemplating? Because you look like you're up in your head."

He mimicked her posture and studied the creamy white ceiling. Maybe the answers to all of his problems would appear there. "Everything."

"Seems about right."

"I'm trying to pin it down to one thing I can focus on. One thing that makes a modicum of sense so I can feel like I've accomplished something besides massively freaking out."

When Phillip tilted his head forward, Thalia

had straightened and tucked her legs under her. She was staring at him. "You did *not* have a massive freak-out. You had a normal response to heinous external stimuli, both past and present. The evidence in your face looked credible, as though your stalker had returned. And while that would be a massive coincidence, I'm not sure we can write it off. Still, don't act like you did something unusual. You're human."

Whatever. She had no idea how embarrassed he—

"Stop thinking you can do everything by yourself and you shouldn't need help." She leaned closer, a challenge in her eye that dared him to interrupt. "You've always had an issue with pride and asking for help. I think you want everyone to believe you're superhuman. You're not. You bleed like the rest of us, literally and metaphorically."

The words would have been harsh had her tone not been so straightforward. This was Thalia. She wasn't condemning him. She was stating the facts as only she could.

If anyone else had said it, he'd have bucked. When she spoke, the words sank into his soul. "Where have you been hiding that little psychoanalysis, Doc?"

She smiled. "There have been times when I wanted to slap you in the face with it, but I've held my tongue."

"You? Held your tongue?"

She fired him a withering glare. "I was waiting for a time when I could say it without wanting to hit you with my shoe while I spoke. Right now was the first opportunity, largely because I'm not wearing shoes."

Thalia would never kick him while he was down. If she was saying this now, then he needed to listen.

She sat back and let her hands fall into her lap, then studied her fingers. It was an uncharacteristic shrinking for someone who usually faced life directly. "I think it's time you realized you don't have to go it alone. How many years have we been partners? And you're just now telling me what you went through? You've buried it all this time, and I feel like it was something I needed to know." She looked up. "You hid it from me because you thought it made you weak. It doesn't. It makes you strong because you survived."

This time, he looked away. Maybe she was right. Maybe he'd never said anything because he'd wanted her to believe he was made of steel. Perfectly strong.

He winced. There was the lie. No one was perfect.

Thalia was right. Serious pride was rearing its head and he should have recognized it sooner.

"As for weak moments, everyone has them. We wouldn't be human otherwise."

"Interesting." *What was good for the goose...* "Where was this deeply psychological side of you when you decided not to tell me what happened to you at the ski lodge this morning?"

She sucked air between her teeth, but not because he'd startled her.

He knew that look. He'd struck a nerve.

This time, he leaned closer to her. "Don't forget how graciously I took your criticism. Respond in kind, partner."

Her stare was icier than the wind whistling around the French doors. She shook her head and seemed to wrestle with what she really wanted to say. "I didn't keep quiet because the incident made me feel weak. At the time, it seemed like an unnecessary distraction that could be dealt with later."

Phillip puffed out his frustration and didn't

speak. Danger was never an *unnecessary distraction*, especially when it assaulted his partner.

Wisdom, however, dictated he not challenge her. Thalia was great at dishing out truth, but she wasn't always quick to receive it. There was a certain finesse when it came to correcting Thalia. He'd learned the hard way over the years.

Instead, he changed course. "Here's what I think we focus on first."

"Let me guess. What it means to be 'Team Orange'?"

It wasn't surprising her thoughts ran with his. "Did you get a look at the Quinones file?"

"I was looking over ours when you texted me to show me the phones, so I never cracked it."

The phones. One more twist in the plot. "I wish we'd been able to power one up."

"Or we'd brought one with us."

"Yeah. *There's* a risk we should take." If they wanted to tip off the Turners, stealing a hidden cell phone would do the trick.

Thalia picked up her phone from the arm of the chair. "I'll text Dana and have her send us intel on Finn and Valerie Quinones. It's possible they're also military, though Stardust has never comped more than two couples on a retreat."

Her thumbs flew across the screen. "We need to start considering why the owners of an adoption agency are hiding burners."

Phillip settled into the couch. Brainstorming motives for criminal behavior was one of his favorite things to do with Thalia. Their ideas ranged from the outlandish to the mundane, but somewhere in the middle, they usually found plausible theories that directed the next segment of their investigation.

Her phone buzzed and she stopped typing. "Just got a text from Gabrielle Hubbard."

"Is she okay?"

"She's fine. Drew had planned to go night skiing, but…" As if to punctuate her words, the wind howled. It sounded as though someone was trying to break through the French doors.

That wasn't a visual Phillip needed. He breathed in and out slowly. *It's only the wind.*

Since when was he a child needing reassurance during a storm?

He shook his head to clear the muck. "Anyway… What's up?"

"She says somebody busted out the board games in the third-floor lounge and there's about to be a round of… Apples to Apples?" She wrinkled her nose and frowned at the screen. "Like old-school bobbing for apples? Because...gross."

His family had played that game at every gathering. "It's part comedy, part strategy and part silliness. You'll hate it. We should go."

She arched one eyebrow and dipped her chin to him.

"On second thought, your natural bent toward sarcasm means you'll slaughter all of us. I say we challenge everyone up there to a duel." He stood and held his hand out to her. "Finish sending your text to Dana, then we'll go see if we can gain insight into more of our fellow hopeful parents. Maybe Finn and Valerie Quinones will be there. If they're not, maybe someone will have intel about them."

"Fine." Thalia sighed and stood without taking his hand. "But I'm staying in my leggings."

"And I'm staying in my flannel pj's. You can talk about how embarrassing your husband is running around a fancy resort in his comfy jammies."

"That won't stretch my acting abilities." She tossed him his phone from the counter as they passed.

"Ha." Something about their polar bear run and their hands-on investigating in the Turners' suite had lightened his mood considerably. Or maybe it was the idea of being with Thalia for some good ol' board game fun with other couples.

Not that *they* were a couple.

Because that could wreck their careers and ruin their friendship.

Forever.

The recreation room was finally quiet.

And not a moment too soon.

Phillip propped his feet on a leather ottoman and slid down until his neck rested on the back of the sofa.

Thalia sat facing him with her back against the arm of the couch and her knees bent. Her cheeks were red from laughing at the game that had been short and loud. It seemed the harder the storm raged, the more the six other couples had tried to outshout the weather.

Nearly everyone had left after an hour, either heading to their rooms or to a late screening of *The Princess Bride* in the resort's theater. It had been tempting to follow, but he'd had his fill of social hour.

On the other side of the large ottoman, Drew

and Gabrielle Hubbard snuggled on a sofa, settling in like they were prepared for a long chat.

If this wasn't an investigation, he'd have hit the rack already. The fun meter had pegged. The social battery had redlined. He was every cliché for an introvert on overload.

Grabbing a throw pillow from the floor, Thalia pulled it against her stomach. "That was fun."

"You were the Apples to Apples queen." Gabrielle laughed. "I knew you would be. Sarcasm wins every time."

"I said the same thing to her before we came up here." Phillip poked Thalia's knee.

She responded by lightly kicking his thigh. "At least I'm good for something."

"You're also a good cook." He raised his eyebrows as high as he could.

She laughed, just as he'd hoped. Thalia was the opposite of *a good cook*. Even powdered eggs were beyond her, and all that required was adding water.

She shook her head as she chuckled, in on the joke and loving it.

Her hair swept her shoulders and her eyes sparked in a way he'd never seen before.

Something in her had let go during that silly

game. Either she had honed her role as Thalia Atkins, or she had genuinely enjoyed herself. She never laughed with her whole being, not like she had tonight. The tears sparkling in her eyes at one point had reflected a rare, genuine joy.

When she caught his eye, she laughed harder, probably thinking about her last disastrous effort at cooking, while they were on the MMA op. He still wasn't sure how someone could wreck boxed mac and cheese, but she certainly had.

She tossed her head and her hair slipped from her shoulders, exposing her neck.

Phillip was blindsided by the irresistible urge to plant a kiss on the curve of her shoulder.

Where had *that* come from? He had no idea, but it flooded every fiber of his being. This was not something—

"You two forget anyone else is in the room." Drew's voice dragged Phillip out of his struggle.

Thankfully, no one seemed to notice he'd fallen completely out of character. Those thoughts had been all his own, not the forced fakery of their sham marriage.

What did it mean that he'd revealed the thoughts of Phillip Campbell and the room still thought he was behaving like Phillip Atkins, a man very much in love with his wife?

He dragged his hands down his cheeks. *There* was a bag he didn't need to unpack.

"He's deployed or is gone for training way too often." Thalia stepped in to explain his near stupor. "I guess it really is kind of like we're still newlyweds. The time we get together is…special." Her head tilted to the side and she watched him as though she'd never seen him before.

Or as though he'd sprouted a unicorn horn from the center of his forehead.

She must have picked up on his very weird vibe.

He cleared his throat and took a deep breath, drawing himself back into character. "I'm sure a lot of military couples are the same. Even you two."

When Drew draped his arm around Gabrielle's shoulders, she snuggled closer. He planted a kiss on the top of her head.

A week ago, Phillip would have called the display sickeningly sweet. Now it was a moment he wished he could have for himself.

Nope. Not going to go there. Between pretending that Thalia was his wife and wrestling with the memories from his past, his emotions were clearly in need of a good shakeout.

She nudged him with her toe again, then

settled deeper into the couch, slipping her feet under his thigh as she did.

His heart nearly stopped. There was something intimate about the gesture. It spoke of a closeness between them, as though she belonged to him and he belonged to her and they stepped into one another's space at will, naturally, often.

Emotion shot through him. Like so much else over the past few days, this felt right and comforting. He'd been wary of women and relationships ever since Ashlyn's advances and attacks. This, the warmth of Thalia's feet tucked beneath his leg... It was so natural it made him feel whole, as if the last piece of a long-worked puzzle had slipped into place.

Without letting himself consider the ramifications, he rested his forearm on her knees as though they sat like this every day.

The gesture felt as though he'd done it a thousand times.

The wind seemed to shake the roof above them. The storm showed no signs of letting up, even though it had been raging for nearly two hours. If the snow was falling as hard as the gale was blowing, they'd be buried by midnight.

He glanced at Thalia, who still held the pillow to her chest and had closed her eyes. Not that he'd mind being snowed in—

Wow.

"I hate this weather." Gabrielle pulled her feet up and curled against her husband's side.

"Snowstorms like this aren't unusual." He let his elbow slide lower and pulled Thalia's knees toward the back of the couch, leaning slightly against her legs. It was more comfortable than sitting straight up.

So he told himself.

It must have been more comfortable for her, too, because she gradually relaxed.

"It's not the snow." Drew grabbed a bottle of water from the side table and handed it to Gabrielle. "Wind spooks her."

Rather than drink the water, Gabrielle pulled it to her chest as though it could somehow shield her. Interesting that Thalia was holding the pillow the same way. "It's been creepy to me for as long as I can remember. The noise it makes…" She shuddered.

"It's never bothered Thal. She loves a good storm. Right, babe?" He tapped her leg.

No response.

"She's out, man." Drew smiled, and Gabrielle leaned forward to verify then nodded.

Phillip eased back to look. Sure enough, Thalia's head had lolled to one side, her face slack with sleep.

His heart softened even more. She was exhausted. After the day they'd had, she deserved a few minutes of rest.

He didn't want to wake her, so he carefully sat back and looked at the Hubbards and smiled. "She's had a long day."

"I gathered that. She was the trail victim? How'd she get away from the guy?" Drew seemed to measure Thalia up as though he was trying to decide how someone so tiny could fend off an attacker.

"Thal did some MMA training at one time. Trust me. Nobody wants to come at her head-on." But she was also human, and if an assailant got the jump on her like he had today, then things could go bad.

"Nice. I tried to get Gabby to take self-defense classes. I'm gone so much..." Drew's words trailed off and worry clouded his expression.

Phillip understood. The military life was difficult. Deployments, classes and training cycles could make for long weeks and months apart. He had no idea how couples survived it all. While some marriages collapsed under the strain, others thrived.

"I'm perfectly capable of taking care of myself." Gabrielle smacked her palm on her husband's knee then abruptly stood. "Speaking of long days, I'm ready for my bed and a good book."

"Right behind you." Drew grabbed Gabrielle's arm and hefted himself up. "You going to wake her up or let her sleep?"

Phillip glanced at his slumbering partner. No way was he going to cut her rest short. She looked more at peace than he'd ever seen her. "I'll give her a few minutes. You guys go ahead."

With another round of good-nights, the Hubbards left, shutting off the overhead light as they went out the door. The soft glow of a table lamp bathed the room in warmth.

With a heavy sigh, Phillip sank against the couch cushions and watched Thalia breathe. This op was harder than he'd thought it would be. She was his closest friend. His teammate and partner. They'd been through things most people would never have to face. They'd looked death in the eye together and had rescued one another on more than one occasion. It made for a strong bond.

It did not make for a romance. Pretending to be in love with her was blurring the lines, making their friendship feel like more, turning their touches into more than simple gestures.

It all made this moment as he watched her sleep more poignant. Although he'd seen her racked out on missions before, it had never quite felt like this. Protectiveness in his mind. Peace in his heart.

As though she could sense his internal conflict, Thalia stirred and opened her eyes, looking straight at him. "Why is it dark?" Setting the throw pillow on the floor, she sat up and scrubbed her cheeks with her palms. Without warning, she slapped Phillip's arm. "Why did you let me fall asleep in front of everybody?"

Her ire amused him, though he was wise enough to keep the chuckle inside and, hopefully, off of his face. "You were out before I knew you were gone."

"Did I drool?" She wiped her hand on her face and turned, dropping her feet to the floor.

He felt colder without her touch. "Nah. But you snored so loud—"

In one smooth motion, she swiped up the pillow and whacked him in the face. "Stop. I didn't." Standing, she backed away from the couch toward the door. "And if you hit me with a pillow in return, I will end you."

He was thinking about it. Oh, how he was thinking about it.

Somehow, he couldn't see a cutesy pillow fight between the two of them ending in any way but with some sort of embrace.

That was enough reason for him to keep his hands to himself. He held his arms out to his sides as he stood, a gesture of surrender. "Let's go. The Hubbards went to sleep. We should too."

He trailed her to the elevator, where she pressed the button and stared at the doors, not saying a word. Thalia woke up slowly and was often irritable when she did.

When they stepped inside, Phillip kept his distance. After the thoughts he'd been having, there was no way he was getting close to her. He'd need a vacation when this was over, time to remind himself—

There was a jolt and a screech...

And the elevator went dark.

Chapter Nine

Thalia grabbed the rail at the back of the elevator as the emergency lights clicked on. *Small space. No way out. Not good.*

While she had essentially no memories of her early childhood in Moldova, one image had never dimmed. She'd been locked in something similar to a closet. It had been dark and uncomfortably humid. The sense of suffocation had been overwhelming.

That horror sometimes muscled its way into her nightmares.

She'd endured tight spaces on missions and in training, but she'd fought her way through by moving forward and maintaining a sense of control.

But this?

There was nowhere to move. Nothing to control. No task to occupy her mind.

The air was growing warmer. It was harder to breathe by the second.

A few feet away, Phillip stared at the buttons, oblivious to the distress that had her clinging to the rails. "I'm guessing the storm knocked out the power. There should be a generator that kicks in and gets us moving, I hope. I mean, we're due a break today."

Thalia's mouth was dry. Yes. They were definitely due a break.

Popping open a door on the panel, Phillip grabbed the emergency phone. "I'll see what I can find out."

While he did, she'd try to remember how to breathe. *In through the nose, out through the mouth*.

She glanced around the ever-shrinking space, grateful for the emergency light that kept them from being plunged into darkness. Now she needed a distraction. Her eyes scanned the space.

The carpet was a deep royal blue with thin gold lines swirling through it. Blue and gold. Those had been her high school colors.

Phillip was speaking to someone, but his voice seemed far away.

She'd forgotten to breathe. *In. Out.* She could handle this. It was an elevator, not a prison cell.

This was temporary. She could endure anything for a few minutes.

They'd better only be in here for a few minutes.

She stared at Phillip's dark hair as he listened to whoever was speaking. "Ten minutes?" He nodded. "Understood. We'll let the front desk know when we're out."

He hung up. "There's a battery backup that kicks in after ten minutes and takes the elevator to the lowest level, which is a basement storage area. There aren't emergency lights down there, but they told me where to—" He turned and caught sight of her. "Thal?"

"I'm fine. Keep talking." The words came out in huffs. She hated the weakness, the fear, the fleeting wisp of memory that she could never grasp and destroy.

She was better than this. More well-trained than this.

Nothing should scare her.

Yet here she was, death-gripping a metal railing in a stationary tin can of doom.

She was never boarding an elevator again.

Phillip was at her side before she could say more. He studied her face in the dim glow of the emergency light. "How have I never known you're claustrophobic?"

"Same way I'm finding out all sorts of new things about you today."

"I deserved that." He pursed his lips. "What can I do?"

"Tell me how much longer we'll be in here." Even if she had to count every second, it would give her something to focus on besides the walls.

"About nine more minutes. I wasn't on the phone long." He peeled her fingers off the railing and took her hand in his. "Let's sit down. Relax. Breathe together."

"Or we can talk." She didn't want to sit. Standing was less vulnerable. She could fight off an attacker while standing.

But she didn't need to. As long as they were in the elevator, no one could get to them. They might be safer here than anywhere else on the property.

Focusing on that one positive, she forced herself to sit beside Phillip.

He slipped his arm around her shoulders and pulled her close to his side.

Despite the strange undercurrent running between them, she let him hold her. Giving him the lead allowed her to relax. Still, it wasn't enough to stem the desire to rip the railing off the wall and pry open the elevator doors. "Ask me something. I don't care what. I'll answer." Even the hard stuff. Anything to take her mind off their situation.

Phillip chuckled and the sound rumbled in his chest, making her believe this might turn out okay. "There's an offer I'm never going to get again."

"It expires in four minutes."

He glanced at his watch. "Eight."

"I was really hoping time had moved faster."

"I'm sure." Phillip settled against the wall and his arm tightened around her. "I'm going to have to think. I want to be sure I use this unique opportunity wisely."

He was enjoying this way too much, which meant it might be a bad idea. Truth-telling with Phillip could go places she didn't want, especially if he asked whether she'd noticed the odd vibe between them lately.

Speaking of, she ought to pull away, but she simply didn't want to. For a few minutes, in this elevator, she was going to let herself be sheltered by someone else. This was a step out of time. Once those doors opened, she could be her strong and capable self again. For the moment, it was nice to let her guard down.

"I've got it." His voice had deepened, weighted with gravity.

Gravity. Like the thing that could drop this elevator. "Go ahead." She might regret it, but at least she'd stop thinking about her body being smashed in the basement.

It sounded like Phillip either choked or chuckled. It was hard to tell. "You heard about my past, and we're here talking to adoptive parents. Tell me what it was like for you, being adopted."

"Wow." He really went for the jugular. Likely, no other question would cost her so much mental and emotional energy. The answer would require thought and focus as she delved into the past.

Phillip knew it.

Only fear could drive her to open up. She'd never tell the story otherwise.

That made her a hypocrite.

She straightened, her back pressed against the elevator wall. Hadn't she lit into him for not revealing his past to her sooner?

"What's wrong?" Phillip bent his knees. "I can retract the question if it's too—"

"No. It's me. Not you."

"Wait." He chuckled. "Did you really give me a variation of 'it's not you, it's me'?"

"We're not dating, Campbell."

"But we *are* married, Mrs. *Atkins*."

In name only. Their relationship was an illusion to be maintained, even when they were away from prying eyes.

It was also one she didn't want to think about for long. "So…adoption."

"Yeah." Phillip settled in as though he was ready for a long story. "And you have six minutes."

Time was crawling, so she might as well start talking. It was the only way to survive with her sanity intact. "I was four when I was adopted. My few memories before that are vague images." Including the one feeding her claustrophobia. "I was abandoned. The agency in Moldova has no record of who my birth parents are. I was found wandering the streets in Pohrebeni when I was three." Thinking of it cracked her heart for her younger self, lost and afraid. It made her physically ill to consider any child in that sort of emotional panic.

Phillip whistled low. "I'm so sorry, Thal. That's rough."

"It's such an empty thing to have no beginning, no origin story. To not know where you came from." There were no family legends, no medical history, no nothing. It was as though her existence began at the age of four. Sometimes she awoke at night feeling like there was a giant hole in her chest where her childhood self should be. Some awful nights it felt like the darkness would ooze out and envelop her until she disappeared.

"What about your mom and dad?" He'd met them on multiple occasions when she'd received an award or a promotion.

"Once I moved to South Carolina, I had an idyllic childhood. Mom and Dad love the outdoors. There weren't video games or cell phones. It was bike rides and hikes and picnics." A sudden lump charged into her throat. She never talked about her childhood. Although she'd been happy, she'd never been able to reconcile the little lost girl on the streets with the privileged young child who'd been thrust into a loving family. The contrast was too much, and it was difficult to believe both of those children lived inside her.

"I was abandoned by my birth parents on the streets. Like I was garbage. I was so angry for so long. At the ones who left me. At my parents. I figured one day they'd walk away too. I mean, why shouldn't they? I wasn't their blood. So, I rebelled. Hard. I made them miserable, and they kept right on loving me. I was in high school before I realized they weren't going to abandon me too. They love me unconditionally. I'm their daughter, and nothing will ever change that." She squeezed Phillip's fingers and tried to pull away, but he held on. It felt like peace. "I wish I'd realized it sooner."

Phillip said nothing. He simply tucked their linked hands against his chest and rested his free hand over them. His thumb ran lightly up and down the side of her wrist.

She could feel his heartbeat. This touch was a whole new sensation she'd never imagined before, electric and comforting at the same time. Familiar. "You know…" Words poured out before she realized she was thinking them. "You're the only person I've never expected to walk away."

His thumb stopped. His whole body tensed. It was as though her words had seized time.

Phillip blinked twice then lowered their hands to the floor between them and looked

at her, staring as though he wasn't sure he recognized her.

It was a look she could drown in.

He swallowed so hard, she could see his throat
move, even in the dim light. "Thal, I—"

With a jerk, the elevator started down.

Phillip shook his head, released her hand and
stood. The motion was abrupt and final. "Guess
the battery kicked in."

He didn't reach down to help her, not that
she needed it. She stood and put space between
them, unsteady and shaking. It was the adrenaline crash from her earlier fear. An emotional
hangover from sketching out her story.

From realizing how much she trusted Phillip.

Thalia shook her hands as the elevator stopped
at the basement. There was no need to think of
that now. They needed to finish this mission
so they could stop pretending to be something
they weren't, before her brain started believing
in something she could never have.

The doors slid open to reveal a deep darkness
too much like the one that often threatened to
swallow her in the night.

The elevator was preferable.

Part of her wanted to reach for Phillip, but
she was stronger than that. This mission was

bringing out her weakness. The sooner it was over, the better.

Phillip activated the flashlight on his phone and she did the same. The darkness eroded for several feet ahead of them; their lights weren't enough to dispel the inkiness around the edges.

Phillip led the way to the right.

She followed. He'd received direction from whoever had been on the other end of the phone. He'd get them to safety.

Something moved at the fringes of their lights. A dark shadow. A glint on metal.

Phillip stopped walking. "Thalia! Knife!"

A dark figure lunged toward them, knife low. It was a practiced move, meant to avoid deflection.

In the deep silence of the basement, the rustle of movement jarred through Phillip.

Dropping his phone, Phillip stepped in front of Thalia and moved to block the attack. This wasn't his first knife fight.

But it was the first to come completely out of nowhere. The first to come while his emotions were out of whack and his head was nowhere near the ballfields let alone in the game.

The knife swung toward him and Phillip

ducked sideways, catching their attacker in the forearm as he dodged, deflecting the first blow.

There would be more.

The light wavered as Thalia jumped back. She was probably itching to jump into the fight but she was also tactically-minded. At the moment, Phillip needed light more than he needed backup. She'd keep him from battling in the dark.

The black-clad figure stumbled and righted himself between them, then focused his attention on Thalia.

With the light from her phone in his eyes, Phillip couldn't see her, but he knew she was holding steady. She wouldn't waver, though she stepped aside to make room for the ongoing battle.

While light was critical, it made her an easy target, giving their attacker a direction to aim.

Crouching, Phillip lunged before the man could move toward Thalia, driving his shoulder into their assailant's side and taking him to the ground. The knife skittered along the concrete and disappeared in the shadows.

The light bobbed as Thalia kicked the weapon deeper into the basement, farther out of reach.

It was time to finish this. "Call security."

Phillip had his attacker on the ground. All they needed was backup. He didn't dare risk announcing himself as a federal agent and—

The man bucked, whipping his head and throwing his body into a twist.

The motion tossed Phillip off balance enough for their attacker to roll free. He scrambled along the floor on all fours before breaking into a run deeper into the basement, disappearing into the darkness.

Phillip bolted after him, but Thalia grabbed his arm as he passed. "Don't."

He tugged at her hold. "We can end this now."

"No." She shone her light in the direction the man had fled, but it only lit a shallow area within a few feet of them. "You're unfamiliar with the layout down here, and I'm guessing he knows it well. You can't go running out there blind. That's a quick way to die."

He jerked his arm free and stayed where he was, breathing hard as he stared into the darkness. She was right. There was no telling the number of places their attacker could be lying in wait for one of them to run into another trap.

Phillip dragged his hand down his jaw. They

faced yet another dead end. He couldn't take many more of those.

They needed to go on the offensive. Someone was trying to harm both of them, and if anything happened to Thalia... "Are you okay?"

In the dim light, she nodded. "He never got close to me, but we can debrief later. We need to get moving before he doubles back. Without light, we'll never see him coming."

Again, she was right.

Grabbing his biceps, she turned him in the direction of the stairs. "Let's go. I'll watch from here."

No way. He wasn't letting Thalia follow when their adversary was behind them. The guy could take her out before Phillip realized she was no longer there.

She shoved him between his shoulder blades. "If you even *think* about suggesting I take the lead, I'll tell you two things. One, the person on the elevator phone told *you* how to find the stairs, not me. And two, if you dare hint I'm not capable of guarding the rear, then you know you'd better sleep with one eye open for the rest of your life."

Both of those things were true. For the entirety of their partnership, Thalia had been an equal. He'd never before felt the need to protect her. As the combat expert on their team, she was probably better trained than he was.

He turned and started walking. They needed to watch what they said, even down here. Anyone, including their attacker, could be nearby. Even Thalia had avoided mentioning the op or the true nature of their relationship.

These lapses in judgment weren't like him. Thalia was bound to notice. No doubt she'd have something to say when they got to their suite.

By the time they made it to the lobby, the area was packed with people who milled in the dim glow of emergency lights. It was likely they'd emptied the theater as a precaution and folks were waiting to see if the movie would resume anytime soon.

Thalia trailed Phillip as they threaded their way through the crowd toward the reception desk.

He reached behind him and pressed his hand against the small of his back, palm out in invitation.

Lacing her fingers through his, she drew close to him.

This was who they were supposed to be. A

husband and wife trying to stay together in a crush of people who were equal parts concerned at the storm's ferocity and upset by the inconvenience of a power outage.

Yep. That was all they were. An imaginary married couple.

The relief he felt at having her close and safe was an offshoot of that. They'd both survived another set of scrapes that could have left them dead instead of bruised.

Thalia leaned closer, her breath warm against his ear. "We've got eyes on us." She jerked her hand to the right slightly to indicate direction.

He glanced over the crowd, reminding himself he wasn't looking for Ashlyn. Near the front door, a redheaded guy in his midthirties watched them make their way across the lobby.

However, when Phillip looked directly at him, he didn't appear to notice, so maybe it was an illusion. The guy—

Wait. A few feet from the man, Chase Westin stood directly in front of the sliding doors, his gray parka zipped to his neck and dusted in snow as though he'd just come inside.

He was definitely watching.

After a moment of surveillance, Westin made

his way at an angle across the room, clearly headed to the reception desk to intercept them.

Thalia's breath tickled his ear again. "You notice he just came in, right?"

Phillip merely nodded. He tried to keep his expression neutral as he let his gaze slide past Westin as though he hadn't seen him.

Inside, though, his emotions threatened to steam out of every pore of his skin. It was doubtful anyone on the property knew the layout of the resort as well as the head of security. If Phillip was doing Westin's job, he'd have walked the resort over and over, searching for entry and exit points, escape routes... Anywhere thieves or other criminals could slip in or out. If there was an exit in the basement level that led to the front of the building, Chase Westin would be aware of it.

He'd also have been apprised of guests stuck in elevators. The ten minutes that had elapsed between Phillip's talk with the front desk and the attack in the basement would have given Westin more than enough time to be in place when they'd exited the elevator and stepped into the darkness.

They reached the desk before Phillip could process more suspicions. He had to set aside his tactical thoughts for the moment. Right now, his main job was to be a husband who'd been trapped in an elevator. The resort didn't need to know someone had come at them in the basement. If Stardust found out the Atkins couple had been the victims of yet another attack, there was no telling what would happen.

But by *not* saying anything, they might tip their hand as well. If someone at Stardust was behind the attacks, their suspicions would be raised by Phillip and Thalia's silence.

It was a delicate dance and he had to be careful where he placed his feet.

They waited behind another couple before he was able to step to the desk. Scanning the clerk's name tag, he looked up with what he hoped was an impassive expression as Westin walked behind the desk.

Phillip ignored the head of security. "Hi, Evan. I'm Phillip Atkins. My wife and I were stuck in the elevator on the Birch wing and were told to let you guys know when we'd made it out safely."

Evan looked up. His eyebrow rose in question as though he didn't understand what he was seeing. "I— Did you—" He shook his head then lifted a smile. "I'm sorry. I'm the one you talked to on the phone. Glad to hear you made it up here without any issues, and I'll be sure to let our manager know. You were the only ones in the elevators when the lights dropped."

"Well, aren't we special?" Phillip tried to keep his voice light. But what were the odds? "Oh, and you were right. The basement's pretty dark."

"So's the rest of the hotel right now. Apparently there was some sort of power surge. As for the basement, we had an issue with the backup lights down there when we upgraded our alarm system. The security company should have them fixed by the end of the week."

So the lights in the basement were down during the week of the Stardust retreat? And the building was updating the security system, which likely left areas vulnerable for short periods of time? *Interesting.* He'd love to know who the alarm company was and if they had any relationship with Hudson Macy, whose identity had been stolen by Thalia's trail attacker.

Thalia squeezed his hand. She'd heard it too.

Evan passed him a slip of paper. "Your group's event is all-inclusive or we'd offer you a free meal in our restaurant for your inconvenience. Instead, the manager asked me to give you this voucher for the gift shop. We're really sorry this happened."

Phillip wasn't. The things he'd learned from Thalia probably would have never been aired any other way. He slid the paper across the counter. "Thanks, but unless you can control the weather, this wasn't the resort's fault."

Thalia reached around him and snatched up the voucher before Evan could retrieve it. "Speak for yourself, pal. I was in that elevator with you, and I have my eye on a ski jacket that this will definitely be going toward."

Evan's entire face wrinkled with a smile. "Well, I hope you enjoy it. Do either of you need anything else?"

"I do." Chase Westin stepped up and offered the widest, most insincere smile Phillip had ever seen.

Whatever that man had to say, the conversation was guaranteed to be interesting.

Chapter Ten

It was getting hard for Thalia to keep her facial expression relaxed. Everything about Chase Westin screamed he was up to something. The events of the past half hour made Thalia wonder more than ever what it could be.

Holding loosely to Phillip's hand, she walked to the end of the reception desk, following Westin's lead.

They rounded a corner into an alcove tucked away from the rest of the lobby but still in view of the laughing couples who milled around the area. The resort-goers seemed to be dispersing. Some headed to the dining room, where the hotel was offering desserts by candlelight. Others had decided to navigate their way to their rooms by flashlight like search parties in the wilderness. Most seemed to view this as an adventure. The only grumbling was from a few who lamented that night skiing had been canceled, and they were quickly redirected by staff.

Clearly, Rocky Mountain Summit was prepared for events like this.

The conversations were dimmer in the small area that held a table and four chairs, the perfect place to gather with friends and drink coffee.

Or to be interrogated.

Phillip inhaled quickly then exhaled slowly, likely resetting himself into character. Like her, the thing he wanted to do most was demand explanations from Chase Westin. Or, better yet, to grill him about his whereabouts while they were in the basement.

Neither of them could do that. They both needed to be slightly nervous and put out about being trapped in an elevator, as though they'd never been in a sticky situation before.

Man, this was harder than she'd expected it to be.

It would be even harder on Phillip. Westin's not-so-veiled accusations had been the catalyst for Phillip's struggles throughout the day. There was no telling what would happen if those accusations became more pointed tonight.

She gripped Phillip's hand tighter and didn't let go until she settled into the chair Westin pulled out for her. She clasped her hands on the table and stared at her fingers, turning her wedding ring as though she was full of nervous energy.

Phillip sat, his knee bouncing up and down as though he, too, was fighting off the fear of being stuck in a very small elevator.

Thalia frowned, feeling the lines deepen in her forehead. Actually, it didn't take much to let the fear of that moment rush in, throwing dust to cloud her thinking. Small spaces were... *No.* Her inhale was shaky, and this time, it wasn't an act.

"Can I get you some water, Mrs. Atkins?" When she looked up, Chase Westin was eyeing her with concern.

It was tough to tell if the sentiment was genuine.

She shook her head and looked down at the ring she still wasn't used to wearing. "I'll be fine once the power is on and I'm in our suite. Small spaces aren't my friends." At least that part was true. "Especially after this morning. Walking through a dark basement with only our cell phone flashlights wasn't my idea of fun. Too many things could be hiding in the dark, waiting to jump out at me."

She stared him in the face. If he'd been wielding that knife, he'd hear her loud and clear.

He held her gaze then shifted his attention to Phillip, showing no flicker of guilt. "You found your way out fine."

"We did." Resting a hand on Thalia's shoulder, Phillip eased closer to her. "I think my wife would like to get to our room, Mr. Westin. Do you need to debrief us about what happened in the elevator?"

"I think I can pretty much guess that part. I really wanted to check to see if you wanted some ice for that bruise on your face, Mr. Atkins."

Thalia's head jerked up. She hadn't really looked at Phillip since they'd come up the stairs. She'd either been behind him or had been focused on her surroundings. Grabbing his chin, she turned his face toward her.

An angry red mark marred the skin over his cheekbone. This was why Evan at the registration desk had been thrown off his hospitality game when they'd initially walked up.

At some point in the fight, while she'd been providing light and no other help, their assailant had landed a decent blow to Phillip's face.

She'd felt totally helpless, uncertain for the first time in her career. Normally, she'd have jumped into the fray, but had she done so they would have been battling in the dark, which could have proven disastrous for both of them.

Phillip turned his chin gently from her grasp. "I hit the corner of the wall before we got to the stairwell. I didn't realize it was hard enough to leave a mark." He leaned across the table toward Westin. "Sir, is there a reason you keep singling my wife and me out? Have we done something wrong?"

"Not at all. It seems like a lot has happened to you today, and I wanted to be sure you're both okay."

This time Westin's concern appeared to be real, but something about him still crawled under Thalia's skin. She tipped her head. "Thank you. We appreciate that." She reached under the table and squeezed Phillip's hand where he'd balled it into a fist against his thigh. She recognized the gesture. He was channeling all of his questions into his fingers.

A brief hum buzzed the air, the lights flickered and gradually powered on.

The remaining crowd in the lobby cheered.

Phillip exhaled slowly then stood. "Like my wife said, we appreciate your concern, but we're fine. It's been a long day full of some incredi-

bly bad coincidences. We don't blame the resort
for any of it." He wrapped his fingers around
Thalia's and pulled her to her feet.

Westin remained in his seat, looking up at
them.

Thalia offered a smile she hoped looked better than it felt, because what she really wanted
to do was launch into an interrogation of her
own. "We're going to head to our room, which
I'm glad doesn't involve taking the elevator. I'm
fairly certain I won't be getting on another of
those for a long time." Another thing that might
be true. She had the physical strength to climb
as many stairs as was needed to avoid a repeat
of the evening.

A wind gust rattled the lobby doors.

Phillip looked toward the sound as they
turned. "I'm surprised the power company was
out in this weather."

"Oh, the power wasn't out in the whole area."
Westin finally stood. He tilted his neck from
one side to the other as though he was working
out some kinks, then stopped when he noticed
Thalia watching him. He cleared his throat,
uncharacteristically off balance for an instant.
"The main unit that powers this building was
hit with a surge, probably somewhere farther

up the transmission lines. Our in-house maintenance department handled the issue." He directed a cryptic look at Phillip then stepped past them and walked away.

Phillip watched him go. "I'm really beginning to dislike that man."

"I'm really beginning to *suspect* that man." Especially when he'd had the time and ability to attack them in the basement. One thing was certain, Chase Westin was likely a threat that bore watching.

The world outside the French doors was blanketed in fresh white, blinding as the sun rose and setting sparkling fire to the trees.

Man, did he ever need a decent night's sleep. His brain was starting to sound like Shakespeare.

"Did you sleep at all last night?" Thalia's voice turned him away from the windows.

She walked in from the bedroom, dressed in jeans that hugged her legs and a dark green sweater that hung to her midthigh. Her hair was loose and waved to her shoulders. It was a softer look than when she pulled it into a ponytail.

In fact, everything about her aesthetic in those clothes was soft and feminine.

It was all a façade. Thalia was a lethal force,

and her clothing choices only covered it up, keeping people off balance. She had the ability to make the bad guys believe she wasn't a threat, and that worked to the team's advantage.

He alone knew the reason she wore that flowy sweater. She'd chosen the shoulder holster instead of the ankle holster, probably because she felt safer with the weapon closer at hand.

He could relate. He'd decided on a looser shirt of his own today. He wouldn't make the mistake of leaving the room without his sidearm again.

"So, did you sleep?" Thalia stopped between her room and the couch, watching him with her head tilted.

It was the same posture his childhood dog had used whenever someone said the word *treat*. Of course, he'd never tell her that. She'd resent being compared to an animal, even a cute one.

She'd especially resent being referred to as *cute*.

Thalia leaned slightly to get straight into his line of sight. "I'm guessing your answer is *no*, because you look zonked out even standing up with your eyes open."

Uh, yeah. He should probably say something. "I probably slept an hour." Phillip took a long sip of coffee to prove his point. The burn punctuated the words. There really wasn't enough caffeine in the world for this op. "It was productive insomnia though. I had some more thoughts about the investigation."

"I heard you pacing." She went into the kitchen, poured some coffee and returned to the den. Sinking into the chair, she tucked her feet beneath her, the picture of early-morning contentment and normalcy.

For them, this probably counted as normal. Adrenaline crashes, coffee and theories. That sounded about right. On this op, though, the surroundings were cushier and the coffee was definitely better.

She grinned. "You're thinking about the coffee, aren't you?"

How did she know? He arched an eyebrow, waiting.

"You're staring at the cup like *it* should be your wife instead of me." She held up her mug. "I get it. I need to find out where they get this stuff." Her expression shifted and she rested the coffee on the wide arm of the chair. "Joking aside, something's bothering you. It's what kept you up pacing the floor all night."

"You should have come out here. We could have talked it through." Or maybe she'd been right to stay behind closed doors. After all, he'd nearly kissed her once. Had given serious consideration to it again in the elevator, when there wasn't an audience to blame it on.

The last thing he needed was the surreal aspect of a middle-of-the-night brainstorming session. Sleep deprivation and that weird dark-of-night brain fog that often rode in with it would have led to a magnification of feelings he was better off setting aside.

"I was..." She pulled her mouth to the side, pursing her lips. "I was too busy lying really still in one spot and hoping that would make me drop off quicker." She didn't look at him. "So what did you figure out?"

"Nothing, but I came up with a new suspicion. I'm not exactly excited about it though." He almost wished the thought hadn't come to him, because no matter which way he turned it, he couldn't deny it might have weight.

"I may be tracking with you." Thalia dragged in a deep breath then released it slowly. "The only reason we were on that elevator was because Gabrielle Hubbard invited us to that get-together, then she and Drew both left before we did."

Bingo. He should have known her thoughts would run parallel to his.

She shifted, dropping her feet to the floor and sitting straight in the chair. "For the record, I'm not a fan of where that train pulls into the station any more than you are."

They both liked Gabrielle and Drew, and after hearing the couple's story, it was tough not to be sympathetic. Neither of them had a reason to doubt the account of their losses. According to Thalia, Gabrielle's emotions had been genuine, and Thalia was excellent at sussing out liars.

"Another thing is," Thalia said, "I see no motive they'd have for coming after us."

Neither did he. *Except…* "Let's not lose sight of why we were sent here."

"Because Stardust is suspected of defrauding couples, including some in the military."

He'd nearly forgotten their goal. A lot had happened since they'd arrived. A lot that could derail them, from the seeming randomness of what had happened to Thalia on the trail to the eerie similarities with his own past. "I think we've shifted focus and we need to come back to the core of this investigation."

"So, if we get back to the Turners and Stardust, and we look at everything through that lens instead of as random occurrences..." Thalia studied the ceiling. It was a familiar gesture that said she was flipping through thoughts and sorting them into workable evidence. "Gabrielle and Drew approached us at the ski lodge. We didn't approach them."

"And they were awfully friendly, awfully fast."

"Maybe Gabrielle was promised a fast-tracked adoption if they helped Stardust learn more about us?" Thalia sucked her upper lip between her teeth, a look that reeked of skepticism. "I don't know."

"It seems like a long shot, but we have to look at every angle. Also, consider this..." Phillip set his mug on the mantel then pointed in the general direction of the lobby. "Nearly everyone who is staying here was in the lobby last night. As nervous as Gabrielle was about the weather, would they have stayed in their room with the power out?"

"On the flip side, would she have felt safer in the room than wandering a dark hotel?"

True.

When Thalia sank into her chair, he knew she'd thought of something else. "As friendly as Gabrielle is, she hasn't texted this morning to see how we fared last night." She frowned and swirled the remaining coffee in her mug. "I don't want to think these things about them. Gabrielle seems sincere. I believe her."

This was new for both of them. Thalia typically shared his suspicious nature. Her view of people skewed heavily toward cynicism. She suspected everyone of something, no matter how innocent they appeared to be. Often, her instincts were right.

She almost never offered the benefit of the doubt.

This op was changing her. Maybe, like he'd felt, her line between reality and undercover was blurring. Maybe her emotions were swirling like the snow in last night's storm.

They should talk. If he brought his strangely warm feelings out into the open, they could work through them and return to the status quo. Their heads might clear enough to focus on their work.

It was possible both of them had learned to be Oscar-worthy character actors and were falling victim to their own abilities.

Or maybe he should keep his mouth shut, focus on the op and deal with the fallout when he could spend a few days away from Thalia.

Maybe then he'd be himself again and their partnership would continue to thrive.

That was a lot of *maybes*.

"You're thinking about something." Thalia was astute. She never missed much when it came to him.

Just like a wife.

The line between reality and undercover shifted again.

Did he dare ask? She'd probably laugh at him then get up and crack a joke about needing to head to the dining room so they weren't late for real eggs and maple bacon.

With a heavy sigh, Phillip lowered himself to sit on the hearth at an angle to her chair. His entire body ached. Maybe thirty-three was too old to be half drowned, half frozen and half beaten. One thing was sure, it was definitely too old to develop a schoolboy crush on his partner. "I think we need to talk about this op. It's getting a little bit—"

His phone vibrated and he pulled it from his hip pocket, not sure if he was grateful for or irritated by the interruption. The screen was lit with an unknown number. Beneath it were the words *Fort Carson, CO.*

Why would someone from Fort Carson be

calling them? Sure, he had a day job on post, working his cover, but they knew he was on leave and he'd left no work unfinished.

He swiped the screen and answered the phone on speaker. "This is Staff Sergeant Phillip Atkins."

"Staff Sergeant Atkins?"

Thalia's brow furrowed. She flicked him a quick glance.

Something was definitely wrong. "This is he."

"This is Staff Sergeant Tyndall with the 148th MP Detachment."

Phillip leaned closer to Thalia, holding the phone between them as his heart rate accelerated. "How can I help you, Staff Sergeant?"

"I'm sorry to bother you when you're on leave, but we needed to inform you—" papers crinkled on the other end of the phone "—we received a phone call from your neighbor this morning around 0300. There's been a break-in at your home."

Chapter Eleven

"We really need to know if anything is missing." A female MP escorted Thalia through the living room and into the kitchen at the rear of the house while Phillip talked with another MP on the porch. "To be honest, ma'am, this is the strangest break-in I've ever seen."

Thalia was inclined to agree. She stepped into the small den off the kitchen, which they'd been using as an office. The printer still sat on top of the two-drawer filing cabinet. The television was still mounted on the wall. Her decoy laptop still rested in the center of the desk.

Not a single high-dollar item had been touched.

They'd left everything set up as though they were a married couple going out of town for a week. No one who entered the house would realize they were investigators or had been sleeping in separate rooms. Even the laptop was designed to yield benign emails, random internet searches and visits to real estate websites to bolster their cover story if anyone gained access.

While nothing seemed to be missing, the sense of violation was sharp. This wasn't her real house, but she'd lived in the duplex for several months. The space had started to feel like home. While she spent her life dealing with criminals, knowing someone had wandered through her somewhat personal space uninvited didn't sit well.

Yet again, Thalia was swamped by the odd sensation of living two different lives.

At the moment, she needed to focus on this one. "I'll check upstairs. I don't have a lot of jewelry or anything, but it's worth a look." Turning to the MP, Thalia read the other woman's rank and name tape. "Staff Sergeant Baker, are you certain someone broke in?" This could all be a mistake made by an overzealous neighbor who'd dialed 9-1-1 too quickly.

She knew most of the neighbors, and none of them was the type to overreact.

"Staff Sergeant Pearsall next door called it in. He was up early this morning helping his wife with their new baby and happened to look out the window. He saw someone with a flashlight moving through the house from the front to the back. According to him, he initially thought you had returned early, but your husband had told him you'd let him know when you got back. Pearsall came over and knocked on the door. The suspect fled out the rear of the house. The staff sergeant chased him up the block but lost him in officer housing."

Maybe whoever it was had been interrupted before they could take anything.

Given the amount of electronics in plain sight, that was unlikely. "There was no sign of forced entry?"

"No, ma'am, but we haven't closely checked the locks yet. Something could have been tampered with." Baker tipped her chin toward the rear of the house. "Only thing we found was the back door open when we arrived, probably from when they fled." She scratched her cheek. "You know, this has to be someone who has easy access to post, someone who lives or works here, or they'd have had a hard time getting through the gate. I've heard stories from other posts of kids breaking into houses to throw parties, but we've not had that happen here. Proximity tends to deter mischief crimes. The neighbors are too close, in space and in relationships, particularly in this housing area."

Boy, did Thalia know *that*. She and Phillip had hoped to slip into the neighborhood under the radar and spend a few months simply living there to bolster their cover story while he worked a "day job" with an intelligence unit. But wow… This housing area was particularly tight-knit. There were cookouts and block parties and sports nights… Everyone knew everyone.

The forced socialization had been good practice as they'd settled into being "married," but it had been incredibly taxing on two people used to being loners. So many nights, she'd fallen into bed in the main bedroom exhausted, while Phillip had disappeared into the guest room to unwind. Both the arrangement and the silence had been comfortable.

A couple of times, though, having him under the same roof had made her consider what it might be like to return home after a night out as a real couple and to live life as one. To fall asleep together and to wake up together…

She shook off the thought. Those thoughts had been fleeting and born of exhaustion, nothing more.

Baker must have mistaken the motion for a shudder, because her expression shifted from business to sympathy. "We checked the house. No one is here and the rest of the place is as immaculate as this room is. Would you like me to walk through with you?"

"No. I'm fine." She didn't need a shadow. As an investigator, Thalia *Renner* was perfectly capable of inspecting her own house. Surely, Thalia *Atkins* was capable as well. After all, Mrs. Atkins might not be an investigator, but she was an Army wife, and there was strength enough in that. "I'll look around upstairs and let you know. Thank you."

As Staff Sergeant Baker waited in the living room, Thalia toured the upstairs. Nothing was out of place, and she called down to let the staff sergeant know. If their neighbor hadn't called it in, no one would have been able to tell an intruder had been there.

By the time she descended the stairs, Phillip was in the kitchen and the MPs had left the scene.

He was texting on his phone. Leaning against the island in the center of the room, he looked right at home.

Well, technically, this was home…yet not for

much longer. After this week, the op would likely end and they'd move on, leaving the neighbors to wonder where they'd gone.

This might be the last time they were in this space together.

The thought of no longer being at home here with Phillip saddened her more than she wanted to admit.

Phillip looked up from his work and set the phone on the island. "How's upstairs?"

"Like we left it."

Rubbing the space between his eyebrows, Phillip nodded. "So this wasn't about a quick buck."

"Are we alone?" She'd noticed the MP vehicles rolling out when she'd walked through the living room, but she wanted to be sure it was safe to talk openly. When Phillip nodded, she turned toward the small den where the desk was. "So now we stop looking for what's missing and start looking for what's out of place."

They'd always had a way of handling things when they left their home base. Certain angles they left things or certain items they placed strategically, so if they were moved, it would be immediately obvious someone had rifled through their stuff.

She'd checked the hotel room the night they'd found the matchbox, but nothing had been touched. She had a hunch today would be a different story.

Sure enough, when she looked down at the computer desk, her laptop was turned to a straight ninety-degree angle, not slightly off-center as she'd left it. "Already found it."

As soon as Phillip stepped beside her, she opened the laptop and keyed in the passcode, their fake wedding anniversary. She'd wanted to cement the date into her mind as well as make it easy for an outsider to guess.

Stepping aside, she let Phillip take over. While she could handle the inner workings of a computer in a pinch, he was the one trained to hack into a system or to search for hidden software. She was the brawn to his brains.

It took him all of three seconds to step back and brace his hands on the desk chair he'd leaned over as he'd worked.

"Someone tried multiple passwords before they guessed the right one. They entered your undercover birthday. Mine. A couple of old addresses. Then they landed on our anniversary and were in. Clearly, they had access to our personal data somehow, in order to know all of those things. We'll have Gabe check our bogus credit reports, especially since we know identity theft is a possible motive." He pointed at a line of white letters on the black screen. "Otherwise, they did a search of the hard drive, but they didn't offload anything."

"What were they searching for?"

"First, emails with a .mil extension, so anything pertaining to my job. Then they went through folders and files. I can track everywhere they went, but they didn't seem to find what they were looking for."

"So, is this related to the case? Or is it a random event because the house has been empty?" Like too much that had happened, the motives were ambiguous.

"I don't know." Shutting the laptop, Phillip turned and leaned against the desk, crossing his arms over his chest. He stared at the plaques on the opposite wall, which told the story of an invented military career. He seemed to read all of them before he shook his head. "A lot went into building our covers. This is probably the most complicated ruse I've ever been involved in."

Thalia furrowed her forehead. He was right, although it wasn't the direction she'd expected him to go. She mimicked his posture, keeping the chair between them. "It's a thorough backstory, but it had to be. Stardust runs deep background checks. So does every agency who looks at adoptive parents. It had to be solid." He knew this.

Phillip continued to study the plaques. "Staff Sergeant Phillip Atkins is in intelligence. My cover would know things. *Classified* things."

Thalia scanned the wall, reading the story of his fake career told in unit plaques and awards.

Phillip Atkins had an entire career based on knowing *classified things*. At least a few things suddenly made sense. "We need to make our way back to the resort and swing through Colorado Springs to see if we can find Hudson Macy, the guy whose identity was stolen. Maybe we can talk to him without him realizing who we are. He works in security for sensitive buildings on multiple posts."

"And Drew Hubbard works for Space Command, very likely doing work that involves heavy-duty clearances as well. I'm guessing, when we get intel on Quinones, he's involved with security or intelligence."

"The guy on the trail…he had fakes of Hudson Macy's credentials."

Phillip's eyebrow arched. "Which would

allow him to get through the gate without anyone noticing, since Macy is authorized as a contractor."

Uncrossing her arms, Thalia pressed her palms against the desktop and wrapped her fingers around the edge. "This isn't about scamming adoptive parents." Although that might be a side issue.

"No." Phillip's voice hung heavy between them. "This is about stealing military secrets."

In all of his years investigating and working undercover, Phillip had never felt the way he did as he slowly cruised the street where Hudson and Camryn Macy lived with their young son. His head was in the game as he watched the mirrors to make sure no one was following them, but his stomach…

His stomach felt like it had the time he'd cut class in high school to go to an Orioles game. Like he wasn't where he was supposed to be and he might get caught at any second. Having spent large chunks of his career in places "where he shouldn't be," the sensation made him feel like he'd stepped outside of his body.

He glanced over at Thalia, who was watching the houses pass. "Do you feel weird right now?"

"Like we're playing hooky?" She chuckled but didn't turn from the window. "Yes." She frowned. "There's a lot about this op that's weird though."

Phillip tightened his grip on the steering wheel and forced himself to watch the street. Surely she wasn't talking about the very subject he'd nearly brought up earlier. Maybe he wasn't the only one feeling that strange blur between who they really were and who they were pretending to be.

He waited for her to continue, keeping an eye on the sidewalks and yards they cruised past.

In spite of the cold, the snow that had fallen the previous night had brought parents and children out to enjoy the late-morning sunshine. In a park that was the centerpiece of the neighborhood, children threw snowballs and attempted to build clumsy snowmen.

It was all normal family stuff.

Beyond fleeting thoughts, he'd never before considered wanting something like those families had.

But now?

Now he wondered if he'd be content with going home to his empty apartment. He'd been living in the same house as Thalia for nearly three months. While they hadn't shared a bed-room, it had been nice to have someone to talk to in the evenings and to hang out with at cook-outs and parties.

Who was he kidding? It hadn't been nice to have *someone*. It had been nice to have *Thalia*.

"Hang on." Thalia's voice broke through his thoughts.

Phillip jerked and almost slammed on the brakes. Could she read his thoughts?

No. She was looking between her phone and the park. "There's a lady sitting at a picnic table with several other women. Gray coat. Green knit hat. Pretty sure that's Camryn Macy." She held up the phone, displaying a photo Dana had included with the background check on Hudson Macy. "We need a way to approach that won't put her on the defensive."

True. If they walked up and started asking questions, every mom in the place would think *kidnapper* then grab their kids and go, calling the police on the way out. Phillip and Thalia would learn nothing, and they'd have an unthinkable mess to clean up.

Phillip surveyed the area, trying to come up with a plan. *Lost dog?* Too basic as well as too suspicious. His mom had drummed it into his head as a kid never to help a stranger look for their dog, so it was probably still a red flag to moms today. *Salesman* might put their guards up. They could—

And there it was. A large For Sale sign held court on the lawn of a two-story Colonial directly across from the park, in view of the group they were targeting. He pointed to the house. "There's our in."

"Perfect. And we're close enough to Fort Carson that we can stick with our cover story about house hunting." Thalia reached for her seat belt as Phillip slowed and pulled into the drive. "Look excited, Staff Sergeant Atkins. We may have found our dream home." She was out of the car before he could kill the engine, excitedly motioning for him to follow her with an effervescence that was almost comical because it was so atypical of her personality.

The difference actually made him laugh. He pulled out his phone and filmed her exuberance.

Immediately, she dropped her arms to the sides and shot him a look that was all Thalia.

Now he had both on film. His "wife" and his partner.

Frowning, he stepped out of the car. He

shouldn't delve too deeply into how both were the same person.

She met him at the front of the vehicle. "Delete it."

"You don't want evidence you can be bubbly?" When she reached for the phone, he held it behind his back. "I think Rachel and Dana will get a kick out of—"

Lunging, she wrapped her arm around his waist to grab the phone.

He was faster. With his free hand, he pulled her against his chest, pinning her arm between them as he looked down into her eyes. "Now what?"

Her breath hitched. He could feel it in her back. Her eyes narrowed and she drew her lower lip between her teeth, searching his face, suddenly serious.

Maybe he shouldn't let her look too deeply. She might see the confusion he couldn't seem to get a handle on.

For several breaths, they stared at one another, an odd electricity flowing between them.

Suddenly, Thalia turned her hands, pressed her palms against his chest and pushed out of his hold. "Keep it." Running her hands through her hair, she walked toward the house, a plastic smile on her lips.

Phillip took a deep breath. When had he forgotten to inhale? And since when did he pay so much attention to her lips? Exhaling through his own pursed lips, he turned his face to the sky and followed her to the door. *Lord, this thing is messing with my head, and it has to stop. I* really *need You to make it stop.* If it didn't, he was going to either blow this mission or wreck the best partnership he'd ever worked in.

He couldn't lose Thalia because of a reckless kiss born out of roller-coaster emotions.

This was ridiculous. He wasn't the type to confuse his real self with his undercover persona, yet here he was.

As he stepped up onto the wide wooden porch with the swing and the hooks for hanging plants in warmer weather, he wanted this to be real. He wanted to live in this house.

Maybe even to live in it with her.

As Thalia made her way down the porch, peering in the windows of the empty house, he shoved that thought right over the railing and into the bushes. He might be feeling weird things, but he certainly wasn't in love with his partner. That would be disastrous.

The more likely explanation had to do with the close friendship they shared. They were a rare team. One that could practically read each other's thoughts. They had each other's backs in situations both benign and dangerous. Adding a sham marriage had created a layer of intimacy that would surely dissipate as soon as they went back to normal.

Right?

She returned to where he stood and took a position next to him, surveying the neighborhood. "Do you think they bought it?"

When he turned, several of the women were watching with interest, and one waved. He smiled and lifted a hesitant hand in greeting. "I'd say so. Want to go meet our new neighbors?"

"Let's go." Unlike earlier times at the resort, she didn't take his hand. Instead she walked close to him with her hands shoved into the pockets of her red ski jacket as though she was cold.

It took all he had not to put his arm around her shoulders and draw her to his side. It would sell the cover story, right?

But he didn't. Instead, he mimicked her posture, occasionally pointing out a feature of the neighborhood as though this was their only concern in the world.

All three of the women huddled around the picnic table looked up when they approached. A tall brunette waved them over and slid down to make room beside her on the bench. "You guys looking at the Kensingtons' house?"

"Across the street?" Thalia slid in next to the woman, and Phillip straddled the bench, facing her. She smiled. "We live on post now, but we're looking for something with more space for the kids to have their own yard. This park in the center of the neighborhood? It's perfect. Oh…" Her wave encompassed all three of the friendly but openly curious women. "I'm Thalia Atkins, and this is my husband, Phillip."

The brunette was clearly the unofficial lead mom. "I'm Jana." She pointed to another brunette and then to the blonde whose name they already knew. "Wynn and Camryn."

Camryn breathed into her gloved hands. "You guys have kids?"

"Not yet." Phillip pushed some expectancy into his voice, balancing his tone so he wouldn't scare off the woman he needed information from. "We're in the process of adopting."

Camryn Macy glanced at a dark-haired toddler playing in a snow-ringed sandbox with an older child. "We adopted our son not too long ago. Our agency was amazing."

"We love ours. In fact, we're at a retreat with them right now." Thalia's smile shifted to a frown. "Well, we're supposed to be. We had to take a break from the luxury life for a few hours. Someone took advantage of our absence and broke into our house."

Sympathetic murmurs floated through the chilly air along with the obligatory questions about what was stolen and if they were safe.

Phillip scooted closer to Thalia protectively. "MPs think it was kids looking for a place to party. Our neighbors are great. They saw a light in the house and checked it out. Nothing was taken, so we got off easy." Now he'd stay silent and let Thalia run with the conversation. The women were far more likely to open up to her.

"It's still a violation." Thalia twisted her lips into a disgusted pucker. She said no more, although he was certain she wanted to start firing questions at Camryn Macy about their experience with Stardust and about whether or not she was aware her husband's identity had been stolen.

The best thing to do was sit silently and let Camryn take the lead. It raised less suspicion and it generally led to deeper intel if the mark came to them.

An uncomfortable silence settled over the table. The ladies seemed unsure what to say next. Finally, Camryn planted both hands on the treated wood surface. "So, you're on a retreat? You must be with Stardust Adoptions."

Thalia's head snapped up. "How did you know?"

The other brunette, Wynn, shoved Camryn's shoulder. "That's the retreat where you did all of your interviews and got to know the other parents, right? Trent and I were jealous. Rocky Mountain Summit is a bucket-list place that we'll never be able to afford."

Camryn laughed, seeming to forget that there were strangers present. "Yeah, and you know we wouldn't have been able to go if we hadn't saved for years and then gotten that last-minute opening."

Interesting. So the Macys had landed on a Stardust retreat at the last second, possibly when someone realized what Hudson's job was?

Their working theory was growing stronger.

"It's good you got to go." Thalia leaned closer to Camryn. "Did you try the bacon?"

The other woman's eyes lit up. "Girl! That bacon was—"

"Cam!" A shout rang out from the sidewalk and a man approached, carrying a thermos and a canvas grocery bag.

It took everything in Phillip not to look at Thalia in shock.

As though they'd written the perfect ending to this day, Hudson Macy advanced.

Chapter Twelve

Even though she'd seen his picture and was reasonably certain Hudson Macy wasn't the man she'd tangled with on the mountain trail, encountering him in person confirmed everything. He was about six feet tall, much like the brute from the previous morning, but he was also reed-thin. Unlike her attacker, Hudson had kind blue eyes surrounded by lines that said he laughed often.

Thalia liked him instantly, a rare occurrence for her. Flicking a glance at the youngest Macy, who was throwing clumsy snowballs at another child, she smiled. It was clear that little boy was being raised by good parents who loved one another and him.

Would he ever wonder where he'd come from? Would he wrestle with dark nothingness in the night? Or would the love of his parents be enough? She prayed he wouldn't endure the self-doubts that had left her cold for too long, that he would be confident and happy and—

A warm hand on her knee drew her into the present.

Phillip was watching her with concern. He tipped his head toward Hudson as the other man drew near.

Right. She was supposed to be on the job, not taking a deep dive into past pain.

Camryn waved then turned to Thalia. "That's my husband. He'll be jealous about the bacon." She grinned then slid off of the bench and faced Hudson.

When Camryn approached him, Hudson cast a curious glance at the two newcomers, then laid a quick kiss on his wife's pink cheek. "You're cold."

"I'm staying out here as long as I can. If *somebody* doesn't get a whole lot of wiggles out this morning, then there won't be a nap and free time for Mommy this afternoon." She wrinkled her nose.

The other moms murmured their agreement.

Jana elbowed Thalia's arm. "That's good parenting. Remember that. Wear them out in the morning and you get time to yourself in the afternoon."

"Noted." She tucked away the information for future reference.

Except…did she actually need it? Kids had never been in the plan. Marriage, the whole picket fence thing… They'd never been a dream she'd entertained. Her career had always been enough.

Now something warmed behind her heart, and the spark started where Phillip's hand still rested on her knee.

When Camryn pulled Hudson closer to the table, Thalia turned her focus fully to him. "Hud, this is Thalia and Phillip. They're looking at the Kensington house. Oh, and they're also adopting through Stardust and were invited on the retreat. We were talking about the bacon at the resort."

Hudson's eyes widened comically. "You should smuggle some out. Freeze it for those times when you can't get the memory of it out of your head. Trust me. When your kid has been up all night and you need something extra to make it through the day, you're going to fixate on stuff like that." He handed the bag and the thermos to Camryn, then extended his hand to shake Phillip's and Thalia's.

He backed away as soon as they'd greeted

one another. "I'd love to stay, but I'm working from home today and I'm between meetings, so I have to get back online. It took me longer to make coffee and get here than I thought it would. Wild idea to bring the moms something to keep them warm. Hope it doesn't cost me my job." He grinned then turned to Camryn and pointed at the bag. "I brought a few cups and some creamer." He kissed her forehead. "Love you. Don't freeze out here." With a wave to the group, he was gone.

Thalia fought the urge to pound the table with her fist. They hadn't been able to ask him even one question. They still had no clue if he was aware his identity had been stolen. The entire encounter had been pointless.

The tension must have run through her muscles because Phillip's fingers tightened on her knee, a silent *calm down.*

She took a deep breath and focused on everything that had gone right. They'd come face-to-face with Camryn and had seen for themselves that Hudson wasn't their man. Both of those things weren't on their radar for the day, yet here they were. They might not uncover any additional information, but what had she expected? The Macys were victims of a crime, whether they knew it or not. Likely, nothing they said would add to the investigation.

Although it would have been nice to hear more about Hudson's job. *So close...*

Reaching across the table, Jana grabbed the thermos Camryn had set in the center of the group. "That man is a keeper, Cam."

"Most of the time." Camryn reached into the canvas bag and pulled out three travel mugs featuring logos from different vacation spots. Clearly, these were people who loved to travel and, like others, bought mugs as souvenirs. She frowned at the mugs then looked at Thalia. "If you guys want to share one, I can drink from the thermos lid."

"That's really nice of you, but we need to head out. Thank you though." Phillip made a show of glancing at his watch. "We should get to the resort. I want to call our Realtor to get some more details on the home for sale, and we probably need to put a lock on our credit, in case whoever broke into our house got ahold of enough information to steal our identities."

Smooth. He'd forced an opening where everything had looked like solid rock.

She could kiss him.

Or...not.

Camryn showed zero signs the words landed in a personal way. She simply winced in sympathy and poured coffee into one of the mugs, shoving it and the creamer toward the two women on the other side of the table. "Smart. I've heard that can be a mess to clean up."

Well, that answered one question. They seemingly had no clue someone had lifted Hudson's identity.

Neither Phillip nor Thalia could tell them, not without raising unnecessary suspicion.

Phillip stood and helped Thalia up. "It's happened to me once before and you're right. It's a mess to clean up. If you've never checked your credit report, it's a good idea to start. It's free."

The other three nodded as they prepared their coffee. The ladies would likely forget the admonition as soon as Phillip and Thalia walked away, but at least they'd done their best to issue a warning.

They said their goodbyes and headed across the street to the car. Once they were safely behind closed doors, Phillip started the engine and rested his hand on the gearshift. He didn't put the car in gear. Instead, he stared into the rearview mirror, probably watching the small group in the park. "What do you think?"

"The Macys have no idea they're victims, so we have no timeline of how long someone has been using Hudson's credentials. We also have no idea if the identity theft is connected to Stardust. It could have happened years ago or last week. This could all be a giant coincidence."

"And we don't believe in those." Phillip shifted into Reverse and eased out of the driveway. "I'll have Rachel make some calls to Hudson's company and to the posts where they have security contracts. She can let them know we've identified a possible breach without offering specifics. That will put them on alert without implicating you or me. Beyond that, we need to see if we can get to the bottom of this. We're running out of days, and we're getting nowhere."

When Phillip merged onto the highway, Thalia relaxed into her seat and closed her eyes. For the two-hour drive to Rocky Mountain Summit, she could be herself. She didn't have to force a happy face or pretend she couldn't defend against attackers. That might be the worst part. That, and the whiplash of being Phillip's partner one moment and his wife the next. The always-on nature of this assignment had her flipped around and twisted like a pretzel.

"That was a hefty sigh." Phillip's voice forced her to open her eyes. "I get it though. We're both exhausted."

They'd been on missions way more physically taxing than this one. This op was already taking an emotional toll she had never prepped for. How would she survive the remainder of the week?

Thalia stared out the windshield without lifting her head from the headrest. The road wound slowly upward, and the trees were coated in fresh white snow. Gray clouds hung low, threatening more wintry weather. With the change in weather, the ski slopes would be hopping, giving them more opportunity to mix and mingle.

They needed to find Finn and Valerie Quinones so they could start making connections between the orange-highlighted couples. Had the Macys been in that "club" as well?

"You okay?" Phillip reached for her hand and lifted it from the seat, wrapping his warm fingers around hers. "You're rarely this quiet. I should know."

She sniffed a laugh. Yeah, he should know. He'd been the recipient of more than one of her frustrated rants when an investigation spun in circles. "Whose idea was it to make me an investment banker instead of a cop or an MMA fighter?"

"You've already been under as an MMA fighter more than once." He squeezed her hand then drew back and held on to the steering wheel as he navigated a sharp curve. "This last time when I was with you, it might have been a fun assignment for you, but it was pretty rough on me."

"It was a lot easier on me than this one has been." The op had only lasted three days, but she'd gone into the octagon with three other female fighters in three different tournament bouts before they'd been able to determine who was supplying performance-enhancing drugs to the group. The pharmacist from a military hospital was in prison now, awaiting his trial. "I knew how to act. That persona was a lot closer to who I really am."

"This is true. You scrap better than you cower." He jostled her elbow off of the console between them. "Is it really so hard to be my wife?"

The question was supposed to be funny, she was sure, but a thin thread of gravity made the words hang heavy between them.

"No." The instant the word was out, she

wished she could take it back. The confusion she felt whenever he touched her wasn't something she should air. It was unprofessional and spoke against her abilities as an undercover officer.

Highly trained operatives didn't develop feelings for their partners because they exchanged a few hugs.

She cleared her throat. "What I mean is, I already know you better than anybody. It wasn't like we had to rehearse to make it look like we're something more. We know each other better than most married couples do. We've definitely faced more together. It's not too tough to make it look convincing." Maybe she'd said too much, but she had to backpedal.

She studied him from the corner of her eye, seeing if the ruse had worked.

The line of his jaw tightened all the way from his ear to his chin, as though he was grinding words between his back teeth.

Yet he didn't look angry. Instead, he looked... disappointed? Sad?

He didn't say a word. He simply slowed at a stoplight then navigated the turn up the mountain to the resort and back to a lie that was slowly becoming all too real.

★ ★ ★

He'd have been a lot better off if she hadn't brought up their last op.

They'd been in the midst of prepping for this mission when the call had come, knee-deep in practicing their role as a married couple. His head had been in this game, not in a side trip to a drug bust.

But Overwatch had needed someone for a few days to infiltrate a gym. A pharmacist at a military treatment facility was suspected of skimming performance-enhancing drugs and funneling them to local gyms near Houston. The unit simply needed the middleman between the pharmacist and the owner of the gym so they could flip him and get concrete evidence the pharmacist was the supplier.

To secure the credibility that would lead to the name of the middleman, someone had to spar in a tournament.

Thalia was the natural choice. Before she'd joined Overwatch, she'd spent months undercover with a different military investigative unit as a fighter in Albuquerque, gathering evidence against a ring smuggling drugs out of Mexico. Her work had shut down a major cartel and had brought her to the attention of Overwatch.

They'd been partners ever since, in ops around the world.

But watching those fights a few months ago had nearly killed him.

He'd been beside Thalia in physical altercations before. He knew she'd trained in martial arts and combatives, and a long list of disciplines.

Thalia was no weakling.

However…

He'd never had to stand on the sidelines and watch her throw down in an all-out brawl for sport.

Every blow she'd taken had ached in his own body, and he'd had to bury it all. Playing the role of boyfriend to the tough girl, Phillip had been under scrutiny as well. He hadn't dared wince when her opponents landed a punch or kick to her that bruised his soul.

It had taken all of his willpower not to throw in the towel to make it stop.

Not that Thalia had ever been in any danger. Having trained with the best, she won her bouts easily, earning them the name of the supplier after the second one.

She'd thrown the title match, unwilling to take the prize money from a fighter who needed it.

At the time, standing ringside and trying not to make himself sick with worry, he'd chalked up his reactions to their prep for this op. A married man would feel every blow his wife took, right? They'd been close to making the move to Colorado, nearing go-time on the mission, so he'd been living with the thought of Thalia as his pretend wife for several months.

But now...

Her flippant dismissal of their time together cut. Sure, it was the way he should be thinking, as well, but it hurt. In fact, her words gutted him in a way they shouldn't have.

The realization rattled him so hard he nearly let go of the steering wheel. Only practice in keeping up an act held him steady. If he freaked out, Thalia would certainly notice and he might be forced to confess these brand-new feelings.

Another realization nearly stole his breath. These feelings for her... They weren't brand-new. These were things he'd felt for...

How long?

He tried to pinpoint when this had started. Definitely before those MMA fights. This had been building for a while, so slowly he could only see it in hindsight.

So, when?

Phillip flipped through the past couple of years. He hadn't had these feelings on the mission with their team leader, Rachel, when they'd protected Marshall Slater and his daughter.

With quick clarity, like watching a movie, he could see himself on a mission shortly before this one started, standing in Gabe Buchanan's front yard. They'd been protecting Gabe from a vengeful hacker who'd wiped his name out of every computer.

Phillip had paused his search for a bullet buried in the siding on Gabe's house after an intruder had tried to gain entry.

Hannah Austin, their team leader on the op, had been looking for evidence in Gabe's backyard with Thalia. It had been easy to see Gabe was watching Hannah in a way that spoke of feelings way beyond friendship.

Feelings Gabe was trying and failing to hide.

Phillip had to force his attention to the winding road in front of him as his own words echoed in his memory. He'd looked up, following Gabe's gaze. While Gabe had been watching Hannah, Phillip's attention had stopped on Thalia, who was intently searching for evidence near the shrubbery. She'd been wearing the tight expression that indicated she was focused on the job while the world around her faded. It was a familiar posture. Something he witnessed on a regular basis.

That night, it had all hit differently.

He could watch her work all day. The essence of who she was shone through. She was unguarded and fully herself. It was like seeing Thalia in her purest form. She had grasped his attention in a way that hadn't let go, although he hadn't realized her hold on him until now.

Phillip had issued a warning to Gabe, who was considering a job with the team. The warning had come from deep inside him, words he hadn't fully realized he'd spoken until now. *Working with someone you have feelings for can be very…problematic.*

His thoughts stuttered. *Someone you have feelings for…*

Had he really said that? About—

"Do you need to pull over and let me take the wheel?" Thalia poked him in the side.

He jumped, returning his focus to the road, where he was riding the white line. "I'm fine. Thinking through the case."

"The case." Her echo was flat. "It's a weird one for sure."

The way she said it sounded odd, as though she was talking about something else.

Maybe even about what he was thinking? She'd always had a way of reading his mind. Did she realize he was on a course to crash their partnership onto the rocks, sinking it forever?

Maybe that's why she'd been acting strange, leaning in then pulling back. Repeatedly. As though she sensed he was getting too close.

There had to be a way to talk himself out of this. He opted for the route she'd taken. Non-chalance. "Yeah, it's been a wild—"

Something in the car *dinged* as they neared the large stone arch marking the entrance to the resort's property.

Thalia leaned across the console, studying the dash. "What's that?" She pointed to a light on the instrument cluster, a circle with an exclamation point in the center.

Phillip glanced at the icon, although he really didn't need to. As he slowed to make the turn, the feel of the brake pedal told him everything.

"We're losing brake pressure. Someone must have tampered with the lines."

Chapter Thirteen

Thalia planted her feet on the rock-salted asphalt and leaned against the passenger seat, letting the open door block the wind rushing off the mountain and across the resort's parking lot.

At the rear of their SUV, Phillip inspected the brakes. They'd both had rudimentary training in mechanics, and Phillip had an old Chevy Blazer he liked to tinker with in his off time like he knew what he was doing, knowledge courtesy of YouTube and a small library of automotive books.

There was no reason to crawl under the car though. They both already knew what he'd find.

Sure enough, he crouched beside the tire and held up two fingers, both smeared with an oily substance. He sniffed it then wrinkled his nose. "Brake fluid."

"How bad is it?" There was no way this was

coincidence. Someone had to have tampered with the brake line, likely hoping they'd fly off the side of the mountain on a hairpin turn.

Thankfully, cutting a brake line didn't work the way the movies often portrayed it. There were too many signs before complete brake failure, like the light in the car and the mushiness Phillip had noticed in the pedal shortly before the warning illuminated.

"Bad enough to require a tow truck." He wiped his fingers along the ground, then on the hem of his jeans. "Whoever it was has watched too many movies if they thought this was going to hurt us. They managed to nick the line, which caused a slow leak. It's not going to cause an immediate brake failure, but it can be corrosive. We shouldn't let it sit and drip on the ground."

Thalia rolled her eyes to the low-hanging clouds. "For sure nobody is going to notice a giant tow truck hauling our vehicle out of here." This was awesome. They didn't need another thing to call attention to them. "You realize if we were truly looking to adopt a child, we'd be in a lot of trouble."

"But since we're investigators…" Phillip stood and scanned the parking lot, probably to ensure

no one could overhear what they were saying.
"If we didn't already *know* we were being targeted, I'd say this is solid evidence."

"When do you think it happened?" If it was
while they were on the secure resort property,
the field of suspects was small. But off property?

Then it could literally be anyone.

Brushing his hands together, Phillip shrugged.
"Hard to say. It's a small enough cut that the
thing could have been leaking for more than a
day, one slow drop at a time. I will say if it happened here before today and the goal was to hurl
us off a mountain curve, then they'd have had
the time to do a more effective job."

True. Under cover of darkness and the previous night's storm, a saboteur would have had
ample time to damage their vehicle in more effective ways.

"It could have happened at any time this
morning too. They could have been surprised
by someone while they were working. Because
of the MP vehicles, we parked down the street
from our house on Carson, then we left the
car unattended and partially out of sight behind
shrubbery while we were at the park, so... No
good clues here." He nodded his head toward

the main building. "But we have bigger problems headed our way."

Thalia turned and peered across the car through the driver's window. Chase Westin had exited the main building. Serena Turner was trailing him, in deep conversation with her husband. "Westin manages to be everywhere the action is, doesn't he?"

"I can't decide if that makes me suspect him more or less. He's definitely not bothering to keep a low profile."

"Worse, he's got the Turners with him. If the bigwigs at Stardust want to talk to us, then the boot might be coming at us." That would be the worst possible scenario. It had taken over a year for one of their teams to get an invite to the retreat. If they were kicked out because of the trouble surrounding them, there was no telling how long it would take Overwatch to get someone else invited and in place. If this was happening because someone knew they were investigating, there might never be another chance to shut down the operation possibly stealing money and government secrets.

As the trio approached, Thalia moved to stand beside Phillip, watching them warily. She hoped she looked more exhausted than annoyed.

"Bad things seem to follow you, don't they?" Naturally, Chase Westin was the first to speak.

There wasn't a whole lot more Thalia could take of him without letting her true self shine through. She had words. So. Many. Words.

The look Serena Turner fired Westin's way said she wasn't a fan of him either.

Interesting.

Serena stepped in front of Chase as they drew closer. "We saw you out here looking at your SUV and had a few minutes between parent interviews. We wanted to see if anything is wrong and how we can help. You're certainly having an eventful week." The words were kind. Unlike Westin's veiled accusations, they seemed genuine as well.

Were they? It was tough to trust that much sympathy from a suspected thief.

"It's been a lot." Phillip dragged his hand down his cheek as though he was too tired to talk. "But we're getting through."

"How's your house?" Westin wasn't content to take a back seat to the owner of Stardust. "I heard you had a break-in." He studied her, almost as though he wanted to see how the words landed.

Thalia tilted her head. They'd notified Stardust that they'd had to leave the property for the morning because of an issue at their home...but how had Westin found out? And how did he specifically know there was a break-in?

Serena's eyes went wide and her husband stepped beside her, his forehead etched with concern. "A break-in?" Brantley Turner shared a quick look with Serena then turned to Phillip. "I assumed you had a water main break or something, not a... Was anything taken? Is there anything we can do?"

Crossing his arms over his chest, Chase Westin watched with a look of calculated interest.

"No. Nothing was taken." Phillip reached for Thalia's hand and pulled her closer. "As far as the military police are concerned, it was some kids looking for a place to party. Our neighbor ran them off."

Good answer. It made them look like less of a target, which would throw Westin off his game.

The head of security nodded slowly. Something like compassion flashed in his expression before he slipped into impassivity.

At least the comment seemed to take some swagger from the man. His cockiness rankled Thalia's nerves and made her want to see how

long he'd last if they went toe-to-toe in a sanc-
tioned bout.

She would take him down quickly, largely
because he'd underestimate her.

Pressure on her fingers drew her into the conversation, almost as though Phillip knew she was
calculating how to wipe away Westin's superior-
ity complex. She'd hear about this later, she was
sure, with a smirking, exaggerated admonition
against beating up the people who crossed her.

Brantley Turner stepped forward, taking control of the conversation. "Given all that's happened to you this week, my wife and I have
been talking and…" He surveyed them with
narrowed eyes as though he wasn't sure he
wanted to say his next words.

This was it. They were being asked to leave.

Thalia dug deep into her acting abilities. This
was her time to shine.

She widened her eyes in faux fear and forced
unfamiliar tears. With the cold wind blowing
in her face, it wasn't difficult. "Mr. and Mrs.
Turner, please don't say anything more." She
leaned heavily on Phillip, who let go of her hand
and slipped his arm around her waist. She took
a deep breath and thought of Gabrielle and the

others who were here hoping for a family, who wanted nothing more than a child of their own.

She was doing this for them.

Before either of the Turners could speak, she charged ahead. "It took us a long time to get here. We never thought we would. And I promise this is not how our life usually looks. A couple of random coincidences have happened, but we're still here. We came back today because we want a family. We want to love a child who needs to be loved."

In a rush of emotion, the tears became real. The words caught on the sharp edges of her own childhood. She wasn't just fighting for parents. She was fighting for children who deserved to be safe and loved. For herself, who had needed the same things.

If it hadn't been for her parents adopting her, there was no telling who or where she'd be today. "Please." The word choked out on a sob she couldn't swallow.

Phillip seemed to freeze, then he tightened his arm around her waist as if he knew the act had suddenly become very real.

The sincerity in his touch broke through a dam she hadn't realized existed. She choked on the next word, rendering it an unintelligible sob, and turned to him, tears blazing down her cheeks in a hot trail that cooled quickly in the icy air.

When Phillip looked her in the eye, there were questions all over his face, but he pulled her to his chest without asking anything.

Thalia pressed her forehead into his sweater and sobbed. She was embarrassed. Humiliated.

Yet she couldn't stop the tears. Who was this person who had suddenly fallen apart in public?

She couldn't find herself in the storm. The darkness inside had broken free.

What was happening? Phillip had been silently cheering Thalia's performance as she put the pressure on, fighting to save their op. Then everything shifted and... She fell apart.

Thalia did not *fall apart*.

Yet here she was, sobbing into his sweater, soaking the material until his skin beneath was damp with rapidly cooling tears.

There was no way to hide her complete collapse. All he could do was hold her and let this play out. He buried his face in her hair and inhaled the clean scent of shampoo, closing his eyes as the emotion she was spilling worked its way out of her and into him. His entire body ached with her pain. Silent, frantic prayers raced through his mind.

He'd never expected this. A well of emotion had been capped off inside her. Sure, he'd suspected she buried her feelings, but this...

This was not Thalia.

It also wasn't the calculated maneuvering of an undercover agent. The way her face had crumpled and her shoulders had slumped had been heartbreakingly real.

He had no clue how to fix it.

There was a rustle nearby and he lifted his head as Serena Turner stepped closer.

He'd completely forgotten they had an audience. The urge to turn her away from them and to shield her from prying eyes nearly overwhelmed him, but he held his ground and waited. Thalia might be falling to pieces, but she'd have words for him if he didn't do all he could to protect their cover.

Serena rested her hand on Thalia's back, her perfectly sculpted eyebrows knitting together with concern and another emotion he couldn't identify. Though she was comforting Thalia, she addressed Phillip. "The adoption process can be emotional and difficult. I understand. We want you to do what you believe is best for you and your family."

"Staying is best." As difficult as this was, the mission came first. Both of them knew it.

Thalia nodded, pulled in a shaky breath and straightened. Swallowing hard, she wiped her face and turned to Serena, seeming to search for her voice.

Even the sympathetic crease in Chase Westin's forehead appeared to be real.

That man was too hard to read. Everything about him crawled up Phillip's spine like fire ants.

No one noticed his disgust, because all eyes were on Thalia as she spoke. "We're staying. This is about family. Nothing is going to keep us from that."

Phillip heard what the others didn't. Threaded through his partner's words was a raw determination to solve this case. To stop the Turners from dashing dreams and manipulating others. Whatever had broken inside Thalia was piecing back together with strength and resolve.

Both of the Turners nodded, but Westin seemed to watch Brantley for some sort of signal he never received.

Instead, Brantley eyed Thalia intently before

he finally addressed Phillip. "Can we do anything for you?"

"Actually, we could use a tow truck. The warning light for our brakes came on as we arrived here. I'm thinking maybe they overheated?" He gauged their reactions.

If one of them had anything to do with the brake line, they were very good actors. Not even a trace of guilt blew across any of their faces.

Westin smirked. "I doubt that's the case, but I'll call a tow truck for you." With a nod, he headed toward the resort, his phone pressed to his ear.

"We'll leave the two of you alone." Serena squeezed Thalia's hand and stepped back. "If you need anything, let us know. Your appointment with the adoption counselors is tomorrow?"

"At three." Thalia's voice was stronger now. "Thank you for understanding."

After saying their goodbyes and offering help one last time, the Turners left, their heads together as they walked to the resort's entrance.

Probably talking about the "problem couple" who was bringing so much trouble to their retreat.

When they were out of earshot, Thalia sagged against the side of the SUV that faced away from the building. She stared out over the mountains that rose and fell in the distance, her jaw tight.

Phillip stood at the rear of the vehicle, hands shoved into his pockets, simply watching. Whatever was running through her mind, she needed a minute. If he approached her too soon, she'd snap a sarcastic comeback and lock herself up tighter than the safe in their suite.

He had his own emotions to work through. Between the realizations he'd come to on the drive and the way she'd felt in his arms, crying into his chest with no reserve and nothing hidden…

He felt as though he'd jumped off the ski lift at its highest point and was tumbling down the mountain with no way to slow his descent.

He had no idea how to play this, what to say to her, nothing. Everything had changed.

Except the mission. *That* remained the same. If they were going to succeed at stopping the Turners from dashing another family's dreams or figure out whether or not there was espionage on the table, they had to be focused.

Easier said than done. *Focus* was on short supply lately.

As suddenly as she'd fallen apart, Thalia straightened and faced him. She clapped her hands together, the sound echoing off the trees around the parking lot. "We should get lunch, and then there's either another afternoon of skiing or a group hike to the lake in the valley. We should find Finn and Valerie Quinones so we can start figuring out why they're tagged." She was babbling, which was something she never did. "We also need to find Gabrielle and Drew, see why they've been MIA since before the power outage."

When she started to walk past him, Phillip grabbed her biceps. "Slow your roll, McFly."

She sighed heavily and stared past him, her lips pursed with impatience.

Should he really be noticing her lips?

Phillip shook his head to fling the thought away. "What just happened?"

Her eyes flicked to his then to whatever was so interesting behind him. "I was acting, and it worked. *Work* is something we should be doing, by the way."

She started to step around him, but he tightened his grip. "How long have we been together?"

The question caused her to stiffen, but she didn't pull away.

Too late, he realized how the phrasing sounded, more like they were a couple than a team.

"Right now, I'm wondering if it's been too long." She pinned him with a hard gaze, her dark eyes issuing a challenge he couldn't quite decipher.

The statement cut. So did the cold determination in her expression. Whatever had happened, she was intent on burying it...and him.

Well, Phillip was equally intent on stealing the shovel. He couldn't let her cover this up. She'd broken through, released something that had needed to breathe. If he cared about her at all, he wouldn't let her shove it into a dark hole.

"Thal, I know you better than anyone."

Sniffing, she tipped her head and stared at the sky, then closed her eyes. A strand of her brown hair clung to her eyelashes and fell across one cheek. She huffed, drawing her eyebrows together. "It was embarrassing."

Rare emotional fragility peeked through, unguarded. This time, it seemed to be by choice.

Thalia was always on guard, always watching for threats, always cautious about her surroundings.

But not now.

With her eyes closed and her head tilted, she was vulnerable to attack. It was Personal

Safety 101. It was a posture that should only be taken with…

With someone you trusted.

A rush of adrenaline squeezed his heart. Thalia trusted him.

She. Trusted. Him.

She believed he would keep her safe, would do whatever it took to protect her. So much so, that she had made herself vulnerable.

While she was more than capable of taking care of herself and took pride in that fact, she was now letting him be her protector.

The magnitude of the moment hammered through Phillip's heart. For the first time ever, she was being her unfiltered and unguarded self with him, handing him every part of who she was.

Did she even realize it?

His emotions settled into the truth he'd been trying to articulate to himself earlier. He trusted her as well. Completely. She wouldn't turn on him or become someone else. She would always have his back.

She was the one person he'd never doubted and had never questioned.

She was Thalia. Unlike any woman he'd ever met. Beautiful. Competent. Strong.

What he did next… What he said next… It would change everything.

He had a choice. He could let the moment fall and shatter in the brittle air, and they'd keep right on going as they'd always been, but it would never be the same.

Teammates. Partners. Friends. And he'd know, beneath it all, there was the potential for more. That would always be between them.

Or he could risk it all.

That strand of hair lying across her cheek… His fingers ached to brush it away.

He was suddenly incapable of taking a full breath. If he walked away and let things stagnate in the status quo, he might never breathe again.

"You should never feel embarrassed around me." His words scraped out in a hoarse whisper. Sliding his hand down her arm, he laced his fingers with hers and pulled her to him. Barely brushing her cheek, he thumbed her hair back and let it fall beside her ear. He trailed his fingers down to her chin, tipping her head slightly, giving her every opportunity to retreat.

Her breath hitched. When her eyes fluttered open, they looked straight into his with a depth of emotion he'd never seen before.

There was no doubt. He was completely gone over her…for her…about her.

Her fingers gripped his tighter and she drew him the rest of the way to her, meeting him halfway in a kiss that spoke everything he wanted to say but couldn't put into words.

Chapter Fourteen

This…

This was…

Everything.

Everything she'd been feeling. The highs… The lows… They all crashed into this moment, rushing between the two of them.

The near kiss in the lobby had been uncertain and possibly fake.

But this… There had never been anything more real than this. This moment wasn't for an audience.

In the brokenness, Thalia had finally let go of her fears and pain. As the tears poured out, they'd washed away lies she'd always believed. That she was a nobody with no past, with a future and identity dictated by the things she could never know.

With the darkness unleashed to light, the truth ran free. She had an identity.

She had birth parents who had released her, but the *why* no longer mattered. She had adoptive parents who'd ensured she was loved. She had a personality and a sense of self that had been built by her experiences and by the people in her life.

Maybe even by the God she was starting to suspect actually cared after all. When she'd unlocked that door in her heart, truth began to flow in. Truth spoken by Rachel and Phillip and Dana and other members of their team. There was a God who cared, who had walked beside her on that street in Pohrebeni and in every moment since. She could clearly see Him now.

So, no, this moment wasn't for anyone else. This moment was for her.

For them.

This was her heart meeting Phillip's. Her whole self poured out for the first time in her life. Everything good about her. Everything bad about her. The dark, empty, unknown inside of her had poured out, leaving space for something else.

For Phillip to accept or reject.

She gripped the front of his sweater, holding on in a silent plea. *Please accept.*

Turning his head slightly, Phillip broke the

kiss. He pulled her closer, tucking her head against his shoulder, holding her as though he was afraid she might run. His pulse raced against her cheek.

Not going to lie, part of her considered taking flight. She'd never felt so exposed. So flayed open, as though her heart was on the outside of her body for the world to see.

But she'd never felt safer or more accepted. She flattened her palms against his chest, reveling in the beat of his heart. The rhythm was quick. Steady. Solid. Everything Phillip had been since the day she'd met him.

"Thal, you need to know…" His voice was rough, like a creek rolling over rocks. "That was not an act."

The words rumbled against her palms.

Her eyes drifted closed. It had been as heart-consuming for him as it had been for her. As real as—

Was it real? They'd been playacting for months, and these emotions flooding her were overwhelming. What if she was wrong? What if, a few weeks or months from now, they came to their senses?

No matter how much she wanted this, the tactical side of her urged caution, even though she wanted to fly down the mountain at break-neck speeds, rushing into life with him.

And that was the problem.

Thalia pressed against his chest gently, pushing Phillip away. "We need to take a minute. This is wrong right now."

She stepped around him, but he grabbed her wrist and wouldn't let go. "Meaning?" He wasn't going to make this easy and she knew better than to expect he would.

"Phillip, we can't. There are too many variables, and we have too many responsibilities and—"

"You know going back is impossible, right?"

Actually, it wasn't. She'd spent a large chunk of her life walling away her feelings. It was very possible to continue doing so now, at least until the mission was over and they could be fully themselves again. "What if we get out of this mission and move to our separate homes and we figure out this was a moment when we got caught up in this game we're playing and we're both completely confused?"

He pulled her closer, his eyes dark. "Are *you* confused?" His voice was a low rumble that demanded the truth.

No. She wasn't.

Yet this couldn't have happened at a worse time. They were twenty-four hours from their final consultation with the adoption counselors. Twenty-four hours from having to put on the show of their lives, when their "marriage" would be scrutinized from every angle. They couldn't throw the wrench of a real relationship into the works now.

It might be too late.

But they were good at their jobs and they'd make it work. They always did.

"You never answered the question." Sometimes Phillip was relentless. A good trait in an investigator. Not such a good trait when Thalia was done talking.

"I can't. Not—" Her phone vibrated in her pocket and she shook her head. Taking a step away from him, she retrieved the device and held it up to show him the screen.

It was their team leader, Rachel Slater.

She surveyed the parking lot to make sure no one was within earshot and then answered on speaker, turning the volume low and motioning Phillip closer. It was time to transition from the personal box to the work box, something they were both adept at doing. "You've got me and Phillip. We're outside away from listening ears."

"Understood." Rachel's tone was all business. "I'll make this quick. I've sent Hannah to your house on post. She's acting as your sister."

"Got it." Phillip was standing close beside her and had focused on the phone, but for the first time Thalia could remember, he was being careful not to touch her. "It'll be good to have someone there."

Thalia heard what he wasn't saying. If team leader Hannah Austin was on-site, she could do a thorough search for anything that might be missing from their fake home. She could also spend time on the devices they'd left behind to further inspect the hard drives and make sure no viruses had been uploaded. Better yet, she'd be able to search for planted devices. At any rate, Hannah might be able to help them get to the bottom of what was happening.

"Anything else?" Phillip shoved his hands into his pockets and looked over his shoulder, checking the front of the resort through the SUV's windows. Eventually, someone would come out and they'd have to cut this conversation short.

"A big something else." Rachel's voice dropped low with the gravity of whatever was coming. "I had Gabe run backgrounds on both of the names you gave me. The reports are in your emails. It's interesting. That's all I'll say. But, guys? Be careful, because you're right. What's happening might be a whole lot bigger than bilking adoptive parents out of money."

So, their suspicions were confirmed. They'd passed the realm of thievery and stepped into a scheme with far deadlier implications.

The laptop slid across the granite counter a couple of inches as Phillip entered his passcode with more than a little bit of force.

Seated on the floor in front of the coffee table where her laptop rested, Thalia didn't look up.

Truth be told, she was likely ignoring him.

He dragged the laptop closer and clicked on his email program, trying not to think about how this normally worked.

Normally, Thalia would be leaning over his shoulder as he navigated through the program to open Rachel's secure email. *Normally*, she'd elbow him and tell him he was too slow or tease him for being the tech geek.

The fact she was sitting on the other side of the room spoke at a deafening volume. He wished he could turn it down from eleven to one so he could hear himself think.

Or so she could hear his heart speak.

Then again, his heart had done all of the talking when he'd kissed her.

He'd known he shouldn't. He'd done it anyway.

But she was right, whether he liked it or not. If they were going to risk their friendship by elevating it to more, then they needed to be sure.

And they needed to wait until they weren't on a mission a year in the making. There was too much at stake to risk it all now.

Clamping his teeth down on a frustrated exhale, Phillip opened the most recent email from Rachel and downloaded the attached files. They'd asked for extended background checks on the Hubbards and the Quinoneses, hoping to find something linking the couples to one another and to themselves.

Each file was over a hundred pages long, filled with documents ranging from marriage certificates to college transcripts. He looked up at Thalia, who had also opened her email. "Divide and conquer?" Why did his voice sound so strained? He cleared his throat. "You want Hubbard or Quinones?"

"I'll take Quinones." She looked at him for the first time since she'd answered the phone in the parking lot.

Grabbing the laptop, Phillip walked over and sat in the chair at an angle to her position on the floor. No matter what was humming between them, they worked best when they were together.

Propping his feet on the coffee table, he planted his laptop on his thighs. He scrolled to the summary where Gabe always bullet-pointed the highlights.

Before Phillip could start reading, Thalia tapped the top of his screen with her closed fist. "Hey, guess what Valerie Quinones does for a living."

"Well, you didn't give her a rank, so I'm guessing she's a civilian but...she works for the government?"

"Ding, ding, ding!" Thalia lowered her voice. "Thank you for playing, sir." Her expression sobered. "Yeah. Like our new friend Hudson Macy, she works for a company that contracts with post security, but she's at Fort Bragg, North Carolina."

Interesting. There was some serious secret squirrel stuff happening at Fort Bragg. What were the odds Valerie Quinones was somehow connected to that kind of intel? "So three files flagged in orange. Three couples on this retreat affiliated with the military, either in intelligence or security."

"We can't say the orange highlighting was a way to mark the scholarship families, because Stardust makes a big deal about comping the trip for active-duty military. They've never mentioned a program for civilian contractors, and we know the Macys paid their own way." Thalia opened a window and tapped out a message. "I'll have Gabe see if he can get the necessary warrants to dig deeper into Valerie Quinones's finances, see if any payments went out to the resort or to Stardust."

"There's a reason we were all invited to this retreat. Whoever broke into your laptop at the house knew personal details like birthdays and past addresses. Someone went in and took nothing, but they went through your laptop. Either they were searching for something on it, or they added something to it. We all have intelligence or security experience. I think we were right. This is bigger than simply bilking a few hopeful adoptive parents out of money."

"This is espionage." Thalia puffed her cheeks with air then let it leak out slowly. "If we'd suspected this before, we could have planted dummy intel and then watched to see if it filtered through any known intelligence brokering channels."

Like dye on a medical scan, purposely leaked false data could be traced either by keyword or software trackers. "We can bait that hook now and see if we get a bite. When Hannah gets to the house, we'll have her upload something onto your device that looks confidential. If they're tracking your keystrokes or data transfers, then we'll know pretty quickly."

Nodding, Thalia typed another message. "Okay. There's that." She shut the laptop and looked up, her expression resolute. "What does the file on Drew and Gabrielle say?"

The light he'd noticed the past few days was missing from her eyes now. She'd slipped behind the wall and was operating in safe mode, doing what was necessary to survive. He'd seen it so many times. She almost ceased to be human, stuffing her emotions into a lead box to complete the mission.

Too often, he'd been envious of her focus, but now?

Now he saw it for the dangerous self-protection that it was.

He wanted to kiss her until the locks disintegrated and the walls crumbled into dust. Until she recognized her value to him and to everyone else who loved her.

But Thalia didn't need to surrender to *him*. She didn't need to measure her worth by how people felt. She needed to surrender to *God*. To see how much He loved her and to learn who He said she was. She hid from Him by choosing a course in life that merely went through the motions without actually living.

That was a matter for prayer, which would have to come later, when he had time to himself.

His display had darkened, so he swiped his finger across the track pad and started reading as soon as the words appeared.

Everything was exactly as Drew and Gabrielle had said. They were a perfectly normal couple. Nothing in their finances or backgrounds indicated anything nefarious.

It couldn't. Drew had a Top Secret security clearance with SCI access. "I don't think Drew or Gabrielle has cut some kind of deal with Stardust. It could jeopardize his security clearance. His clearance also has Sensitive Compartmented Information added on."

"Which means he's a pretty secret squirrel. What does he do specifically? Was Gabe able to find out?" Thalia's phone buzzed and she pulled it closer, swiping the screen.

Phillip scrolled through a couple of the pages until he located the information. "Drew works with satellites, and not just weather satellites either." Communications. Intelligence. Drew Hubbard dealt with some of the deepest levels of security the military had. If this was about espionage then—

"Phillip?" Thalia was staring at her phone. "I heard from Gabrielle."

At the tone of her voice, he pulled his hands from the keyboard and looked up. "What's wrong?"

Her expression was grim. "They've left the retreat. Last night, their house was also the target of a break-in."

Chapter Fifteen

Thalia scanned the dining room, searching for familiar faces. They needed more than high-lighted names and burner phones. Concrete evidence Stardust was involved in both theft and espionage was necessary, and the week wouldn't last forever. Their plan for dinner was to work their way into a seat at Serena and Brantley Turner's table or to get into a conversation with Finn and Valerie Quinones. If two of the three highlighted houses had been hit, it was likely the other couple had suffered a break-in as well.

More than they needed evidence, she needed to keep moving. If she stopped, she'd drown in the events that had happened in the parking lot. Her breakdown...that kiss...

She shook her head. The mission. She had to focus on the mission.

Serena Turner swept into the room, dressed

in dark jeans and a lavender button-down shirt, elegant even in her casual attire.

It was showtime.

Before Thalia could move, the woman sat at a full table with only one seat left for her husband.

Okay, then. Maybe they could orchestrate a meeting with the Turners, say they had some concerns. They'd have to play that one gently though. They were walking a tightrope, and leaning too far could land them hard on the ground.

She stepped deeper into the room. At a back table, Finn and Valerie Quinones sat huddled together, looking concerned. No one else had joined them, likely because the table was isolated in a darker corner.

She'd taken two steps toward them when Phillip appeared at her elbow, holding out her customary cherry Coke. "You look like you're headed somewhere."

"Finn and Valerie are over there." She sipped her drink. It was twice as sweet as the night before. "Less cherry juice next time?"

"Whatever you desire, your majesty." Phillip dipped into a fake curtsy. "Shall I make certain your bacon is extra crispy in the morning as well?"

"And please be sure my eggs are scrambled with exactly half a teaspoon of sea salt." Humor like this was how she and Phillip survived. Why did things between them have to change?

"Really?" Phillip chuckled then held his glass out to her. "You want to try mine? The bartender, Claire, suggested orange and vanilla soda. It's pretty good." He arched his eyebrow, already knowing her answer, he was certain.

Thalia shuddered. While she choked down orange juice when there was no other option, it wasn't her first choice. "I'll stick to this, even if it's about to spike my blood sugar into the stratosphere." She took another slow sip of her cola. "This bartender you know by name. Claire? She's making you personalized drinks?"

"It's her job. Jealous?" He cleared his throat and his neck pinked, a clear sign he wanted to take the words back.

If only he could. They hit a little bit too close to home.

Phillip studied his drink. "I chatted with Claire last night, looking for inside intel."

If you wanted to know something fast, you asked the people behind the scenes. She'd spent a few minutes talking to room service after they'd first arrived. People tended to look past staff members and to be less guarded around them. They typically knew everything, even simple rumors. Often, gossip held a nugget of truth. "She been helpful?"

"Not yet. But I talked to her about our break-in. Told her I heard it had happened to another couple, as well, trying to ferret out if she'd heard of any other Stardust couples getting hit."

"And?"

"She shrugged it off and said it wasn't unusual for thieves to hit empty houses, which is true. I couldn't press her without looking suspicious."

While thieves liked an easy target, the fact that break-ins and identity theft were happening to families who worked in intelligence and who'd been flagged by Stardust was worth looking into.

"You can keep working the Claire angle. For now, we'll go and talk to Finn and Valerie. They don't look like they're up for a chat, but they're about to make new friends whether they want to or not." She tipped her head toward the couple, still talking with furrowed brows. At the motion, her brain seemed to swim inside her skull.

Thalia righted herself quickly and reached for Phillip's arm.

He laid his hand over hers. "Something wrong?"

"Sugar high." She linked her arm with his and tugged him to follow, carefully stepping around other diners.

"Really? Sugar? I've seen you suck down lattes with three billion shots of syrup and double the whipped cream without flinching."

She didn't dignify his comment with a response. There was no way she'd ever tell him that emotional exhaustion likely had more of an effect on her wavering brain than the amount of syrup in her Coke did.

He pulled his arm from hers and lagged behind to guide her with his hand on her lower back. It was an intimate gesture, protective and warm.

Reading too much into that might get her into trouble, so she focused on putting one foot in front of the other. It was hard to do. The day was catching up to her. Hopefully, they could learn something then get out quickly. She'd never been one for an early bedtime, but now it sounded like the perfect plan.

Phillip stopped walking and pulled his phone from his pocket. He glanced at it then held it up for Thalia to read.

Gabe's number flashed on the screen.

"He's probably got more thoughts. Want to see what he has to say?"

As tempting as that was, she needed to talk to Finn and Valerie, her mission for the evening. "Brief me. I'm going to stay on target."

"Save me a seat." He dropped a kiss on her cheek and walked out of the room, the phone pressed to his ear.

Was his kiss for show? Or for something more?

The room wobbled as though an earthquake rolled through. Her drink sloshed over her hand.

Thalia grabbed the back of the nearest chair to steady herself, searching the room to see if anyone else felt the tremor.

No one else seemed fazed.

Her vision wavered and her throat thickened. Something was wrong, and it wasn't exhaustion. This felt more like...

More like...

Hand shaking, she set her drink on the vacant table and stared at it. This was more like someone had doctored her drink.

She tried to turn but moved too quickly. The floor rocked.

If she passed out in front of everyone, it would spell the end of this investigation. She had to get out, to find Phillip.

Fighting to stay conscious, she made her way to the door, gripping the backs of chairs as she went.

Everyone probably thought she'd been drinking. *Great.* That was an awesome look for a hopeful mother.

In the lobby, she looked around.

No sign of Phillip.

She'd go to the room. Bracing a hand against the wall, she made it to the hall and knew she wouldn't make it much farther.

To her right was a room with a television and a couch for those who missed news from the outside world. Stumbling inside, Thalia pulled her phone out, trying to text, though her fingers refused to work. She mashed letters she hoped would tell Phillip where she was...

Her legs refused to work any longer.

She crumpled to the floor.

He should have grabbed a jacket. As Phillip stepped outside the lobby doors and away from the building, the cold night air soaked through his button-down shirt. It was warmer inside, but the last thing he needed was to risk someone overhearing this conversation. "I'm clear now. What have you got?"

Hopefully, some answers, because those seemed to be in short supply.

"Confusion." Gabe's voice was deep with the kind of exhaustion that weighed Phillip down as well.

"Welcome to this op, pal. That's all we've got here too." His heart sank. If Gabe had no answers then Phillip wasn't sure what their next move should be.

"Confusion isn't always bad. Sometimes, it gets you thinking."

"Go on…" Leaning against the low brick wall along the edge of the hotel's drive, Phillip crossed one arm over his stomach, trying to keep warm. He wanted to urge Gabe to talk faster, but they might both miss something important.

"I'll give you the short, geek-free version." Gabe often liked to explain his process. Thankfully, it didn't sound like that was the case this evening. "I think you're dealing with two different criminals who may or may not be operating independently of one another."

Phillip stood. "What? You're going to have to walk me through at least the basics of your geek-think here, because that's a stretch."

"I've looked at this from multiple angles, and

the operational models don't match up. If you've got a good thing going by bilking people out of money in a way that looks legit, why would you risk it all to break into houses and steal identities for espionage? One is a small-time racket. The other casts a wider net with a lot more moving parts. Along with several other factors, I just can't see this being the same person."

"But what if they're stealing from prospective parents in order to fund their other operations?" Even as he asked the question, it made no sense. If someone was making money on the black market selling secrets, why would they bother with the "small change" that came from hitting a few parents in the wallet? "Never mind, I figured it out."

"You and Thalia need to be looking at this investigation from two angles, not one. That's all I have at the moment. I can add that the identity thefts and intel breaches would require several people with some basic tech skills to break into the houses and to create the fake IDs necessary to pull off whatever it is they're doing. That crew is likely who's coming after you and Thalia. After all, if the Turners suspected you were investigating, they'd simply ask you to leave."

True. "What should we make of the burners in their closet?"

"You'd have to get your hands on one. That could be anything from an affair to a smuggling ring. I'm still digging into them. Honestly? I don't like them for either crime. Never have."

Well, that was interesting. "They definitely have fans around the resort. It seems they've been pretty generous with the staff." He outlined what Claire had told him, ignoring a buzz indicating he'd received a text.

"Yeah, that's not typical behavior for thieves unless there's a Robin Hood syndrome going on. Since some of the birth parents who backed out and took money pulled the scam on military families, the whole 'rob the rich to give to the poor' thing doesn't quite fly. I'll keep digging though."

"Appreciate it. This op is taking a toll on both of us. It's tough." That was more than he'd meant to say, but Gabe was his closest friend. They'd bonded while the team had worked Gabe's stalker case. "The sooner we get out of here, the better."

"So the fake marriage is hitting a little too close to home, huh? I kind of saw that coming."

Phillip's mouth dropped open, although the

comment shouldn't have surprised him. As a profiler, Gabe was adept at reading people, especially his friends. "What tipped you off?"

"What didn't? Phil, think about this… You've had an unhealthy sense of distrust for every person you've ever met, even me. People have to earn their way when it comes to you, then you still expect them to disappoint you. That doesn't hurt my feelings. I can make my guesses about possible traumas in your past, but I won't." Gabe rushed ahead, not leaving an opening for interruption. "But let me ask you this… Who's the one person you've never questioned? Have always trusted? Think about it."

The call dropped. Gabe didn't want a discussion. He wanted Phillip to mull over what he'd said.

Sliding the phone into his pocket, Phillip crossed his arms over his stomach, his brain spinning and dragging his heart along with it.

Thalia. Despite all of the suspicions and fears Ashlyn had ignited, all of the ways he knew he could be betrayed and hurt, he'd never once thought Thalia would turn on him. From the moment he met her, he'd known she was special. He'd probably started falling in love with her from their first handshake in Rich's office.

Falling in love with her.

The thought settled like a warm blanket. It was a truth he'd denied for far too long. It was the reason this op was so hard for him, the reason her backing away earlier had cut so much. He *did* love her. He *did* want to spend his life with her, sharing all of the things they were pretending to share.

Lord, let her want it too.

He believed she did, but he also believed she was scared.

No wonder this whole thing had him completely turned around.

Pulling his phone from his pocket, he started to let her know he was headed in, but there was a message already on the screen.

Oh, yeah. One had come through while he was talking to Gabe. He swiped Thalia's name and the text opened.

Drink drugged. In hall TV.

What? He read the text again, adrenaline surging as he tried to make sense of the ending. How had her drink been drugged? Where was she?

And was he too late?

He burst into the lobby, expecting to see

signs Thalia had gone into distress in the dining room. The space was tranquil and still. The dining room doors were open and the murmurs of relaxed conversations drifted out.

She must have gone to the room.

He ran to the front desk. "Call 9-1-1. Something's wrong with my wife." Without waiting to see if the woman complied, he headed for their suite. She had to have gone there. His heart raced with fear and exertion, scattered prayers blending with the whirling thoughts in his head.

He burst into the room, calling her name.

There was no reply. Quickly, he searched the space and came up empty. Whoever had drugged her must have—

The truth hit like the icy wind had the night before. *Claire.* She'd made both of their drinks, insisting Phillip try something new. It was her way of making certain he didn't mix them up. Thalia had mentioned hers was too sweet, likely extra syrup to overpower whatever the cola had been laced with.

Claire might now have Thalia…if Thalia was still alive.

Phillip headed for the door then hesitated and went to the secure bag in the bedroom for his identification and the equipment he'd need for the coming showdown.

This ended tonight. There would be no more undercover work. The op was over. He had to identify himself and save Thalia.

He made a call to Rachel as he exited the room, notifying her of the situation. She'd handle calling the proper authorities and explaining things to the resort, ensuring he had backup as soon as possible. They'd find Thalia.

They had to.

He raced toward the lobby, but stopped halfway there. *In hall TV.*

Thalia wasn't in the dining room. Each floor had a media room offering guests a place to watch television, since the rooms didn't have TVs. Thalia must have made it to the one on their hallway.

He was at the door to the room before he realized he'd covered the distance. Through the window, Thalia lay on the floor, motionless.

His stomach threatened to revolt. *No. God, let her be okay. Please.* It was the only prayer he could force out of the emotions threatening to choke rational thought.

Shoving through the door, he dropped to his knees beside her, feeling for her pulse with one hand while he gently shook her shoulder with the other. "Thal, it's me. Come on…"

Mumbling, she turned her head toward his voice but didn't open her eyes. "Drink."

"I know. Claire poisoned your drink. Help's coming. I already had someone call—"

"It's probably too late for that."

At the voice, Phillip whirled toward the door and stood to face the newcomer.

Claire. Holding a pistol.

And pointing it at him.

Chapter Sixteen

"Phillip?" The word rasped out of Thalia's dry throat.

Where had he gone? He'd been there, cutting through the fog and bringing her back into the present. Then was gone. Another voice, muffled through the roaring in her head. A female.

A paramedic?

No, she sounded angry.

Training urged her to rise and fight, but her body was encased in concrete. Her mind operated on half its normal speed. None of her muscles wanted to obey the slow-moving thoughts in her head.

She managed to convince her eyes to open, blinking slowly as the room spun and twirled. Colors and objects mixed and overlapped. The world worked its way into focus, like pieces in a kaleidoscope tumbling.

Finally, an image formed.

Phillip stood between her and a figure at the door who was silhouetted in the fluorescent light that spilled from the hallway through the window. She could only see the side of the woman's head and her left arm. Something about her was familiar, but the way Thalia's thoughts tumbled over one another, there was no way to know for certain.

Without turning, the other woman pulled a string on the blinds, blocking the view from the hall and reducing the light to the glow of a small table lamp.

The softer light gave Thalia's eyes a moment to adjust and the scene came into focus. It was like watching a movie, seeing the action but being outside of it and unable to affect the situation.

Phillip held his hands out from his sides and backed slowly away from the woman. The posture was familiar. He was feigning surrender, but his hip holster was within quick reach. She must be training a weapon on him. "Why are you doing this? What's the point?"

The woman shifted and looked around Phillip, her face finally visible. She looked straight at Thalia. "Recognize me yet?"

Thalia blinked and tried to get the face to

process. Somewhere in the far reaches of her memory, recognition tried to work its way forward. The face reminded her of something. Of blond hair, not red. Of a fight. Of…

Of Albuquerque.

The truth returned in a rush. Claire had been a low-level runner for the drug crew when Thalia had been undercover for all of those months before she'd joined Overwatch. Along with a handful of others, the woman had spent time in jail when the bust went down.

Had she figured out Thalia had been undercover then? Was undercover now?

Thalia's lungs tried to gasp, but they seized. It was getting harder to breathe. Harder to stay awake. *Lord. I know You care. You hear me. Help…* Her mind screamed prayers. For herself. For Phillip.

Claire smiled. "I see you remember now."

Phillip seemed to sense Thalia's stress. He eased sideways and looked down at her. "Claire, whatever you're trying to do, she needs help. The paramedics are on the way. She's going to die if you don't—"

"Not immediately, but the fentanyl will eventually do the job. I want her to suffer. All of us in the crew lost everything, did time and had to start over with nothing to show for our work. Obviously, she found you and has been living the high life as an Army wife ever since. Did you know your wife's a criminal, Staff Sergeant Atkins?"

Was it a relief to know Claire believed their cover story?

No. Because her expression was murderous. "I'm pretty sure she's the one who ratted us out to the cops in the first place, since she vanished after the bust and we never heard a word about her doing time like the rest of us." Claire focused her attention on Phillip. "But since you've called for help, I guess we'd better speed this up. Sorry your wife is a drug runner, Phil. And while I enjoyed talking to you, this isn't about you."

Phillip's hand moved for his hip.

There was a loud pop. The sound of a gun fitted with a silencer.

He dropped with a thud beside Thalia, gasping for air before he went still.

No! The scream stuck in her throat, lodged in her paralyzed vocal cords. She willed her body to move to Phillip, who was only a few feet away, but she couldn't. He might as well have been on another planet.

She couldn't reach him. Couldn't save him. She was helpless. She had nothing. *God, please. Please.*

A warm tear trailed down her cheek. He couldn't be dead. Claire couldn't have shot him. None of this was happening.

It was getting harder to breathe.

Stepping around Phillip's body, Claire knelt in front of Thalia and pressed the gun to her forehead. "I could put you out of your misery, but I won't. That would be too easy." She shook her head. "You showed up, the newcomer, and you almost took over the crew. And then we mysteriously got raided. And we all went to jail. Except you." She leaned closer, her fake smile fading into a scowl. "Then one of my guys tells me he saw you waltz into the lobby the other day like you owned this place, and I figured it all out. You never suffered. You've got this great new life with a soldier who loves you, and you're adopting a kid." Claire shook her head. "You don't get any of that now. None of it. Mark didn't finish you off on the trail when he should have, so I'm going to do what he couldn't."

Thalia's breathing was slowing. Panic surged through her, but her body couldn't react. She was dying. Phillip was dead.

This couldn't be the end. There had to be more for her. Gabrielle had said her children's lives had meant something. They'd changed the world. Although she'd never met them, had never gotten to know their personalities or even their physical traits, she'd known them. They'd been her children. They'd had an identity.

Thalia had an identity. Where she'd come from didn't make her. The experiences of her life did. The people in her life did.

Love did.

And it was too late to do anything about it now.

Another tear chased the first one, though she could barely feel it. It was hard to draw a full breath. The edges of the world were dimming.

"I have to go now, before the paramedics show up." Claire stood, looking down at Thalia. "I'd say I'm sorry, but I'm not. Enjoy watching it all disappear."

She kicked Thalia's shin, but the pain didn't register. There was nothing. Only the agony of a heart in pieces and the terror of a body slipping toward death.

Pain. So much pain.

At the moment of impact, the gunshot had

stolen Phillip's breath and whipped white-hot pain through his body, robbing him of the ability to breathe. To stand. To do anything but suffer.

He'd hit the ground hard, almost certain the bullet had pierced the vest he'd put on before he'd left the suite.

Instinct begged him to dig the bullet out, to make sure he wasn't bleeding from the heart. Likely, the vest had stopped the round from penetrating, but from close range, the pain was enormous. He'd probably broken a rib. There was no way to know.

Agony and the fact that playing dead was the only way to survive kept him still.

He'd never wanted to move so much in his life, but Claire thought she had already dealt with him, so she'd focused on Thalia. All he needed was a few seconds for his body to absorb the pain and then he could save his partner.

Please, God, fast. Before she hurts Thalia worse.

Where was help? Where was backup? It felt like hours since he'd bolted through the lobby, since he'd prepped for this confrontation.

Behind him, Claire was speaking. She could shoot Thalia any second. The threat was ongoing. He had to do something.

He couldn't let Thalia die in front of him. She was his partner.

She was the woman he wanted to spend his life with.

Gradually, his breaths returned, though he had to fight the urge to pull in deep lungsful of air. He had to be still and quiet until the right moment. The initial explosion geared down into dull agony, but it was enough.

Claire rose and moved to step over him.

This was the moment.

Forcing his body to move, Phillip threw his arm out. White-hot pain blinded him as he turned with the motion, rolling onto his back.

The blow caught Claire in the leg and threw her off balance. She pitched forward and landed on her hands and knees.

The gun skipped across the carpet and came to rest near the door.

Phillip tried to get to his feet, but the throbbing in his chest was intense. Maybe the vest hadn't stopped the bullet after all.

There wasn't time to check.

With an unintelligible cry, Claire rolled onto her back and leapt to her feet, whirling to stare down at Phillip.

He couldn't get up in time. Couldn't fight her off.

And she knew it.

She drew her foot back to kick him in the side, a move that would surely end him if she drove a splintered rib into his heart.

Summoning all of his remaining strength, Phillip drew his pistol and fired, half-blinded by pain.

Claire roared and fell to her knees, clawing at her shoulder.

Phillip's arm dropped to the floor. That gunshot better have drawn some attention. Help had better come. He couldn't last much longer under the onslaught to his body.

He wanted to check on Thalia, but the immediate threat was Claire. Until she was dealt with, she was still dangerous.

As best he could from his vulnerable position, he lifted his sidearm, ready to pull the trigger if necessary. Clearly, his aim had been compromised the first time, but he didn't want to shoot her again unless she gave him no choice.

Breathing heavily, Claire rose to her knees.

"I'm a federal agent, Claire." Phillip took aim at center mass. "Don't make me do this." *Please,*

God, calm her down. Send help. Something. I don't want to take her life.

Claire glared at him. "You shouldn't be protecting her. Thalia's a criminal. She's been lying to you." She backed toward the door.

Or toward the gun.

"Claire…" His voice held a warning. He kept the weapon as steady as he could while his brain tried to go dark and his mind spun with the truth. Thalia had never lied to him.

She never would.

Claire continued to inch toward the door.

If she fled, the amount of blood dripping between her fingers from her wounded shoulder said she wouldn't get far. If she went for the gun… "Stand still and raise your hands, Claire. It's over."

Shaking her head, she reached behind her for the door. "I'm not going back to prison."

Her hand gripped the knob.

The door flew open.

Claire stumbled forward with a cry.

A police officer entered, weapon drawn, followed by Chase Westin.

Phillip immediately lowered his pistol and raised his empty hands, the room rocking with waves of pain. "I'm a federal agent. My identification is in my left hip pocket. My partner is behind me." He sketched the details as Westin stepped around the police officer and found Phillip's badge.

Westin held it up to show the officer and then helped Phillip to sit as the officer took Claire into custody. "Your team leader notified us of the situation. I'm sorry I—"

"Not now." Phillip cut off Westin's apology. "My partner needs medical attention. Claire drugged her. Fentanyl." He turned away from Westin and reached for Thalia.

Her breathing was shallow. Her skin was pale.

"Please, God." He whispered the prayer as more people rushed into the room. "Don't let it be too late."

Chapter Seventeen

The world came back in a violent rush.

Thalia gasped, trying to fill empty lungs. She inhaled once. Twice. Short breaths that didn't satisfy.

What was happening?

Where was Phillip?

Nothing registered. She couldn't remember where she was or how she'd gotten here. She was walking to the table to talk to Valerie Quinones, wasn't she?

Her eyes flew open. She struggled to sit up, finally getting a deep enough breath to expand every inch of her lungs.

The relief was fleeting. "Phillip?" A nagging, raging fear for him flooded her, but she couldn't piece together why.

Hands grasped her shoulders and eased her down. An unfamiliar female face hovered over her. "You're going to be okay, ma'am, but I need you to be still."

"But Phillip—"

"Just be still." The woman's voice was soothing, and Thalia let herself lean into the peace it invoked. "You ingested fentanyl, and we've administered naloxone. We're going to transport you to the hospital."

"Phillip?" Why wasn't he here? Something in her memories screamed he was dead. She'd lost him.

Everything was wrong but she couldn't figure out why.

"Let me talk to her." A male voice came from her right. It wasn't Phillip's.

She managed to turn her head. Why was she on the floor? Had she passed out in the dining room? *Wait.* "Fentanyl?" She'd ingested fentanyl?

The drink. Her soda had been too sweet. Somebody had tried to cover the taste.

Her brain slowly started to process as someone knelt on her other side.

Chase Westin looked down at her with pity in his eyes.

Pity. That meant— "Where's Phillip?" As

much as she didn't want to hear what she feared the answer would be, she needed to know.

"He's fine. He refused transport and is in the hall, getting looked at by the medics. He's in a lot of pain, but he's going to be fine."

Phillip was safe. Not dead. Safe. After taking a bullet. Probably for her. She'd cry if she was the type of person who cried in front of others.

A brief memory flashed past of Phillip crumpling to the floor, but it was gone before she could process it. Had it happened? Or was her imagination working double-time as the effects of the fentanyl and the naloxone coursed through her system? "I want to see my partner."

The paramedic spoke. "You will, but right now you need to be still."

Though she still felt weak, she struggled to rise. Lying on the floor with no way to defend herself against Chase Westin was more than she could take. She looked at the blonde paramedic who had remained beside her. "I want to sit up." It was a command, not a plea.

The other woman must have heard it as such. She helped Thalia ease into a sitting position so she could lean against the couch for support.

Thalia looked Westin in the eye. "Why are you here?"

His dark eyebrow arched, likely at her pointed question. "It's good to see you're going to be okay." He offered her a brief genuine smile. "I'm head of security. Why wouldn't I be here?"

Yes, he was head of security, which meant he should be informed who had attacked her. "Claire doctored my drink. The bartender in the main dining room. She—"

"Is in custody." Westin rocked back on his heels and motioned for the paramedic to step away. When she hesitated, he gave her a terse nod. "You can stay close, just out of earshot. I'll give you the high sign if something goes wrong."

The other woman gave a quick glance to Thalia for the okay, then stood and walked a few feet away, keeping a wary watch on her patient.

While Thalia didn't think Chase Westin would try anything, she wasn't entirely sure. She was grateful for the extra set of eyes on her. "What do you have to do with this?"

"Nothing." Westin held her gaze then reached into his pocket and passed her a wallet that looked all too familiar.

She flipped it open then closed her eyes to reset her brain. At this moment, she needed to be one hundred percent certain she was seeing clearly. When she looked again, the words hadn't changed.

Chase Westin was an FBI agent.

Wordlessly, she folded the case shut and passed it back. Until she knew what he knew, she wasn't saying a thing.

He tucked his credentials into his hip pocket. "I know you and your partner are federal agents."

"What makes you say that?" If he was bluffing, she wasn't going to fall for it.

"I suspected something about the two of you. You were…off. I can't tell you how I knew, but you pick up a vibe from people undercover after you've been undercover yourself. The long and short of it is that I asked for some deeper background checks from my team on the two of you, deeper than the average entity would be able to run. Didn't take much to figure out Phillip and Thalia Atkins don't actually exist."

Still she waited. He could be fishing.

"At first, I wondered if you were working with Claire and her crew, so I kept a close eye on you. I did it out in the open, so you'd think I suspected your hus— your *partner* of domestic issues. I received a call from an Alex Richardson about fifteen minutes ago. He confirmed your presence here, and said you needed backup, but he gave no further intel. We heard the gunshot and headed this way."

Thalia sagged against the couch. Dropping Rich's name gave her the assurance she needed. Westin was legit.

While she still felt weak, her mind was coming back online, although how she'd gotten into this room was still fuzzy.

The desire to see Phillip was overwhelming. If she had the strength, she'd already be up and heading after him. If she did, he'd read her the riot act for not finding out all she could from Chase Westin. She set aside her personal needs. "What's the story here?"

"I have about thirty seconds before they put you on a stretcher and haul you out. Short version? A couple of years ago, Claire presented herself as a potential birth parent and bilked families at multiple agencies out of a great deal of money by pretending to back out at the last second. She was never pregnant in the first place. Despite all of the precautions the Turners take, they were fooled by some members of Claire's crew who had fake documents and medical histories. It was a sophisticated con. Several families lost money and had their hearts broken."

"That's why we were sent in. We thought the Turners were involved." She'd give him that much, but what she really wanted to know was about those highlighted names. "There's more, though, and it has to do with intelligence."

"I'm sorry. What?" Westin's eyes widened. He glanced at the paramedic, who hovered nearby as the door opened and several EMTs entered. "Claire blackmailed the Turners, threatening to bring forth evidence she'd planted to show they were behind the scam. The Turners went along with Claire for a while, handing over confidential information on certain guests. Claire and her crew are running an identity theft ring. Brantley Turner eventually had enough intel and came to the FBI to have us investigate, which is why I'm here. He's playing both sides in exchange for immunity, informing on Claire, who thinks she's working for him."

"That explains the burners in his closet."

"That's how he passes along info. One call, then destroy the phone. Claire never talks to the Turners directly." Westin nodded. "Claire has a whole ring of thieves here. They work at the resort, partying it up, but they're making bigger money somehow. I knew it went beyond identity theft, but I hadn't figured it out yet."

"But we did."

"Did she discover you were investigating?"

Thalia shook her head. "No. She—"

"I want to see her. Now." Phillip's voice rang through the room.

Looking up, Westin nearly smiled. He squeezed Thalia's hand and stood, moving away from her. "Let him in. If you don't, he'll rip the door off to get to her."

A jolt shot through her, painful yet sweet. She closed her eyes against the sensation. Phillip really would do whatever it took to be by her side. She had no doubt.

The light shifted, and when she forced her eyelids to open again, Phillip was beside her.

She'd never been happier to see anyone in her entire life. "You're alive."

"So are you." His voice was haggard and tired, and he sounded like he might be out of breath. "I wasn't sure for a minute and…" He shook his head, his gaze never leaving hers. With a slight smile, he brushed her hair back from her cheek and tucked it behind her ear. He winced with the effort. "I think the mission's officially over."

"And I think you're hurt." It took all of her strength to reach up and grab his hand. She pulled it down beside her and held on tight. As much as she prided herself on her independence, right now, she never wanted Phillip to be out of reach again. They were both safe here, in this cocoon between them, despite their bruises and scars.

"I'll be fine. I'll get checked out once I know you're okay." He lifted her hand and pressed a kiss to her knuckles, running a jolt from her hand straight to her heart. "We need to talk about some things."

No, they didn't. Talking would ruin everything because she'd never be able to put it into words. Right now, she just wanted to be with him and to let this feeling settle. This peace. This wholeness. This sense that she was finally complete. There was no way to say it that sounded right, so she squeezed his hand. "Hey, partner. Me and you? We're going to be okay."

He seemed to hear what she couldn't say. As the medics rolled a stretcher into the room, he smiled at her then bent closer and pressed a kiss to her forehead. "Better than okay."

Phillip stood in the center of the suite's living room and stared at the hallway door, which had just closed behind Chase Westin, who'd gone to his car to grab Phillip's prescribed pain meds.

Leaving the hospital without Thalia had been one of the hardest things he'd ever done. He'd managed to work his way into the ambulance with her, each turn a searing jab in his chest, but it had been worth it to hold on to her hand and to know she made it there safely.

Easing down to the sofa, Phillip winced against the pain in his side. A series of exams and scans had revealed a large contusion and a cracked rib at the site of the bullet's impact. He'd thanked God more than once he'd taken a minute to grab his credentials and to armor up before he'd headed out to find Thalia.

If he hadn't, they'd both be dead.

The docs had released him before her. Rachel had ordered him back to the hotel to facilitate the transfer of evidence and notes over to the FBI, who would now be working jointly with Overwatch in a task force aimed at building a case against Claire and her crew. As much as he'd wanted to buck that order and to be by Thalia's side, he understood the mission dictated they move quickly to round up the rest of Claire's crew and to process evidence before it was destroyed.

Chase Westin had followed their ambulance to the hospital and had been waiting for Phillip when he was discharged from the ER. Who'd have thought that guy would be an ally? Or an FBI agent?

Or that he'd be the one to ride to the rescue?

Phillip closed his eyes against the thought, his stomach quaking from leftover adrenaline and residual fear. He could have lost Thalia today. That frightened him more than the threat to his own life.

It was a good thing Westin had left the meds in the car. Phillip needed a few minutes of quiet to process the events of the day before he returned to work. To pray for Thalia and to shift gears in his brain.

If only she was here…

Phillip winced, both from the pain in his chest and the pain in his thoughts. When it came to Westin, he'd trusted the wrong person. He'd tried to get answers from Claire, believing her to be a harmless bartender, while he'd suspected the acting head of security of any number of crimes.

Despite it all, the man had come through for them in the end. Phillip's worst fears had come true. He'd made huge mistakes about character and motives…and everything had worked out anyway.

He was going to get it wrong sometimes. He had to let go of the fear of that.

Maybe it was time to give up control and let God take the wheel. To trust.

Thalia would likely agree.

Thalia…

He'd heard what she hadn't said earlier, and his heart had been too wild to respond. He wanted to tell her plainly to her face he had no doubt he was truly in love with her, not just fake-undercover-marriage-in-love with her. There would be no more pretending. No more hiding. No more lying…to her or to himself. He would tell her how he felt as soon as he saw her. She needed to know he'd risk everything to be *her* everything.

He wanted to hear her say the same.

The door opened softly, but he didn't bother to turn. "You can throw them on the counter. I'll be down to the security office in a few minutes to go over the evidence."

There was a slight rattle as the pill bottle was obviously tossed to the counter, and then a shadow appeared at the end of the couch. "Are you kicking me out, partner?"

His head jerked up so fast, his neck and chest protested.

Thalia.

She gave him a wan smile, her face pale and her eyes tired, but she was there, standing in front of him, well and whole.

And hopefully his.

If he could, he'd jump up and hug her. No, he'd kiss her until she was convinced of their love for each other. But his body wasn't prepared for quick movements. "How did you get back?"

"Rachel showed up just as I was being discharged. We ran into Westin in the parking lot, and she's in the security office with him now. You and I have been ordered to take a few minutes to decompress before we go."

Decompress. Rachel was savvy. She likely knew they needed to talk. He'd thank her later.

Phillip started to stand, but Thalia held up her hand. "Stay there. We're giving up all of this cushy luxury soon. I think I'll enjoy it for another minute. Maybe call room service for one more round of bacon."

Slowly, as though the room might still be rocking, she settled on the other side of the couch then turned so she faced him with her knees bent and her feet between them.

The last time she'd taken that position, the night before, she'd slipped her feet beneath his leg as though she belonged to him. As though they did this all the time and it was her right to touch him. It had been more intimacy than he could handle in the moment.

If only she'd do that again.

He waited for her to say something, but she remained silent, staring at him as though she was seeing him for the first time. Before he could speak, she started talking. "I thought you were dead." When he started to respond, she shook her head and plowed forward. "I don't remember anything after I left the dining room, but I do know I thought you were gone. That I'd lost you. And it…" Her head swung from side to side again and her eyes shone with unshed tears.

Thalia. And tears.

He felt his own eyes sting. *Come on.* This was not cool on any level.

Phillip cleared his throat. "I thought the same about you."

Her gaze met his. "And?" There was an undercurrent in the word, one his brain couldn't process.

But his heart did.

He could kiss her right now…if he could move without a thousand lightning bolts shooting through his chest.

He didn't need a kiss though. He had the rest of his life to kiss her. The way she was looking at him erased the last of his doubts.

Right now, he simply wanted to belong to her, truly, not as fake husband and wife but as their real selves. "Know what?"

She tilted her head, shooting him the same half-flirty look she'd been faking him all week.

This time, it was real. "You're thinking you love me?"

So, she really could read his mind. Oh yeah, if he could move, he'd definitely kiss her. "I do."

"Funny. Because I'm pretty sure the feeling is mutual."

Phillip moved slowly, partly because he didn't want to spook her into running like she had in the parking lot and partly because he was still in some serious pain. Gently, he wrapped his hand around her ankle and pulled her feet toward him. He hesitated. "What would the team say if we made the married thing real?"

She smiled softly. "They'd all claim they saw it coming all along."

"So...should we?"

Thalia didn't answer. Instead, she slipped her toes beneath his leg and settled in as though they did this all the time. As though it made her his and it made him hers.

Forever.

★ ★ ★ ★ ★

Romantic Suspense

Danger. Passion. Drama.

Available Next Month

Colton Mountain Search Karen Whiddon
Defender After Dark Charlene Parris

A High-Stakes Reunion Tara Taylor Quinn
Close Range Cattleman Amber Leigh Williams

LOVE INSPIRED

Baby Protection Mission Laura Scott
Cold Case Target Jessica R. Patch

Larger Print

LOVE INSPIRED

Tracking The Truth Dana Mentink
Rocky Mountain Survival Jane M. Choate

Larger Print

LOVE INSPIRED

Treacherous Escape Kellie VanHorn
Colorado Double Cross Jennifer Pierce

Larger Print

Keep reading for an excerpt of a new title
from the Intrigue series,
MURDER IN THE BLUE RIDGE MOUNTAINS
by R. Barri Flowers

Prologue

Jessica Sneed was a proud member of the Eastern Band of Cherokee Indians, a tribe based in North Carolina. But she was even prouder of being the mother to a rambunctious little dark-haired boy named Garrett. Being a single parent at age twenty-five was anything but easy. Had it been up to her, she would be happily wed with a strong marriage foundation and Garrett would have both parents to dote on him. That wasn't the case, though, as his father, Andrew Crowe, wasn't much interested in being a husband. Much less a dad. Besieged with alcohol-related issues and a self-centered attitude, he'd left the state two years ago, abandoning her, forcing Jessica to go it alone in taking care of her then three-year-old son. Well, maybe not entirely alone, as her parents, Trevor and Dinah Sneed, did their best to help out whenever they could.

Shamelessly, Jessica took full advantage of

the precious little time she had to herself, such as this sunny afternoon when she got to hike in the Blue Ridge Mountains. She loved being in touch with nature and giving back to the land her forefathers had once roamed freely, through retracing their footsteps in paying her respects. She made sure that Garrett, whom she'd given her family surname, was aware of his rich heritage as well. They spent some time in the mountains and forest together when he wasn't in school.

But today, it's just me, Jessica told herself as she ran a hand down the length of her waist-long black hair, worn in a bouffant ponytail. She was wearing tennis shoes along with a T-shirt and cuffed denim shorts on the warm August day as she trekked across the hiking trail on the Blue Ridge Parkway, the hundreds-of-miles-long scenic roadway that meandered through the mountains. She stopped for a moment to enjoy some shade beneath the Raven Rocks Overlook and took a bottle of water from her backpack.

After opening it, Jessica drank half the bottle and returned it to the backpack. She was about to get on her way when she heard a sound. She wondered if it might be coming from wildlife, such as a chipmunk or red squirrel. She had even noticed wild turkey and white-tailed deer roaming around. Humans had to adapt more than the other way around. Some did. Others chose not to.

She heard another noise coming from the woods, this one heavier. Suddenly feeling concerned that it could mean danger, Jessica headed back in the direction from which she'd come.

But the sounds grew louder, echoing all around her, and seemed to be getting closer and closer. Was it a wild animal that had targeted her? Perhaps rabid and ravenous? Should she make a run for it? Or stay still and pray that the threat would leave her alone? As she grappled with these thoughts, Jessica dared to glance over her shoulder at the potential menace. It was not an animal predator. But a human one. It was a man. He was dark haired, with ominous even-darker eyes and a scowl on his face. In one large hand was a long-bladed knife.

Her heart racing like crazy, Jessica turned away from him to run but pivoted so quickly that she lost her balance and the backpack slipped from her shoulders. She fell flat onto the dirt pathway, hitting her head hard against it. Seeing stars, she tried to clear her brain and, at the same time, get up. Before she could, she felt the knife plunge deep into her back. The pain was excruciating. But it got much worse as he stabbed her again and again, till the pain seemed to leave her body, along with the will to live. What hurt even more was not getting to say goodbye to her son. She silently asked Garrett for forgiveness in not being around for him before complete darkness and a strange peace hit Jessica all at once.

HE TOOK A moment to study the lifeless body on the ground before him. Killing her had been even more gratifying than he had imagined in his wildest dreams. He recalled his mother once telling him as a child that he was messed up in the head. The memory made him want to laugh. Yes, she'd been right. He had to agree that he wasn't all there where it concerned being good and bad, much more preferring the latter over the former. His sorry excuse of a mother had found out firsthand that getting on his bad side came with dire consequences. Too bad for her that he'd put her out of her misery and made sure no one ever caught on that he'd been responsible for her untimely death.

His eyes gazed upon the corpse again. How lucky for him that she'd happened upon his sight at just the right place and time when the desire to kill had struck his fancy. It had been almost too perfect. A pretty lamb had come to him for her slaughter. He wondered what had been going through her head as she'd lain dying, a knife wedged deep inside her back. Maybe it had only been his imagination, but there had almost seemed to be a ray of light in her big brown eyes before they'd shut for good, as though she'd been seeing something or someone out of his reach.

He grabbed the knife with his gloved hand and flung it into the flowering shrubs. There were plenty more where that had come from. And he intended to make good use of them. Too bad for the next one to feel the sting of his sharp blade. But that wasn't his concern. A man had to do what a man had to do. And nothing and no one would stop him.

He grinned crookedly and walked away from the dead woman, soon disappearing into the woods, where he would slip back into his normal life. Before the time came for a repeat performance.

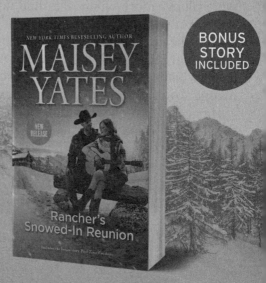

Subscribe and fall in love with a Mills & Boon series today!

You'll be among the first to read stories delivered to your door monthly and enjoy great savings.

WE
SIMPLY
LOVE
ROMANCE

MILLS & BOON